RESOLUTE JUSTICE

LESLIE MARSHMAN

CONARD COUNTY
CONSPIRACY

RACHEL LEE

MILLS & BOON

First Published in Great Britain 2022
by Mills & Boon, an imprint of HarperCollins*Publishers* Ltd
1 London Bridge Street, London, SE1 9GF

www.harpercollins.co.uk

HarperCollins*Publishers*
1st Floor, Watermarque Building,
Ringsend Road, Dublin 4, Ireland

Resolute Justice © 2022 Leslie Marshman
Conard County Conspiracy © 2022 Susan Civil-Brown

ISBN: 978-0-263-30328-5

0122

MIX
Paper from
responsible sources
FSC™ C007454

This book is produced from independently certified FSC™ paper to ensure responsible forest management.

For more information visit: www.harpercollins.co.uk/green

Printed and Bound in Spain using 100% Renewable electricity at CPI Black Print, Barcelona

RESOLUTE JUSTICE

LESLIE MARSHMAN

For Ann.
Thank you for the late-night calls to check
on my sanity, and your invaluable feedback that
made this a stronger book.
Am I approaching the innermost circle yet?

Chapter One

A jagged thread of excitement ripped through Sheriff Cassie Reed's chest as she tugged the Velcro strap. Tightening the Kevlar vest against her ribs, she felt along the sides, confirming there were no gaps.

This was her first raid since being appointed Boone County sheriff. She and her deputies worked quickly, speaking in whispers. They'd parked around the corner, out of sight from the small house that was their target.

Cassie's younger brother Noah approached her. "You sure you don't want me at the back door with Lonnie and Adam?" Noah, like Cassie and their brother Adam, had followed their father into law enforcement. Only Nate, Noah's twin, had yet to decide what he wanted to do with his life.

"Your vest is buckling. Turn around." Cassie reached up and adjusted the straps on his broad shoulders. Then she patted the back pocket of the Kevlar encasing Noah's muscular frame, huffing her annoyance. "Where's your rear trauma pad?"

He fidgeted beneath the body armor. "It's too freaking hot."

Anger laced with fear shot through Cassie, and she spun him around to face her. Gripping his shoulders, she looked up into brown eyes the same warm hue as their father's. "It's never too hot to die. Dagnabbit, Noah, you know better."

Noah's enthusiasm for the job still exceeded his experience. And truthfully, after everything that had happened over the past few months, she was usually glad for that. There were days when the gleam in her brother's eyes and his winning rookie smile helped hold back the pain of so recently losing their dad. But she would take no chances where his safety was concerned. And that went for everyone on her team.

"By the book, Deputy."

"Yeah, yeah. But what about the back door?"

"We're going according to plan. You're with me at the front." She ignored Noah's muttered curse and added, "Get the pad in that pocket. We're ready to roll."

Cassie gave the go signal to Chief Deputy Lonnie Dixon. Though not yet forty, Lonnie's once lean and trim physique had softened, and his dark beard boasted more than a few gray hairs. But he could still bring down a fugitive who had a decent head start. He'd become Cassie's indispensable right-hand man since she'd assumed the job of sheriff.

At her signal, Lonnie led half the men down the dirt alley that bisected the block. From there, they'd get into position behind the detached one-car garage and the backyard storage shed, staying hidden from the security camera at the rear of the house.

Using large oak trees in neighboring yards as cover, Cassie and her group leapfrogged toward the front. They knew from earlier surveillance that the window curtains along both sides of the house never moved. But the camera near the front door would announce their presence as soon as they crossed the property line.

Cassie pressed the button on her mic. "Approaching door now. Get ready."

"Ten-four." Lonnie's voice came back in a whisper.

She and Noah ran up the front steps and to the left of the door. Longtime deputy Sean Cavanaugh's powerful biceps bulged as he carried the breacher to the right side.

Cassie leaned forward just far enough to knock, then bellowed, "Sheriff's Department! We have a warrant to search the premises. Open up!"

No response. She checked her watch. After waiting the required number of seconds, she reached for the knob. Locked. She backed away and nodded at Sean, speaking into her mic. "Breaching."

"In position." Lonnie's calm voice assured her they were ready in the back.

As the battering ram hit the door, it splintered like dried kindling. Cassie entered in a crouch, swinging her gun toward the living room on the left. Noah followed, covering the small room to the right.

Sean dropped the ram and ran past them to the first doorway. "Bedroom. Clear."

Cassie moved down the hallway, Noah on her heels. Room by room, they confirmed the house was vacant. Sean unlocked the back door, letting Lonnie, Adam and Deputy Peter Grant into the cramped, trash-filled kitchen.

"They're not here?" Lonnie's tone gave shape to the disappointment cramping Cassie's gut. *Not again.* She'd been sure this time. Done everything by the book. Taken no chances on a leak that could have warned them off.

"Nope." She bit off the word, then blew out a breath of frustration. "But they were." Eyes sweeping across her men, she issued orders. "Listen up, everybody. Gloves on. Touch nothing. If you see something that's potential evidence, set down a marker and call Brett. He's the investigator Travis County sent us, and he's our finder today."

She pressed her mic and called in Brett Miller, the forensic technician waiting back at the vehicles, then continued with her commands. "Pete, Noah, bedrooms. Sean, the front two rooms. Lonnie, you take the garage and shed." She glanced at Adam. "Sorry, bro. That leaves the kitchen and bathroom for you."

"Hey, that's why you pay me the big bucks, right?" Nothing ever seemed to affect his cheerful mood. Not even a sink filled with dirty dishes and putrid, scummy water she could smell from across the room.

Two years younger than Cassie, Adam had been upbeat even as a child. He'd never complained about helping her with household chores and had taken over as the family cook when Cassie's attempts at the stove proved inedible.

He tucked his slightly-too-long, dark blond hair behind his ears and rolled up his sleeves.

"How long since you've been to the barber? Your hair's almost past regulation length."

"So's yours, sis." He flipped her high ponytail, then laughed when she grabbed the end to measure by touch against her shirt. "Don't worry, it's barely hitting the top of your collar." Adam fought the August humidity to pull on a pair of nitrile gloves. "Besides, who's gonna yell at you for long hair? You're the boss now."

"I don't follow the regulations to avoid getting reprimanded." Convinced her ponytail had stayed where it should be, she let go of it. "I follow them *because* they're the regulations."

"Well, go follow them somewhere else, *boss*. I'm fixin' to be elbow-deep in this sink water. Just hope nothing's alive in there."

As her men searched their assigned areas, Cassie began her own process. She walked back to the front door, closed her eyes, and turned around. Inhaling a deep breath, she sorted through the odors that fought for her attention. Stale fried food. Unwashed bodies. The acrid scent of fear.

She opened her eyes, taking in the front rooms as if for the first time. No furniture other than a couple of card tables and some folding chairs. Internet cables and extension cords lay coiled on the floor like Mexican black kingsnakes.

A soft knock right behind her yanked Cassie's attention back to the open front door. Brett Miller stood on the sill holding his crime scene case, ID clipped to his pocket. She waved her hand for him to follow her into the living room, stepping over pizza boxes and empty beer cans, porn magazines and used condoms.

"I want every single thing in this house bagged." Cassie glanced at the CSI, a young man she hadn't worked with before.

Brett rubbed the back of his neck, his gaze sweeping across the trash-covered carpeting. "You don't think it's just kids using this as a party house?"

Cassie tipped her head to the side, peering at him. "You been working crime scenes long, Brett?"

A red flush crept up his cheeks. "No, ma'am. This is my first solo case."

Cassie pursed her lips and nodded. "Follow me." She led him into a bedroom. "Tell me what you see."

"Some pretty disgusting mattresses."

"Anything else?"

"More trash." Brett shrugged. "I mean, it looks like some kids had a sex fest. Ma'am."

Cassie pointed to where the wall and ceiling met near the door. "See the damaged drywall up there? That happens when security or video cameras are ripped out in a hurry." She tapped the toe of her well-worn cowboy boot on a large metal eyebolt screwed into the floor. There were two bolts by each mattress. Four filthy mattresses in each of the three bedrooms. "Now, I've never been to a sex fest myself, but I doubt that cuffing girls to the floor puts them in a festive mood."

The color drained from Brett's face. "I didn't realize—"

"Garage is clear." Lonnie's deep voice interrupted them. He stood in the doorway, his lip curled with disgust as he eyed the wall-to-wall stained mattresses.

Cassie acknowledged Lonnie by holding up one finger,

then refocused on Brett. "I don't doubt you're well trained. But if you want to work my crime scenes, you need to be a lot more observant. Your job isn't jumping to conclusions and ignoring potential evidence. It's collecting every piece of garbage, every disgusting hair from the drains, every fingerprint, footprint and drop of blood. Lives are at stake, Brett."

She paused, a painful lump forming in the back of her throat. It wasn't just the lives of the faceless victims she'd sworn to protect that were endangered. The painful memory of her father's sightless eyes and bloody uniform pushed its way forward. The lives of people she loved most in the world were also at risk. "Look, I've been chasing these monsters for two years. And when we catch them, I sure as heck don't want the case thrown out because someone didn't handle evidence correctly. I'm depending on you to do your job by the book, without cutting any corners."

Brett looked down and nodded. "Yes, ma'am."

Cassie followed Lonnie to the living room, Brett tight on her heels. She cocked a questioning brow at the investigator.

"I'm gonna need more evidence bags." Brett walked through the front doorway, calling over his shoulder, "They're in my van."

"Newbie?" Lonnie asked, hooking a thumb toward Brett's retreating back.

Nodding, Cassie swiped at a trickle of sweat sliding past her eye. The late August heat had turned the small house into an oven. "Yep. But I think he got the message. I have a feeling Brett's going to turn out to be an excellent criminalist." She turned her full attention to Lonnie. "What were you saying about the garage?"

"It's empty, but there are some muddy footprints. Took some pictures. We might be able to ID the shoes."

"Great. Then all we have to do is find the man wearing those shoes." She clenched her teeth until her jaw ached.

Lonnie shrugged. "Better than nothing."

Cassie walked down the short hall to the kitchen at the back. "What about the shed?"

"It's locked. Your brother went back to the truck to get the cutters."

Noah walked past them just then with a pair of long-handled bolt cutters resting on his shoulder. He cocked a brow toward his older sister. "I call first dibs if it's full of money."

Anger at being one step behind these scum-sucking human traffickers sharpened her tone. "This is no time to joke about your get-rich-quick schemes. The young women taken by these brutes are facing a horrible future, if they even have a future." Her brother's grin faded, and she and Lonnie followed a subdued Noah through the back door and across the yard in silence.

A quick snip through the padlock's shank and the doors swung open with a rusty squeal. A lawn mower sat center stage, yellowed newspapers covered with oil spots beneath it. Pushed up against one wall, a potting bench held remnants of broken terra-cotta planters and a tipped-over container of fire ant killer.

"Man, I hate that stuff." Noah eyed the insecticide on the bench. "Always smells like something died."

"Yeah, but it works." Lonnie eased past the mower and around a stack of boxes. "Nothin' back here but cobwebs, dead roaches, and..."

"And what?" Cassie asked.

"And I think you're gonna want to see this."

Cassie joined Lonnie, who was bent over a blue canvas tarp. He lifted a corner with gloved fingers, revealing a body. Cassie crouched down for a closer look, but layers of clouded plastic sheeting encased the body like a mummy and obscured the features. Only escaped strands of long blond hair indicated their vic might be a female.

"Based on the smell, I'd guess she's been dead a while."
Lonnie ducked his head away to inhale.

Cassie shook her head. "I don't think so. I think it's the
heat in here." Her fingers itched to open the plastic, get a
better look, but she couldn't risk destroying evidence.

"I thought you said that stench was the fire ant powder."
Noah peered around the stacked boxes. *"Whoa."*

"Actually, you were the one who said that." Cassie
glanced up at her brother's ashen face. Despite being a
deputy for several years, this was Noah's first homicide.
"You okay?"

He nodded like a dashboard bobblehead, apparently
afraid to open his mouth in case more than just words
came out.

"If you're going to get sick, get your butt back outside,"
Lonnie snapped. "Worst thing you can do is contaminate
the scene."

"I'm not gonna get sick." Noah glared at Lonnie.

Proud of her brother's fortitude, Cassie stood and pulled
her phone from her pocket. "Noah, go get Brett. And call
the justice of the peace. Tell him we need a death verifica-
tion ASAP." She began snapping preliminary pictures of
the body and the scene.

Noah headed for the house, but his yell across the backyard carried all the way into the shed. "Brett, Cassie needs
you out here. We got a body burrito."

Lonnie shook his head. "He's got a lot to learn."

"You don't have to tell me." Cassie bit her lip to hide her
amusement. "But he has what it takes. It's in his DNA."

"It takes more than that."

Cassie gave him a gentle punch in the arm. "Oh, lighten
up. At least he's not cranky and cynical, like a certain chief
deputy I know."

Equipment box in hand, Brett jogged up to them and
addressed Cassie. "Where's the body?"

"Inside, back behind the boxes. Wrapped in plastic, under the blue tarp."

"You call the JP?" The investigator was already slipping paper booties over his shoes.

Cassie nodded. "But it'll probably take him a while to get here. Usually does."

"Okay." Brett squatted next to his kit, grabbing gloves and evidence markers. "I called my office, too, told them we need a couple more techs and a transport vehicle. I'll get started with the initial walk-through out here."

Pleased that her assessment of Brett's potential seemed on point, Cassie motioned Lonnie outside. "Can you go check on the progress in the house? If they find *anything*, make sure they wait for the rest of the forensic team to get here to process it. I want to keep an eye on the body while we wait for the JP."

"You don't trust the newbie?" Lonnie kept his voice low.

"It's not that. I'm just not taking any chances this time."

Lonnie gave her a sympathetic look that irritated Cassie more than she'd ever admit. "Don't worry, boss lady. We'll get 'em."

She blew out a frustrated breath. "Two years, Lonnie. And catching these creeps is proving harder than putting socks on a rooster."

TYLER BISHOP PRESSED the doorbell, laughing out loud when Beethoven's "Für Elise" chimed inside his brother's garish Houston McMansion. Bob hadn't known Beethoven from Black Sabbath before marrying his second wife. Not that *Monique* knew anything about classical music, either. But then, what did one expect from a pretentious gold digger?

While he waited on the front porch, his gut churned like he'd overdone the hot sauce on his breakfast taco. He'd bet the ranch there was more to his brother's invitation than just being sociable. But after a two-year moratorium on visits, at least he'd get to see his niece.

Ashley had taken after her mother, Beth. Blonde, pretty and with a bubbly personality, she loved life. Well, she had until Beth's devastating fight with cancer left Ashley motherless at an age when a girl needed her mom the most.

He reached into the right pocket of his blazer, anticipating her reaction to the turtle key chain he'd brought her. Her fascination with turtles began when she was a toddler, resulting in her nickname. *Little Turtle.* He had brought her one whenever he'd seen her. So far, her favorite had been a silver turtle necklace, inset with pieces of Mexican opal. He'd given it to her four years ago, on her fourteenth birthday.

The front door swung inward, framing Monique in the opening. Her knee-length, sleeveless blue dress revealed well-toned arms and legs. *Personal trainer? Tennis pro? Pool boy?*

"Tyler." Bob's wife was a displaced Yankee, but despite her bogus Southern accent she still managed to impart resignation, disappointment and distaste in only two little syllables.

And the wrong two at that. He'd gone by Bishop since seventh grade when he and another Tyler agreed to use last names to avoid confusion. Only Bob and his parents still called him Tyler. And now, Monique.

"Monique." Bishop matched her tone but didn't try for the exaggerated drawl.

"Come in." She stepped back, motioning him into the three-story foyer.

"Thanks." Bishop's gaze took in the sweeping staircase to the second floor, modern art on the walls and the crystal chandelier hanging far above their heads. "I gotta admit, the invitation surprised me."

Monique sighed. "Now is not the time to be petty, Tyler."

"Petty? Listen, I've respected your demands to have no contact with my brother and niece…"

"I simply don't think the lifestyle of a homeless private investigator sets a good example for an impressionable teenager. Nor does it reflect well on our family name."

Our. As if *he* was the latest addition to the family instead of her. "You know I'm not homeless, Monique."

"Well, the *house-sitting* does seem to be a permanent situation, doesn't it?" She even used freaking air quotes, just in case he missed her disparaging tone.

"Tye!" Bob's cheerful greeting didn't match the tight smile that cracked across his haggard face. His shoulders slumped and dark circles rimmed his bloodshot eyes. Bishop fought to keep his mouth from dropping open. *He looks like an old man.* Warning bells clanged. What had aged his brother since their last covert meetup for coffee a few months ago?

"Thanks for coming. I…" Bob glanced at Monique. "*We* need your help."

On high alert now, Bishop followed his brother into a formal living room that he vaguely remembered from his only other visit to the house.

Please, let it be something simple, like divorce. Just the possibility improved his mood.

He sat on an uncomfortable, overly ornate chair with asymmetrical arms while his brother dropped onto a weird-shaped couch with only half a back and a ridiculous flaring armrest. No, not a couch. A *settee.* Funny how a word you've never used can pop into your brain at the appropriate moment. Monique lowered herself gracefully next to Bob. The settee's odd form suddenly made sense. Monique needed nothing behind her. The stick up her butt kept her upright.

"You going to tell me what's going on?"

A housekeeper came to the doorway and waited, brows raised.

"Coffee?" Bob asked Bishop.

Monique inhaled a tiny gasp, and Bishop glanced at the Oriental rug beneath the glass coffee table. When someone with the legal name of Monica insisted it be pronounced *Monique*, what were the odds her furnishings were authentic? But why poke the bear?

"Better pass. I'd hate to accidentally soil your rug." Bishop leaned back in the chair and rested one ankle across the opposite knee. Bits of dried mud from the edge of his boot heel flaked onto the floor, giving him a sense of satisfaction that he had to admit was, indeed, petty.

No comeback from his brother. Instead, Bob slouched forward, elbows on knees, and rested his face in his palms. Bishop almost regretted his sarcastic reply, but it wasn't easy to get past being unfairly ostracized by the only family he had left.

Lowering his hands, Bob blurted out, "Ashley's missing, and we need your help to find her."

"What do you mean, she's missing?" Bishop dropped his foot to the floor and leaned forward. "Since when?"

"Really, it's not like she hasn't done this before." Icicles dripped from Monique's words. "Several times, in fact. She'll be back when she's done being annoyed with us."

Bishop's gaze slid from his sister-in-law to his brother. "Bob?"

Monique rose. "*Robert* can fill you in on the details. I have an appointment I must keep."

"Botox injections?" Bishop asked.

Monique narrowed her eyes at him, pivoted like a model at the end of a runway and sashayed out of the room.

Bob's sidelong glance followed her, disappointment written across his face. "It's true. Ashley *has* run away before.

But in the past she always stayed at her friend Kim's house, and Kim's parents would let us know." Bob scrubbed his face with his hands. "But not this time. We haven't heard from her. We called around. No one's seen her."

"Did you contact the police?"

"The first day. But between her age and her history of running away, they shut me down. Said I should reach out to her friends and relatives." He raised red-rimmed eyes to Bishop. "Is that right? Can they really refuse to do anything?"

"Unless there's evidence that Ashley left against her will, there's not much they can do. They might take a missing persons report, but they won't actively search for her." Bishop pulled a small notebook and pen from his jacket pocket. Old habit left over from his days as an HPD detective. "When did you last see her?"

"Four days ago. Sunday." Bob blew out a hard breath. "She was upset because her boyfriend had to go back home for some sort of family emergency, and Monique wouldn't let her see him before he took off."

Bishop glanced up from his notes. "Any chance she took off with the boyfriend?"

"I guess it's possible. But we don't have his phone number, so we haven't been able to reach him. We started by calling Kim and all of Ashley's other friends. None of them have seen her. Not a one." His hands clasped together in a death grip. "Every single one of them said she hadn't even mentioned running away to them. I thought teenagers told their closest friends everything. This isn't normal, is it? For a runaway, I mean."

"You believe them?"

Bob nodded. "They're a good group of kids, for the most part."

"And the boyfriend? What's his name?"

"Michael Pugh. Nice enough kid, from what I've seen."

"So what was Monique's issue with Ashley seeing him before he left town?"

"He's a couple of years older than Ashley. He moved here from some small town near Victoria or San Antonio. Stays with an uncle here in Houston, I think. Works at Old Sam's auto repair shop." Bob shrugged. "Monique thinks he's not good enough for Ashley."

Definitely not country club material. But then, neither was Monique. "Why did Ashley start running away?"

Bob's eyes shifted to the side. "The first time was right after Monique and I got married." He sighed. "She accused me of betraying her mother's memory. Resented Monique for trying to take her mother's place. And it doesn't help that Monique has no experience being a parent." He raised his hands, palms up, as if pleading with Bishop to understand. "It's not easy being a stepmother to a teenage girl."

"Yeah, well, I doubt it's easy being a teenage girl, either." Bishop fought the urge to shake his brother. "Why didn't you tell me she was running away?"

"It was a family matter, Tye. Monique doesn't believe in airing our dirty laundry in public."

Bishop stood, tucking his notebook away. He'd thought himself immune to the pain of his brother's betrayal, and yet the words hit him like a sucker punch to the gut. "Wow. A *family* matter, huh?"

Bob jumped to his feet. "I didn't mean it like that."

"Yeah, I'm pretty sure you did. And in case you didn't notice, you just referred to your daughter as dirty laundry." Bishop fought to control his breathing. "Tell me, did Monique even want you to call me?"

Bob looked away. "She thinks Ashley will get over it and come home on her own."

"And you? What do *you* think?"

"It feels different this time," Bob admitted. He continued to glance anywhere other than Bishop. "Ashley and Monique's arguments are usually loud. But this one wasn't. When Monique told her no, Ashley just went to her room. No screaming or slamming doors. First time that's happened."

Bishop waited until Bob's darting gaze finally met his. "Man, what happened to us? We used to be close. And you know I love Ashley like she was my own kid. For the life of me, I can't figure out why you've let Monique drive this wedge between us. Why you allowed her to keep my niece, my *godchild*, from seeing me for the past two years." Bishop stepped toward Bob. "But I'm an adult. I can deal with Monique's guff. But your eighteen-year-old daughter is missing, and you wait four days to ask for my help because your wife didn't want you to? Do you see a problem with that, *Robert*?"

His older brother had always been "Bob" until Monique insisted he be called "Robert." Using that name now, Bishop acknowledged the wedge had done its work. The split between the brothers was complete.

"I'll find Ashley. Not for you. For her, because that kid deserves to know she's the most important person in *someone's* life."

And because he'd been a fool to let anyone stop him from seeing his niece. Maybe if he'd been a better uncle, a true godfather, Ashley would have come to him for help the *first* time she'd run away. And then maybe he wouldn't be here now, feeling like a total failure.

"I need to see her room."

With a defeated nod, Bob led him upstairs, then down a long hall. The closed door at the end bore remnants of Scotch tape and sticky residue.

"What was on her door?" Bishop asked.

"A keep-out sign and some stickers." Bob shrugged. "Normal teen stuff, I guess."

"When did she take it down?"

"She didn't. Monique ripped off the sign, then had our housekeeper remove the stickers as best she could."

"When, Bob?" Bishop repeated the question through gritted teeth.

"Ashley put them up right after we moved here. Monique kept telling her to clean off the door, but Ashley refused. Monique took them down at some point. I don't remember when." Bob turned the knob, pushed the door open and walked into the room.

Bishop followed him in. "Does anything look unusual? Out of place?"

Bob gave the room a once-over, his brows pinched together. "I don't know. I haven't been in here in ages." His gaze landed on Bishop. "I respected her privacy, even after the sign came down."

"She wouldn't let you in even when you knocked and asked permission?" Bishop tried to keep his tone even.

"I gave her some space, Tye." Bob's cheeks reddened. "You've never been a father, so don't judge my relationship with Ashley."

Bishop held his brother's angry glare for a long moment. "Does she still wear that turtle necklace?"

"The one you gave her? She's never taken it off."

Nodding, Bishop said, "You should wait for me downstairs. I need to look around in here by myself."

Bob gave the room another long look, as if it might be his last. Then he left without a word, pulling the door closed behind him.

Bishop stood with his back to the door, taking in a first impression of the entire room. Posters filled two walls. Some were of bands he'd never heard of. There were a few with inspirational quotes, and a couple featured meditation mandalas. He'd taught Ashley a little about mindfulness and meditation. Seeing these posters filled him with the hope that she'd continued to study and find peace through them.

Disregarding his niece's privacy and forcing himself into professional mode, Bishop dug through her dresser drawers, a place where women liked to hide things. After he came up blank, he moved on to her desk. Nothing of interest in the drawers. A docking station sat on top, but the laptop it belonged to was gone. He looked through her closet, not surprised when it yielded no earth-shattering clues.

Bishop's last stop was Ashley's bed. Although the other furniture in the room reflected a young woman on the verge of college, her bed was the one she'd had before her mom died. A twin four-poster, decked out in pink and white ruffles and a canopy stretching above it. Bishop recognized the bed from his visits, back when Bob and Beth had always welcomed him into their home. Ashley was still holding on to her mom through the ruffles and pillow coverings Beth had sewn herself.

He lifted the top mattress and ran his hand between it and the box spring. Ashley hadn't made it easy. She'd hidden the journal there, but on the wall side. He sat on the edge of the bed and opened the hardbound book of teenage trauma.

Skimming past pages of Ashley's heart breaking into pieces on the pages as her mother's health failed, Bishop fought the burning behind his eyes. She'd journaled about forcing herself to keep moving forward because her mother had asked her to. But it had been difficult, according to her entries. She'd tried to find comfort from her father, but apparently Bob was too busy comforting himself.

Several blank pages separated "Before Monique" and "After Monique." Ashley had still been grieving for her mother when Bob interjected Monique into the family. The rest of the entries spoke to Ashley's depression, isolation and longing for love.

Bishop flipped through the pages to the end. There were three last entries, each one addressed to a particular person.

To Dad: I'm sorry, but I just can't live with Monique. You've made it clear that you've chosen her over me. I hope you find happiness together.

To Monique: I wonder what made you so insecure that you feel threatened by my relationship with my father. Regardless, you win. He's all yours. Following this entry, a detailed drawing of a hand, the middle finger pointing up, filled an entire page.

To Uncle Tye: I've only survived this long because of what you've taught me. I'm sure it's Monique's doing that I haven't seen you for so long. You would never abandon me on purpose. Namaste.

Bishop's chest ached like he'd just run a marathon. He'd never considered that his niece might not know why he hadn't visited her all this time. He wanted to find Ashley all the more, to make sure she knew that he hadn't abandoned her.

Despite not seeing her for two years, Bishop's gut told him Ashley might be in real danger. Her journal entries sounded more like she was running *from* her parents than running *toward* anything, even her boyfriend. And that's when horrible things could happen to young, vulnerable women. Ashley was looking for love, for comfort. Bishop had to find her before she found those with the wrong type of person. The type who preyed on girls like Ashley.

His fingers curled into fists and he fought the urge to punch something by shoving them into his jacket pockets. His right hand brushed up against the turtle key chain. He held it in a tight grip, as if it were a talisman that could guarantee his niece's safety.

No matter what it cost him, he would find Ashley and bring her home. He owed her that much.

Chapter Two

Bishop parked in a diagonal space in front of the Boone County Justice Center and climbed out of his pickup. He'd had to exit I-10 west of Houston because of construction, then decided to stay on the longer scenic route the whole way. It added about an hour's drive time, but it was a no-brainer compared to freeway traffic.

Needing to stretch his legs before meeting with the local sheriff, Bishop strolled across the street to the town plaza. Benches sat in the shade of towering live oaks, and the pathways leading to a central fountain were lined with colorful flowers, wilting in the late-summer heat. It wasn't a big park, but then Resolute was a fairly small town for being the county seat.

An elderly gentleman sitting on a bench nodded a friendly greeting and Bishop smiled in return. A far cry from big-city life, where everyone was suspicious of strangers. Or was that just the cynical ex-cop in him talking?

After a brief look around, Bishop headed back to the justice center. According to his research, the sheriff's office, courthouse and jail were all housed in the three-story structure built around the turn of the century. Well, turn of the *last* century. Hand-hewn native limestone bricks, arched windows with keystones, wraparound balconies on the upper floors. *I bet these walls have some stories to tell.*

While on the Boone County website, he'd also skimmed

the sheriff's bio. Wallace Reed had filled the position for the past three decades and then some. There were two possible reasons for that. Either he ran things like a dictator, beating his competitors in election years by nefarious means, or he truly was a good guy and the people around here wanted him right where he was. Giving Sheriff Reed the benefit of the doubt, Bishop climbed the front steps.

Pushing open the heavy wooden door, Bishop was hit by a welcoming blast of air-conditioning. As his eyes adjusted from bright sunlight to the dim interior, he noticed a petite woman with graying hair sitting behind a desk. Her fingers flying across a computer keyboard, she seemed oblivious to his approach. Bishop waited a moment for Helen, according to the nameplate on her desk, to address him.

She didn't.

He cleared his throat. "Morning, Helen. I'd like to speak to Sheriff Reed."

"Have an appointment?" She still didn't bother to glance up from her computer screen.

"I don't." Bishop took in the color-coded file folders standing at attention in an upright holder. A coffee mug bearing the county emblem sat centered on a sandstone coaster. Not a stray paperclip in sight. Bet the old gal ran a tight ship.

A few seconds passed before Helen gave a long-suffering sigh, punched her keyboard one last, forceful time, then deigned to raise her eyes.

Bishop favored her with the full force of his best smile, usually a surefire guarantee of getting one in return.

Helen did not smile back. "The sheriff is extremely busy today."

"It's important. I only need a few minutes." And seriously, how much lawbreaking could be going on in a town this quiet?

She picked up the desk phone's receiver and cocked a brow at him. "Name?"

"Bishop."

"And the nature of your business?" She jabbed one button on the phone.

"I'm looking for someone," he said at the same time Helen spoke into the receiver.

"I'm sorry to bother you, Sheriff, but there's a man here to see you. Says his name is Bishop." Pause. "I *did* tell him you're busy." Helen moved the receiver away from her mouth. "The sheriff wants to know what you're here about."

"It's about a missing person." Bishop answered loud enough for it to carry through the phone.

The sheriff must have heard and issued an order, as the stalwart clerk snapped to. "Right away." With a heavy clank, Helen dropped the receiver in its cradle and stood. "Come with me, please."

Bishop followed her as she marched sharply down a long hallway, her sensible flats making little noise. She stopped at a closed door bearing the words Sheriff Reed, gave one quick rap with her knuckles, opened it and ushered Bishop into the office. As soon as he'd crossed the threshold, Helen pulled the door shut behind her, her soft footsteps fading away.

Bishop's practical joke meter pinged and his smile vanished. *What the...?* The slender redhead standing next to the desk wore a starched white shirt and ironed black jeans. *Who irons creases into their jeans?*

She'd pulled her hair into a high ponytail so tight, he doubted any strand would dare try to slip loose. Almost as tall as Bishop, she was a lot curvier, and her full lips flashed what might have been a quick smile as she sat down and picked up a pen.

"Please have a seat, Mr. Bishop." She motioned to a chair facing her desk. "How can I help you?"

Under other circumstances, Bishop would have several good, if inappropriate, ideas on exactly how she could help him. But with Ashley's whereabouts on the line, he was angry about getting the runaround. "I was under the impression I'd be meeting with Sheriff Reed."

"I *am* Sheriff Reed." Her tone was stern, all business.

"Really?" Bishop crossed the room and dropped into the chair. "Then I can say without a doubt, your picture *really* doesn't do you justice."

Green eyes widened beneath raised brows. "My picture?"

"On the Boone County website? Your profile picture there makes you look a lot older. And definitely more masculine." When she didn't respond, he added, "The website says Wallace Reed is the sheriff. Wild stab here, but I'm guessing you're not Sheriff *Wallace* Reed."

Her eyes closed, and the knuckles gripping the pen whitened until it seemed the poor pen would snap in two. After a deep breath, she opened her eyes, piercing him with a determined stare. "Until a few months ago my father, Wallace Reed, *was* the sheriff. The website hasn't been updated yet, but I assure you, I'm Sheriff *Cassie* Reed. I was appointed after Dad's death."

Bishop gave himself a mental thrashing. An honest mistake on his part, but he regretted joking about what was obviously a deep, personal wound. "I'm sorry for your loss."

Her face devoid of emotion, the sheriff sat taller in her chair. "You said you wanted to talk about a missing person." She flipped her notebook to a fresh page, pen poised to write. "Who *is* the missing person, Mr. Bishop?"

"Just Bishop. No need for the 'mister.'"

She looked up, her glare hardening as she tapped the pen on the paper. Apparently, smiles didn't come easily to the women of Resolute. But even with the glare, *this* woman kicked his resting heart rate up a beat or two.

Bishop tried again. "I'm a private investigator. When I arrive in town, I like to introduce myself. Helps me avoid getting pegged as a peeper or a stalker when I'm on a case. Saves everyone a lot of time and embarrassment."

The sheriff's heart-shaped face tilted ever so slightly to the right. "You're here on a private job?" Bottle-green eyes bored into his with an intensity that held him like a magnet. "Apparently I misunderstood why you wanted to see me. But I certainly appreciate you making me aware of your presence in Resolute. Now, if that's all, Mr. Bishop…"

"Just Bishop. No…" His words tapered off as her eyes narrowed. "Look, I think we got off on the wrong foot. I'm a PI, but this case is personal to me." He leaned forward. "It's my niece who's missing. Her boyfriend's family lives in Resolute, and she may have come here with him. I have their address, but I figured there's a good chance you know them and might be able to give me a little advance intel before I talk to them."

Setting her pen on her desk, the sheriff leaned back in the chair, her brows drawn together. "I'm sorry to hear about your niece. We take missing persons cases very seriously around here. Especially young girls." Tapping a finger against her generous lips, she seemed lost in thought for a moment. "First, I'd like you to file a report. Then we can discuss approaching the boy's family."

"I already filed the report in Houston, but I doubt much will be done. Ashley's eighteen, and according to her parents, a chronic runaway."

The office door swung open. A young man—dressed like the sheriff right down to the ironed-in creases—leaned into the office. "Hey, sis. You get an ID on our Jane Doe yet?"

"Noah, how many times have I told you about knocking? I'm in a meeting." Her words were reproving but her tone laced with affection.

Noah's eyes flickered to Bishop, then back to his sister. "Sorry. Lonnie needs to know if you still want the sketch artist to work up a drawing of the vic."

"Yes. I haven't heard from the medical examiner yet, but I want the sketch ready in case he can't identify her."

Bishop waited for the deputy to leave. "So, your father *was* sheriff. Now, you *are* sheriff and your brother's a deputy? Let me guess. Lonnie's a brother, too?"

Amusement tugged at one corner of her mouth. Just a hint, but enough to make Bishop hanker to see a full-on smile from her before he left town. "My cousin."

Bishop chuckled. "Does anyone work here who isn't a relative?"

"What can I say? Resolute's a small town, and Boone's a small county." She shrugged. "I apologize for the interruption, but we're in the middle of a murder investigation." She picked up her pen. "Now, please tell me about your niece."

"A murder?" A chill swept through Bishop. "Did that deputy say the vic was female? How old?"

The sheriff stilled, a look of dawning comprehension on her face. "We're not sure." She spoke in a measured tone that Bishop recognized from his days on the force. The tone used to keep victims' families calm. "Teens, maybe early twenties."

Fumbling for his phone, Bishop pulled up a picture and held it out for the sheriff to see. "This is Ashley. She's petite, long blond hair, blue eyes."

Sheriff Reed's full lips tightened into a thin line. When her gaze lifted, Bishop's heart stopped beating and his blood ran cold.

Chapter Three

Waiting for the medical examiner to call back, Bishop almost hyperventilated while doing deep breathing exercises. Even muttering a quiet mantra for Ashley's safety over and over couldn't cut through the overwhelming fear and anxiety clawing apart his insides.

Sheriff Reed grabbed the phone when it rang. "You're positive? I understand. Thank you, Doctor." She ended the call. "The ME confirmed that the vic has no tattoos."

It wasn't Ashley.

Bishop gave a hard bark of laughter. The sheriff probably thought he was crazy, but he didn't care. Now wasn't the time to explain how Monique had screamed like a banshee when Ashley got a small tattoo of a turtle on her ankle a few months earlier. How his brother, so cowed by his own wife that he'd escaped her rantings by meeting Bishop for coffee, had admitted it was actually a cute little tattoo.

Bishop resolved then and there, the first thing on his agenda after finding Ashley would be getting his own turtle tattoo in celebration of his niece's rebel ways.

To her credit, the sheriff had looked just as relieved as Bishop when the ME said it wasn't Ashley. Bishop had been ready to throw his arms around her, but something about the stiff set of her spine quashed the impulse. Instead, he asked Sheriff Reed about Michael Pugh and his family in Resolute.

"It's just the three boys since the mother died. Mike's in the middle. He's got an older brother, Garrett. Billy's fourteen, maybe fifteen." Her voice, though still matter-of-fact, had softened considerably since Bishop's scare about Ashley and the Jane Doe. Everything about Sheriff Reed screamed tough as nails, but Cassie the woman seemed almost compassionate.

He pulled his notebook from his pocket. "The kids live by themselves?"

"Garrett took custody of Billy when Ms. Pugh died." Cassie shrugged. "The place is paid for, and somehow they find a way to keep the utilities on. Mike used to work at a local garage. Garrett probably does odd jobs or construction work, because I haven't seen him working in town."

Bishop made a note of that. "What about the father?"

"Ms. Pugh never had much luck with men. Each boy has a different daddy, and none of them stuck around much longer than it took to be a sperm donor. Pugh was her maiden name, and she passed it on to her sons."

"The brothers get into trouble much?"

Cassie shook her head. "Some minor drug possession charges on Garrett a few years ago. Nothing on Mike or Billy."

Trying to ignore how the end of her high ponytail swished across her shoulders each time she moved her head, Bishop slapped his notebook closed and stood. "Well, guess it's time to pay them a visit."

"The family's always been downright antisocial." Cassie glanced at her watch, a basic utility model that looked out of place on her slender wrist. "I can't do much on this murder until the autopsy's complete and I get the lab and evidence reports." She stood and came around her desk, a set of keys dangling from her tapered fingers. "I think I'll tag along, if you don't mind. If Ashley *is* in trouble and in my county, I want to know."

"Don't mind in the least." Understatement of the century. Spending the afternoon with the shapely sheriff who got stuff accomplished would be a pleasure. "I'm parked right out front."

"Oh, I'll be driving," Cassie informed him. "No guarantee when it comes to the Pugh brothers, but less chance of my official truck catching a load of buckshot than a stranger's vehicle pulling onto their property."

Grinning, Bishop stepped back and allowed the sheriff to precede him. He'd enjoy riding shotgun for a change. "Thought you said they weren't troublemakers."

One hand on the door handle, Cassie turned around and caught him staring at her backside.

Bracing for the reprimand he deserved, he thought fast. "I was, uh, just admiring those sharp creases in your jeans."

Although her raised brow told him she didn't buy that for one second, she simply replied, "Having a gun for protection doesn't make someone a troublemaker out here." Cassie's accent thickened like cold honey. "You're not in the big city now, Bishop. Us country folk keep shotguns by the front door." Her eyes sparkled with amusement before she turned and sauntered out of her office.

Her tone was sarcastic, but he didn't care. She'd finally called him Bishop.

"THAT'S THEIR HOUSE up ahead on the left," Cassie told him. They came to a stop along the shoulder of County Road 21, about three miles southwest of Resolute. Three agonizingly slow miles, since the sheriff came to full stops, used her turn signals and obeyed the speed limit even on the empty roads outside of town.

Bishop gazed through the windshield at the small frame house sitting to the side of what looked like a failed town dump. Old tires and a threadbare couch surrounded a rusted-out truck, and smoke wafted up from a burn barrel. "I can see why Michael wanted to try his luck in Houston."

Cassie tapped the gas pedal, easing back onto the blacktop. Pulling into the dirt drive, she stopped behind an old Ford Mustang whose glory days were long gone. When they climbed out of the truck and she slammed her door shut, Bishop shot her a questioning look. In his business, stealth was key.

"Sometimes it's best to let people out here know they have company before you knock on their door." With that bit of advice, she led the way up the porch steps, going around a mangy bloodhound asleep in the shade.

A guy who didn't look much like the pictures Bishop had seen of Michael answered her knock, leaving the screen door closed between them. This Pugh brother had a black eye, swollen lip, and bruises covering his arms and bare chest.

"Hey, Garrett. How y'all doing?" Cassie's tone was friendly, but her back was straight, her shoulders squared.

"Doin' fine, Sheriff. What's up?" His jeans hung low on his hips, the frayed hems bunched under his bare feet.

"Looks like quite a shiner. Hope the other guy looks worse."

Garrett touched beneath his eye and shrugged. "This? This ain't nothin'. Just roughhousing."

Cassie paused, allowing the quiet between them to grow. Bishop knew the tactic. Silence made the person being questioned nervous. But Garrett waited her out, and finally Cassie asked, "Michael home? I need to talk to him."

"What about?" Garrett's gaze slid to Bishop. "Who's this guy?"

"I'm asking the questions, Garrett. Where is Michael?"

"He don't live here no more. Went to Houston after Mama died."

"I heard he came back." Cassie hooked her thumbs on

her belt. "Some kind of emergency with you or Billy, as I understand."

Bishop strained to see the dim interior of the room behind Garrett.

Garrett's tongue skimmed over his front teeth, pushing out his upper lip as he looked Cassie over. "No emergency 'round here. We ain't seen Michael for months." He folded his inked arms across his narrow chest, also covered with tats.

Bishop's patience reached its limit. He pulled his phone from his pocket and turned it toward the door. "This is Michael's girlfriend. Did she come by here looking for him?"

The kid squinted at the phone through the dirty screen door, then blinked several times, fast. A tell many liars had. Cassie shifted next to him. The observant sheriff had caught it, too.

"Nope. Never seen her." Garrett swaggered a little, as if emphasizing his claim.

Cassie's smile didn't reach her eyes. "If you see either of them, ask them to give me a call, okay?"

"Sure thing." Garrett pushed the inside door shut before they'd even turned away.

Bishop turned to Cassie, keeping his voice low. "He's lying."

"I know. But we can't force our way inside. There's no indication either one of them is here." Cassie paused before stepping off the porch, raising her voice to a volume that would carry. "Well, if they haven't been here, they haven't been here. Let's go."

Farther up the drive, between the Mustang and a one-car garage, another mutt rolled on his back in the dust. This one looked like a Heinz 57, with short legs, floppy ears and a stub tail. A teenage boy squatted next to him, rubbing the dog's stomach. Bishop headed toward him.

Cassie caught up. "Hey, Billy. Y'all getting along okay without your mom?"

Billy looked up at her. "Yes'm."

"You going to school every day?"

"Don't gotta go. It's out for summer."

She pulled her lips in as if fighting a smile. "I meant during the school year. You keeping up with your classes?"

"Oh. Yeah. I go when I gotta go." Billy's attention returned to the dog.

"I was hoping to catch Michael home."

"Just missed him by a day or so."

Bishop muttered a curse. "He was here?"

Billy's gaze shifted to Bishop, but he spoke to Cassie. "Who's he?"

"A friend." Cassie crouched down to the boy's level. "When was Mike here?"

The kid cocked his head and closed his eyes, his faced scrunched as if it hurt to think. "Got here on the weekend."

Bishop shoved his phone in Billy's face. "Did you see her? Was she here, too?"

After staring at the phone for a full minute, Billy finally nodded. "Yep. She showed up after Mike got here."

Bishop blew out a breath. If Billy were to be believed, Ashley was alive and well. "Do you know where they are now?"

Billy shook his head. "She left. Mike and Garrett had a big fight, then Mike left. Been gone a day or so." Standing, the boy scratched at the acne on his cheek. "Why you lookin' for Mike?"

"He's not in trouble. Just need to ask him something." Cassie straightened. "If you hear from him, tell him to call me, okay?"

Billy shrugged. "Doubt he'll call, but if he does I will."

So Garrett had been lying to them. Bishop couldn't stomach liars at the best of times. Throw Ashley into the mix and he was ready to do some serious damage. He stormed back to the house, taking the porch steps two at a time. Cassie caught up with him as he pounded his fist against the flimsy door.

When Garrett opened up again, Cassie jumped in before Bishop had a chance to start yelling. "Garrett, I'm about ten seconds away from arresting you for impeding an investigation." Cassie planted her hands on her hips. "I want the truth this time."

"You can't arrest me. I ain't done nothin'—"

"We know Mike and Ashley were here. Where are they?" Bishop gnashed his teeth, fighting the urge to smash his fist square into that belligerent face. "Where'd they go?"

Cassie's threat didn't seem to scare the kid, but Bishop had made grown men cry in interrogation rooms. He'd do the same to Garrett if he didn't start talking. He reached for the screen door handle, but Garrett shoved the whole door at him. The flimsy hinges broke away. Bishop's head popped through the screen and the door frame encircled his shoulders.

Garrett streaked through the house toward the back. As Bishop struggled to get free of the door frame, the edge of it knocked Cassie off balance. Arms pinwheeling, she stepped backward onto the slumbering hound. Baying his indignation, the dog stood and sent Cassie down the steps head over heels.

Bishop, finally free of the door, ran down to help Cassie. "I'm all right. Go after Garrett." Already on her feet, she charged back up to the porch. "I'll go through, you go around."

Billy stood as Bishop ran past him toward the backyard. The teen signaled him and pointed to the garage. With the small building closed up, Bishop raised his brows in question. Billy motioned for him to go around to the side door.

Cassie skidded to a stop in the backyard. She approached

the short chain-link fence that ended at the corner of the garage. Bishop tipped his head toward the garage, and Cassie moved to the side door, behind the fence.

"Are both doors unlocked?" he whispered to Billy.

The kid nodded, and Bishop grabbed the door handle. When Cassie went in from the side, Bishop swung the front door up. Garrett darted out, but Bishop was ready. He caught up with him before Garrett made it past the Mustang, tackling him on the driveway. Bishop flipped him onto his back, holding his scrawny chest down with one hand. He raised the other as if to punch Garrett.

"Dadgummit, Garrett. Why did you run?" Cassie caught up to them.

Bishop held his position but glanced up at Cassie. Did she really just say *dadgummit*?

"I knew this guy was gonna beat me up." Garrett held his hands in front of his face to block any potential blows.

"I'm not going to beat you up unless you keep lying to us." Bishop brandished his fist in the air.

"Okay, okay. They were here. But Mike made me swear not to tell nobody."

"Tell anybody *what*?"

"That they run off together. Said they was gittin' hitched."

"It makes sense that Garrett would lie if Mike asked him to." Cassie sipped her sweet tea and looked with disdain at Bishop's unsweetened glass. "The Pugh brothers have always stuck up for each other."

It had taken some convincing, but she'd talked Bishop into grabbing lunch at The Busy B diner. Her stomach had been growling for hours, and she was starting to enjoy the PI's company. Not sure why. She wasn't one to be swayed by a pretty face, but there it was. Bishop's face *was* pretty. And she enjoyed looking at it.

"I don't buy it." Bishop leaned back in the booth, scowling. Even then, he was pretty. "Ashley's not the kind of kid to run off and get married."

Cassie fought the urge to roll her eyes. "But isn't that exactly what she did, and why you're here? She ran off after her boyfriend. Look, she's of age, and at least they're making it legal." Not that getting married was always the best route to take. Her own mother was proof of that.

Marge Dawson, owner of the diner, approached their table. She not only opened and closed The Busy B every day, but tough times often saw her working the grill and waiting tables during the midafternoon lulls. Though more than twice Cassie's age, Marge served as her sounding board for all matters of a personal nature.

"What'll it be, Cassie darlin'?"

Cassie ordered her favorite, a bacon cheeseburger with fries.

If anything, Bishop's scowl deepened. "You have anything that's not fried or part of a cow?"

Marge's thick caterpillar brows rose sharply as she took in Bishop for the first time. A smile of pure appreciation widened across her face and she patted her tight battleship-gray perm as though primping for a glamour photo. "And who might this be?"

"He's a private investigator from Houston. Just passing through." Cassie kept her tone nonchalant.

"Well, Mr. Fancy Pants." Marge's eyes sparkled with mischief. "We got catfish. It ain't cow, but it *is* fried."

His look of dismay was priceless. "Any chance I could get it grilled? And a dinner salad with balsamic vinaigrette?"

Still smiling, Marge wrote on her pad. "You want a side of bland and tasteless with that?"

Cassie snickered. Loudly. Bishop threw her a scornful look, but she only laughed harder. Imagine Mr. Tough

Guy PI being both pretty *and* fussy. Too bad he'd be leaving town so soon. Might have been fun getting to know him a little better.

She stopped laughing when Bishop morphed from peeved to charming, giving Marge a wicked smile and a playful wink at the same time. "Got to take care of my heart, darlin'. Saving it for my one true love."

Pu-lease. Cassie rolled her eyes so hard, they hurt. But dadgum if Marge didn't fall for that hogwash, hook, line and sinker.

"For you, handsome, anything. I'll toss that sucker on the flattop myself. But I can't promise you'll like it, and no sending it back. I'll bring the *eye-talian* dressing on the side. It may not be up to your standards." The heavyset woman walked away chuckling, her orthopedic shoes squeaking on the bleached linoleum floor.

With no idea what to say after that undisguised display of masculine persuasion, Cassie endured several minutes of awkward silence that settled over the booth.

"If you don't mind, I've got two questions for you." Bishop looked across the table, his expression dead serious.

Cassie blew out a breath of relief at the conversation starter. "Ask away."

"Not sure I ever met a sheriff, or any other officer of the law for that matter, who tripped over a dog, fell down several steps, chased a delinquent and wrapped it all up by saying 'dadgummit.' What's up with that?"

Cassie frowned. "Which part are you confused by? The dog, the steps, the delinquent or the fact that I don't spew profanity?"

"Most cops I know utter a swear word now and then."

"Well, my daddy taught me that ladies don't swear. And that gentlemen don't swear in front of ladies." She aimed a satisfied smile at him. "My brothers learned that by way of a few good swats and several bars of soap. I learned it by way of my brothers getting punished."

"So you never—"

She leaned forward. "Let's get one thing straight right here and now. I'm no shrinking violet who faints at the sight of blood. I can shoot straighter, fight harder and chase down a fugitive faster than anyone in my department, including my brothers and cousin." Her smile had disappeared. "But I don't swear. Now, what's your second question?"

"Why'd they leave the e's off of Bee?"

Cassie threw her head back and laughed. "Okay, first thing you need to know about this place is that Marge is the sole owner, so there's no 'they' making decisions around here. Second, the 'B' doesn't stand for Bee. It stands for Body." Cassie smiled at Bishop's puzzled expression. "Our Marge is ground zero for all gossip and rumors in Resolute and proud of it. So she named the place The Busy Body."

"Makes sense. But if she's so proud of the fact, why not spell out the word?"

"Because the 'y' in Body put it at eleven letters, and the price point she could afford for the sign out front was ten. The Busy Bod sounded wrong in more ways than one, so she just went with B. *And* made the sign guy give her a discount for having only eight letters."

Bishop laughed, his dimples deepening in his five-o'clock shadow.

Like Marge, Cassie felt the full force of those dimples. But no way would she give him the satisfaction of knowing. "You heading back to Houston this afternoon?" She tore into a package of soda crackers to tide her over until the food arrived.

"Why would you think that? I still have to find Ashley."

Pursing her lips, Cassie chose her words with care. "She's eighteen, Bishop. She's got the right to do what she wants, including getting married."

"That's the problem. I'm not sure she's doing what she wants." The words from Ashley's last journal entry haunted him. "There's more to this whole thing."

"I'm just not seeing it. There's no evidence that even hints at your niece being a missing person." She slid over in the booth and turned sideways, stretching her legs out along the seat. "I'd offer to help you keep looking, but I've got my hands full with that murder case." *And trying to break up a human trafficking ring. And figuring out who killed my father.* "Have you considered that you're thinking about this all wrong? Maybe you should be happy for your niece. Maybe Ashley and Mike are simply a modern-day Romeo and Juliet story."

Squeezing lemon wedges into his iced tea, Bishop paused, meeting her eyes. "You do know how that story ended, right?"

Cassie's mouth watered as he crushed the citrus, but it was the flexing tendons in his powerful hand and the scattering of dark hair at his tanned wrist that had her licking her lips. Pretty faces might not turn her head, but she'd always had a thing for masculine hands.

Marge returned with a full tray and set Bishop's food on the table. "Catfish, grilled, not fried."

"With a side of bland and tasteless," Bishop added with another wink for Marge.

"And here's your nekked salad, dressing on the side." The Busy B owner cackled with delight. "Get it? It's nekked 'cause it ain't dressed yet."

Bishop laughed with her, revealing yet another facet of his personality. Whether he found her remark funny or not, he made sure Marge thought he did. Cassie straightened in her seat when Marge set the burger and fries in front of her. Dousing everything on her plate with ketchup, she took a huge bite of the burger and held off replying to the Romeo and Juliet comment until she'd swallowed. With the greasy food filling her stomach, everything seemed right with the world.

"Can I get y'all anything else?"

"I'm good." Bishop forked catfish into his mouth. "This is delicious."

Marge's cheeks blushed red. "Of course it is. I cooked it." With a satisfied nod and grin, she headed to the kitchen.

Cassie turned her attention back to the conversation with Bishop. "Two young lovers eloping doesn't exactly equal tragic death all around. But I understand that you're worried about your niece." The pleading sorrow in Bishop's eyes when he'd thought his niece might be lying in the morgue had pierced her heart.

"That, I am. And by the way, I'm not buying the Romeo and Juliet story. Since Resolute is the last place she was seen, this is where I plan to start digging." Bishop dipped a fork tine into the salad dressing, touched it to his tongue. Pushing the tiny ramekin aside, he dug into the *nekked* salad. "I appreciate your help today, and I get it that you're busy. I actually prefer working cases on my own." Around a mouthful of greens, he added, "I do have a favor to ask, though."

Eyeing his healthy lunch with distaste, Cassie dragged a fry through the puddle of ketchup and popped it into her mouth. "I'm listening."

"Run a trace on Ashley's cell phone for me."

Cassie stopped midway from popping another fry into her mouth. *Seriously?* She dropped the fry on her plate. Wiping greasy fingers on a paper napkin, Cassie shook her head. "You know I can't do that, Mr. Bishop. Just as I presume you know that you can't officially make the request since you don't own the phone."

"You can run it if she's in imminent danger." He seemed oblivious to her now-frosty demeanor.

"There *is* no imminent danger that I'm aware of. Garrett

told us she eloped. I have no reason to doubt that." This is why pretty faces rarely did anything for her. They almost always spelled trouble.

Despite her irritation, the hunch of his shoulders and slight rounding of his eyes tugged at her heart. Still…

"Garrett's a liar. Billy's fourteen and just repeating what Garrett told him. How's that for doubt?"

"I'll grant you that. But based on what I know, it would be against the law for me to trace her phone, and you know it." She pushed her plate to the side, her appetite gone. He probably wouldn't believe her, but she was well acquainted with the frustration of being thwarted at every turn while trying to find a loved one. But the law was the law.

"Then at least issue be-on-the-lookout orders for Michael and Ashley's vehicles. If they ran off together, it makes no sense that both cars are gone."

"If they don't plan to come back to Resolute, it makes perfect sense that they took both vehicles." Cassie flagged down Marge for the check. "Most likely they'll head back to Houston. They might already be there by now." She eyed Bishop, whose mesmerizing dimples had been vanquished by disappointment. "Have you checked with her father?"

"My brother would have called me if she'd shown up. *Especially* if she'd shown up married." Bishop ran his fingers through his thick hair, leaving it standing out at odd angles that somehow charmed her and threatened to undo her resolve. "Why can't you just do me a solid and put out the BOLOs?"

"Because I have no legal cause to do that." Cassie bristled. He was pushing too hard. Time to push back. "Listen up, because I won't say this again. I don't break the law. Not for anyone."

Bishop's laugh lacked any trace of humor. "Seriously? You're telling me that you've never given a shoplifter a second chance? Coached someone giving a statement to make sure their attacker went to jail?"

Heat flooded Cassie's face. "I absolutely have not. What kind of sheriff do you think I am?" She stood, furious with him for even suggesting such things. But as she threw a twenty on the table, her anger turned toward herself. She should have known as soon as her stomach started fluttering like a dadgum hummingbird that he'd be no good for her. "And if you'd ever been a real cop, instead of just some private *dick*, you'd understand how important it is to follow the law. To the letter, *Mister* Bishop."

With that pronouncement, she strode toward the door, leaving him in the booth with no regrets.

Chapter Four

Well, *that* didn't end well.

Bishop took another sip of iced tea and leaned back in the booth. Not that he cared what Cassie Reed thought about his career choice. She was wrong, though, about him not knowing how crucial cops' rules were. He knew firsthand.

Crucial in screwing up investigations.

Crucial in getting a confidential informant killed.

Crucial in pushing a reputable detective to the brink of rage and madness.

He had only agreed to pause for lunch with the hope that he could enlist the sheriff's help. He'd been an idiot to think that a small-town sheriff might not be such a stickler for all those stifling rules. That maybe, just maybe, she'd be willing to extend him a little professional courtesy and bend the rules to make sure Ashley was found safe. It wasn't as if he'd asked her to do more than cut through the red tape.

At least now it was clear that he'd be on his own, and that was just fine with him. That clear-eyed, fresh-faced beauty with all those womanly curves was just another by-the-booker. He knew the type and wanted no part of it. Besides, working with her would only distract him as her scent, that of a warm summer evening washed clean by rain, enveloped him. Bishop dug his wallet out of his back pocket and added another twenty to the one Cassie had left.

Marge's rubber-soled squeak announced her arrival.

"Hold on, Fancy Pants." She picked up the cash. "I'll get you your change. Just be a minute."

"Keep it. I appreciate the special order."

Marge's eyes widened, as did her smile. "That's mighty kind of you, sir." She waved the money in her fist. "Tip like this, and I'll happily serve up bland and tasteless anytime you want. If you're not planning on leaving town, that is." Giving him a taste of his own medicine, she favored him with a conspiratorial wink.

Marge might shuffle along like an old lady in her orthopedic shoes, but there was nothing wrong with her hearing.

"As a matter of fact, I was wondering if you could recommend a good motel in town. Maybe something with a small fridge in the room?"

"I can do you one better." Marge flopped down opposite Bishop in the booth, letting out a loud sigh. "Lordy, it sure does feel good to get off my feet for a minute. Must have been crazy, opening a diner in this economy. Can't even afford to hire full-time help." She grabbed a napkin from the dispenser and wiped down the salt and pepper shakers before setting them back in their wire holder. "Now, the place you want to stay is Doc's Motor Court, out on the west edge of town. Just take Main Street to Pecan and hang a right. Can't miss it. He's got a row of rooms, but trust me, you don't want none of those."

"I don't?" Bishop relaxed against the booth back. The engaging conversation with Marge washed away the bitter taste left in his mouth after his encounter with the sheriff.

"'Course not. You'll be wanting one of them detached kitchenettes. That's where you'll get your refrigerator and coffee maker. Even a microwave and electric burner." She folded her arms across her full bosom. "Be gettin' a lot more privacy that way, too. The walls in them row rooms are as thin as cardboard. Guy in the next room farts, you'll be waving your hand in front of your nose."

Bishop chuckled at Marge's colorful way of expressing herself. Not like the uptight sheriff. "Gotcha."

"I'm dead serious. If Doc tries to stick you in one of them, you tell him I said to put you in his best detached or he's cut off for a month."

"Cut off?" Bishop's smile wavered. "From eating here?"

Marge tipped her head back, roaring with laughter until she sputtered and gasped for breath.

Bishop leaned across the table. "You all right? Do you need anything? Water? A pat on the back?"

His questions set her off again. "Whooee! I ain't had a laugh that good since I don't know when." Marge pulled a paper napkin from the holder and wiped tears from her eyes. "Me and Doc are married, ya see. And just 'cause we ain't exactly spring chickens don't mean we stopped having fun in the sack. *That's* what I meant by cut off." Her chortles tapered off.

Bishop adored Marge's candidness. "I figured that's what you meant. I just didn't want to assume—"

"Hogwash. You young'uns think passion dies at fifty. You'll learn differently someday." Marge gave Bishop a sharp nod. "Now then, back to the motor court. Doc's may not have a swimmin' pool or one of them free breakfast spreads, but it's cheap, clean, and has everything you'll need. Just promise me you'll come by here once in a while for some good, old-fashioned home cookin'. Don't just be nuking junk food in the microwave."

"Appreciate the recommendation, Marge. And I promise to eat—" Bishop tapped the Formica tabletop twice "—right here as often as possible. If the sheriff doesn't run me out of town first."

Marge reached over and patted his hand. "Don't you judge our Cassie too hard. There are reasons she's the way she is."

"I don't mean to judge her at all. But you have to admit, she is a bit…rigid."

"Rigid?" Marge snickered. "Oh, come on. Call it what it is. That girl's got a stick so far up her butt, it must tickle her tonsils. She just needs to loosen up and have some fun." She cocked her head to the side, scrutinizing Bishop's face. "And you might be just the fella to make that happen."

Bishop snorted.

Shaking her head, Marge pushed herself up from the booth, groaning with the effort. "Don't laugh it off just yet. You'll see. I'm right about darn near everything."

So thought almost every woman Bishop had ever known. But Marge didn't deserve the sharp edge of his cynicism, so he kept the snide remark to himself. Instead, he thanked her and left the diner.

A wave of heat blasted him as he eyed the parking spaces, remembering he'd left his truck at the justice building. With a groan, he began the sweltering trek back to his truck. Burning him up more than any blazing sun was the sheriff's refusal to trace Ashley's phone or put out the BOLOs. Two small asks that would've given him a jump start in his search and saved him crucial time.

Rounding a corner, Bishop paused in the shade of a shop's awning and pulled his phone out to check it. A couple missed calls from unknown numbers, but no voice messages. He scanned the list of new emails, none of them urgent. Several texts from Bob, sending the most recent pictures of Ashley he could find, as Bishop had requested. He clicked on one of the photos to enlarge it. He stared at the dark blue eyes that ran in his family, the innocent smile of a happy teenager. Or had Ashley just pretended to be happy for the picture, hiding her true emotions behind the smile? Hiding them within the pages of her journal?

Bishop's chest tightened, and he continued toward his

truck, his long strides eating up the distance. He'd wasted precious time stopping to eat with the sheriff, and all for nothing.

He'd find Ashley, and he didn't need Cassie Reed to do it.

A TWINGE OF guilt hit Cassie as she parked next to Bishop's truck in front of the justice center. The late August heat rose from the street in shimmering waves. He'd be lucky not to blister his feet right through his boot leather walking here from the diner.

But she didn't feel guilty enough to go back for him. She should have known he'd be like all the other men she'd been attracted to. Only interested in the easy way, not the right way.

Pushing through the front door, a blast of air-conditioning raised goose bumps on her arms.

"Whew! Feels good in here." She approached Helen's desk. "What do I need to know?"

"Sean, Dave and Noah are canvassing the neighborhood around the stash house again." Helen glanced at her desk calendar, where she faithfully kept track of all comings and goings of the deputies. "Lonnie's following up a lead on the victim, Adam's out on a vandalism call, and Pete's hanging around the bullpen in case any calls come in."

Already moving toward her office, Cassie U-turned as Helen's words sank in. "Lonnie has a lead on the victim?"

"He provided no other information, just that he'd be gone for a while."

"Hmm." Curiosity crawled through Cassie. Could Lonnie be close to discovering who their Jane Doe was? All they knew so far was that she wasn't local. None of her deputies had recognized the young woman from the crime scene photos, and no one from Resolute had been reported missing. If they were lucky, the victim's identity would lead them straight to the traffickers. Shutting down those degenerates was consuming her, much as it had her father. *What had Dad discovered that led to him being gunned down?*

"Notify the deputies, please." Cassie checked her watch. "Full team meeting at three o'clock sharp. We need to update one another and strategize a new game plan for these traffickers." She smoothed back the already taut hair at her temples, then winced when Helen's stiff brows arched at the telling gesture.

"What's got you more agitated than usual?" the older woman asked, never pausing as she straightened a stack of reports and placed them in her filing basket. The one attempt to hire a file clerk had ended with the clerk quitting in tears after Helen criticized the girl's work ethic and inability to grasp a basic understanding of the alphabet. Even Cassie steered clear of the file room out of fear of messing up her system.

Cassie jerked her hand away from her hair. "We clearly have a leak, and I can't be sure that it isn't the reason our Jane Doe is dead."

"There's no evidence to support that thinking, so stop adding stress to a plate already full of real issues." Helen slid a file drawer closed with a *thunk*. "What did you learn at the Pugh house?"

"At first, Garrett claimed he hadn't seen Mike *or* the girl. We talked to Billy outside, and he told us Mike and Ashley *had* been there. Apparently, it caused quite a row between Mike and Garrett. You should have seen Garrett's face. What a mess."

"Odd that he lied about seeing them." Helen rose to sort through a stack of files on the credenza behind her desk.

"That's what we thought, too. When we went back to the house to talk to Garrett again, he took off like the bogeyman was on his heels. And that's after he clobbered Bishop with the screen door."

"He's just 'Bishop' now?" Helen kept her tone neutral, but arched her brow again. Sometimes it was doggone annoying working with people who knew you so well. "And he got clobbered with a screen door?" She shrugged as she handed Cassie several case files. "Never a dull moment with those Pugh boys. Did you find out why Garrett lied?"

"He told us Mike and Ashley ran off to get married. Allegedly, Mike made him promise not to tell anyone." Cassie turned away, then turned back. "I'll be in my office. If *Mr.* Bishop happens to show up, ask him to leave a message. I have work to do." She held up the case files.

She'd taken only three steps toward her office when Helen said, "So it's like that, is it?"

Cassie whipped around. "Like *what*, Helen?" The unsuccessful raid and a dead Jane Doe. A possible leak. Garrett's hinky behavior. Bishop's casual request that she break the law. And now this. She was not in the mood.

Helen stood taller and raised her chin. "You've no cause to take that tone with me, Cassie Reed. You may be my boss, but I've been looking out for you since the day your mother took off. Tell me to mind my own business if you want, but the least you can do is use a civil tone while you're doing it."

Cassie drew in a deep breath, then exhaled slowly. "You're right. I apologize. And it is none of your business."

"I figured that would be your attitude."

Lord, give me patience. "Okay, out with it. I'll get no peace until you do."

Helen settled her skinny butt in her chair. "Electricity was crackling between you two before you even walked out the door this morning. Now you're avoiding him, hiding out in your office."

"As you said yourself, I've got a lot on my plate right now. The last thing I need is to get involved—"

"Think about it, Cassie." Helen held up one finger. "Eyes

bluer than a Texas swimming hole." She added another finger. "Dimples for days." Third finger. "And he'll be leaving town sooner or later. Sounds like the perfect man for you."

"What's that last one supposed to mean?" Cassie crossed her arms. "Leaving town sooner or later?"

Helen scoffed. "I've known you since you were knee-high to a grasshopper. You've never been in a relationship that wasn't over before it started." She shrugged her bony shoulders. "You're the love-'em-and-leave-'em queen of Boone County."

Even the icy air-conditioning couldn't mitigate the heat flowing through Cassie. "That's not true. And I don't appreciate—"

Helen held her hands up in a defensive position. "I couldn't have worked for your father for so many years without coming to know and care about you and your brothers. So anything I say is said out of love." Her eyes softened, draining the ire out of Cassie.

"I know." Cassie bit her lip. Helen had always been the one she'd turned to when she needed advice from a woman. Advice on raising three younger brothers. Advice on the facts of life when she'd hit puberty. "But I *don't* love 'em and leave 'em."

"No, technically *they* leave because you always choose men who are just passing through."

"Well, it would be pretty darn awkward living in a small town full of exes."

There went Helen's judgy brow again.

"I just haven't found the right man yet."

"Whatever you say, sweetie." With a knowing smile, Helen lowered her gaze back to her computer screen.

Cassie huffed and strode toward her office.

"You keep rolling your eyes like that, they're gonna get stuck." Helen's singsong voice followed her down the hall.

Closing her office door, Cassie tossed the files on her

desk and crossed the room. The justice center's architecture reflected an era when buildings were designed with character, rather than today's sleek lines of steel and glass. As a result, she was blessed not with a sterile, fluorescent-lit workplace where so many in law enforcement spent their days, but a spacious corner office with magnificent windows on two walls.

Desperate for a moment to gather her thoughts, she stared across at the empty town square. After 8:00 p.m., when evening came and the temperature finally dropped below ninety degrees, the grassy, tree-lined square would fill with people walking dogs, pushing strollers or just enjoying the fresh air. Cassie often joined in, finding contentment mixing with the townsfolk. Her dad had taught her that good peace officers didn't just protect their town, they participated in it.

A flash of movement caught her eye, and just like that, her growing sense of calm evaporated. Bishop hustling toward his truck. Jaywalking. She might have known. Helen may know nothing when it came to Cassie's relationships, but she was on the mark when it came to the intriguing PI. He was definitely easy on the eyes. And he could probably charm the dew off the honeysuckle.

Well, she wasn't honeysuckle. And she dang sure wasn't Marge, cooking special meals after getting suckered by a pretty face. Even Helen seemed to soften where Bishop was concerned. Well, not her. Not with his lack of ethics. The man didn't seem to know how wrong things could go when the rules weren't followed. But Cassie did. All too well.

As Bishop approached, he looked directly at her window. The sun reflecting off the glass must surely prevent him from seeing her. Then again, maybe not. For at that very moment he raised his arm and waved at her, flashing that dimpled grin.

Startled, Cassie jerked away from the window, then immediately berated herself. It wasn't as though she'd been watching for him. She'd chewed him out at the diner, so what in tarnation were the wave and grin about? Probably a sorry attempt to get under her skin even more. *Not likely, Mr. Bishop.*

She stepped back to the window, catching a glimpse of his truck backing up, then peeling out with a screech of rubber on hot pavement. She didn't know where he was going in such an all-fire hurry, but Resolute had speed limits. Shaking her head with annoyance, Cassie stepped over to her desk and dropped into the well-worn leather executive chair. It had been her dad's, as had the desk, and the office, for longer than she'd been alive. When the county council had chosen her to take over as sheriff a few months earlier, she'd considered getting a new chair. Or at least moving the one she'd used as chief deputy into this office. But she couldn't bring herself to do it.

The first time Cassie had sat on the leather seat and run her hands over the scuffed wooden arms, the legacy of Wallace Reed had flowed into her. She'd learned from the best sheriff this county had ever known, and she'd resolved to keep his office exactly as he'd left it. His ethereal presence lingered, guiding her, giving her the confidence to solve his murder and shut down the traffickers.

Cassie spent the next hour reviewing crime scene reports from the raid. The forensic investigators in Austin were processing all the evidence since Boone County had no specialists of its own. There'd been so many items collected, not everything had been tested yet. Despite numerous fingerprints at the location, so far there were no matches in the databases. DNA results from still-viable body fluids wouldn't be back anytime soon. Other items collected—a few loose coins, one black hoop earring etched with skulls, and a pocketknife—were waiting for the overworked techs to examine.

Exhaling in frustration, Cassie unlocked her top-left desk drawer and pulled out the file on her father's murder. He'd been shot to death in what was clearly an ambush, set up on a call about the trafficking case. She reread the report every few days, each time hoping to find some small detail that she might have overlooked.

Helen's buzz interrupted her futile search.

Cassie punched the intercom button. "Yes?"

"Everyone's back. They're waiting for you in the briefing room."

"Be right there." Cassie closed her father's file, placed it back in the drawer and locked it. She rose and headed to the small conference room they used for briefings, the muscles across her shoulders achingly tight. Plug the leak and shut down the traffickers, and she might finally learn who had brutally shot her father. Nothing else mattered.

Chapter Five

Cassie entered the room flushed with renewed purpose. Lonnie stood at the end of the first table, his right foot on a chair as he leaned forward, speaking with Pete. Noah sat on the other side of Pete, chin to chest, arms crossed, and legs stretched out and crossed at the ankles. He appeared to be dozing. *Gonna have to have a talk with that boy.* At the second table, Sean and Adam sat with an empty chair between them. Each had an open folder before them, studying the papers spread out on the table. Dave, as expected, sat alone at the far end of that table.

Cassie stepped to the lectern and set her own folder down. The room was small enough that she didn't need a microphone, and when she cleared her throat all chatter ceased.

"Noah?" Her loud voice startled him awake. "Will you please take notes on the whiteboard?"

"Huh? Sorry." He rubbed the sleep from his eyes and made his way to the large board at the front. "Guess the heat got to me some."

Dave snickered. "Heat didn't bother Sean or me none."

"That's because you—" Noah started.

"That's enough!" Cassie's voice reverberated around the room. Then at normal volume, she said, "I want to go over yesterday's raid and review everything we have on the victim and scene." She glanced at Dave Sanders, their newest deputy, and the last one her dad had hired. It wasn't his slight frame, thick glasses and pale skin that made Cassie question his career choice. It was his seemingly total lack of common sense. "I know you stayed here to answer calls during the raid, Dave. But I assume you've familiarized yourself with the case details by now."

Dave, slouched in his chair, nodded.

Normally easygoing with her deputies, today Cassie's tone was stern. "I've reviewed the evidence reports. So far, not much to go on, but the investigators still have a lot to wade through." Her gaze swiveled to Adam. "Any updates from the ME's office? Have they ID'd the girl?"

Adam straightened in his chair. "Not yet. I checked again just before the meeting, and they said they'd contact us as soon as they learn anything."

Pursing her lips, Cassie nodded. Some things were beyond their control. Her gaze lit on Lonnie. If his lead on the vic had turned up anything he would've told her immediately, so she continued with the other deputies' reports and left Lonnie's for last. "Sean. Y'all learn anything new during the neighborhood canvass?"

The no-nonsense deputy stood as if still in the military. It was the one habit he couldn't seem to break, and it sure wasn't one to complain about. "Yes, ma'am." He pulled out his pocket notebook and flipped it open. "Approximately one week ago, the neighbor across the alley behind the stash house, a Mrs. Crenshaw, saw a box truck in the alley, backing in and across the yard until it was right up tight to the house. She heard the backup warning and wondered why it was beeping for so long. Said the truck had to maneuver for a while to avoid taking down any fences."

Cassie motioned Noah to write this information on the whiteboard. "I don't suppose she caught a plate number or a description of the driver?"

"No, ma'am. But she said the back bumper was dented

in on the driver side, and there was a logo on the side of the truck." Sean referred back to his notes. "Victoria Appliance Sales." He sat, his back still ramrod straight.

"Nothing out of the ordinary about that. Most folks in Resolute order stuff like appliances and furniture from Victoria." Dave added his two cents. "It's a lot closer than San Antonio."

Noah's mouth dropped open as he turned toward his fellow deputy. "Way to miss the point, Dave. There weren't any new appliances in that house."

"Or empty spaces left by repossessed ones." Sean shook his head at the newbie. "Think before you open that big yap of yours, Sanders."

"I was just stating a fact, *Cavanaugh*. Remember, I had to stay here while you guys went on the raid. How am I supposed to know what was or wasn't in the stupid house?" Dave crossed his arms.

"Dave, it seems you just stated a fact that proves you did *not* read the reports." Cassie gripped the edge of the lectern. She needed to pair the newbie up with an experienced partner and hope he increased his street smarts. "But we'll discuss that later. Privately."

He aimed a sullen glare at his boss.

"Let's get back on track, shall we?" Cassie turned again to Sean. "How long was the truck parked at the back door? And no need to stand this time."

Sean answered without glancing at his notes. "It came in late evening and was gone by the next morning. She didn't see it leave."

"That explains why we didn't see it when we staked out the house." Peter so seldom spoke during briefings that everyone paid attention when he did. "We made note of all passenger vehicles coming and going before the raid. They all checked out. Besides, we knew it was too risky to move the girls individually, so we figured they were in something bigger. We never caught a van or box truck anywhere near the house."

Only once had Cassie been on a stakeout with Pete. One of the most boring nights of her life. The man was an enigma, keeping his own counsel even more than she did.

Noah moved away from the whiteboard and grabbed his notebook. "I can confirm that account of a late-night delivery truck. Um, give me a sec." Flipping pages for a few moments, Noah finally found what he sought. "Here it is. Mr. Boyd Jackson, who lives next door to the stash house, said it was full-on dark. He couldn't make out the logo, and when the driver opened the double back doors, they almost touched the house. He couldn't see what they were loading or unloading, but he knew the house was empty. Thought maybe the owner hired a cleaning crew or renovation company. He did think it was odd, it happening so late at night."

Cassie cocked a brow at Noah and waved a hand toward the board. "This is good work, Noah. Write it down." Hoping for more useful tidbits, she asked, "Did we find anyone who *heard* anything?"

Noah finished writing before turning back toward the others. "Yeah, Mr. Jackson's wife. She said that same night, after they'd gone to bed, she awoke to the sound of cats."

"Cats?" Dave's sarcastic tone made Cassie close her eyes for a moment. Although Noah had been on the force longer and had more experience, Dave was older. For some reason he seemed to think he was entitled to better assignments than Noah and took out his frustration verbally. She needed to shut that down, and quick.

"Yeah, *cats*." Noah glared at Dave. "She said she got up in the middle of the night and thought she heard a child crying. But it was off and on, sometimes more than one at a time. She finally decided it had to be feral cats in the alley."

Noah wrote "Cats!" on the board with no urging from Cassie.

"Helen said you were chasing a lead on the victim?" Cassie asked Lonnie.

"I thought she might be a dancer at Bush Whackers out on State Highway 87. Drove out there, talked to Shorty, but he said he hadn't hired anyone new."

Adam leaned forward to smirk down the row at Lonnie. "Fess up, Dixon. You were just getting your jollies while the rest of us were working."

Everyone, including Lonnie, laughed. "Hey, I take my job very seriously."

Cassie allowed the moment before moving on to the next subject. "Okay, time to address the elephant in the room." Frustration was burning a hole in her stomach. "Yesterday's raid was my first since becoming sheriff, and it went south. Three more like it when my father ran things. This many is no coincidence, which means we have a leak."

This brought her team to their feet, voicing loud, indignant denials. Cassie raised her hands. "All right, all right. Settle down. You can't tell me I'm the only one to draw this conclusion." Her men reluctantly took their seats and the room finally quieted.

Lonnie broke the silence, his voice cold. "Are you saying someone in this room is dirty?"

"No, I'm not. I trust every man in this room with my life. The leak could be coming from other sources." She paused. Though she believed what she'd just said in her heart, she knew she couldn't rule out a leak among her group. She just wasn't about to announce that worry. "Anyone have any thoughts?"

"My money's on Judge Harmon's office," Sean said.

"He issues the warrants, and that man's known for his indiscretions, especially when he's had too much to drink."

"Which is pretty often," Pete added.

Adam shrugged. "Could be someone in clerical, maybe."

"Possibly," Cassie agreed. "I'll speak to Helen. She knows everyone in the building."

"Have you asked Marge if she's heard any rumors?" Noah asked. "If anyone knows something, it would be her."

"I don't discuss ongoing cases with anyone. And especially now, none of you better, either." Cassie went eye to eye with each man to emphasize her words. "Besides, Marge would have told me if she'd heard about anything hinky going on."

Cassie's cell phone vibrated. She pulled it from her pocket and read the text from Helen.

Two Texas Rangers waiting for you. They don't look happy.

"Meeting adjourned."

CASSIE SETTLED INTO her office chair before calling Helen. "Please bring them back."

"Yes, ma'am." The line went dead.

A moment later a sharp rap on the door sounded and Helen entered ahead of two tall, lean men wearing the prerequisite Stetsons and silver cinco-peso badges. "Ranger Ward." She tipped her head toward the man to her right.

"Ma'am." He removed his hat to reveal cropped sandy blond hair.

Before Helen could introduce the man to her left, he stepped forward, also removing his hat. "Ranger Mills, Sheriff."

"Thank you, Helen. Gentlemen, have a seat and tell me what I can do for you."

Both men sat, resting their Stetsons on their laps. They

waited until Helen left the room, pulling the door closed behind her.

Ward took lead. "Sheriff Reed, are you aware of a human trafficking ring operating within Boone County?"

"I'm well aware. We've been tracking their movements for some time," she acknowledged. "In fact, just yesterday—"

"Let me stop you there, Sheriff," Ward interrupted, the frown lines between his brows deepening. "We're not here to work on the trafficking case."

"Not directly," Mills added.

Cassie cocked a brow and waited.

Ward resumed. "We've received information that someone is tipping off the traffickers. Letting them know when raids will take place, among other things."

Shocked that the Rangers knew about the leak, Cassie's pulse quickened. "Yes, my father, the former sheriff, came to the same conclusion. We were working that angle when he was killed." Cassie cleared her throat of the telling emotion. It was still hard to talk about her father's death. "Are you here because you know who the leak is? Or do you need my help finding the source? Because, gentlemen, if we plug this leak, then shutting down those traffickers just got a whole lot easier."

Neither Ranger had smiled since entering her office. Maybe they never smiled. But now, their mouths pinched into tight, straight lines, they both looked downright grim.

There's more going on here than they're telling me. Cassie held their gaze as good as she got. "We going to sit here all day, or are you going to tell me why you're really here?"

Mills looked to Ward, who nodded ever so slightly. "We have information that suggests the leak is someone within these walls."

Cassie leaned against the back of her chair, hands in her

lap. "We've considered that and are currently investigating it. It's quite possible someone within the clerical office or judge's chambers—"

"We're not talking about the entire building," Mills said.

Cassie's fingers curled into fists, the short nails digging into her palms as a visceral dread ran through her. It unsettled her to think a member of her team could be responsible for tipping off the bad guys. She sure as heck didn't want to share that worry with outsiders. If it was someone she trusted, she needed to track them down on her own and deal with it. By the book, yes, but with fairness. Her team was family in more ways than one.

"As of this moment," Ward added, "you and your deputies are no longer authorized to work on the trafficking case. All related files will be confiscated and online access denied until we've completed a full investigation of the Boone County Sheriff's Department." He handed her an envelope he'd been holding beneath his hat. "This gives us the authority."

She snatched the offending paper from his outstretched hand, fighting the urge to rip it to shreds. "This is ridiculous. It's obvious that your informant is playing you for fools."

"Ma'am, we take corruption very seriously and would advise you to do the same." Ward stood. "We require space in the building to work from." He opened her office door and paused, as if expecting her to jump up and fulfill his demand.

Cassie made no move to stand. "If you'll both have a seat in the reception area, I'll see what I can find." She caught the look that passed between the two men, and Ward's scowl filled her with a petty satisfaction.

"We'd like to get started as soon as possible." He exited her office, Mills on his heels.

Cassie could barely breathe. Her palms throbbed where

her nails had drawn blood. Ward said they weren't going after the trafficking ring themselves. Pulling her whole department from the case would give the traffickers free rein to cross through her county.

She needed to find the real culprit responsible for the leaks.

But first things first. Cassie punched the phone button for Helen and asked her to come to her office. Between the two of them, they'd find the perfect space for the Rangers to use. She was pretty sure a corner in the basement was available.

Chapter Six

Bishop chuckled to himself as he climbed into his truck. He'd barely glimpsed Cassie's face at the window, but the flash of red hair had given her away. He wouldn't mind getting to know the vexing sheriff a little better, but finding Ashley was his number one priority. Too bad Cassie wasn't willing to cut a bureaucratic corner or two to assist.

Bishop drove southwest out of town, intent on questioning Garrett again, this time without the inflexible sheriff looking over his shoulder. But when he approached the house, a faded red Corolla was parked in the driveway behind the old Mustang. Unable to stake out the house without being made, he braked, took a picture of the car's plate and headed back to Resolute. Best to identify Garrett Pugh's visitor before getting in the kid's face again.

After making a few stops in town for necessities, Bishop followed Marge's simple directions to the motel. Doc's Motor Court looked to be straight out of a movie from the fifties. The facade above the office arched over the driveway to connect with a thick stucco wall surrounding the property. Just as engaging as his wife, Doc talked his ear off while checking Bishop into one of the stand-alone kitchenettes.

He hauled his bags inside the sweltering room as quickly as possible and cranked the window unit to high. After stripping down to boxers and socks, he crammed his groceries into the small fridge and set his new smoothie blender on the counter. Still sweating, he dropped into the chair by a small table.

It had been a long day, and he wasn't any closer to finding Ashley. He rubbed his chest just above the sternum, trying to ease a tightening band of anxiety. Anxiety he hadn't experienced since leaving the police force.

Pulling his laptop from the duffel bag, he powered it on and plugged in the Toyota's license plate. Technically, he shouldn't run searches on vehicles not directly related to a case he was working. But Bishop didn't pay attention to many technicalities.

Armed with the owner's name, he started a background check. Turned out Kevin Palmer was quite an enigma. Born in El Paso, his past addresses included San Antonio, Midland and Fort Stockton. He was currently renting a house in Flowertop, a small town not far from Resolute. His spotty work history consisted of short-term stints in manual labor.

Although the employment gaps could have valid explanations, they nagged at Bishop once he linked them to corresponding stretches when Palmer's Texas driver's license was expired. The man might have just moved out of state during those periods, but Bishop's gut said Palmer had been doing time.

Bishop pulled up the Texas DPS Crime Records database and tried to log in. After exceeding his password attempts, he remembered he'd changed it recently. Calling to reset it meant working his way through an automated list of options longer than a country block. It would be faster to request the records in person.

He pulled on his T-shirt and jeans and jogged to his truck. If he calculated correctly, he should make it to the justice center right before it closed, though he may have to break the local speed limit to do it. That didn't mat-

ter. If Palmer had a criminal record, Bishop would have
a copy of it by end of day.

"THIS ROOM SHOULD be fine for them." Helen had vetoed the
basement, suggesting instead a large unused office in the
back of the building. "I'll have a second desk moved in.
There's plenty of space."

Cassie eyed the old desk and rickety chair already in
the room. "Fine. And since you insist on keeping them up
here, maybe you could swing by a few times throughout
the day, ask if they'd like coffee or something."

Helen's eyes widened. "Well, let's just take a giant step
backward in women's equality, shall we?"

"I'm not asking you to wait on them." Cassie chuckled at
the indignant expression on Helen's face. "But if you have
an excuse to loiter outside their door from time to time, you
might pick up some intel."

"I'll be sure to keep my ear to the ground." She patted
Cassie's arm as they walked toward the front lobby. "Don't
worry. I'm sure they're wrong about our department. If not,
they'll find the leak *for* you. Either way, they'll be gone before you know it."

Less than an hour later, Helen was eating her words.

BISHOP THANKED THE clerk for the printed copy of Palmer's
report. She gave him a tight smile that lasted only long
enough to close up her station, muttering something under
her breath about people waiting until closing time.

Bishop's own smile faded as he lowered himself onto
a bench in the lobby, reading Kevin Palmer's rap sheet.

The man had spent more than half of his thirty-eight
years behind bars. His most recent stint ended about a year
ago. The arrests corresponded to Palmer's addresses on
record. El Paso, San Antonio and again in El Paso. The
crimes included felony shoplifting, possession with intent

to distribute, assault, assault with a deadly weapon, and sexual assault.

Palmer had roofied a young woman, then raped her after she was passed out. She'd been nineteen. He'd been thirty-one. Five years in prison for ruining a life before it had barely started. Palmer had claimed the sex was consensual and his buddies backed up his testimony. After the victim had filed the police report and put herself through the added trauma of an exam and evidence collection, she'd refused to testify. Palmer's friends had most likely scared the ever-loving daylights out of her, threatening her life as well as her family's if she showed up in court. He'd seen it more times than he liked to count during his days on the force.

But even without the victim's testimony, the rape kit evidence, together with the victim's blood test revealing Rohypnol, was enough to get the creep the minimum sentence.

And within a matter of months after getting out, he was living in Boone County and hanging out with Garrett Pugh, Ashley's boyfriend's brother. This was one game of Six Degrees of Separation Bishop could do without.

"What are you doing here?"

Bishop's gaze shifted from the report in his hand to a pair of starched and ironed black jeans in front of him. Tipping his neck back, his eyes locked with the flashing green of Cassie's. Beneath the harsh fluorescent lights, a smattering of freckles across her nose stood out starkly against her pale skin.

"Is there a reason I'm not supposed to be here?"

Her lips pursed in tandem with her narrowing eyes. "I just don't want you to get in the habit of asking me to help you break the law."

"Me? Never." Bishop flashed her an offended look. "Besides, I really don't need your help, Sheriff. I just came by to pick up the rap sheet on a suspect related to my missing niece."

"You got Garrett Pugh's criminal record?" Cassie scoffed. "I could have given you that off the top of my head."

"Nope. Not Garrett Pugh."

"Who then?"

"Kevin Palmer."

"Who on earth is Kevin Palmer?"

"He's the owner of the vehicle parked in Garrett Pugh's driveway when I drove by after lunch."

Cassie crossed her arms. "You went back out to the Pugh house? If Garrett files a complaint that you're harassing him—"

"I told you, I just drove by."

"Then how do you know who owns a car in his driveway?"

Bishop flashed a cat-ate-the-canary grin.

"Tell me you didn't run his plates."

Maintaining his silence, Bishop just kept smiling.

"You know you're not supposed to—"

"Run plates on a vehicle that isn't directly involved in my investigation." He shrugged. "Turns out, this vehicle *is* involved in my investigation. So no harm, no foul."

As a red hue crept up Cassie's neck and colored her face with what could only be anger, Bishop stood.

"Bottom line, Sheriff, I'm going to do whatever's necessary to bring Ashley home safe and alive. In my line of work, the end justifies the means."

Without waiting for a reply, Bishop crossed the lobby and pushed through the front door. He looked back over his shoulder before descending the steps. Cassie faced him through the glass, arms at her sides, boots spread slightly apart. Like a beautiful gunslinger looking for a fight.

Chapter Seven

Cassie balanced the warm pie in one hand as she opened the front door to her family's ranch house, dreading tonight's conversation. Her brothers' voices rumbled out from the kitchen, a mixture of good-natured ribbing and laughter. Though she had her own place in town now and loved it, Cassie would always think of this ranch where she grew up as home.

"Finally! Hurry up. We're starving." Leave it to Nate to prioritize things.

Despite being fraternal twins, Nate and Noah couldn't be more different. Noah had planned from the get-go to join the sheriff's department and work with the rest of the family. Nate had seemed to want anything *but* a career in law enforcement. After wandering aimlessly for a few years, he'd come home for their father's funeral and decided to stay put. Hopefully, for good.

"Nice to see you, too." Cassie held out the dessert.

"You know I'm happy you're here." Nate gave her a one-armed hug as he took the pie from her. "Apple?"

"Peach." Cassie followed him through the house to the kitchen.

"Hey, sis." Noah leaned against the butcher-block counter, a beer bottle in one hand.

"Hey. Where's Adam?"

"Out back, grilling steaks." Noah waggled his almost empty bottle. "Want one?"

"No, thanks." Cassie crouched in front of an antique washstand repurposed into a liquor cabinet and pulled out a bottle of tequila. "A day like today deserves shooters."

"I'll drink to that." Nate grabbed a lime from the fridge and sliced it into wedges. "Bad day at work?"

Cassie filled four shot glasses to the brim. "That's an understatement."

The twins whistled low in unison.

Without further ado, Cassie licked the back of her left hand between the thumb and forefinger and sprinkled it with salt. Picking up one of the glasses, she licked the salt, tossed the tequila and sucked on a wedge of lime. Her eyes closed, she exhaled as the burn slid through her, taking too little of the day's stress with it.

Adam came through the back door with a platter of steaming bone-in rib eyes and potatoes wrapped in foil. "Glad you made it in time for dinner." His smile, aimed at Cassie, dimmed when he caught sight of the empty shot glass in her hand. "Or am I?"

In response, she poured herself another and carried it, along with Adam's, into the dining room.

"Why do I get the feeling you're gonna ruin our appetites?" Noah joined them.

"Nothing ruins *your* appetite." Nate sat next to his twin. "And more pie for me if y'all aren't hungry for dessert."

Adam set the platter in the middle of the table, next to a basket of rolls. "Pie?"

"I swung by Marge's on my way here. My contribution to the feast."

"You really should learn how to bake one of these days. Or at least some basic cooking," Adam said. "'Cause unless you marry a chef, your kids are gonna be malnourished."

Cassie snorted. "Don't hold your breath. I had enough rug-rat-raising with you three."

"What are you talking about? I was a perfect child." Noah grinned. "But I'm good with you bringing professionally made stuff."

"I'm with Noah." Nate scoffed at his siblings' raised eyebrows. "*Not* about you being perfect." He pointed his fork at his brother, then swung it in his sister's direction. "But I'm still traumatized from your cooking when we were kids. Sure glad Adam took over when he was old enough."

Cassie tipped her head in acknowledgment, glad for the pleasant family banter. She'd be ruining it soon enough. "I agree. Why waste time learning something I don't enjoy when there are others who excel at it?"

"You *could* use a hobby." Adam passed the platter to Cassie. "Even Dad went fishing on his days off. You don't seem to do anything but work."

An image of her backyard shed turned pottery studio popped into Cassie's mind. Transforming lumps of clay calmed her mind when stressed. Soothed her soul while grieving. Connected her to a part of herself she kept hidden from everyone, especially her family. It was a part that came directly from her mother, the free-spirited artistic part that had destroyed her parents' marriage.

"Maybe that private investigator could be your new hobby." Noah talked around a mouthful of meat. "Spent most of the day with him, didn't you?"

Adam eyed Cassie. "What private investigator?"

"Just some PI from Houston, looking for his niece." Cassie focused on topping her potato with sour cream and bacon.

"Better grab him while he's in town, sis. He's a lot better-looking than most of your exes." Noah chuckled.

"I hadn't noticed." She shoved a bite of roll in her mouth, avoiding her brothers' eyes.

Noah snorted. "Come on, sis. Even *I* noticed."

"I'm *not* interested in him. Can we please change the subject?" Not that changing the subject would help clear Bishop's pretty face from her mind.

"But what if he can cook?" Nate grinned at her from across the table.

"If he can, it wouldn't be anything I'd want to eat. He doesn't eat anything fried. Or *cow*. Marge had to make him grilled fish for lunch, and he ate his salad naked."

Noah's face transformed into the definition of horrified. "Where's he from?"

"Believe it or not, Texas. Born and bred."

Noah shook his head slowly. "That's just wrong." Then, as if proving his point, he shoved a chunk of medium-rare into his mouth.

Conversation waned as they all got serious about the food. Knives and forks clattered against plates, jaws chomped meat, Noah gnawed at his steak's bone. The Reed family was never one to stand on ceremony.

Even so, Cassie loved her brothers something fierce. How someone could think any of these three gold-hearted boneheads could turn rat, she had no idea. And as hard as Adam and Noah worked for her every day, Cassie dreaded bringing up the dire direction the trafficking case was taking.

As if reading her mind, Adam spoke first. "So, you want to tell us what's going on with the Rangers?" Setting his knife and fork down, he leaned back in his chair.

"And why can't we get into the files?" Noah asked.

A bite of blood-rare steak halfway to her mouth, Cassie paused. "Y'all know, huh?"

Adam nodded, his early humor gone. "But we wanted to give you a moment before we brought it up. Especially with you doing shooters."

"We also wanted you to eat something. No one likes a

hangry Cassie." Noah's smile was a bit forced this time, but she loved him all the more for it.

There had never been any question that Cassie would take over when their father died. None of the male bravado hogwash that most women in her position would've faced. Because her brothers knew her to be the best candidate. Knew her drive and conviction for justice that had nothing to do with whether she was a man or a woman. They respected her. And more importantly, even at times like this when she had to be sheriff before sister, they loved her.

Cassie put her fork down and sat up straighter, doing her brothers the courtesy of looking each one in the eye before starting. "The Rangers informed me that they know about the leak. They think it's someone in our office."

Adam nodded, as if he'd already thought of the possibility. "No way the leak wears a badge, if that's what they're implying." He bit the side of his lip, apparently contemplating his next words. "Dave's the only possibility, and only because he's still pretty new and we don't know much about him—"

"Other than he's a pain in the butt," Noah chimed in.

"Other than that," Adam agreed, his tone more serious than jovial. "But the guy is all talk. On calls, he shies away from confronting anyone."

Excitement lit Noah's face. "Maybe that's it. He's trying to impress people when he's out drinking by exaggerating his involvement in cases."

Cassie waited and listened. She may be sheriff, but Adam and Noah were both excellent deputies. And although Nate didn't wear a badge, his intelligent observations offered a different point of view. She'd be shortsighted not to consider more ideas than just her own.

"I guess it's possible," Adam agreed. "But my money's on someone who's not a deputy."

"Can't be Heather in the county clerk's office," Noah said around a mouthful of roll. "She's too stupid."

"Noah!" Cassie had taught him better than that.

He looked at his sister and shrugged. "It's true, though. I mean, she's efficient enough, but have you ever tried to have a conversation with her? She's not the sharpest tool in the shed."

Cassie gave him the look that, as a child, had worked better than a scolding.

"Come on, sis." Noah flashed her the puppy-dog eyes that had also worked well when they were kids. "It's not like we're going to say this to her face."

"Doesn't matter." Cassie huffed, annoyed that her voice lacked the sharp tone she needed when faced with his faux-innocent expression. "No need to be so blunt about it."

"What about Judge Harmon's file clerk? I think her name's Mandy." Adam rose and paced around the table. "She sees all his paperwork, including requests for warrants."

"What about his secretary? She *prepares* all his paperwork." Noah leaned back in his chair.

"I've seen Mandy hanging out at the Dead End. She gets pretty wild after a few drinks." Adam stopped circling them. "Some biker jerk picks her up after work. Has long greasy hair and wears one of those military helmets. Tats all over his arms and neck."

"What makes him a jerk?" Nate asked, the only Reed still eating.

"He sits outside the back door and revs the engine while he's waiting for her."

Noah straightened. "I've seen that dude in the Dead End. Playing pool with another guy who had a bunch of tattoos. It was weird, 'cause they both had the same tat on their left hand."

"You got close enough to examine their tattoos?" Nate snorted. "What were you doing, trying to—"

"They were both bridging their cue sticks with that hand, wise guy." Noah sneered at his twin. "It was kind of hard to miss, even from a distance. Didn't get a good enough look at precisely what the tats were, though."

Cassie put both hands on the table and leaned forward, looking to wind them back down. "I appreciate the theories, but right now the Rangers are certain it *is* someone wearing a badge. They said there would be a thorough investigation of our department, and until they complete it we're off the trafficking case."

Noah rose so suddenly his chair fell over behind him. "Are you kidding? They're going to be working it instead?"

Cassie gritted her teeth. "Apparently not. They seem to be focused only on the leak."

"That's great." Picking up his chair, Noah sat again. "So they're just going to let the real bad guys run free and mess with innocent girls' lives because they think someone with a badge is leaking info." He snorted so hard he coughed. "Real heroes, those guys."

Cassie glanced at Adam. His eyes bored into hers as if he was sussing out additional information she hadn't delivered yet.

Steeling herself for the difficult part still to come, Cassie took a deep breath. "What I'm about to tell you stays between us. Understood?" She waited for their nods before continuing. "Right before I left tonight, Helen came into my office. She told me the Rangers asked her for copies of personnel reports."

"Well, obviously if they're investigating your department, they need those. Right?" Nate glanced from Cassie to Adam. "Right?"

"The only reports they wanted were mine, yours—" she

looked at Adam "—yours—" her gaze moved on to Noah "—Lonnie's and Dad's."

"What the...?" Noah's brows pinched together. "Dad's? That makes no sense."

Adam stilled, staring at Cassie as if wordlessly communicating with her. When he got like this, he reminded her of the duck joke. Calm on the surface but paddling like crazy below. "Why isn't Lonnie here tonight? He needs to know this, too."

"I invited him. He said he had other plans that he couldn't change."

"Probably a poker game or a hot date." Noah scoffed. "That guy has perfected bachelor life."

"If you'd told him what tonight was about, he would have changed his plans." Nate glanced at her. They all considered Lonnie another brother, but Nate was especially close to his cousin.

"I told him it was important and he needed to be here." Cassie shrugged. "It was his choice. Don't worry, I'll make sure he knows."

Adam leaned forward, his forearms on the table. "So... why do they think *we're* involved?"

"Someone had to have fed them false info." Cassie rubbed her eyes. "What we need to figure out is *who* and *why*."

"And in the meantime, no one's working the case." Adam blew out a hard breath.

"I bet Helen hasn't been locked out of the computer files," Nate said. "If one of you gave her a thumb drive, she could download them for you."

"That way, we could keep working on them from home." Noah's voice rose with enthusiasm.

"Working a case we've been pulled off of goes against protocol." Were her brothers seriously suggesting this? And here she'd been silently praising them for being such good law enforcement officers. "Plus, it could cost all of us our jobs, along with Helen."

"Only if we get caught." Noah pushed his plate away from him. "How many more girls are those creeps going to hurt or kill while we're sitting here twiddling our thumbs?"

Adam rubbed the back of his neck, avoiding her eyes. "Sometimes the end justifies the means, Cass."

There it was. The same phrase Bishop had used earlier, and she'd accused him of being an unprincipled scoundrel. Now her brothers were considering similar actions. She rose and reached for the tequila, pausing after she poured herself another shot.

She couldn't fault them for wanting to take action. That's what made them good deputies. But she refused to let them go about it the wrong way.

"I understand your frustration. I'm frustrated, too." She looked each of them in the eye. "But we're not resorting to unethical methods just because we don't like the situation."

"You don't have to. But Adam and I—"

"Noah, I said no. And don't forget, I'm not just your sister. I'm your boss." She drained her shot glass and stood. "You go rogue on this, you won't have to worry about the Rangers. I'll fire you myself."

Chapter Eight

Bishop had left the justice center intent on finding and staking out Kevin Palmer's house overnight. But exhaustion from the long day had caught up with him when he stopped by his motel room for protein bars and water. Though anxious to find Ashley, he'd reluctantly admitted that sleep would help him be sharper when he did confront Palmer.

Bishop headed out early the next morning, well rested and loaded for bear. As he drove west, the vivid oranges and pinks in his rearview mirror reminded him of the rainbow sherbet he'd loved as a kid. He rarely got to appreciate sunrises these days. The tall buildings where he lived blocked the view, and if he was already on the road, the notorious Houston traffic held all his attention.

The house he'd shared with his ex had a clear view to the east, and he'd watched the sun creep over the horizon while enjoying his first cup of coffee every morning. But after he quit the force and she kicked him out, he'd lost that view along with pretty much everything else.

Stopped at a railroad crossing, Bishop took a sip of his green smoothie. Buying a new blender yesterday had been worth it. When he'd asked the grocery clerk if they carried organic kale, the look on the kid's face had been priceless. The teenager had directed him to a frozen aisle for "them exotic foods." Despite the odds, he'd found bags of frozen, chopped, organic kale.

The last railcar, covered in talented graffiti, flew past and the crossing arms swung up. Bishop bumped across the tracks and worked his way west on a network of back roads.

His healthy lifestyle was just one piece of the new and improved Bishop. Anger management classes had also helped him come a long way from the walking time bomb he'd once been. He became acquainted with yoga and meditation as paths to find inner peace. He quit drinking and began purifying his body with antioxidants. He interned for a buddy's PI agency to see if going private was a good match for him. And that was when the ex kicked him to the curb. Apparently, living with an out-of-work detective who was trying to find himself was not what she'd signed up for. And to be fair, it *was* her house.

It took less time than expected to reach Flowertop, a town even smaller than Resolute. Bishop cruised down the main drag, where shop owners went about the business of opening up for the day. A middle-aged man, sporting horn-rimmed glasses—the same style that Bishop's grandfather had worn—twisted a rod to raise awnings above a five-and-dime store. A few doors down, a squat, round woman wearing a white apron over a red dress swept the sidewalk in front of a bakery. With her curly white hair, it was a safe bet she played Mrs. Claus in December.

The scent of warm dough and sugar crept into his truck like an invisible finger beckoning him. These days he avoided sugar, but he couldn't deny that the smell of freshly glazed doughnuts and cinnamon rolls could still tempt him. He grabbed his travel mug and took another swig of pulverized kale, fruit and protein powder—a taste he'd actually come to like.

He followed his GPS to the address he had for Palmer, a small, shabby house with a postage-stamp yard on the outskirts of town. The Boone County property records showed the house on Shady Oak Street was owned by a Norma

Winston. Further searching revealed no link between Winston and Palmer. Not knowing if Palmer was flopping on a friend's couch or hiding out with criminals, Bishop intended to be cautious.

He drove past the address and continued down the length of Shady Oak. Lights were on in several houses. A man who looked to be about Bishop's age balanced his coffee tumbler and white hard hat while he unlocked his pickup. No sounds of kids playing outside yet. They were probably still watching cartoons in their pajamas.

Bishop turned right at the corner, a large rottweiler inside the yard's chain-link fence keeping pace with his truck, saliva flying with every bark. Looping into the alley behind the row of houses, he eased along until he was behind Palmer's one-car detached garage. He shifted into Park and hopped out to peek through the garage's side window, confirming the Corolla was inside.

Leaving the alley, he returned to Shady Oak and parked on the other side of the street, several houses down from Palmer's. From this vantage point he had a clear view of the front door, as well as a corner of the garage. With any luck, Palmer would come out of his hole and lead him to Ashley. If not, Bishop would make his own luck with the creep.

He opened his truck windows, hoping for some cross-ventilation. The late-summer temperature was already creeping up from the mid-eighties, the humid early morning air heavy and still. Even a slight breeze would be welcome as he settled in for a little sweaty reconnaissance work.

As a detective, he'd passed time on stakeouts drinking coffee and eating junk food. These days he turned to mindfulness. Thankfully, the neighborhood cooperated, providing quiet now that the rottweiler had calmed down. Bishop straightened his spine and got as comfortable as a six-foot man could get inside the confines of his truck. He focused his awareness on the sensations of his physical body, allowing thoughts to drift through his mind without judgment. But once his focus shifted inward, his chakras spoke to him.

Chakras, the body's seven main energy centers, needed to remain open and aligned for physical and emotional well-being. Bishop began with the first, or root, chakra. It was open. Next, the sacral chakra, connected to pleasure and sexuality—and just like that, his calming thoughts vanished as images of the contrary sheriff poured into his mind. Her tight ponytail swishing back and forth with the sway of her walk. Her slender body, its curves filling out her starched shirt and creased jeans. But more than her physical appearance drew Bishop to her. Her admirable, yet frustrating, integrity. Her compassion the previous day when he'd thought Ashley might be their Jane Doe. Her obvious affection for her younger brother.

Yep, Cassie was seriously messing with his sacral chakra. He'd wanted her from their first awkward conversation, and that desire just kept growing. He wanted the by-the-book sheriff naked except for a red-tape bow of justice wrapped around her. But he also wanted something more. Something intangible. Something he couldn't put a name to just yet.

Bishop pushed images of Cassie from his mind. He might not be bingeing on sugar-filled treats or gallons of coffee like he had when he was on the force. But allowing his attention to drift from his target for any reason wasn't just unhealthy, it was dangerous. Bishop refocused on Palmer's house.

THE MORNING AFTER the family dinner, Cassie tried to stifle a yawn as she parked in front of the justice center. Although not a morning person, she'd never been so much as a minute late to work. But today she'd crawled out of bed an hour before sunrise, aiming to beat the Rangers to the office. Giving in to the yawn, she leaned against the head-rest and closed her eyes—just for a minute.

Loud rapping against the driver's-side window made her jump in her seat, her eyes jerking open. Texas Ranger Ward's wide knuckles continued to strike the glass until she rolled it down.

"Mornin', Sheriff." Mills stood next to Ward, an apologetic smile on his face.

Cassie sighed, her heart still pounding from being startled. "Morning, Ranger Mills. Beautiful day."

"It is indeed." Mills tipped his hat toward her, then followed his partner up the front steps.

Ward yanked on the building's locked door handle. "What time y'all open this place up?" he hollered at her.

Cassie ignored him. He had to have already known the door was locked. Otherwise he wouldn't have scared the bejesus out of her by knocking on her window. If he wanted to start his day with a hissy fit, fine by her. She took her sweet time getting her laptop and grabbing the satchel she used for carrying case files home at night.

She locked her vehicle and climbed the stairs at a slow pace, enjoying Ward's impatience through her reflective sunglasses.

"We're going to need a key to the building if everyone who works here keeps bankers' hours."

Cassie looked at her watch instead of unlocking the door. "Not sure six in the morning qualifies as bankers' hours, Ranger Ward." She took off her sunglasses and arched a brow.

When he only glared at her, Cassie smiled, unlocked the door and held it open for the two men. Ward strode into the building and directly down the hall toward their office.

Mills reached above Cassie's head to grab the edge of the door. "Please. Ladies first."

"Well, well, well. Your mama did a good job raising a gentleman."

His smile was warm. "She tried her best."

Once inside, Cassie relocked the front door. "I understand travel doesn't agree with some people." She tipped her head in the direction Ward had gone. "You think he needs some roughage in his diet or something?"

Mills's laugh echoed through the empty lobby.

Cassie leaned a little closer to him and stage-whispered, "Seriously though, are you really as nice as you seem? Or did you lose the coin flip and have to play the good cop this time?"

Mills matched her volume level. "I'm always the good cop. Especially when I'm working with guys like him." Mills winked, then took off after Ward.

Cassie cocked her head to the side, frowning as she watched him walk away. Was he truly a good cop? Or just better at playing one than Ward? Better to be safe than sorry and assume it was the latter.

She continued to her office, shut her door and locked it. At this point, she had no idea who she could trust outside of her family.

She drummed her fingers on the desk blotter, contemplating what she was about to do. Her eyes slid to her locked top desk drawer where she kept the short stack of files on her father's murder. All practically memorized by now.

Ward and Mills had only warned her away from the human trafficking investigation. While Cassie's gut told her that the traffickers had ambushed and killed her father, there was no proof. Until an official link was made, she had no problem treating her dad's murder as a separate case. She was about to tread a very thin line in not-so-narrow cowboy boots. But she'd sworn to find his murderer, and she aimed to uphold that vow.

Cassie unlocked the drawer and grabbed the manila folder, slapping it down on her blotter.

Although positive that the killer was linked to, if not part of, the trafficking ring, Cassie sat at her desk and reset her perception of the case to zero. Assuming anything about a crime at the get-go could cause tunnel vision, forcing the facts to fit the assumption. Never mind that the anonymous call her dad and Dave had responded to that day had been about a suspicious group of men dragging a young woman into a neighboring house. Forget that at the time, her dad had been sure he was onto whoever was tipping off the bad guys.

Sean and Pete had been first at the scene after her father was shot. She'd read their incident reports countless times already, but she started through them again, looking for that one elusive fact that would shed light on the truth. While she flipped pages with her left hand, her right lay fisted on her thigh, nails digging into her palm. Just enough pain to keep her emotionally detached from what she read.

Nothing new. Same reports, same facts. Dave and Dad went on a call following an anonymous tip on the trafficking case. When they arrived, the house appeared vacant. Dad had Dave skirt around back while he took point at the front. Next thing Dave knew, shots were fired and when he came back around to the front, Dad was down on the ground, riddled with bullets.

Though most of the initial shotgun blast through the door hit Dad in his vest, some of the scatter landed low, nicking his femoral artery. But that was followed with close range shots from a 9-millimeter that screamed assassination.

Cassie closed her eyes in frustration as her stomach growled in hunger.

She pushed back from her desk and scrubbed her hands down her face, personally wanting to erase the autopsy pictures from her mind, but professionally trying to hold on tight to each detail.

She blinked several times, unable to stop the moisture in her eyes from sliding down her cheeks. She could only do so much compartmentalizing.

Using her sleeve, she gave her cheeks a rough swipe. She was stronger than tears. She would find her father's killers and ensure *they* were the ones crying behind bars.

But first, carb load.

Chapter Nine

Cassie pushed through the front door of The Busy B, gave Marge a quick smile and headed for the last booth. First thing her dad had taught her. *Always sit with your back to the wall.* She set her satchel beside her on the bench.

Rachel, who worked the breakfast shift, stopped by Cassie's table with a glass of water and a mug of black coffee. "Mornin', Cassie."

"Thanks, Rach." Cassie picked up the mug and blew at the rising steam. "So, is Brad enjoying being a big brother yet?" The server's four-year-old had decided he didn't really like his new baby sister after all.

Rachel huffed. "Well, he *did* stop demanding we return her."

"Sounds like progress."

"Oh, yeah. Lots of progress." Dark circles under Rachel's eyes revealed her new-mother exhaustion. "Now he's insisting we exchange her."

"For a boy?" Cassie took a careful sip, willing to risk a burned tongue for a desperately needed caffeine boost.

"For a dog."

Cassie almost spewed coffee across the table.

"Yeah, yeah. Easy for you to laugh. Come on over and babysit them one of these days. Then you'll understand."

Cassie already understood. She'd all but raised her brothers, even before their mother had left. Her mom's ability to get lost in her artistic endeavors had led to dinners of cold cereal and no clean clothes for school. Lifting her hands as if surrendering, Cassie said, "No thanks. Been there, done that, got three brothers to prove it."

Rachel pulled out her pad and pen, her mocking grin all but calling Cassie a chicken. "So, what'll it be?"

"Number three, over easy. Extra bacon, extra crispy. And a biscuit with gravy instead of toast."

"In other words, the Cassie Special," Rachel said, her grin genuine this time. "Juice?"

"Tall orange. Thanks."

"Comin' right up." Despite her fatigue, Rachel headed for the kitchen with a spring in her step. Motherhood apparently agreed with her.

Cassie's mind drifted away like the steam on her coffee, returning to her father's death, the Rangers' suspicions and the dead-in-the-water trafficking case.

When Marge appeared with plates of steaming food, Cassie straightened, trying to physically shake the lingering melancholy.

Marge set the plates on the table, then planted a fist on each hip, looking down at Cassie with a motherly frown. "You okay, hon? You look like death warmed over."

Cassie gave her a halfhearted smile. "I always look like this when I get up before dawn."

"Hmph. More like you're workin' too hard." Marge smiled as Rachel set down Cassie's juice and topped off her coffee. "Rachel hon, cover my tables for me while I sit a spell, will ya?"

"Sure thing, Marge."

"That girl's a keeper." Marge slid into the booth across from Cassie. "Watch. She'll bring me coffee without me even havin' to ask." She grunted as she swung her stocky legs under the table and got situated. "Now, then. What in tarnation are you doing here this dang early? When you walked in, I about had a heart attack. Thought the clock done broke and I was movin' slower than a herd of turtles."

"Ha ha." Cassie forked hash browns into her mouth and washed them down with coffee, regaining tight control of her emotions. "Things have taken an unexpected turn at the office."

As predicted, Rachel dropped off a hot mug on her way to take an order.

"I heard. Texas Rangers in town, huh?" Marge stirred cream and sugar into the coffee. "They have anything to do with your mood?"

"That's a definite yes." Cassie dived into her easy-over eggs.

Marge's all-knowing brows arched. "Not hungry, are you?"

"As a matter of fact, I'm starving." Breaking off a piece of bacon, Cassie popped it into her mouth. "Or maybe I'm just eating my emotions."

"Or maybe you're hungry for a little down-home country justice."

Marge always jumped right to the heart of whatever had Cassie tied up in knots. "Maybe."

"Why don't you take a breather from stuffing your face and tell me what's really going on?" Marge invited confidence by leaning forward and resting her forearms on the table. "I swear on Doc's grave I won't tell a soul."

"Doc's not dead, Marge."

"I know that, sweetie. But I already paid for his plot in the cemetery and believe you me, it cost a pretty penny. So I'm still swearing on it."

Marge had her own rules of logic, and Cassie had never been able to convince her that some of them didn't make sense.

"It's not really a secret." She took a sip of orange juice. "The Rangers are taking over the human trafficking case.

Kicked the whole department off of it." Cassie stabbed at her plate, loading her fork with another mouthful of food. "Losing that case sure sticks in my craw."

"Did they say why?"

The whole town knew about the trafficking ring to some degree. But Cassie couldn't tell Marge about the leak. Instead, she pivoted. "I'm going to concentrate on Dad's death instead."

Marge pursed her lips and nodded. "That explains the sad look on your face, sweetie. Working on your own daddy's murder." Marge sipped her coffee. "But didn't you say you thought them traffickers killed him?"

"I'd bet my badge on it."

"And didn't you just say them Rangers told you not to work that particular case?"

"*Technically*, no one knows who shot Dad, so *technically* Dad's case isn't related to the traffickers. Not officially, anyway. Therefore, I'm not working the case I've been booted off of. *Technically*." She lifted her shoulders in a shrug. "Not my fault if the two cases just happen to intersect."

Marge cackled. "Well, well, well. Never thought I'd see the day when you'd find a way around a direct order. Better be careful. Next thing we know, you'll throw caution to the wind and race down Main Street goin' thirty-two instead of the posted thirty."

"Very funny." Cassie fought the urge to remind Marge the town's speed limit was twenty-five, not thirty. "I just need to figure out how all the moving pieces fit together."

Marge aimed a sly smile at her. "Maybe your PI friend can help you figure it out."

Cassie choked on her hash browns. "Don't even start with me about that man."

"And why not? He might be useful, especially with him

being an outsider. He might notice things you'd miss, seeing as you're so close to the situation and all."

Fair point.

"And sweetie, don't even pretend you haven't noticed how mighty fine that man is." Marge's sly grin returned.

Cassie groaned. "Looks aren't everything. He thinks he can do whatever he wants with no repercussions. Working with him, especially now with the Rangers in town, could spell disaster for my career."

"And you know all this just by spending a few hours with him yesterday?"

Cassie narrowed her eyes at Marge, for all the good it did. "The few hours yesterday were more than enough." She nibbled on a slice of bacon. "You don't understand. When he asked me to help with his case, it was the unethical, if not downright illegal, kind of help. And later he admitted doing something…well, something he shouldn't have. He's a loose cannon at a time when I can't afford any slipups. There's too much at stake. I have no intention of spending any more time with Mr. Bishop."

"You're being too harsh in your judgment of him." Marge settled her rear end more firmly into the vinyl cushion. "And I'm fixin' to tell you why."

Cassie inhaled a deep breath and reined in her irritation. Like Helen, Marge had been there for every high and low point in her life since Cassie's mother abandoned the family. The two older women got along together about as well as oil and water, but they each loved Cassie in their own way.

"What you're forgetting is that he isn't here for some random case," Marge said. "It's about his flesh and blood. One look at that man's eyes and you can see he's worried sick about that niece of his. And you know darn well that people don't always color inside the lines when their loved ones are in jeopardy."

Cassie's gaze dropped to her plate. She did admire the

PI's determination when it came to Ashley. Like a dog with a bone, he wouldn't stop searching until he laid eyes on her himself, despite no evidence of foul play.

And she couldn't argue Marge's point, because she couldn't tell her about the jeopardy her whole family was in right now. Sharing that information was a line Cassie refused to step over. Just as "coloring outside the lines" to save her family would never happen.

"Besides which, someone like your Mr. Bishop might help balance out your..." Marge paused, apparently fishing for the right word.

"There is no part of me that needs balancing out." Cassie broke off a piece of biscuit with her fingers, dragged it through the creamy gravy, and topped it with a tiny bit of bacon. "And he's not *my* Mr. Bishop. You know I love you, Marge. But this conversation is over." She shoved the lump of carbs and fat into her mouth and chewed, not caring if she resembled a chipmunk with cheeks full of nuts.

Shaking her head, Marge slid to the edge of the seat and heaved herself up with a groan. "Suit yourself. Maybe I'll mosey on over to Doc's after closing and check on Mr. Bishop myself. Make sure he's all settled in, nice and comfy." She winked. "If you know what I mean."

Cassie's eyes widened. "He's at Doc's?" she mumbled, her mouth still full. Not that she cared where he stayed or if he was comfy. Just professional curiosity. Came with the badge.

"I didn't quite understand that, but I *think* you asked if he was staying at Doc's." Marge turned away before Cassie could nod. Over her shoulder she added, "Maybe you should just figure that out yourself with your own mighty detecting skills," then trundled off toward the counter.

"I don't really care," Cassie called after her. Who was she kidding? That aggravating man had gotten under her skin, and Marge knew it.

She pushed her plate across the table, her mind on Bishop. No doubt about it, he was a fly-by-the-seat-of-his-pants kind of guy who had no problem skirting the law if it suited his purpose.

Cassie yanked out her scrunchie and snapped it around her wrist, shaking her hair loose. Either her ponytail was too tight, or mental images of Bishop had brought her to the brink of a feverish headache. *Has to be the ponytail.* No low-principled private investigator could make the breath in her chest hitch and the pulse in her neck throb.

She massaged her temples, willing away all thoughts of Bishop. But as they left, her father's case rolled back in. She'd go home and review the files again. Figure out what the next step would be in solving his murder. And when she found his killer, there'd be more hell to pay than the devil even owned.

Chapter Ten

Stakeouts sucked, and mindfulness only took a man so far. After sitting for two hours waiting for Palmer to leave the house, Bishop's smoothie was gone and he'd exhausted all of his Cassie fantasies.

He climbed out of his truck to stretch his legs, his mind turning to Ashley. Her first dance recital at age four. The crisp fall afternoon when he'd joined Bob and Beth to help teach her how to ride a bike. Her fourteenth birthday, when he'd given her the silver turtle necklace, but then also surprised her with a trip to the gun range. The girl was a natural. Luckily, Beth had still been alive then. She'd been the one to convince Bob their daughter should learn how to handle guns safely.

Ashley wasn't perfect. Sometimes moody, other times sulky. What teenager didn't go through those growing pains? But she was a good kid, and he cursed himself again for ever letting Monique block his involvement in Ashley's life. Never again.

I'm coming for you, Little Turtle.

Time for a face-to-face with Palmer. And just let the weasel try something, because right about now Bishop had a powerful urge to forget about anger management and issue a good old-fashioned beatdown.

He pulled on a chambray shirt and let it hang unbuttoned to cover the gun in the back waistband of his jeans, crossed the street and jabbed the doorbell. After pounding on the door brought no response, Bishop rang the bell again until even he was irritated by it.

He walked along the right side of the house toward the backyard, stopped by a six-foot chain-link fence with a padlock. Grabbing the top with both hands, Bishop stuck the toe of his boot into one of the fence's diamond-shaped holes and hoisted himself up and over. He dropped to the ground and paused, listening for any hint of life.

The silence held.

Staying tight against the side of the house, he crept toward the backyard. A quick peek around the corner revealed nothing but a solitary lawn chair on the patio, surrounded by cigarette butts. His gun in one hand, Bishop moved toward the back door.

Movement to his left caught his attention. He froze.

There it was again. A curtain fluttered against a window. He flattened himself against the back wall, the familiar rush of adrenaline sharpening his senses, readying him.

He leaned away from the house just enough for a quick glimpse through the window. The curtains moved with a steady rhythm, pressing up against the glass, then falling away. Not the furtive movement of someone peeking out.

A deep breath, then Bishop spun, gun at the ready. The half-closed curtains continued to swing. Through the gap in the fabric, he spotted an oscillating fan. Blowing out the breath he'd been holding, Bishop lowered his gun. He peered through the dirty glass. A bedroom, clothes all over the floor and piled high on the bed.

No Palmer.

He continued on to the back door. Confirming it was locked, Bishop made quick work with his lock picks. He pocketed the tools, donned a pair of nitrile gloves and pulled his gun again before easing the door open. Sticking his head in, he looked both ways. Empty. Remnants of food in takeout containers and pizza boxes filled the kitchen with eau de garbage dump. Bishop approached an entryway to another room and paused. A sound behind him. *There it was again.* Trying to pinpoint it, he returned to the stove. Two cockroaches had fallen into a burner pan and were skittering in circles, hissing at each other.

Back to the entryway. Keeping tight against the wall, Bishop held his gun in both hands, aimed at the ceiling. He swung into the next room in a crouch, gun pointed toward the wall to his right, then swinging it to the left. The sparse living room had nothing but two threadbare recliners and a TV sitting on the floor.

With no other rooms to his right, he moved with stealth toward the side of the house he'd peeked into. Four closed doors off a short hallway. The first one he opened was a linen closet, its shelves empty. Closing that door, he froze as a squeak sounded somewhere in the house. He glanced up. A crawl space entry, covered with white plywood. Another squeak. Not from above him.

He moved to the next door. Turned the knob and pushed it open, his gun aimed into a small bathroom. It smelled worse than the kitchen. Flies swarmed around the disgusting toilet, and Bishop gagged as he moved past it. He ripped aside the shower curtain, revealing nothing more than a filthy tub.

Only two rooms left to clear. Palmer had to be in one of them. Bishop's heart rate increased, and he stopped, hand on the knob. He would normally take a deep breath to slow his pulse, but the bathroom's fetid smell had followed him.

He pushed the door open. A different stench rolled over him and into the hall. Death, with undertones of unwashed laundry and rank body odor. A closet door hung open, no one in its depths. Bishop flipped the wall switch, and a bare bulb came on overhead. Clothes littered the floor, along with empty beer bottles and cans, and ashtrays overflowed with cigarette butts.

He picked his way across the floor, stepping between the clutter and trash. As Bishop approached the bed, the piles of clothes he'd seen through the window morphed into a body. The dark areas surrounding it transformed from shadows to sheets soaked with dark, drying blood.

The man lay faceup, his blank eyes staring at the ceiling. A gaping slash in his neck resembled a macabre smile. Based on the mug shots Bishop had seen, this was Palmer, and he cursed himself for not pursuing him the evening before.

On the nightstand, a tipped-over pill bottle's label read "oxycodone." The top drawer was partially open, and he pulled it the rest of the way. Inside, a bag of weed, more pill bottles and a gun Palmer hadn't gotten to in time.

Bishop slid the drawer back in to where it had been. He'd have to call Cassie, tell her what he'd found. When she and her team arrived, they wouldn't be happy if the scene was compromised. He still needed to check the last room, probably another bedroom, and the attic crawl space. There'd been no other noises; maybe the squeaks had been from rats.

Intent on exiting the room without stepping on anything, Bishop shifted his balance before turning back toward the door. The hair on the back of his neck stood on end. A whisper of movement flowed toward him. He spun, gun already aimed toward the intruder. A large man came at him, wearing black jeans, black shirt and a black ski mask over his face. Before Bishop could pull the trigger, the man lunged. Pushing Bishop's arm out, the man slammed it into the nightstand, and the gun flew against the wall.

Bishop wrenched his arm free and charged the stranger, driving him into the closet across the room. Using the wall behind him as leverage, the man kicked Bishop in his gut.

Doubled over, Bishop slid across the floor as the man kept kicking him.

The kicking stopped. A blinding pain exploded in Bishop's head. A darkness, filled with unrelenting anguish, crept toward his brain. Erasing thoughts. Wiping out the light until only a pinpoint remained. Bishop grabbed on to that tiny bit of light. He couldn't let the darkness win. Ashley needed him. Ashley nee…

CONSCIOUSNESS RETURNED TO Bishop in agonizing fits and starts. Pain pounded from inside his skull, stopping only when the blackness regained control. He fought that dark layer each time it moved in, even as his brain screamed to let it carry away the pain.

Forcing his eyes open, he cringed when the staggering blaze of light attacked them like a thousand sharp needles. Bishop propped himself up on one arm, a wave of nausea crashing over him. His eyes still blurry, he had no idea how long he'd been out. He sat, then stood, gritting his teeth against the protests from both his head and his stomach. He didn't know if he was alone. If Ashley had been in that last bedroom, his failure to clear it had sealed her fate.

Finally on his feet, he gazed in confusion at the bloody knife in his hand. His *ungloved* hand. He checked the corner where his gun had landed, but it was gone. Bishop looked at the bed. Palmer was still there. Still dead, from a wound that most likely had been made with the knife he held. His attacker had done a sloppy job of trying to frame Bishop.

It was a sure sign Bishop was getting close. It couldn't be a coincidence that Palmer was dead less than twenty-four hours after visiting Garrett Pugh. Garrett was a link to Ashley. Ashley was still missing. Bishop grabbed on to the nightstand, vertigo pulling him sideways. He needed help.

He pulled out his phone and hit Cassie's speed dial. Yeah, he'd put her on speed dial. *So what?* He braced himself as her phone rang. She would yell at him, but oddly enough he was almost looking forward to tangling with the beguiling by-the-booker.

"I thought we were done, Mr. Bishop." She hadn't even waited for him to ID himself. Apparently, he was programmed in her phone, too. Well, well.

"No time for pleasantries, Sheriff. I'm in Flowertop. Palmer's last known address. You might want to send your CSI guys over. And the coroner. He's already smelling a bit ripe."

His head throbbed, but he actually smiled the whole time she laced into him.

LIGHTS FLASHING AND gas pedal stomped to the floor, Cassie drove west. Her fingers grasped the steering wheel in a white-knuckled death grip. She hoped they'd uncurl eventually, because as soon as she arrived at Palmer's house, she intended to wrap all ten of them around Bishop's neck.

She'd arrived home from The Busy B with her dad's case, thinking her mood couldn't get any worse. But she'd barely opened the files when her phone vibrated in her back pocket. Caller ID did nothing to improve her frame of mind, which went further downhill with Bishop's ramblings about Flowertop, Kevin Palmer's house, a dead body. The man just couldn't stop meddling where he didn't belong.

Cassie turned off the emergency lights and eased her foot off the gas as she approached the town limits of Flowertop. It, like Resolute and so many small towns in Boone County, couldn't afford its own police force. As the sheriff, she enforced the law for these towns as well as unincorporated areas of the county. Which was darn lucky for Bishop. If Flowertop had its own police department, he'd already be sitting in an eight-by-ten interview room.

Parking in front of Palmer's house, she had a clear view of Bishop in the backyard behind a chain-link gate. He sat on the ground, leaning against the trunk of a live oak, holding something on his head. Cassie blew out a breath of exasperation, stepped out of her SUV and slammed the door.

She strode through the gate, eyeing the padlock hanging open on the post, and stopped in front of the defiant PI. "How exactly did you get back there? And don't tell me that gate was unlocked when you arrived."

Bishop peered up at her, his eyes broadcasting pain. The rolled-up sleeves of his shirt revealed bruises on both arms.

"Let me see." Cassie lifted his hand, which was holding a bag of frozen french fries, from the top of his head. The wound wasn't hard to find. A large knot, covered with blood-matted hair. Her anger faded at the sight of his injuries. "What did he hit you with?"

Bishop shrugged. "I have a feeling he kicked me. There was a lot of that happening, and he was wearing steel-toed boots." He lifted up his T-shirt, exposing arc-shaped bruises across his abs. His *very impressive* abs.

"My guys are already on their way. Helen called the JP, and the forensic team should be here soon. But I didn't realize you needed an ambulance." Cassie pulled her phone out.

"I don't need an ambulance. It's just a little—" he struggled to stand, wincing "—bump." He sucked in air between his teeth.

When Cassie started to tap her phone, Bishop grabbed it from her hand. "I told you, I don't need an ambulance." She reached to take it back and he held it above his head. "Don't you think you should take a peek at the dead guy?" He directed her to a back window. "Probably easier to identify from out here when you know what you're looking for."

She peered through the glass, confirming there was indeed a body on the bed.

"Explain to me how you just *happened* to see this." Cassie referred to his earlier phone call, which had made him sound like an innocent passerby. Not that she'd believed it for a single second.

He motioned toward a small building in the alley. "His car is in the garage, so I figured he was still home. I parked on the street to watch the house, waiting for him to leave so I could follow him. He didn't, so eventually I rang the bell." Bishop donned an innocent expression. "When he didn't answer, and only out of the utmost desire to ascertain his well-being, I—"

"Cut the crap, Bishop." Cassie planted her hands on her hips. "Yesterday you were champing at the bit to blame this guy for your niece's disappearance, only because his car was at Garrett Pugh's house."

"Also because of his criminal history." Bishop's half smile segued into a tight line beneath flaring nostrils. "And she has a name."

It took Cassie's brain a second to process his last few words, but they still made no sense. "What?"

His arms at his sides, Bishop's fingers curled into fists. "My niece. She has a name." The words fell from his mouth like abrasive grains of sand. *"Ashley."*

Cassie's hands slid off her hips, and she took a small step toward him but stopped when Bishop's eyes drilled into hers with the red-hot burn of a branding iron, his pain and fury palpable.

"I didn't mean to depersonalize her." She kicked herself mentally. "I mean, Ashley." Referring to victims by pronouns or descriptors often caused their loved ones agony, as if law enforcement didn't see them as real people. Even if Bishop was a PI, he came to Resolute as an uncle.

His glare never wavered, and Cassie continued to meet it, standing tall with a neutral expression. Her dad had taught her to never show weakness by looking away first, even when apologizing.

As Bishop's gaze finally softened, he looked down at his

hands as if surprised to see them fisted. He straightened his fingers and stretched them a few times before glancing her way again. "Sorry. I, uh, didn't mean to go off like that."

The tension in Cassie's body trickled away but she remained still, gauging Bishop's change in demeanor. "No big deal. It's just that you're usually so even-tempered. But hey, at least you didn't start punching walls or smashing windows."

He started to rake the fingers of both hands through his hair, then flinched when he touched his goose egg. He dropped his arms and blew out a breath. "Yeah, I've got a pretty good handle on the physical part of it."

"Physical part of what?"

Bishop scoffed. "Obviously, I still have a few anger issues."

"They have classes for stuff like that." Cassie peered through the window at the body again. "You might want to check them out."

"Been there, done that." He screwed his lips to the side. "Shoulda seen me *before* the classes."

Cassie raised her brows. She avoided men with complications like wedding rings, arrest records and emotional issues. But dang if Bishop didn't pique her curiosity more every time she was around him.

"Okay, walk me through it from when you approached the house."

"Can I get another bag from the freezer first? The french fries have defrosted, but I think I saw some onion rings in there."

Cassie crossed her arms and tapped her boot. She sympathized with his pain, but she wanted the whole story before everyone arrived.

Bishop's mouth tipped up on one side. "Okay, okay. Figured it wouldn't hurt to ask." Then he gave her a full accounting, from hopping the fence to getting jumped from behind.

"So, you cleared the last bedroom after you regained consciousness? What was in there?"

"Two sets of bunk beds. That was about it." Bishop leaned against the side of the house, wiping sweat from his brow.

"You don't need that looked at, huh?"

"I'm *fine*." He glared at her. "What happens now?"

"Now we wait for the troops to arrive."

"You aren't going inside first?"

"I'm sure the scene's already been disturbed enough, what with your fight and all. No need to compromise it even more." She turned her head and inhaled fresh air. The funk of death and filth clung to Bishop like cheap perfume. "Let's go wait on the front porch. But walk behind me. You need a shower."

"Hmph."

Cassie couldn't force Bishop into an ambulance. But she did make him sit on the front porch steps so he wouldn't fall over, while she stood a few feet in front of him on the walkway. It was sheer luck the wind was blowing in the right direction.

The Rangers arrived before anyone else. *Of course they did.*

"Sheriff." Ward's gaze slid from Cassie to Bishop. "Who found the body?"

Cassie folded her arms across her chest. "Afternoon, Ranger. What brings you out here?"

"Heard there was a murder."

"I reported a death, not a murder." She lifted her chin. "Either way, this isn't your case."

"Might be connected."

"I'll let you know what I find after our investigation is

complete." Cassie narrowed her eyes at Ward. Behind him, Mills headed for the backyard.

"Since we're already here, I think we'll hang around. Talk to the techs." His lips stretched into a thin smile that didn't reach his eyes. "See what's what, if you know what I mean."

Oh, I know exactly what you mean. The Rangers planned to muscle their way into every case her office caught. They weren't just *investigating* her family. They were planning on taking their badges.

"So, again, who found the body?" Ward stared hard at Bishop.

"I'll make sure you get a copy of my report." Cassie returned his forced smile. "As soon as I find time to write it up." She pushed past him and joined Lonnie and Pete on the lawn.

"Why's *he* here?" His voice full of contempt, Lonnie watched Ward walk toward the back of the house.

"I sure didn't invite him."

Pete headed toward the arriving forensic team, and Cassie stepped closer to her cousin. "These guys are getting involved in a lot more than the human trafficking ring."

"They can't take over a case unless you ask for their help." Lonnie tucked his thumbs into his belt. "Just ignore them. They'll be gone as soon as they realize the leaks didn't come from our department."

"I'm not so sure about that." She lowered her voice even more. "Do me a favor? Stick around, keep an eye and an ear on them for me. I'm working on Dad's murder and want to get back to it. Plus, not sure how much more I can take of Ward today."

"You got it. You still taking lead on this?" Lonnie tipped his head toward Palmer's house.

"For now."

Lonnie nodded. "Let me know if you want a second set of eyes on your dad's file."

Cassie gave her cousin's shoulder a firm pat and motioned Bishop over.

"Who's he?" Lonnie asked.

"A PI from Houston."

"What's he doing at the crime scene?"

"It's a long story." Cassie waited until Bishop reached them. "This is my cousin Lonnie. Lonnie, Tyler Bishop."

The two men shook hands. Cassie knew her cousin, and before Lonnie could start questioning him, Cassie steered Bishop toward her SUV.

"Get in." She unlocked the doors, and they climbed inside.

Bishop settled into the passenger seat. "Why are Texas Rangers here?"

Cassie stared ahead through the windshield, biting her cheek. "I'd like to talk to you about something."

"Okay. But can we turn on the AC first?" He dragged his shirt sleeve across his brow.

"Sorry." She pushed the ignition button and cranked up the air, her nostrils rebelling at the scent of decomp. "I don't mean talk now. Think you'll feel up to meeting tonight? *After* you've showered."

Bishop chuckled. "I told you, I'm fine. How 'bout I buy you dinner? Where's the closest sushi place?"

Cassie turned to face him. "I am not eating raw fish and seaweed."

He gave her a two-dimpled grin and a wink. *Heaven have mercy.* She wasn't even used to the dimples yet. But the wink *with* the dimples pushed her pulse to hummingbird rate times two. This man was going to be even more trouble than she'd expected.

"I'll meet you at The Busy B." *Keep it nice and casual.*

"Is that the only place in Resolute to eat?"

She cocked a brow at him. "You don't like the diner?"

"I *love* the diner." The exaggerated enthusiasm in his voice told her otherwise. "But I was hoping for someplace with a bit more atmosphere."

Bishop wanted atmosphere, did he? For the first time all day, Cassie smiled. "I know the perfect place."

Chapter Eleven

Sitting in her parked SUV and watching Bishop over the top of her steering wheel, Cassie chuckled. The big bad PI stood next to his truck in the packed, crushed-rock parking lot, his mouth hanging open like a kid on his first trip to Disneyland. She figured a man from Houston would have seen at least one two-story neon sign blazing over a gigantic converted barn, but apparently not.

To be sure, the Resolute Chute was a unique and popular local landmark. The place served the best food in town—something she'd never admit in front of Marge—but at 9:00 p.m., the tables were pushed aside and the place turned into a boot-stompin', two-steppin' honky-tonk with live music.

As much as she enjoyed observing Bishop's undisguised show of amazement, not to mention his heart-stopping backside, she stepped from her SUV and self-consciously adjusted her soft teal shirt. With the top buttons open and the lapels falling away on either side, a disturbing amount of cleavage was exposed.

Marge had given her the shirt as a birthday present one year, assuring her she looked sexy, not like a hussy.

Well, sexy didn't come naturally to a gal raised in an all-male household. So she'd toned down her appearance by exchanging the black jeans she wore to work for a pair of broken-in blue ones. Her well-worn boots crunched against the gravel as she approached. "How do you like our little dance hall?"

"Little?" His head swiveled toward her, and he did a quick double take. His gaze turned intense, penetrating. "I guess it's true, the stars *do* shine bright deep in the heart of Texas."

A light breeze lifted her hair, hanging loose across her shoulders, but her cheeks still warmed at his wide eyes and parted lips. *Come on, Cassie, think of something to say.* Never at a loss for words before in her life, she just stood there like a statue, staring into Bishop's fathomless blue eyes.

"I've never seen you with your hair down." A smile tugged at Bishop's mouth as he took a step back, giving her a head-to-toe once-over. "You look…softer."

Oh, man. He walked right into that one. Fisting her hands on her hips, Cassie huffed with false indignation. "Are you saying I usually look hard?"

His smile vanished. "No, not at all."

She could practically hear the normally unflappable man slamming on the brakes.

"What I meant to say is that you look less…less severe."

She pursed her lips and tapped her boot.

"Okay, that's not right, either." He ran a hand through his hair. "Less serious? Maybe less professional?"

"Yes." Cassie nodded, still stifling her amusement. "A sheriff is *supposed* to look professional while at work."

He nodded with her, his shoulders relaxing. "Then let me start over. You look much less professional tonight." He flashed his dazzling smile, the same one he'd given Marge at The Busy B when he asked for his fish grilled, not fried. The one where his dimples took center stage. "Not what I was originally going for, but I hope you'll take the compliment in the spirit it was given."

"I will. Thank you." His obvious appreciation made fussing with her hair and makeup, as well as the ridiculous amount of time spent deciding how far down to unbutton her shirt before spritzing her throat with her favorite perfume, worth it.

His gaze raked over her in a slow move that made her glad for the lengthening shadows that masked her heated cheeks. "So, dinner *and* dancing?"

"You said you wanted atmosphere." Cassie gave him a self-satisfied grin before spreading her arms wide toward the building. "I give you atmosphere."

She led the way inside and through a vintage wooden cattle chute that ended at a hostess stand. The petite brunette standing next to it was dressed like a rodeo queen.

Flashing a smile at Cassie, and a much bigger one at Bishop, she said, "Hey, Sheriff."

"Evenin', Crystal. How's your mama?"

"Doing just fine. Should be home from the hospital tomorrow."

"Glad to hear it. Tell her I said hey."

"I sure will. Y'all here for dinner, or just gettin' your drink on before the band starts?"

"I'm here for both." Cassie hooked a thumb in Bishop's direction. "Not sure about him."

Crystal's gaze lingered on Bishop like he was a juicy slab of meat. "This your first time here?"

"Yes, ma'am, it is."

"Well then, you're in for a real treat. We have the juiciest, most tender steaks in all of Texas." The barely-twenty-one-year-old licked her upper lip with the tip of her tongue. "And we make sure the customer always leaves satisfied."

Cassie rolled her eyes, but only in her mind. "It's just a darn shame he doesn't eat beef."

"Oh, I'm sure I'll find *something* delicious here to devour." Bishop gave Crystal a playful wink as he turned his eyes to Cassie. But there was nothing playful about the intense look they shared. It was hot. Smoldering hot. Cassie's mouth went dry, and the tempo of her heart jumped a notch or two.

Crystal led them to a small table near the dance floor. "I'll seat y'all here, so you've got quick access when the dancin' starts." She set two menus on the table and headed back to her stand.

Bishop held Cassie's chair for her before taking his own seat. "This is quite a place."

"Disappointed that I didn't take you to one of those salad bars?"

"You have one of those here?" His eyebrows shot up in excitement.

"Of course we do. You just have to wait until the Webbs are sound asleep, then you hop the fence and nibble away at their vegetable garden." She bit her bottom lip to keep a straight face. "It's perfect for a man like you, who likes his salad *nekked.*"

They both burst into laughter, setting the stage for an evening that Cassie looked forward to, despite the serious conversation she had planned.

Bishop twisted in his chair to get a view of the entire building inside. Cassie followed his line of sight as it moved from the crowded bar to the shuffleboard and pool tables to the souvenir stands geared to visiting tourists. Then he turned his blistering gaze back to her. "I thought they had live music."

Cassie gave him a pleasant smile, hoping it wasn't obvious how much his attention affected her. "That comes after dinner. With the dancing."

"I see. And…" He trailed off as his eyes latched on to something over her shoulder. Cassie turned, smiling to herself. Just past the far end of the dance floor, in a separate, good-sized pen surrounded by rail fencing, a mechanical bull bucked its current rider into the hay surrounding it.

Bishop shook his head. "I thought those things went out of style after *Urban Cowboy*."

"Don't worry. They've got mats under the hay. Long as you don't land on your neck funny, you'll be fine."

Bishop met Cassie's eyes. "What makes you think I'm getting on that thing?"

She gave a one-shoulder shrug. "Tradition. Everyone rides it their first time here."

"Well, how about we just keep the fact that it's my first visit on the down-low?"

Cassie picked up her menu, hiding her grin behind it. "Too late. Crystal asked, you answered. By now she'll have spread the word."

"Great. Just great." Bishop left his menu on the table. "They have anything *except* beef here?"

Reaching across the table, Cassie tapped on a section of entrées. "Their chicken is good. Crispy on the outside, juicy on the inside."

"Like *fried* crispy?"

She glanced up from beneath her lashes, then batted them at him. "Oh. That's right. You don't like cow *or* fried. Well, shoot. This place has the best atmosphere around, but I completely forgot about your list of won't-eat vittles." His fingers brushed the back of her hand, and a chill raced up her arm, leaving goose bumps in its wake. "They have really good shrimp," she said, trying to recover. "No, wait. That's fried, too. Dang it. Well, check the appetizers and sides." Ducking back behind her menu, she hid both her shocked reaction to his touch and her amusement with his food dilemma.

Several minutes later, a waiter approached their table with two waters. "Howdy, folks. My name is Mark and I'll be serving you tonight. Is this your first time visiting the Chute?"

Cassie grinned up at him. "You know it's not *my* first time, Mark."

"Sorry, Sheriff. You know we have to ask."

"Well, it's a good thing you did tonight." Cassie tipped her head toward Bishop.

"Oh, so this is *your* first time here?"

Bishop groaned.

Oblivious, Mark went on. "Well, sir, you're in for a real treat. Just so you know, we stop serving dinner at nine and push the tables aside, 'cause that's when we bring out the band and the dancing starts. Can I bring y'all anything else to drink while you look over the menus?"

"I'll have a Oaxaca old-fashioned. And I think we're ready to order." Cassie glanced at Bishop, one brow raised. He nodded and she continued. "I'll have the tomahawk steak, rare. Loaded baked potato, and blue cheese on the salad."

"Excellent choice." The waiter faced Bishop. "And for you?"

"Iced tea with lemon. *Un*sweet." He glanced back down at the menu. "I noticed you have a smothered chicken breast on the menu."

"Yes, sir. It's a very popular choice. In addition to the bacon, cheese, grilled onions and mushrooms, a lot of our customers add jalapeños."

Bishop nodded as if mulling it over. "I'll have the grilled chicken breast with just the vegetables on it."

The waiter paused, pen hovering in midair over his order pad. "Onions and mushrooms, hold the cheese *and* the bacon?"

"That's right." He closed the menu and shifted forward in his seat. "And toss the jalapeños on it, too. And I'd like the sweet potato, no toppings. Vinaigrette on the side for the salad." Bishop handed his menu to the waiter.

"Very good, sir." He picked up Cassie's menu. "I'll have those drinks right out." He hurried off toward the bar.

Cassie leaned toward Bishop, her forearms on the table. "Glad you found something that fits your rigid diet."

"Look who's talking about rigid." A smile tugged at Bishop's mouth. "I just like to live a healthy lifestyle."

She huffed, refusing to get into a discussion about her supposed inflexibility. She'd heard it enough from people she knew. And Bishop most certainly knew nothing about her. "I suppose you do all kinds of other weird woo-woo stuff, too."

Bishop's brows pulled together in puzzlement. "Woo-woo stuff?"

"Yeah, you know. Yoga. Meditation. Stuff like that."

"In what world are yoga and meditation considered woo-woo?"

"In this one right here." Cassie slapped a hand on the table. "Good old Texas."

"I live in Texas, too, remember? Maybe you just need to expand your horizons."

"So, you *do* do yoga and meditation."

"Yes, I do both of them. Usually every day. Especially meditation."

"Ooh. Can I watch sometime?" Cassie widened her eyes in mock excitement. "You know, *expand* my horizons?"

Bishop massaged his forehead. "Meditation isn't something you watch. It's something you do to re-center your chi. Your energy."

"Woo-woo." Cassie wiggled her fingers in the air.

The waiter brought their drinks, then scurried to the next table. Cassie took a sip and sighed with pleasure.

"What's that thing called?" He nodded toward her glass.

"Oaxaca old-fashioned." She took another sip before setting it down. "It's an old-fashioned, but with tequila, mescal and xocolatl bitters. Want a taste?"

He shook his head. "*What* kind of bitters?"

"Xocolatl. Chocolate mole bitters." She laughed at his grimace, then looked around at the mechanical bull. "Speaking of expanding horizons, it's about time for you to ride that bull. And I strongly recommend doing it *before* you eat. You'll thank me later."

"I may be from out of town, but I'm not naive. There's no way you're getting me on that bull." Bishop rested his forearms on the table and leaned forward. "Besides, the only people lining up to ride it are women."

"And here I thought you were a modern man with all that yoga, meditation and whatnot." Cassie mirrored his position. "Didn't think you'd play the macho card so soon."

He relaxed against the back of his chair. "Not playing the macho card, darlin'. I'm playing the bullsh...the bull card. There's no way all newcomers are expected to ride that thing."

"Nice save, Bishop."

Just then the manager, Sal, stopped by their table. "Sheriff, good to see you."

"Hey, Sal. How are things?"

"Busy, as always." Sal turned to Bishop. "And who's this? I don't remember seeing you at the Chute before."

"This is my, uh, friend, Bishop. He's just passing through." Cassie ignored Bishop's arched brow. Well, what did he expect her to call him? Colleague? Not a chance. Boyfriend? Laughable. Date? As if. Friend was as good as he'd get.

"Welcome, Bishop. Always good to see a new face." Sal winked at Cassie. "The regulars love the entertainment when a newcomer comes to the Chute." He pointed over to the mechanical bull. "When you go up there, just tell Rowdy I sent you. That'll get you to the front of the line. Don't want to interrupt your date any longer than necessary."

Cassie's satisfied grin slid off her face. "Wait, this isn't a—"

Bishop cut her off, eyeing the manager with suspicion. "So you're telling me all newcomers have to ride the bull?"

"Hasn't anyone told you?" Sal's glance swung to Cassie, then back. "It's tradition. Now go have some fun." He clasped Bishop on the shoulder and moved on to the next table.

Cassie's cheeks hurt from smiling. "Told ya."

"What happens if someone refuses to ride the bull?"

"Ooh, I wouldn't do that if I were you." Cassie shook her head from side to side. "That would make you a bad sport, and no one likes a bad sport."

"Not even my *date*?" Those dadgum dimples appeared again.

"I'm not your date." She crossed her arms. "Sal was just confused."

"How 'bout this?" Bishop leaned in again, this time like a conspirator. "I ride the bull if you call this our first date."

Cassie matched his low volume. "That would imply a second one in the future. Which is impossible, because this *isn't* a date."

"Have it your way." Bishop shrugged. "Then you're spending the evening with a bad sport. Doesn't say much for your taste in men, now does it?"

After staring at each other for a full minute, Cassie let out a groan of frustration. "Fine. This is our first date." *And there will never be a second.* "Now go ride that bull."

"A deal's a deal." Bishop slapped both hands on the table for emphasis and stood.

Cassie raised her glass toward Bishop. "By the way, his name is Old Horny."

Bishop looked over at the bull. "But he doesn't have horns."

She snickered. "That's not how he got his name."

Bishop watched the current rider, his brow furrowed in confusion. Cassie rolled her lips between her teeth to keep from laughing. How long would it take him to realize the girl riding the bull in a slow, sexy motion had a very satisfied smile on her face?

Bishop looked back at Cassie, a crooked smile parting his lips. "Ah, I get it. She does look very happy."

"I'll bet her date does, as well." Cassie chuckled. "Good Old Horny is famous for putting people in the mood."

He glanced again at the bull. "Hmm. Maybe you should give him a ride, too." He winked at her and strolled off toward the bull.

"Maybe I should," she murmured, watching him walk away from her. "Maybe I should."

Bishop got in line behind the girls, but Rowdy motioned him up to the front. When the current rider swung one leg over the bull's back and slid off without falling, everyone watching her cheered. Cassie stretched her legs out under the table and got comfortable for the show.

Rowdy started with the slowest speed, and although Bishop should have looked ridiculous, Cassie's breaths came faster with each movement. Backward and forward. Bucking and swaying. The speed increased and Bishop held on with perfect form. The longer the ride, the more the bull twisted and changed directions. His left arm in the air for balance, Bishop still managed to stay centered. But as the pace picked up even more, his movements crossed over into slapstick.

Cassie's panting turned to laughter. Impressed that he'd held on this long, she cheered along with the crowd as his butt flew up off the seat and slammed down. His thighs lost their grip of the bull's sides and his arm swung wildly in the air. And still, Bishop refused to let go. A wild ride that would have tossed most anyone else to the ground long ago slowed to a stop. Sliding off Old Horny, he seemed surprised at the crowd's clapping and whooping. When he bowed with a flourish, diners and employees alike gave him a standing ovation.

Sal approached the table and Cassie slipped him the twenty she'd promised if he played along with the tradition story. "Here's another ten for Rowdy."

"Always happy to oblige, Sheriff." Sal retreated before Bishop reached the table.

Cassie noticed a slight limp before Bishop eased into his chair with a wince. "Got a little hitch in your git-along?" Not about to admit he'd crushed the ride, Cassie's lips twisted into a smirk.

"Guess I've been out of the saddle too long." He guzzled his iced tea. "How'd I do?"

"Not too shabby for a city boy." Sucking on an ice cube from her empty glass, she asked, "When you say 'out of the saddle,' would that be the grocery store horsey ride?"

"Cute. Very cute. And by the way, I know you set me up. I never figured such a stickler for the rules would orchestrate such a well-planned practical joke."

Hmm. The man was more observant than she gave him credit for. She widened her eyes. "I don't know——"

"Like he…heck you don't." Bishop's eyes twinkled with amusement. "I saw you handing Sal the cash."

Instead of denying it, Cassie doubled over with laughter. "What can I say? It was worth every penny. Especially when you were flying every which way toward the end." The laughs tapered off and she wiped her eyes with her napkin. "Sorry. What were you saying about saddles?"

"I used to ride horses every day. I haven't had a chance to for a long time."

Cassie swallowed the sliver of ice, surprised by his words. "You live on a ranch?"

"Not now." Bishop nodded at some of the girls from the bull-riding line as they passed by on their way to the bar but kept his attention on Cassie. "But I grew up on one just outside of Houston. I rode almost before I could walk. My first job was riding fences. Seemed there was always a section to repair."

"Why'd you leave ranching?"

Bishop waited until their server refilled their water glasses. "Because I wanted to be a cop."

This guy had more layers than an onion. "But you didn't pass the exam, and decided to go private?"

"Oh, I passed the exam with flying colors." He smiled at her shocked expression. "After I'd put in my time on patrol, I took the detective's exam and passed that, too."

Embarrassment burned through Cassie, turning to indignation. "Why didn't you tell me that in the diner when I—"

"Said private dicks don't know as much as real cops?" Bishop chuckled. "As I recall, you didn't give me a chance to answer before you stomped out of there."

Her face warm, Cassie intended to regain the upper hand. "Why were you fired?"

Bishop scoffed. "Good guess, but no, I wasn't fired."

Now he was just yanking her chain. Payback for the bull ride. "No one in their right mind quits a detective job to become a PI. That's a move retired cops make when they can't give up the game."

"Guess I'm not in my right mind, then." He sipped his disgusting, unsweet tea.

Cassie frowned. "It doesn't make sense. Why would you do that?"

Mark arrived with plates of food, and Bishop picked up his fork. "Well, darlin', that's a story for our next date."

CONSIDERING THE PLACE was a steakhouse, Bishop's meal exceeded his expectations. His chicken was surprisingly tender, the vegetables perfectly seasoned, the salad cold and crisp. Add lively dinner conversation, with Cassie pointing out interesting townsfolk and sharing humorous anecdotes about them, and the evening was shaping up to be perfect.

Perfect except for his constant worry about Ashley. It was a drumbeat that grew louder in the back of his mind with every passing moment. He had to eat and sleep, though, and he needed to form a bond with Cassie. If he played his cards right, she could help him more than she already had. It was a bonus that he genuinely liked her and wanted to get closer to her. Maybe after a few slow dances later, he'd have a chance to get to know her as well as everyone else around here seemed to.

After a busboy cleared the table, Cassie ordered pecan pie with whipped cream and a cup of coffee. Bishop declined, claiming he was full from dinner.

Cassie pursed her lips. "Come on. I ate more than you did, and I still have room. To complete the perfect food pyramid, you gotta start with alcohol and finish with dessert."

Bishop cringed inwardly, fighting the urge to lecture her on nutrition. There were more important things to discuss. Like Cassie's reason for this entire evening.

Mark returned with Cassie's pie and coffee and set the bill holder near Bishop. "I'll just leave this here for whenever you're ready." He took off at a fast clip, probably needing to finish with his tables before the dancing started.

Time to get the ball rolling. Bishop rested his arms on the table. "I've enjoyed tonight." He could swear his chakras aligned when Cassie's face lit up with a smile. "But it goes against my nature to stop searching for Ashley just so I can have a good time. I'm only here because you said we need to talk."

After one small bite of pie, Cassie put down her fork. "You're right. And that's what I want to discuss. Ashley. What's your next step in finding her?"

Immediately on guard, Bishop paused before answering. Was this an offer of help, or a trick to find out what he was up to? "Hard to say. I'm figuring it out as I go. Why?"

"I think it would benefit us both if we work together on our cases."

For a minute Bishop just stared, not expecting her offer. "What changed your mind?"

Cassie frowned. "Changed my mind?"

"You don't remember me asking you for help in the diner?"

"Working together doesn't mean I'm willing to break the law." Cassie's professional tone returned for the first time tonight. "I'm suggesting that an extra pair of eyes might catch something we've missed." She sighed, her voice softening again. "I *want* to help you find Ashley." She reached across the table and rested her hand on his.

The sincerity in her voice, the warmth in her touch, broke through Bishop's defenses. Since becoming a PI, he'd handled every case professionally, with no emotional involvement. But his search for Ashley was different. It was personal. It was eating him up on the inside, despite all attempts to maintain a Zen energy.

"I would appreciate your help." His voice cracked and he cleared his throat. "What case are *you* working on?"

Cassie pulled her hand back and sipped her coffee. "My father's murder. I've gone over the reports until my eyes bled. I was going through them again this morning, but was interrupted." The corner of her mouth twitched. "I had to respond to some bonehead's call to a murder scene."

Bishop shrugged. "Sorry about that. Figured you'd want to know."

"I did. But I still don't understand why you're so sure Palmer had anything to do with Ashley."

"He has a criminal record that includes sexual assault on a young woman. He gets out of jail and he's hanging out with Garrett. Ashley is at Garrett's house right before she disappears. Someone kills Palmer and tries to frame me while I'm there looking for Ashley. And then, Texas Rangers show up at Palmer's after he's murdered." He cocked his head. "What's that about, anyway?"

Cassie let out a long, slow breath as if trying to cool her temper. "The Rangers are here to investigate one of our cases that we've been working for the past couple years. My dad thought he was getting close to solving it when he was killed." She straightened in her chair. "Meanwhile, the Rangers have kicked my whole department off the case." Cassie picked at her uneaten pie with her fork. "That's why I'd like you to be the fresh eyes on Dad's murder."

"Why were they at Palmer's? Is he what they're investigating?"

Cassie's troubled gaze found his eyes. "No. They just showed up, claiming it might be related. But that's hogwash. They had no right to be there." A shadow crossed her face. "They seem intent on taking over *all* our cases."

"What case did they kick you off of?"

"There's a human trafficking pipeline running through Boone County. In fact, the Jane Doe we found right before you got here was one of their victims. We were all hands on deck to track them down, but the Rangers trumped our efforts."

Bishop jerked upright in his chair, his stomach tight with anger. The uncontrollable fury he'd thought vanquished spread through him like a malignant old friend, tensing every muscle until even his jaw ached. "You knew there were human traffickers here the whole time, and you never thought to mention this to me?"

Cassie's mouth dropped open, apparently shocked by his tone.

He slammed his hand on the table. "Ashley is eighteen, good-looking, and disappeared into thin air, and you didn't think this was pertinent information? You even checked your Jane Doe to make sure it wasn't my niece."

"Bishop." She spoke slowly, as if still surprised from his outburst. "It was a confidential investigation. And Garrett said—"

"Right." He scoffed. "You just accept some cock-and-bull story about her eloping, knowing at least one woman was dead because of a human trafficking ring." Bishop stood, fists clenched at his sides, glowering down at Cassie. "For all you know, Ashley could have been with your Jane Doe when she was killed. And because you just had to follow the rules, she could be halfway across the country by now."

"No." Cassie shook her head. "The timing doesn't track. I—"

"Save it." Bishop muttered a curse as he pulled out his wallet and slid five twenties into the bill holder. "The extra there is for the tip. If you want to keep drinking, buy your own." He stalked out of the building, not even trying to calm down. The old Bishop was slithering back in, ready to resume control. And the new Bishop was ready to let him.

WHAT THE... CASSIE watched Bishop's fine backside stalk out of sight, still in shock from his Jekyll-and-Hyde personality.

He hadn't even given her a chance to explain before he stormed out. *Fine.* He could find Ashley on his own.

Cassie waved over a waiter and ordered another drink. Mostly out of spite. She could pay for her own drinks, thank you very much, *Mister* Bishop.

After the scene he made, drawing the attention of everyone around them, Cassie seethed on the inside while keeping a smile on her face. *Everything's fine here, folks. Nothing to see. Move along.* She picked up her fresh drink, the telltale signs of her hard-fought control marking her palm. Four crescent-moon dents; only one drew blood. She set the glass back on the table.

She closed her eyes and took a deep breath. *Put yourself in Bishop's shoes.* If one of her brothers or Lonnie were missing, she'd be madder than a wet hen if someone withheld relevant information. And they were men trained to take care of themselves. Ashley was a teenager, out there on her own. Unless she eloped with Michael. *But what if she didn't?* Cassie's eyes popped open.

Having already paid for her drink, she dashed for the exit door. Bishop was probably already gone, but she knew where he lived. Almost mowing down a couple walking in, Cassie skidded to a stop in the parking lot. Bishop stood by his truck, his back to her. She inhaled a deep breath, exhaled and came up behind him.

"I understand, Bishop."

He turned around, his face still contorted by anger. "You understand *what*?"

"Why you're so mad at me. I would be, too."

He shook his head. "It's not just you I'm mad at. I never should have blown up at you like that." His shoulders slumped. "I feel like I'm losing control. Reverting back to who I used to be."

"I should have told you about the trafficking ring. But the timing still doesn't work for them to have grabbed Ashley here. They'd already left the stash house in Resolute."

"But even the slightest chance..." He turned pleading eyes on Cassie.

"If you'll let me, I'd still like to help you find her. Work together on our cases." She held her breath, willing him to agree.

"I can't do it unless you're going to be completely honest with me." Bishop folded his arms across his chest. "About everything."

Revealing the real reason the Rangers were in town,

telling Bishop about the leak and the threat to her family, made her stomach hurt and her chest relax at the same time. It was confidential information she shouldn't share. But working together, Bishop might help her find the real person behind that leak. "Fine. But that goes for you, too."

"Deal. But don't tell me what I legally can and can't do."

Cassie gnawed her lower lip. Was she really going to agree to this? "All right. But don't ask me to do anything illegal. Or unethical. Or—"

"Okay, okay." His mouth kicked up at the corners. "When do we start?"

Chapter Twelve

In her dream the next morning, Cassie balanced on a wobbly step stool and stretched high to shut off her smoke alarm. As soon as she stepped down, it went off again. The cycle continued until she surfaced long enough to recognize her phone's ring. Fumbling it off her bedside table, she answered without opening her eyes.

"Sheriff Reed." Her head fell back on her pillow.

"Hey, Cass. It's Lonnie."

Bolting upright, Cassie forced her eyes open and looked at her phone. Half past nine. "Dang it. I overslept." *First time for everything.* She pressed the speaker button and got out of bed, tripping over the clothes on the floor. *Stupid teal shirt. Only ever wrangled me bad luck and worse judgment.* "Anything wrong?" She kicked the shirt across the room.

"Just thought I'd check on you. You were MIA yesterday until the Palmer thing, and when you didn't show up this morning, I was worried."

Cassie loved her independence, but she appreciated her cousin's concern, too. He was more like a brother anyway, growing up with her family after his dad kicked him out. "I don't care what anybody says about you, Lonnie. *I* love you."

His deep chuckle came through the line. "Come on, Cass. *Everybody* loves me."

"That's 'cause on the inside you're just a big ol' marshmallow." She grabbed a pair of black jeans and a freshly starched white shirt from her closet and laid them on the bed.

"Don't go spreading that around. You'll ruin my gambling reputation."

Cassie snorted. "Are you kidding? Your poker face is so good, no one would ever guess."

"If it was, I'd be playing in Vegas." Lonnie paused, then asked, "So, you coming in today?"

"Of course. The wicked don't rest on Sunday. Neither do I." She stretched her arms above her head. "Want breakfast from the diner?"

"I could go for a Daybreak Double."

"See you soon."

Cassie went into the bathroom. Waiting for the water to warm up, she leaned both hands on the counter and stared at herself in the mirror. She looked like she felt, which wasn't great. She'd thrashed about all night, tangling in sheets and punching her pillow as the previous evening with Bishop replayed on an endless loop.

As difficult as it was, she'd set aside the whole ethics thing as Marge had suggested and focused on what else he brought to the table. By the time they'd finished dinner, Cassie could no longer deny her attraction to him. *I mean, come on.* Not one person he'd crossed paths with had been able to resist those bulging biceps or his alluring smile. He was a good sport, and between his sense of humor and the smoldering looks he gave her...

Cassie turned off the warm water and splashed cold on her face, halfway expecting steam to rise from her skin. Her mind still spun with what-ifs. Maybe she should have considered a possible connection between Ashley and the trafficking case.

No. She slapped her cheeks, trying to wake herself up and disrupt the unhelpful second-guessing. Her investigation had been a continuation of her dad's, following the rules of law and logic. As he often said, hoofbeats most likely mean horses, not zebras.

Brushing her teeth, she thought back to Bishop's angry outburst at Palmer's house. That, along with his comments about anger management classes and the way he'd stormed out last night, belied his normal, sunny temperament. *What demons haunt you, Mr. Bishop?*

She pulled on her clothes, ran a brush through her hair and tugged it into the ponytail she always wore for work. Pinned on her badge, strapped on her gun, and she was out the door.

Her breakfast order sat ready on the front counter when she ran in. Marge would add it to her tab, so she grabbed the bag and made it back through the door before it swung shut. Not only was she late, she hadn't even started her incident report for the Palmer case. The Rangers would just love that.

She slowed as she passed Helen's desk, pulling a fresh prune Danish from the bag and handing it off to her like a relay baton.

Closing her office door behind her, Cassie slid into her chair and dialed Lonnie. "I've got the food."

"I'll bring coffee."

"Bring Helen a fresh cup, too. I got her one of those nasty prune pastries."

"She loves those things."

"I know. But you better promise me, if I ever reach the point where I crave a prune Danish, you'll do everyone a favor and put me down." She hung up on his laughter.

A few minutes later, Lonnie walked in carrying two steaming mugs. Sitting in one of the visitor chairs, he unwrapped the breakfast sandwich Cassie handed him.

"Bless Marge's little heart." He bit into a jalapeño bun

stuffed with sausage, fried egg, melted cheddar, more ja-lapeños, bacon and hash browns.

"How can you even get that in your mouth?" Cassie un-wrapped hers, which was half the size of Lonnie's.

"Just one of my many talents." Lonnie spoke around a mouthful of food. "What were you up to yesterday?"

Cassie took a bite of her sandwich and set it down. "Working on Dad's case. I came in early so the Rangers wouldn't bother me." She took a sip of coffee. "But not early enough."

He swallowed and wiped egg yolk from his mouth. "I can't believe they just ripped our case out from under us. It's ridiculous."

"I know. That's why I'm avoiding them. I don't want them pulling Dad's files away from me, too." Cassie lifted the top bun, picked off a piece of bacon and popped it in her mouth. "I know we're off the case, but *technically* the stash house hasn't been linked to the traffickers. So Sean's still trying to find the truck those neighbors saw there. And I've got Noah and Dave showing Jane Doe's picture around town again, trying to ID her."

Lonnie's laugh turned to coughing as he almost choked. "You've got those two working together? Let's have a meet-ing when they come back. I could use the entertainment."

"I've had enough of the back-and-forth sniping in our meetings. How much do *you* know about Dave?" Cassie trusted her cousin's input. He'd become a deputy a few years before she had, after her dad had tired of Lonnie's endless string of dead-end jobs and convinced him to take the exam and join the department. It had turned out to be the perfect fit for him.

"No more than anyone else. I think he's got an inferior-ity complex." Lonnie shrugged. "He's one of those guys who tries to build himself up by knocking others down. Off the clock, he runs with a rough crowd. I saw him one night at the Dead End, playing pool with a couple bikers. A skanky woman was hanging all over him. He finally passed her something from his pocket and she hightailed it to the restroom."

"Drugs?" Cassie would fire Dave on the spot if he was using. "Why didn't you report it to me?"

"I don't know what it was for sure. And she didn't come back out before I finished my beer and left." Lonnie set his sandwich down. "Probably wouldn't hurt to keep an eye on him."

Cassie drummed her fingers on her desk. "I'm glad you mentioned that. I have some concerns about Dave. From the first time I read his incident report on Dad's murder, I've thought he failed to follow protocol when he heard the shots. I think he froze in the backyard instead of immediately backing up Dad." At the time, she'd thought he'd panicked, and embarrassing him with a confrontation wouldn't have gotten her closer to the truth about her father's killers, so she'd let it go.

"Adam's mentioned that when they go out together, Dave hangs back, almost like he's scared."

"I think it would benefit him to be partnered with a more experienced deputy. Someone able to teach him procedures, judge his decisions."

"You thinking Adam?" He picked up his sandwich, leaning over the paper to take a bite.

"Nope."

Lonnie's mouth stalled in the open position and his gaze rose to meet Cassie's. "No. No, no, no." He dropped the sandwich back on the desk. "The last thing I need is some nitwit tagging along at my heels. Next thing you know, he'll accidentally shoot me. Or himself."

"Sorry." She gave her cousin an overly sweet smile. "You're the most qualified."

Giving Cassie the stink eye, he ripped off a chunk of sandwich with his teeth and chewed.

Cassie leaned back in her chair. "So, about the family dinner the other night."

Lonnie raised his brows.

"It concerned you, too. Thought I could fill you in on everything now."

"Sounds serious."

"The Rangers are actually here because they suspect someone within our department of being the leak." Cassie kept her voice low.

"Who told them we have a leak?" He picked up his mug.

Cassie shrugged. "But the concerning thing is, the only personnel records they requested are yours, mine, Adam's, Noah's and Dad's."

Lonnie swallowed a mouthful of coffee and began coughing. He set down his mug and got up, walking around Cassie's office. By the time he caught his breath, tears were running down his face.

Cassie handed him a tissue. "*That* went down the wrong pipe."

"No kidding." Lonnie dropped back into his chair. "How'd you find out about the personnel files?"

"It doesn't matter. What's important is that we know, so we can be wary of the Rangers. Just remember, you can't discuss this with anyone."

"I won't. But I appreciate you telling me." He wrapped up the rest of his sandwich and tossed it in the trash.

"Why, Lonnie Dixon. I've never seen you throw food away before." Cassie loved to rib her cousin about how much he ate and his expanding girth.

His brow furrowed. "Guess knowing the Rangers are looking at us took away my appetite."

"It may mean nothing." Feeling guilty for making him

waste a sacred Daybreak Double, she tried to appease him. "But you know what they say, knowledge is power."

"You got that right." Lonnie stroked his beard, then seemed to shake it off. "Heard your PI friend put on quite a show at the Chute last night."

"News travels fast in these parts." Cassie grimaced, wondering whether her cousin had heard about Bishop riding the bull or making a scene.

Lonnie's brows arched. "Something going on between you two?"

Cassie's face warmed and she cursed her fair complexion for always giving her away. "Lonnie, the guy just got into town a couple days ago."

"I can think of a few times that hasn't stopped you."

She balled up her sandwich wrapper and threw it at him. "Geez. Between you and Helen…"

"Why? What did Helen say?"

"She thinks he's my type, especially since he'll be leaving town soon."

"Well, you do seem inclined toward less commitment-heavy relationships." He gave her a knowing look.

Cassie huffed. "I don't see *you* settling down with anyone."

"Touché. Maybe it just runs in the family."

Cassie's smile faded. Lonnie was her cousin on her mom's side. His offhand remark meant no harm, but it was a reminder that her mother hadn't been made for a long-term relationship, either. One more thing Cassie had inherited from her.

"I better get back to work." Lonnie rose. "Thanks for breakfast."

Cassie gave him a thumbs-up. "Next time, you're buying."

Twenty minutes later, Helen knocked and opened Cassie's door without waiting for an answer. "Michael Pugh just called. He said he needs to talk to you, but he won't come in. He'll only meet you at that abandoned rest stop south of town, and he said to come alone."

Cassie arched a brow.

"He said it's about Ashley Bishop."

Chapter Thirteen

Obsessed with keeping an eye on Garrett Pugh, Bishop had just cruised past his house when Cassie called. Using her country directions, *Turn right at Jody's Gas-up, about three miles down take a left at the lightning-struck live oak, then a right where the street dead-ends*, he beat her to the abandoned rest stop. Only one car sat in the weed-filled parking lot. A beat-up, vintage green Impala matching the description of Michael's.

Cassie had told him to wait for her if he arrived first.

Not today, Sheriff. If this kid knew anything about Ashley's whereabouts, Bishop would make him talk, whether Cassie approved of his methods or not.

He parked near the car, able to see a silhouette in the driver seat. He climbed out of his truck and rounded the front of the Impala. Michael stared at him through the windshield. As Bishop reached the driver's-side door, it swung open full force, slamming him to the ground, knocking the breath out of him. The door handle hit him where nothing should *ever* hit a man. Waves of pain radiated to his groin, his stomach, finally settling deep in his core.

He'd grabbed on to the edge of the door as he fell, pulling it from Michael's grasp. Now he breathed through his pain and held on, hoping the kid didn't think to turn the key and back up. Before Bishop could stand, Michael leaped over him and started running.

Bishop staggered to the hood of the Impala, lifted it and pulled a spark plug. *That should slow you down, you little jerk.*

Moving easier now, he started after Michael. Bishop was fast, but so was the kid, and he had a good head start. Michael hurdled a crumbling knee-high brick wall and disappeared behind the locked restrooms. By the time Bishop rounded the building, the kid was hightailing it back to his car.

Gotcha. Despite the fury building within him, Bishop slowed his steps, reserving his energy in case the chase renewed. Michael, unable to start his car, was under the hood now. Skittish, he kept glancing over his shoulder as Bishop got closer. The kid was a mechanic, so finding the problem didn't take long. His lanky frame tensed, and he bolted again.

This time, the parking lot's loose gravel tripped the kid, and he went down hard. Probably took off a layer of skin. Served him right. But he was young, wiry, and he hopped up, taking off for an open grassy patch near a concrete table. The fall had done its trick, though, slowing him enough that Bishop was able to leap and tackle him.

The kid didn't surrender easily. He twisted and thrashed, his arms swinging and legs kicking like half an octopus. Bishop flipped him on his stomach, yanked his arms behind his back and cuffed him with one of the zip ties he always carried. The kid kept squirming, kept trying to kick Bishop.

"You want me to tether your ankles together, too, you little punk?"

The kid stilled.

"That's better. Now, where's Ashley?"

"What do you mean, where's Ashley? I thought you had her."

Not what Bishop expected to hear. He flipped the kid over, grabbed his shirt front, and yanked him to a sitting position. Bishop stepped back out of kicking range, glowering down on Ashley's supposed boyfriend. "Explain yourself."

Michael's angry stare changed to one of total confusion. "So, you really don't have her? Who *are* you?"

"I'm a private investigator, Michael. And I need answers from you."

The kid's eyes widened. "How do you know my name?"

"I'm a *good* private investigator. Now, where's Ashley?" The words came out as rough as the parking lot gravel. "She followed you to Resolute, right?"

"Yeah, but I didn't even know until she showed up at my door."

"Then you and she disappeared, along with both of your cars." Bishop took a step toward him. "The way I heard it, y'all ran off to get married." His hands, hanging by his sides, curled into now-familiar fists. "I want to know that she's okay, and where she is. *Now.*" He barely registered his fists rising until Michael scooted back on his butt, cowering.

"Who told you that? Garrett?" The fear in Michael's voice disappeared, replaced by a cold, hard tone. "It's *his* fault that Ashley's gone. *I've* been looking for her for the last two days."

"What do you mean, it's Garrett's fault?" Bishop managed to lower his fist, though it was still clenched and ready. "And how would you know where to even start looking?"

"Garrett told me she might be between Resolute and El Campo somewhere off Highway 59. But after two days I realized I'd never find her just driving around. I needed Sheriff Reed's help." He sat taller. "I mean, I take full responsibility for everything. If she wasn't dating me, she never would have come here. And if I hadn't let her into that house, hadn't let her get near Garrett—"

"What did Garrett do?" Bishop spit the words one at a time, barely opening his mouth to let them out.

Michael stared at Bishop with haunted eyes. "He took her. My own brother…he took her." His face had gone from red to a pasty white, rivulets of sweat running down it. "He was always bad news, but I never thought he would ever do something this evil."

The fury in Bishop raged, and he didn't care who the target was. But as Michael spoke, his face wavered and the image of another kid, a girl about his age, superimposed itself there. His dead CI from Houston, taunting him. *What are you gonna do? Kill him, like you got me killed?* Bishop closed his eyes and shook his head. When he opened them, Michael stared at him with naked fear.

"Son of a sea biscuit! What do you think you're doing?" Cassie strode past Bishop and pulled Michael to his feet. Bishop hadn't even heard the crunch of her tires in the parking lot.

She pulled her tactical knife off her belt and tossed it to Bishop. "Cut that zip tie off of him *now.*"

Bishop glared at her. "I thought we agreed that you wouldn't interfere in the way I handle—"

She stepped up to him, toe-to-toe, her face inches from his. "And I told you to wait until I got here. Now cut that boy loose."

Still glaring, he flicked the knife open and slit the tie, letting it fall to the ground.

"Pick that up," she snapped at him. "We don't allow littering around here."

Bishop blew out an exasperated breath as he bent over for the tie. Afraid she'd make him pick up the rest of the trash, too, he didn't point out the plastic party cups and broken glass bottles near the building.

"I'm so sorry, Michael. Did he hurt you?" Cassie walked the kid toward the covered concrete table.

"Not really, Sheriff. Just scared me half to death. Thought he was one of the men who have Ashley."

Cassie froze midstep. "What men?"

"We were just getting to that." Bishop passed them and sat in the shade.

Michael sat on the far side of the table, shrinking in on himself like a balloon losing its air.

"Let's start at the beginning." Cassie settled near Bishop where she could look directly at the kid.

Michael scrubbed at his face with both hands. "I got news there was family trouble and rushed home to Resolute."

"When exactly was this?" Bishop asked. "And what was the family trouble?"

Michael jumped at his tone, but when Cassie nodded encouragingly, he began to talk. "Last weekend. Garrett called, said he'd gotten himself mixed up with some guys he shouldn't have. They were threatening to kill him."

Cassie rested her arms on the table. "What guys?"

"He didn't say then. Just said he needed me, so I raced back to Resolute to help him." Michael cringed at Bishop's disgusted expression. "What was I supposed to do? He's my brother. Me, him and Billy are all we have since Mom died."

"And the trouble?" Cassie prodded.

"Turns out he'd gotten involved with some gang that pimps out girls or something."

A lump formed in Bishop's stomach.

"But that wasn't even the worst of it." Michael averted his eyes. "He, uh, you see, those guys were mad because, well, because he lost one of the girls."

Bishop rose and leaned toward Michael, planting his fisted hands on the table. "Half-truths aren't gonna cut it, kid. What does 'lost' *really* mean?"

"He killed her, all right?" Michael blurted out. "Garrett was watching over some girls they had at some house, and he accidentally killed one."

Through clenched teeth, Bishop asked, "How did he *accidentally* kill a girl?"

"He said his job was to keep them doped up, but one of them either got too much or had a bad reaction to it. Whatever it was, she OD'd."

"Jane Doe." Cassie put her hand on Bishop's arm, pulling him back down next to her on the bench. "What does this have to do with Ashley?"

Michael's voice shook. "Those guys told Garrett if he didn't replace the girl immediately, they'd kill *him*."

Bishop's chest hurt like a mallet blow to his solar plexus. "So Garrett took Ashley as the replacement?"

"I beat the living daylights out of him, but it was already too late. Only thing that made me stop punching him was when he said they move girls along 59 toward Houston."

Suspicion snaked through Bishop's mind. "Wait a minute. If you beat your brother up, why didn't you stop him from taking Ashley in the first place?"

The kid's eyes filled with tears. "Because I wasn't there. I was mad at her for coming, 'cause her parents already hate me. We had a big fight, and I needed to get out of there, clear my head." He raked his hands through his hair and looked at them, pleading. "You gotta believe me. I *never* would have left her there if I knew what Garrett was going to do. I mean, he's my brother. I knew he was into some bad stuff, but kidnapping my girlfriend? I just didn't see it." Michael stared at him like a hungry man starving for absolution.

Bishop's anger and his fear for Ashley's safety had turned his heart to stone. He had no sympathy for Michael. Instead, he turned the knife again. "So you knew he was into some bad stuff, but you still left your little brother in Garrett's tender care."

"Ah, man, come on. I was seventeen when I left Resolute. I didn't have a job. I didn't have a place to stay. How was I supposed to take care of an eleven-year-old kid? I had to make a life in Houston before I could even think about bringing him there."

"Why didn't you call the sheriff right away, have her arrest Garrett and help find Ashley?"

"I could have helped, Michael," Cassie said.

"I thought about it. But Garrett said those guys could get to him even in jail. He'd be dead within a week." Michael hung his head. "And if we said anything to the cops about those guys, we'd all wind up dead. Even Ashley and Billy."

"Did he say they were local pimps?" Cassie's right hand was clenched on her thigh.

Michael shook his head. "No. He said they were part of a bigger group who had connections."

The lump in Bishop's stomach moved to his chest, squeezing the air from his lungs.

"Michael." Cassie waited until he met her eyes. "These guys aren't just pimps. They're human traffickers. They lure girls and young women, usually runaways or drug addicts, into a false sense of security. Pretend they care about them. Or get them hooked on drugs. Sometimes they just kidnap them."

Michael swallowed, looking like he was about to puke.

"They're like the wholesaler, selling to retailers. They move the girls along a circuit, sometimes working the girls themselves, but usually distributing them to pimps." Cassie's voice remained void of an incriminating tone, but its cold, detached tone made the words that much harder to hear. "The women are kept in cheap motels or massage parlors, or forced to work truck stops."

The color drained from Michael's face again.

Irrational or not, Bishop still partially blamed him for Ashley's situation. But that didn't mean he wanted Michael to get hurt. "Listen, kid. Don't go back to your house. You need to stay away from Garrett."

"What about Billy?"

"The sheriff and I'll pick him up. He can stay with you."

"I'll find somewhere safe for you to stay," Cassie said. "But you need to do as we say. I can't be chasing bad guys and worrying about you and Billy at the same time. Deal?"

The kid nodded, clearly defeated. "Just promise me you'll find Ashley."

Michael might not have been able to pound the truth out of his brother, but Bishop knew a lot of ways to make a man talk. And he'd use every last one of them on Garrett if he had to. Bishop stood. "Don't worry. That's a promise I intend to keep."

When they reached the parking lot, Cassie said, "Go directly to the justice center, Michael. I'll call Helen, let her know you're coming. Stay there until I make arrangements for you and Billy."

"Okay."

Bishop reached into his pocket. "You'll probably need this." He handed him the spark plug he'd removed earlier.

Michael started for his car, then stopped and turned back. "Hey, man, who *are* you?"

"The name's Bishop."

"Bishop?"

"I'm Ashley's uncle."

Michael closed his eyes. "She told me about you."

"Kid, whatever she told you, the truth is a hundred times worse."

After Michael drove off, Bishop braced himself for another scolding from Cassie.

"You did good, especially considering what we just learned." She scrutinized his face. "Are you okay?"

"Of course not. But at least—"

Cassie's phone rang and she held up a finger. "Sheriff Reed."

The voice coming through the phone was deep, muffled, and loud enough that Bishop could hear every word.

"If you want to know who killed your father, meet me at 1620 Oak Street in ten minutes."

The line went dead.

Chapter Fourteen

Bishop took a step toward her, his brows drawn together, but Cassie didn't have time to talk. She noted the time, then called her office.

"Sheriff's Department," Helen's brisk voice answered. "How may I—"

"It's me. Who's in the office?"

"Everyone's out right now. What's wrong?"

Cassie ran her palm across her hair. "Anyone in the vicinity of the old rest stop?"

"Hang on." Computer keys clicked. "Sean's the closest. About ten minutes away."

She checked the time again. Eight minutes left. "Never mind. Gotta go."

Cassie pocketed her phone and walked a short distance away. Her caller ID had said only Private Number. No name. *Has to be a setup.* She walked back. *But what if it isn't?* She stopped, the dust from her pacing settling on her boots.

She had to go. She had to check it out. She had to take backup. Cassie eyed Bishop, who looked concerned. Frustrated, but concerned. "You're coming with me."

As Cassie turned onto Oak Street, Bishop asked, "Think it's legit?" His tone expressed the same doubt plaguing Cassie.

"No way to know until we get there." She glanced at

her watch again. Five minutes left. "But it sounds exactly like what happened to Dad. Best if we expect an ambush."

The address was part of a small residential neighborhood not far from the rest stop. Cassie parked two houses away, the only sound the tick of her engine cooling. No kids playing outside. No dogs barking. No neighbors talking or laughing.

Bishop surveyed the area. "It's too quiet."

"Yep." Cassie's head was on a constant swivel. "No splitting up."

They climbed out of the SUV and eased the doors closed. With guns drawn, they circled the house together, covering each other as they checked windows for signs of life. Nothing.

Returning to the front yard, Cassie observed the street. No curtains fluttered, dropped by the hands of neighbors peeking out to watch the excitement.

"You ever see that movie *Tombstone*?" Bishop whispered.

"When all the townsfolk skedaddled before the bullets started flying?"

They exchanged a knowing glance before climbing the porch steps and positioning themselves on either side of the door. She was glad he'd told her he used to be a cop. Without that experience, he might not know how to handle a situation like this. Turned out, Bishop made a pretty good partner.

He signaled her that he would kick it in. Cassie shook her head and pointed to herself. She was lead on this, and she aimed to follow protocol. Motioning for her to freeze, he cocked his head as if he heard something inside. Cassie paused, straining to pick up the sound. Then Bishop gave her a quick wink and stepped back, ready to assault the door.

Before he could, Cassie pounded on the door and yelled, "Sheriff Cassie Reed!"

As "Reed" came out of her mouth, Bishop's boot hit the door. It splintered from the frame and swung in.

Cassie dropped into a crouch where she'd been standing. "I told you to wait," she whispered.

Bishop's whisper matched her harsh tone. "You took away any advantage we had." He crouched on the opposite side of the doorway.

They held for a few seconds, then Cassie raised a brow toward Bishop. He nodded. Bishop went left, Cassie went right. They cleared the house, room by room, then moved on to the garage. Although the house had been completely empty, stacks of boxes filled the garage. While Bishop opened one to check its contents, Cassie stepped outside. She called Helen and asked her to run a search for the owner.

She rejoined Bishop, who had opened several more cartons. "What's in them?"

"Financial records." He moved to another stack and opened the top box. "But it looks like records for a bunch of different people."

"Maybe whoever owned this place was an accountant." As Cassie glanced around at the dusty garage, frustration fought with relief. She'd come here wanting answers, but at least she and Bishop were still alive.

Holding a ream of paper in one arm, Bishop flipped through it. "Maybe." He didn't seem in a hurry to leave.

"While you're doing this, I'm going back in the house." She needed to find at least a hint of who had lured her here.

She went in through the kitchen and opened drawers and cabinet doors. Not even a stray slip of paper in any of them. She turned down the short hallway that led to a small bedroom. A soft scraping noise stopped her. Rat? Possum?

Critters always seemed to know when a house was vacant. Tipping her head, she strained to hear it again. Silence.

She stepped into the bathroom doorway next to her. She'd already cleared the room, finding nothing but a rusty water stain in the tub. A thump behind her made her spin, her peripheral vision catching movement in the mirror. The hallway ceiling revealed a square black hole. The wooden panel had been removed from the attic hatch. She swung her gaze to the access panel in the wall next to her, but before she could open it, a dark blur lunged from the bedroom and hit her full force.

He tackled her into the bathroom. She went down hard, her head slamming against the toilet. She kicked and flailed beneath him, trying to gain traction. When the figure, completely disguised in black, grabbed her shoulder, Cassie tightened her abs into a sit-up and rammed her forehead against his.

Stunned, he lost his grip on her. She jumped to her feet and tried to get past him, but he grabbed her by the ankles. When he yanked her feet out from under her, Cassie's chest hit the floor with a loud crack. *Son of a sea biscuit. That was a rib.* Searing pain spread through her torso. She broke his hold on one ankle and kicked back, connecting with his face. A satisfying crunch of nose cartilage fueled her fight, and she kicked again. He cried out and let go of her other ankle.

She made it into the hall and spun back toward the bathroom, pulling her gun. The perp still lay on his stomach, his mask dripping blood. He had beaten Cassie to the draw, a 9-millimeter in his outstretched hands.

She flung herself out of the doorway as a bullet just missed splitting her ponytail into pigtails. Cassie ran for the front door, pressing her radio mic and calling Bishop's name. As she reached the front porch, Bishop had already rounded the side of the house. A shot rang out and Cassie dropped, rolling behind a low brick wall lined with a hedge. Bishop took cover behind an oak tree and fired at the front door. Gun in hand, Cassie peeked over the hedge. After a moment of silence, a barrage of bullets flew from inside the house, and she and Bishop dropped flat. When the shooting stopped, Bishop raced to Cassie.

"Go! Don't let him get away." Bishop hesitated and Cassie got to her feet. "I'm fine. Get him."

Bishop ran toward the front door. Cassie followed him exactly two steps before losing her balance and falling. She fought to stand again, but the world spun, and vertigo took her to the ground.

"Cassie!" Bishop raced back to her side. "You *aren't* fine."

"Probably a minor concussion." She forced her eyes open. Bishop's face, lined with concern, hovered over her. "It was nothing. Just a collision with a toilet."

Bishop helped Cassie up. "You're bleeding." He held her arms out to the sides. "You've been shot."

"Can't be. I'm wearing a vest." *Just like Dad.* She watched blood soak her sleeve, cover her hand and drip off her fingers. "Well, if that don't snap my garters. I'm too busy to get…" Her vision blurred. "I think I need…"

Bishop eased her to the ground and called 911, cradling her head in his lap. His fingers brushed across her forehead, soothing her.

She wasn't ready to meet her maker yet. But between the deep hum of Bishop's smooth voice as he talked to the dispatcher and the soft touch of his fingertips at her temples, Cassie was just fine with being babied a bit longer.

MINUTES LATER, or maybe hours, Cassie regained consciousness to the sound of sirens.

Another blink or two later, deputies and medics swarmed the scene.

One more and she found herself on a gurney.

"It's a flesh wound, Sheriff." A medic hooked her up to a bag of fluids. "A through-and-through on the underside of your arm." Cassie struggled to remain awake and professional while Noah and Adam paced around her, talking to Bishop.

And then Ranger Ward showed up. *A concussion, cracked ribs and getting shot wasn't enough for one day?*

Ward approached and crouched next to her. "You doing okay, Sheriff?"

Cassie gave him a thumbs-up. "Peachy keen 'n' hunky-dory."

The Ranger's mouth twitched at the corners.

"Why, Ranger Ward, I believe you're smiling. Didn't think you *could* smile."

"And I believe they've given you something for the pain."

Frowning, she looked at the medic, then at the bag of fluids he held above her. "Did you give me drugs?" she stage-whispered. "I'm on duty. I can't even have a drink when I'm on duty."

"We'll discuss this incident, and the call that brought you out here, tomorrow morning. My office." Ward stood.

"I'll be there bright and early." Dopey from the drugs, Cassie fought through them, unwilling to give any ground to the Ranger. "But we'll meet in *my* office." She gave him a satisfied grin. "And don't be late."

Ward started to reply, but his gaze traveled past Cassie, and his usual sour expression returned. "We'll also discuss why *he* shows up at all your crime scenes."

Cassie twisted her head as best she could to follow his line of sight. "Oh yeah, him." Bishop stood with arms crossed, a look of disdain aimed at the Ranger. "Don't worry about him. He's just my date."

She smiled at the look of amusement on Bishop's face before she blinked once more and was out.

Chapter Fifteen

That evening Bishop pounded on Cassie's front door, every swing of his fist carrying fear, frustration and anger.

Just hours ago he'd held her in his arms, silently begging whoever was in charge of such things to allow her to live. With her eyes closed and face in repose, the fierce, tenacious sheriff had faded to a fragile shadow of herself.

But apparently, the old Cassie had returned somewhere between the ambulance driving off and the obstinate sheriff checking herself out of the hospital against medical advice.

"Cassie! Open the door." He kept pounding.

"Excuse me." The soft voice behind Bishop stopped him mid-pound. "Are you looking for Cassie?"

He turned around to find a middle-aged woman wearing cropped jeans, an oversize blue shirt with the sleeves rolled up, and camo-green Crocs.

"I'm her neighbor." She waved in the direction of the house next door. "I couldn't help but hear you."

"Sorry." Bishop grimaced. "Didn't mean to disturb you." He took a deep breath, trying to calm down. "I'm a friend of Cassie's. Did you happen to see her come home earlier?"

Every neighborhood had at least one nosy buttinsky, eager to share the fruits of their meddling. Bishop hoped Camo Crocs was Cassie's.

"No, I've been working in the garden all day." She tipped her head to the side and tapped a finger against her lips, as if trying to decide if he meant Cassie harm. His disappointment must have looked convincing, because she took pity on him. "But if she's not answering the door, there's a good chance she's out back in her studio."

"Studio?" Bishop came off the porch to continue the conversation.

The neighbor nodded. "Well, she calls it a shed, and she doesn't know I know about it. So mum's the word."

Bishop gave her a polite smile. "Thank you, ma'am. I'll go 'round back, see if she's there."

"There's a gate over here." She led him to the side of the house nearest hers. "I only know about her studio because sometimes I sneak into Cassie's yard and water her plants for her. She's a wonderful girl, but she kills plants like nobody's business."

"Except yours," Bishop mumbled under his breath.

They reached the gate, and Bishop managed to make it through while leaving Ms. Buttinsky on the other side. He rounded the back corner of Cassie's bungalow and paused. Not sure what he'd expected, but this was definitely not it.

A path of slate stepping-stones crossed the center of the lawn, beginning at the patio and ending in front of the shed's door. Flowering bushes lined the fences surrounding the yard, and arching trellises strained beneath the weight of several bougainvillea. Bishop glanced at the patio's single cushioned chair, positioned beside a small table. A book and one coaster sat on the table's mosaic top.

He stayed on the stone pathway to the shed, conflicting emotions still battling within him. And now another, curiosity. A large padlock hung from a metal hasp near the door handle. Bishop tried the handle, finding it locked, too. After no response to his knock, he walked around the small building. No back door. A few windows, one blocked by a window unit AC. The others were covered by curtains. He returned to the front of the shed.

"Just what do you think you're doing?" Cassie's angry voice carried across the yard from the patio. "Get away from there."

She moved from stone to stone, wincing as she charged him in slow motion. Her wet hair hung loose, water drops soaking the straps of her light blue tank top. White shorts ended mid-thigh, and as each shapely leg stretched to the next piece of slate, five sparkling purple toenails twinkled at Bishop. *Glitter?*

He pushed his curiosity aside, his concern and frustration taking center stage. "What are *you* doing here? You're supposed to be in the hospital."

"Says who? You?" Glowering at him, Cassie reached the end of the path.

"Yeah, me. And your doctor. You checked out AMA."

"I swear, I'm gonna arrest you if you keep digging into people's private business. How'd you find out I left against medical advice?"

"Noah told me the last time I tried to see you."

"That boy. I'm gonna—wait." The anger in her voice drained away, replaced by confusion. "What do you mean *last* time? You never came to the hospital."

"Are you kidding? I showed up so many times, the receptionist got sick of my face. You were either with the doctor, in X-ray or some other excuse. They wouldn't even tell me what floor you were on." Bishop threw his hands up in a very un-anger-management fit of pique. "It wasn't until I talked to Noah that I found out the real reason."

"And what was that?" Cassie folded her arms, then flinched in pain and dropped them to her sides. But not before drawing Bishop's attention to her chest. He had to blink before he could force his eyes to meet hers.

"They were afraid your attacker would make another appearance." He managed to bring his thoughts back on track. "Finish the job."

"That's ridiculous. A coward who hides behind a ski mask wouldn't take a chance like that." She shifted her stance, wincing again. "I need to sit down." She turned and followed the path back to the patio.

Bishop came right behind, admiring her long legs, revealed for the first time since he'd met her. "I'd offer to carry you, but if you have broken ribs—"

"I don't need to be carried," she snapped. Then more softly, "They're not broken. Just bruised." She lowered herself onto the chair, breathing shallow breaths. "Not sure bruised hurts any less than broken, though." She picked up a glass from the coaster. "You can grab a chair from the table inside. And there's iced tea in the fridge if you want some."

"Sweet?"

"Of course."

"Think I'll pass." Stepping into her kitchen, Bishop found it pretty much as he'd imagined. Spotless, organized, the countertops clear of small appliances except a coffee maker. He continued on to the table and picked up a chair, pausing to check out Cassie's living area. Again, not surprising. A couch, a coffee table with nothing on it, and a TV against the wall. Orderly, like the lady sheriff herself.

When he returned to the patio, Cassie eyed him as he placed the chair at the opposite side of the table. "You were gone long enough. Check out the whole place?"

"I would never dig into people's private business." He feigned a look of innocence as he tossed her words back at her.

"Yeah, right." She paused, then changed the subject. "I called Helen from the hospital. She said she found a place for Michael and Billy to stay." Cassie smiled. "Thanks for picking up Billy."

"No problem. Figured I'd run a few errands between trips to see you. I hoped to find Garrett there, too, take care of both things at the same time." He blew out a frustrated breath. "But he wasn't at the house."

"We can go tomorrow morning. I know you're worried about Ashley, but if Garrett wasn't there, he's probably in the wind."

"I can handle trying the house again. You should take it easy for a few days."

"I'm fine. Just a little sore."

Bishop raised a brow. "What else did the doctor say besides bruised ribs?"

"Minor concussion. And the bullet didn't hit anything important. Absolutely no reason to stay in the hospital."

"Maybe they were just trying to keep you safe."

"Like I said, whoever it was isn't going to waltz into a hospital for another go at it." She sighed, leaning her head back against her chair and closing her eyes for a moment. "Besides, I'm more comfortable at home. I don't like anyone hovering over me. Never have."

"I bet you loved it when you were a kid and your mom hovered."

A cloud crossed Cassie's face. "If she ever did, I can't remember it. But Mom wasn't the hovering type."

"She's gone?"

Cassie nodded.

"I'm sorry." The image of a young Cassie graveside hurt his heart. "How young were you when she died?"

"She didn't die." Cassie met his gaze and gave him a tight smile. "Just…disappeared. Ran off, I guess. I was eleven. We came home from school one day and she just wasn't there."

"No note? Nothing?"

Cassie shook her head. "I called my dad, and he came straight home. All I remember after that is him hugging me. Dad wasn't much of a hugger. Guess that's why I remember it so well. It was the only time he gave me a really tight, long hug." Her face flushed. "I felt so guilty about enjoying that hug."

"Why?"

Her gaze drifted to the live oak, as if lost in memory. "I thought that if Mom running off was what it took to finally get some attention from Dad, I was glad she was gone." Her sad eyes returned to Bishop. "But that wasn't true. I idolized her."

Bishop couldn't imagine growing up without being smothered by parental love.

"Dad was more of a man's man," Cassie said. "He never really knew what to do with a daughter, so he treated me like another son. At least, until Mom disappeared. Then all of a sudden I was in charge of my brothers, the housework, cooking, everything."

"How could you idolize your mom if she abandoned you?"

A wistful smile touched her lips. "Mom wasn't a creature of this world." She cocked a brow toward Bishop. "Maybe she was from your woo-woo world. She was like a hippie, a fairy, a free spirit who danced without touching the ground. I loved her." The condensation from her glass had pooled on the coaster, overflowing onto the mosaic tabletop. Cassie trailed a finger through it. "She was unapologetically her authentic self, and I wanted to be exactly like her."

After a moment of silence, she straightened her back and moaned in pain. "At least, I did until she left. Then I realized the full consequences of her actions on our family."

"What do you mean?"

"Mom refused to become the wife that Dad wanted." Cassie's voice was back to the no-nonsense quality Bishop was used to. "She put her artistic interests before the rest of us. Dad yelled and Mom refused to engage. She'd just go out to her studio." She flickered a quick glance at her shed. "I guess one day she got tired of the yelling."

Bishop paused for a moment, then took advantage of the obvious segue. "What's in your shed over there?"

Lifting one shoulder with nonchalance, Cassie said, "Nothing. Why?"

"Just curious. You seemed pretty upset that I was near it."

She tried straightening in her chair but stopped with a wince. "I didn't expect to find you in my backyard. That's all."

"Then show me your studio."

Cassie whipped her head toward him and narrowed her gaze. "Why'd you call it a studio?"

"Well…" Bishop leaned forward and lowered his voice. "I'm not supposed to tell you, but your neighbor happened to mention—"

"When were you talking to my neighbor?" The anger was returning.

"While I was pounding on your door and yelling your name," Bishop said, amused at how hostile she became over a shed.

She massaged her temples. "What else did the old snoop tell you?"

Bishop chuckled. "That's all. How 'bout you show me what you're hiding inside?" When she wouldn't reply, he tried a different approach. "Whatever you do in that shed is a part of you. And I want to know *everything* about you."

Cassie lowered her eyes. "What I do in there is personal."

"This is starting to sound a little kinky." He waggled his brows when she glared at him. "Seriously, why such a big secret? You know about all my woo-woo stuff."

Her lips twitched into a smile. The look she gave him was almost pleading, but what was she pleading for? To be left alone? Or did she really want to share her secret? Either way, it had to be her decision.

"You really want to know everything about me?" She

rested her arm on the table. "Because you might not like what you find."

"Then that would be my problem, not yours." Bishop reached across the table and stroked the back of her hand. "And yes, Sheriff Cassie Reed, I really want to know everything."

Her smile was bittersweet as she rose. "Hang on a minute. I have to get the key."

She returned and he followed her to the shed, unable to even guess at what he was about to see. Cassie unlocked the padlock, pulled the door open and stepped in, pausing to flip a light switch. Bishop walked in behind her, his mouth dropping open.

HER HEART PUMMELING her sore ribs, Cassie watched him. The first person she'd allowed into her studio. The first person she'd revealed her whole self to.

Bishop didn't speak. He didn't move. He just stood still, taking it all in. She followed his gaze, trying to see the room through his eyes. Tarps covered the floor. Her pottery wheel stood in the middle of the room. Shelves on one wall held supplies, while another displayed finished pieces. Or rather, *un*finished pieces.

"Wow. Not what I was expecting." He stepped to the wheel and examined it more closely, then looked at Cassie. "Why is this something you hide?"

She dragged her teeth against her lower lip. "Because when I come out here, I turn into my mother. I get lost in it with no sense of time." She pointed to an old-fashioned two-bell alarm clock near the wheel. "I don't start throwing clay until I've set that alarm. When it goes off, I quit, no matter where I'm at. Otherwise, I'd forget about everything else I'm supposed to do, and that's not how responsible people act."

Bishop walked over to the shelves holding her art and

picked up a piece. After examining it, he set it down with care.

"You don't have to be so careful with those. They're all horrible."

"They're not horrible." He picked up one of her favorites, a vase. She'd lost control of its mouth, but the wavy opening had turned out even better. "This one is incredible." He replaced it with the next in line. He looked at her, then back at the piece. "Some of them just look unfinished."

"That's because most of them are." She stored clay projects in plastic wrap, returning to them when time allowed. "Some I've lost interest in. I usually break them into pieces and toss them in my reclaimed clay bucket."

Bishop held up one that resembled an alien with a long snout.

Cassie laughed. "Some I've stopped and started so many times, I can't even remember what they were supposed to be."

Bishop set it back on the shelf and crossed to the wheel. "I don't know anything about pottery. Tell me how all this stuff works."

She assessed him, wondering if he was serious or just humoring her. When he continued to stare at her in earnest, she relented.

"You start with a fresh lump of clay and wedge all the air out." At his questioning look she said, "Squish, basically. Then you fasten it to the bat." She showed him the center of the wheel. "Moisten your hands, and center the clay."

"Make sure it's exactly in the middle of the table?"

"Yes, but there's more to it than that. You wrap your hands around it and cone up, then down, over and over." She showed him the motions with her hands. "As you're doing that, you listen to it. It'll tell you what it wants to become."

"The *clay* tells *you*?" Bishop's face looked like hers probably had when he talked about his meditation.

"That's what I've read. If it's true, I'm obviously not listening well." She scoffed at herself. "Once the clay spins beneath my fingers, I just zone out. All the stress and pressures of life just…disappear."

"Cassie, this is as much a part of you as shooting guns and arresting felons. You should stop hiding it."

It came from her mother, this desire for artistic creation. Cassie's soul cried out for it like an addict screaming for drugs, refusing to quiet until the craving was appeased. At the same time, her mind stalled in fear. Fear that if she allowed it to, the desire would swallow her whole, tear her away from everyone she loved.

"I don't want anyone else to know. Please don't make me regret letting you in." She hated the pleading tone in her voice.

The intensity of Bishop's gaze pulled at her heart. "It's not mine to tell." He crossed the short distance and wrapped his arms around her, careful not to squeeze her ribs. "But I hope one day *you'll* share it with the world. Or, you know, at least the rest of Resolute."

Thankful that the levity in his voice broke the tense moment, Cassie chuckled. "I'm not so sure Resolute is the best place for artistic appreciation."

"Maybe not," he said into her hair, still holding her to him. "But *I* appreciate it."

Slowly, he lowered his head to hers and paused, as if waiting for her to shove him away. But she didn't. She didn't have the energy to fight what she hadn't even realized she wanted. And what she wanted more than anything at this exact moment was Tyler Bishop's lips on hers.

She rocked forward, speeding up the process, and she could swear Bishop's lips curved into a smile before opening, his tongue sliding alongside hers.

Cassie sank into it, her fingers hooking into his belt loops, the only thing keeping her grounded. Bishop's hands loosened from around her, and he cradled her head in them, his thumbs brushing away tears she hadn't known she'd cried.

It was the most vulnerable she'd ever allowed herself to be in front of someone. No badge, no gun, surrounded by the evidence of her own whimsy. And yet with Bishop, she didn't feel scared or embarrassed. She felt free.

Bishop pulled back, concern warring with passion in his expression. "Are you okay?" He brushed away another tear. "Did I hurt you?"

Cassie brought her arms up, her right hand sliding behind his head. "I'm fine." She pulled him closer. "I've never felt better." She touched her lips to his once more, chasing the feeling of freedom.

They continued to touch, to explore, eventually making their way to her sparse, utilitarian bedroom. She glanced at Bishop's face as he took in the room. She'd never allowed a man in her home before, let alone her bedroom. Always in control, she preferred to scoot out of the man's place before sunrise, before things got awkward. But Bishop was different.

Standing by the bed, she followed his gaze around the room. "It's kind of simple."

Bishop stepped to her, stopping only inches away. Lifting her hair from her shoulders, he let it slide slowly through his fingers. "I like it."

He tipped her chin up with one finger and kissed her, a soft caress of her lips that had her hungering for something deeper, something more fervent. But Bishop kept it tender, brushing his lips against hers until the heat building within consumed her.

Cassie grabbed the front of Bishop's shirt, tugging him to the bed and pushing him to sit. She lifted her tank top, nearly staggering when her ribs screamed out in protest.

Bishop stood, his hands reaching out to steady her. "Are

you okay? Maybe we shouldn't…" He trailed off as if reluctant to finish the thought.

His concern made her want him that much more.

"I'm made of sterner stuff than that." She turned around, pulling her hair to the side. "Can you manage a bra clasp?"

He scoffed, as if affronted by her lack of faith in him. "Oh, I can manage."

But instead of reaching right for it, Bishop trailed his fingers up and down her spine. The warmth of his hands settled above her waist before reaching around and undoing the top button of her shorts.

Cassie's short and fast breaths had nothing to do with her ribs.

The sound of the zipper seemed impossibly loud, as tooth by tooth it lowered and her shorts slipped from her body.

His lips replaced his hands, kissing her back, her neck, her shoulders while his hand settled itself lower.

There was nothing to worry over, nothing more to focus on than the fire building inside.

Cassie's head dropped back on a moan, and her legs weakened as her pleasure reached its peak, again and again.

When she finally stilled, Bishop unhooked her bra, kissing her newly exposed skin.

It took a few deep breaths, but finally Cassie's legs felt stable enough to move. Turning in his arms, she faced him. Let her bra fall to the floor between them.

His gaze roamed from the top of her auburn hair all the way to her sparkly purple toes and back up again. She was battered, bruised and pleasure-worn. She had never felt more beautiful.

Hooking her thumbs into her panties, she slid them to the floor.

Bishop licked his lips.

She grabbed the hem of his T-shirt and lifted. She had to grit her teeth when her arms went past rib height.

Bishop saw. "Now, just hold on. I think maybe we've done enough for tonight. It's no fun if you're in pain."

Her want, her need, overruled her injuries. She unbuckled his belt, and in a matter of seconds the rest of his clothes were on the floor. Cassie ran her hands across the well-defined planes of his chest, gently touched the bruises covering his abs.

She smiled and pushed him back on the bed. "Oh, we're doing it, Mr. Bishop." She straddled him, loving the way his eyes centered on hers. "You're not the only one who can ride a bucking bull, you know."

At that, Bishop chuckled.

Then there was nothing but them, two bodies moving together, each healing the other in ways that had nothing to do with their external wounds.

He was gentle.

She wasn't.

It was perfect.

And as sleep finally overtook her, cradled in Bishop's arms, Cassie realized all her pain was gone.

Chapter Sixteen

Early the next morning, Bishop eased Cassie's front door shut so he wouldn't wake her. He smiled to himself. He'd come over bound and determined to stay, keep an eye on her. After all, she did have a concussion. But he hadn't planned on how close she'd let him get. How far they'd take their relationship. Most of the time, Cassie riled him up in both the best and worst of ways. But last night it was as if they'd become one, their chakras completely aligned.

He laughed to himself, imagining Cassie's expression if he told her that.

His mood darkened, though, as he parked in front of Garrett's house. Cassie's injuries had been only part of the reason he didn't want her here. He planned on getting the information about the traffickers from Garrett any way he could, and the sheriff might not like some of his methods. Though Garrett hadn't been at the house yesterday, Bishop wasn't convinced the kid had fled for good. He didn't figure him for being smart enough to do precise risk assessments.

After a night's rest—well, some of it was rest—Bishop was ready to take on the lying piece of crap who could lead him to his niece.

Bishop crossed the front porch and pounded on the flimsy door. He gave Garrett a minute before pounding harder, then tested the knob. When it turned in his hand, he pushed the door open.

Garrett, a few feet away from the door, froze, his eyes widening. "What the…" He came at Bishop with both arms stretched straight out, as if to push him back outside.

Instead, Bishop grabbed Garrett and pushed *him* up against the wall.

"What are you doing, man?"

"I'm getting the truth out of you one way or another. I already know you're working for the human traffickers and that you gave Ashley to them."

"I don't know what you're talking about." Garrett made a feeble attempt to bat at Bishop's arms. "Get off me."

"Who are they? Where did they take Ashley?" Bishop's right hand balled into a fist.

"How should I know, man? I just babysit their bit—"

He punched Garrett in the stomach. Hard. "Never call a woman that. Especially not my niece."

Garrett doubled over and slid down the wall. When he struggled to get up from the floor, Bishop grabbed the front of the kid's shirt and hauled him up. He shoved him against the wall again, one hand on his chest, the other around his throat. Tight enough to scare him. Loose enough that he could speak.

"I heard in addition to babysitting, you dope them up. Only this last time, you gave one of the girls too much. She died from an overdose, and you hid her body in the shed behind the stash house."

"Look, I don't know where you're getting your information—"

Bishop pulled back the hand from Garrett's throat and punched him in the face. This time the punk didn't even try to get up. Bishop hauled him to his feet again. Propped him against the wall again.

"I'm running out of patience. Either you tell me everything you know about the whole operation, or I'll dispose of you like you did that girl."

Blood and snot ran down Garrett's face. "Try it, and they'll find you. And you don't want to know how they get rid of people."

"Then maybe I'll just put out the word that you're co-operating with the police in the murder. And apprehension of the entire ring." Bishop leaned forward, close enough to see Garrett's eyes dilate in fear. "Keep my hands clean, let them do the dirty work for me."

"You don't even know who they are. You just said so." Garrett's voice lost some of its defiance.

Bishop shrugged, the nonchalant movement at odds with the tension in his chest. "I don't have to. I just have to spread the word. It'll get to them." He smiled and Garrett flinched. "I'll just watch you, and after they've disposed of you, I'll take care of them."

Sweat dripped down Garrett's temples. A few more minutes, maybe a few more punches, and Garrett would spill his guts. Bishop pulled his fist back for another jab.

"What do you think you're doing?" Cassie's voice came from right behind him.

Bishop's stomach dropped. Without turning around, he said, "I'm allowing Garrett to live in exchange for information about the trafficking ring."

Cassie shifted to his side. From the corner of his eye he saw her cross her arms, looking like a teacher about to go into full-on lecture mode. "You can't just beat it out of him."

Bishop hung his head, muttering a curse Cassie would not approve of. Why did she have to show up now?

"I told him that, Sheriff. I told him he can't kill me." Garrett's upper lip curled into a sneer aimed at Bishop. "You're gonna be sorry you ever messed with me."

"Shut up." Cassie stepped closer to the two men. "And don't think you'll be getting off any easier when I haul you down to the jail. We've got a couple of Texas Rangers in the house, and they're awfully interested in this whole gang you've hooked up with. I'm sure they'll want to question you, too."

She looked Garrett over from head to toe, pure disgust on her face. "And yeah, they may be more gentle than Mr. Bishop here, but don't be fooled. 'Cause when they haul you back to their Austin headquarters, where the really bad guys go, they'll throw you to the wolves. And how do you think a little small-town pup like yourself will fare, hmm?"

Garrett struggled against Bishop, who pushed him harder.

"Let him go, Bishop." Cassie's voice was firm. But it was the look of hurt in her eyes that finally made him act.

"Fine." He took his hands off the kid so fast, Garrett collapsed on the floor, gasping. Bishop turned to Cassie. "He was about to tell me everything."

"And you think that makes what you're doing okay? You can't beat a confession out of someone you're interrogating. Actually, you're not supposed to be interrogating him at all." Cassie blew out a breath of frustration. "That's why I wanted to come along today, instead of *taking it easy.*" She glared at him.

Bishop held his hands up in surrender. "Go ahead, do it your way. But you might want to cuff him so he can't—"

Pain exploded in Bishop's knee and he went down, his flailing arms grabbing at Cassie, bringing her down, too.

"What—" Cassie moaned, holding her side as she tried to untangle herself from Bishop.

"Punk kicked me in the knee." The back door banged, and Bishop struggled to stand, then helped Cassie to her feet. She hobbled out the front door, one hand still on her ribs. After a few limping steps, Bishop picked up speed and followed Garrett out the back.

Bishop checked the garage first. Empty. The back of the property stretched all the way to a small creek. He ran as fast as his knee allowed, scouring the area. No sign that Garrett had come this way.

Limp-running back toward the house, he heard a car engine turn over. Bishop pushed himself harder. He hopped the short fence to the driveway, groaning when his knee buckled on the landing.

The Mustang was gone.

So was Cassie's SUV.

As he speed-hobbled to his truck, Bishop pulled out his phone. He had no idea which way Garrett had fled, but that wouldn't stop him from joining the hunt. He tapped Cassie's number, frustrated when he had to leave a message to call him with her location.

Before he could pull away from the curb, though, Cassie's SUV came down the street toward him and pulled into the driveway. Bishop shut off his truck and limped up the drive, eager for another go at Garrett.

But when she slammed her door and stomped across the yard alone, his anger toward Cassie returned. He followed her to the porch steps, where she stopped to brush at dirt and grass stains on her clothes.

"I couldn't catch up to him." Failure added a hard edge to her voice. "I checked his car first. He wasn't there, so I moved down the street, checking side yards and anywhere else he might be hidden. I must've been five houses down when I heard his car start. I tried to run back, but he was coming toward me when I was still a couple houses away." She looked into Bishop's eyes. "The dadgum son of a sea biscuit swerved up on the grass and tried to run me down. I got my car and went after him fast as I could, but I never even caught a glimpse of that Mustang."

Bishop was relieved she hadn't been hit. But right now, so much rage filled him from the little weasel slipping through his fingers that he couldn't fully register any other emotions. And Garrett's escape was all on Cassie.

He brushed past her without a word, stepped over the dog who never moved, and went back in the house. Cassie's footsteps followed him.

"Look, Bishop, don't think that just because I don't condone beating a confession out of someone, I don't care—"

"Save it, Sheriff. We both know you only care about doing things by the book. Now, if you'll excuse me, I have a house to search. *Illegally.*"

CASSIE BIT HER tongue until the metallic tang of blood hit her throat. It was that or cry, and she'd be darned if she'd shed tears over this aggravating Jekyll-and-Hyde act Bishop was playing.

Last night, when the world hadn't ended while she showed him her studio, she'd thought they had both turned a corner. That by showing him the part of her she didn't trust anyone else with, things would be different.

What a joke.

Before drifting off to sleep, they'd agreed to question Garrett together. But when she woke, Bishop was already gone. Her gut told her he hadn't gone out for coffee and bagels, and she was glad she listened to it. She should've listened to it last night when she'd seen him poking around her studio and just kicked him out.

Because when she found him at the Pugh house, trying to choke the truth out of Garrett, she broke a little inside. Not because Bishop was beating up someone lower than a snake's belly in a wheel rut. The punk had earned that whupping. No, she broke because she'd ignored her own rules. She'd let Bishop get too close.

What she had thought was freedom was really just unrealistic romantic notions, the kind her mother was known for.

"Make sure you wear gloves." That's all she would say about him searching the house. Cassie snapped on her own pair before stepping into a bedroom. It was no more legal for her to search the house than Bishop, but at least she had a reason to be here. She needed to pack a few more clothes for Billy.

Two unmade twin beds with a nightstand between them filled most of Billy's room. Clothes were strewn across the floor, but a few shirts hung in the tiny closet. Searching dresser drawers, Cassie managed to round up several T-shirts and a couple more pairs of jeans that still smelled of detergent and fresh air from hanging on a clothesline.

She found socks and underwear in the top dresser drawer, all in a jumbled pile. Cassie pulled out a week's worth of each and carried everything out to her SUV. She returned to the house and looked into another room. *Must be Michael's.* It was empty except for a neatly made bed and a dresser. She looked through the drawers, but they were as vacant as the closet.

Bishop had started in the kitchen but was already in the master bedroom by the time Cassie walked in. Garrett had obviously taken over the master after the boys' mother died, because it looked like an adult version of Billy's room. Unmade bed, dirty clothes everywhere, nudie magazines sprawled across the floor.

His hands gloved, Bishop searched the nightstand drawers. He glanced over at her, his expression neutral. Cassie matched it and walked to the dresser.

She found a 9-millimeter handgun hidden beneath an unfolded pile of T-shirts. She'd seen the shotgun leaning against the wall in a corner when she'd come in. A rush of heat burned through her like a flash fire. Had *Garrett* killed her father?

Cassie left them where they were. *For now.* She'd have to get a warrant, and she didn't have probable cause to request one at this point. She moved on to the closet. A few shirts on hangers, but most of them were on the floor covering his shoes. She reached up to the top shelf and felt along until her fingers grasped a bundle. She took it down, set it on the bed, and unwrapped it. Inside the dirty T-shirt she found a brick of heroin. She wrapped it back up, put it on the shelf, and continued searching.

By the time she finished, she'd come across at least a half pound of weed and a baggie of cocaine, in addition to the heroin. Were these the drugs he used to dope the girls? Or were they payment for his evil deeds?

Bishop, done with pulling everything from dirty plates to dust bunnies out from under the bed, stood and popped his back. "Not even a hint of where they're holding the girls."

"No, but enough drugs to put him away for a good while," she said, her voice as neutral as his expression. "And if the guns match to any crimes, even longer."

"But we're just leaving it all here, for him to come back and collect at his convenience." Bishop scoffed and walked out of the room.

Cassie went after him, catching up on the front porch. "You think I don't want to arrest his scrawny butt? But you know darn well it won't stick unless we do everything right."

He turned and gave her a look sharp with disappointment that cut deep into her heart. Then he stepped off the porch, walked to his truck and drove away.

For the first time in a long while, Cassie cursed. And just as she'd never admit out loud that Garrett deserved Bishop's punches, she'd never tell a soul how good it felt to let the profanity slip past her lips.

She'd closed the front door and was stepping over the dog when her phone rang.

"Perfect timing, Helen. I need you to put out a BOLO on Garrett Pugh's car."

"Where *are* you?" Helen whispered in a frenzied tone.

"Taking care of some things. Why?"

"You were supposed to be here early to meet with the Rangers." Helen's voice dropped even lower. "That one guy, Ward, he's fit to be tied."

"Dang it. I completely forgot about that." She scrubbed a hand down her face. "But to be fair, I was on drugs at the time. *And* had a concussion. Think that's a good enough excuse for him?"

"I think you better get yourself to the office PDQ." The call ended.

Chapter Seventeen

"Reed! In our office. Now."

Cassie had made it as far as her office door when Ward's voice bellowed down the hallway. He stood outside their room, his hands on his hips.

She turned to face him. "It's *Sheriff* Reed. You want to talk to me, you come to my office."

"Won't be for much longer." His voice was softer, but still plenty loud for Cassie to hear.

She rounded her desk and sat, composing herself. Boots drummed along the marble floor, the echo no doubt Mills's footsteps. They entered her office and Mills shut the door. Neither bothered to sit.

"Did you not understand me when I told you to stay away from the trafficking case?" Ward asked. He looked like a cartoon character with steam coming out of his ears.

"I understood perfectly. And I did what you, uh, *de-manded*." It definitely hadn't been a request.

His left eye ticked. "Then explain that fiasco yesterday."

"If by fiasco, you mean me getting beat up and shot, what makes you think that had anything to do with the traffickers?" Cassie cocked a brow at Ward. "Or the leak, which is supposedly the only thing you're investigating."

"Just tell us what you were doing at that house." Mills was still playing the good cop, keeping his voice gentle and his face neutral. Too neutral.

Cassie stared hard at him for a moment, finally seeing through a crack in his mask. He was even more devious than Ward, who'd made it clear from the get-go what he thought of her.

"I don't owe you an explanation about any of our cases." Cassie stood. Enough of the psychological advantage of towering over your opponent. "Unless I request your assistance with a case, you have no jurisdiction here."

Ward crossed his arms. "We do when it's an internal affairs investigation."

"Then explain to me how yesterday's abandoned house has anything to do with *that* investigation."

"We have confidential information linking it to the traffickers," Mills said.

"And when did you receive this confidential information?" Cassie smoothed her hair. "Prior to yesterday? Or after I was shot?"

Mills stole a sidelong glance at Ward that answered her question.

"So someone around here is keeping tabs on what I do, where I go, then telling you it's somehow involved with the traffickers." She smirked. "How convenient for you. And your informant. Has it ever occurred to you that maybe your informant *is* the leak? Maybe you're the ones internal affairs should be looking at."

Another look from Mills to his partner. Ward ignored him this time.

"And what about the Palmer house? Somebody tell you that one's part of the leak, too?" Cassie's fingernails were halfway through her palm by now. "How about you give me a list of every address that's off-limits to my deputies and me. Right now. That way we'll know where to stay away from, and if the address isn't already on the list, you'll know your informant is feeding you a bag of grade A cow manure."

"That won't be necessary."

"Why is that?"

"Because we've already met with the county council, and as of immediately you are relieved of duty until we've completed a full investigation." Ward's smug smile made Cassie want to punch him in his Texas-sized nose.

But she wouldn't give them the satisfaction of seeing her emotions. "On what grounds?"

"You're impeding our case. Interfering in the search for justice regarding this internal leak. The council agreed to name a replacement for you."

Mills jumped in. "Depending on how things fall out after we're through here, you may be reinstated."

Cassie reeled. If the council brought in some stranger who didn't know the county, didn't know the people of Resolute... "Who did they choose as my replacement?"

"Lonnie Dixon. He's chief deputy, which makes him the logical choice." Ward's tone turned even more condescending. "And our investigation to date shows he's not connected to the leak."

Cassie sighed with relief. She could trust Lonnie to run the department the way she and Dad had. But that single fact did nothing to allay her anger. A deeper understanding of Bishop's pain and frustration burrowed into her. He'd mentioned the system failing him, failing the people who needed him. She hadn't really understood that until now.

But Cassie held all that inside. "I'll be looking forward to the looks on your faces when you discover the real leak." Her tight smile disappeared. "In the meantime, the death of every single girl in the hands of those traffickers will be on you."

She rose from her chair. "So, sleep well knowing the chaos you've created in Boone County. And get yourselves a good representative. By the time I'm done, you'll be lucky if you're directing traffic in a one-stoplight town." She was bluffing, but she didn't intend to go down without a fight. It wasn't just about her. It was about the office of sheriff. It was about her father's legacy.

Cassie slapped her gun and badge on the desk and strode out of her office, head high, insides roiling with shame and frustration, and her right palm damp with blood. She'd failed her father. Her town. Her county. She had followed the rules. Adhered to protocol. And still, they were able to kick her out the door as if she were dirt on the bottom of their boots.

She reached Helen's desk and asked her in a low voice, "Have they questioned you yet about the leak?"

Helen nodded. "I'm not supposed to tell you anything. They said I'd be out on my butt if I did."

Cassie stared into Helen's eyes, but Helen remained silent. "So you're *not* going to tell me?"

"I didn't think you'd want me to. They were adamant about it, and I know how you feel about any of us doing what we're not supposed to."

Cassie felt the rigid strings that she lived by tug at her from every corner of her life. Going by the book hadn't helped her plug the leak, stop the traffickers, track down her father's killer or find Bishop's niece. Maybe the Rangers had done her a favor after all. Maybe now she would try it Bishop's way instead.

Placing her elbows on the desk, Cassie leaned down. "What if I told you they relieved me of duty, and maybe I'm going to do things differently for once?"

Helen's eyes went round. "They fired you?"

"I think it's more of a suspension-type thing."

"That's just not right." Her face crumpled and she grabbed a tissue. "How could they do that?"

"Pull it together, Helen. We're the ones who keep this place running with spit and baling wire. Remember?"

Helen nodded as she wiped her nose. "They only asked

me if I'd seen any evidence of corruption in the department. I told them no. And that's the truth."

Cassie straightened and patted Helen's shoulder. "I'll keep in touch. We'll straighten everything out. Oh, and if you get a hit on that BOLO, call me. No one else." She walked out of the building, a plan already forming in her mind. She pulled out her phone as she reached her vehicle and hit speed dial.

"Bishop."

"Meet me back at the Pugh house. We need to talk."

Chapter Eighteen

Bishop stood in the doorway of the Pugh master bedroom, watching Cassie put Garrett's drugs and guns in a duffel bag. "I thought you couldn't do that 'cause it went against the rules."

"Yeah, well, I'm done playing by the rules." She opened the bottom dresser drawer, retrieved the baggie of cocaine and tossed it into the duffel.

"Any particular reason?" If it were true, Bishop sure wouldn't complain. But this just wasn't the Cassie he'd gotten to know.

She placed the handgun in the duffel, too, staring into the bag before her somber gaze met his. "Because doing everything by the book just got me relieved of duty. I'm no longer sheriff, and all I was doing was my job."

"Did they tell you why?"

"Whoever gave the Rangers false info about the leak is tipping them off about my actions, claiming it all ties into the trafficking case. Which I was ordered to stay clear of. And I have been."

"What leak?" Had he missed something?

"I meant to tell you about it the day after the Chute. By the time I got home from the hospital, I forgot."

Bishop crossed his arms. "You sure you weren't still holding out on me?"

"Look, *Mister* Bishop, we need to get a few things straight if we're going to keep working together."

"Are we?" he asked, surprised she'd want to after his actions this morning. "Still working together, that is," he added when Cassie looked confused.

"You don't want to?" She backed up a step.

Bishop sighed. "Yes. I want to work together."

Cassie narrowed her eyes. "Even though you accused me of letting Garrett get away?"

"Getting him to confess was my best chance of finding Ashley alive. I had a right to be angry." Even now, his fingers itched to curl in on themselves.

"Next time you get mad, meditate or something, will you?"

Bishop snorted and ran a hand through his hair. "Yeah, yeah. Are you going to tell me about the leak?"

She dropped the bag. "We've figured there's been a leak related to the human trafficking case for quite a while. They were always one step ahead of us when we went after them." Cassie paced in the small room. "The Rangers arrived already knowing about the leak, said they were looking at everyone in my department."

"How'd they find out about it?"

"They said they couldn't reveal their source. Thing is, the only people they're looking at are my brothers and me. Oh, and my dad, if you can believe it." She snorted. "I know no one in my family is the leak, but unless we find the real culprit, Adam and Noah could wind up behind bars. And when the Rangers kicked us off the trafficking case, they made it clear they wouldn't be working it."

Bishop closed his eyes and took a calming breath. "Let me get this straight. No one is actively looking for the girls? Or the traffickers?"

"Nope. Not until now." She squared up to him, hands on hips, looking like the feisty Cassie he'd met on day one. "*Now*, you and I are going to be looking for them."

"How do you propose we do that? Especially since Garrett's gone."

"I put out a BOLO on his car." Cassie's lips curled into a very satisfied smile. "My last official act as sheriff."

"Nice move." Bishop started to smile but stopped. "If you're not in the office, though—"

"Already handled. I told Helen to call me, and only me, when there's a sighting." She picked up the duffel. "Let's go back to my house, figure out our plan."

Bishop allowed himself a moment to appreciate Cassie's resilience. "Why are you taking this stuff now? You can't turn it in as evidence."

"Like you said earlier, keep it out of Garrett's hands if he comes back here." Cassie winced when she shifted the bag. "Might even get him into trouble with whoever he's working for."

"Ribs still hurt?" Bishop didn't wait for her to respond but took the bag from her. She opened her mouth, probably to argue, but snapped it shut.

"Thanks." It was soft and hard to hear, but she said it all the same. And with that one word he followed her out of the room, hoping that this time, just maybe, their teaming up would work.

"They twinge every now and then, but don't worry. They won't slow me down."

"Not worried in the least." He raised a brow. "They didn't seem to slow you down last night."

Cassie shot him a look as a pink flush crept up her cheeks. "I only let you take my bag so I can save my energy for the bad guys." She stalked out of the house without looking back.

"LET'S SIT OUTSIDE. It seems to be cooling off." Now if only Cassie could. Last night she'd felt more intimate with Bishop than she'd thought possible. His consideration, his gentleness, his passion had made her realize the difference between having sex and making love. *Better late than never.*

But today had given her doubts. He'd betrayed her trust, and that was something hard to get past. If there even was any getting past it.

"Probably that front they predicted. Supposed to get some heavy rain with it." Bishop carried a dining room chair out with him. "Nice that your patio's covered."

"Grab another chair if you need to elevate your knee."

"It's practically good as new. But don't worry." He gave her a sly smile. "I'm saving my energy for the bad guys."

"Touché."

"How likely is it we'll get a hit on the BOLO soon?" Bishop stretched his legs out in front of him. "I mean, in this part of Texas?"

"Oh, us country bumpkin cops tend to ignore BOLOs. We just stand around at the corner gas station, drinkin' Cokes and talkin' 'bout how hot it is."

Bishop's lips twisted into a crooked smile. "You know what I meant."

"Actually, it's pretty likely," she said. "A lot of the towns around here don't get much excitement on a daily basis. So when a BOLO goes out, the police departments jump on it like a duck on a june bug."

His smile faded. "I feel like I should be doing something. Not just sitting here, waiting."

"Think of it as a stakeout. It's basically the same thing, except we're not in a car." Cassie leaned back in her chair. "When I'm on one with a deputy, we talk."

"Mine are always solo."

"You're not solo now. What do you want to talk about?"

"You."

Cassie scoffed. "We've already talked plenty about me. I want to hear why you quit the police force to become a PI."

Darkness spread across Bishop's face, and Cassie realized this wouldn't be an amusing story. But she wanted to hear it. She wanted to learn about the hidden parts of him that defined his character. She needed to understand what made a man who had once upheld the law become a man who thought himself above the law. So she waited him out.

"There was this kid, Jessica Santos. Nineteen, trying to save money for beauty school. Her boyfriend had talked her into doing a drug sale for him, said he'd give her a cut of the money that would pay her tuition in full." Bishop's tone foreshadowed where the story was going. "Instead, she wound up face-to-face with me in an interrogation room."

He stared out across her yard, his mind probably replaying the past.

"I believed her story. No priors, just bad choices when it came to men. The current boyfriend had a rap sheet a mile long but was free and clear on this bust. It ate at me that she'd be in prison and he'd still be on the street dealing drugs." He shook his head, as if regretting his next move. "So I gave her a chance to reclaim her life. Become my confidential informant, help me take down the boyfriend and the high-level connections above him, and she'd walk away with no charges, no jail time. She agreed."

A beat of silence followed and Cassie wondered if he'd continue. Finally, he blinked, breaking his stare and looking at her, a veil of sorrow dropping over his features. Something only a fellow officer might recognize.

Bishop swallowed. "Within a month, she was dead."

Cassie reached out a hand. "Bishop..."

He pulled back, as if her touch would weaken his resolve to keep talking. She understood.

"I'd given her a plausible cover story to explain why we released her, and she went back to her boyfriend. She let me know when he set up a meeting with his suppliers and she convinced him to take her along. Told him she wanted to make up for the last time, to learn enough that she could help him more in the future. When he agreed, we put a wire on her for the meet."

He continued, this time his eyes focused on his boots. "The operation was already in motion when a DEA agent called foul. One of their guys was undercover in the organization, and they were after the international dealers. My captain called off the op, but it was too late for Jessica."

Cassie reached out her hand again and this time he allowed her to rest it on his.

"We heard her scream when they found the wire. We were only a block away, but we couldn't go in because of our captain's order. I tried to anyway. I didn't care if I got fired as long as Jessica was safe. But my partner held me back until we heard a gunshot. When we arrived at the scene everyone was gone except the boyfriend. He was lying on the ground, dead from a bullet to the forehead."

Bishop's gaze met Cassie's. "A homeless man found her body in an alley dumpster. Medical examiner said she'd been sexually assaulted multiple times and shot up with uncut heroin."

Though not surprised, Cassie released a sigh of empathy.

"I was already tired of dealing with bureaucratic red tape on a daily basis. When that op was shut down, when Jessica's body wound up in the morgue, I completely lost it."

"What happened?"

"I blew up at my captain, his boss, the whole system. But it had about as much impact as water splashing against a rock. I knew nothing would change. So I turned in my gun and badge. I was done following the letter of the law, especially when it got innocent kids killed."

"I'm so sorry," Cassie whispered. Such a heartbreaking end to both a young woman's life and a good man's career. "Is that when you decided to go private?"

He let out a breath. "Not exactly. First, I drank too much.

Yelled too much. Got into fights with strangers in bars and the next day couldn't even remember what the fights were about. I lost my career, my pride and my dignity so fast, it didn't take long to hit rock bottom." Bishop grimaced. "Then I quit drinking and started the anger management stuff. I tried to figure out what was next for me. I interned at my buddy's agency, liked it, and *that's* when I went private." He smiled a sheepish grin. "I've never told anyone that before."

Cassie's throat tightened with an emotion she couldn't identify. Bishop could have refused to answer her question. Instead, he'd allowed her a glimpse of those demons she'd wondered about. His anger when she insisted on going by the book now made more sense. "Thank you for telling *me*."

Bishop's eyes softened and he traced a finger along the inside of her arm. "Thank you for asking."

Her phone interrupted the moment. "Sher—Reed." How long before she'd stop saying "sheriff" when she answered?

"Hey, Cassie. It's Steve, from Winston."

"Hi, Steve. What's up?" Winston had its own police force, and Cassie had worked with their chief several times.

"Calling about that BOLO on the yellow Mustang."

Cassie straightened in her chair. "Yeah?"

"It sounded familiar. I'd seen one over in Hudsonville a couple months back. So I took a little drive this evening, and sure 'nuff, it's parked by the same house as before."

"The plates match?" Nervous energy jolted her system.

"Wouldn't have called if they didn't. Want the address?"

She pulled up her phone's notes app. "Go ahead." After typing it, she read it back.

"That's it. It's an old farmhouse, 'bout a mile from town. The car's empty, but the owner's most likely in that house. I know it's out of my jurisdiction, but if you want me to—"

"No!" When Bishop jumped in his seat, she could only

imagine how surprised Steve was. "Sorry, didn't mean to yell, but no. We don't want him to know he's been found."

Steve chuckled. "Alrighty, then. Long as you'll be up here directly, I'll mosey on home."

"Thanks, Steve. I owe you one."

Cassie ended the call and looked at Bishop. "He's in Hudsonville."

A predatory gleam lit his eyes. "Where's that?"

"About twenty-five miles northwest of here." She jumped to her feet. "I have to grab my personal gun. I'll meet you out front."

Bishop followed suit, eagerness radiating from him like the sun's heat at high noon. "We need to swing by my room. I have to grab my other gun and more ammunition." He threw her a pained expression. "I suppose you're driving again?"

"Since mine's county-issued, I think we better take yours."

He let loose an exaggerated sigh of relief. "Great. I was afraid we'd still be on our way tomorrow if you drove."

"WHAT'S THE ADDRESS? I'll use my GPS." Bishop had zipped in and out of his motel room, and they were approaching the town limits.

"No need. I know exactly where it is. The fastest way is Highway 111." Cassie picked up a plastic grocery bag he'd tossed on the front console. "What's in here?"

"Protein bars. I don't know about you, but I'm hungry." He followed the road they were on to an intersection.

"This is 111. Turn right." She pulled the bars out of the bag. "You want one?"

"Please." He held his hand out toward her, but Cassie opened the wrapper and pulled it down partway before handing it to him. That was something different. And nice. He usually just ripped it open with his teeth. "Help yourself." He glanced at her wrinkled nose and skeptical look. "They taste like fudge brownies."

"Nothing that's good for you can possibly taste like a fudge brownie." She tossed them back in the bag. Then her stomach rumbled.

"Sounds like someone disagrees with you." Bishop smirked. "At least try one. If you hate it, I'll finish it for you."

Cassie reached back into the bag and pulled out a bar. She tore it open and sniffed. "Hmph. Passes the smell test." She nibbled on the end of it.

Bishop's eyes on the road, he smiled wider as she ripped at the wrapper and chewed with enthusiasm.

"Okay. I didn't hate it. Therefore, it must not be healthy."

Chuckling, Bishop said, "If your hypothesis is based on faulty logic, your findings bear no validity."

Cassie turned her head and watched his profile. "Pretty face *and* smart? Who'da thunk?"

Bishop choked on his protein bar. "You think I'm pretty?" He glanced at her.

Cassie rolled her eyes. "Don't let it go to your head. I usually run as fast as I can from men with pretty faces."

"So, I'm an exception?" He laughed at Cassie's expression.

"Enough with pretty." Cassie leaned back against her seat, like they were two people just out for a drive. "Let's get back to smart. I'm even more impressed because I had to drop logic, statistics and physics in college. My brain is just not wired for that stuff."

"I only remember bits and pieces of it." Bishop passed a car going the precise speed limit, which made him even more thankful Cassie let him drive.

"Where'd you go to school?"

"Sam Houston. Majored in criminal justice. Got my master's in criminology."

"Wow. Not a lot of cops go for their graduate degree." She nodded, a look of approval on her face. "And here I thought you were just a cowboy who wanted to be a cop."

"A little more complicated, but that pretty much sums it up."

"Take a left up here." Cassie pointed. "Why was it complicated?"

"Just family stuff." Bishop made the turn. "Why are you so interested all of a sudden?"

"I told you about my family." She shrugged. "I want to hear about yours. Now spill."

Giving up, Bishop sighed. "Bob was always the golden child. Firstborn, good grades, college scholarships, high-paying job already lined up before he graduated." Bishop passed another car. "It's not that I was jealous of him. Even though he's quite a bit older than me, we were close. But it meant I'd eventually take over running the ranch. Didn't matter what I wanted."

"Which was to become a cop?"

Bishop nodded. "I'd told my folks that over and over for years. They either weren't listening or didn't care. One day, I was a senior in high school, my old man told me not to worry about getting a scholarship like Bob. Said he'd foot the bill for business school, which I'd need to run the ranch." Bishop sneered. "It was like he didn't know my grades were as good as my brother's. I'd already been approved for an academic scholarship, and I'd applied to several colleges."

"Did you tell him that?"

"I didn't get a chance to. I explained again that I had no intention of running the ranch for the rest of my life. That I was becoming a cop, and that was that." Bishop scoffed. "So he threw me out. Tossed my clothes through the window, locked the door and never spoke to me again."

"Wait, what? While you were still in high school?"

Cassie's indignant expression on his behalf warmed Bishop's heart. He'd learned not to reveal much of himself to people. It was the best way to avoid disappointment. But it seemed the more Cassie knew about him, the *less* she judged him. And vice versa. Day one, he'd pegged her as an uncompromising Goody Two-shoes that he wanted nothing to do with. And now? He wanted *everything* to do with her. He just needed to figure out what Cassie wanted.

"I stayed with a friend and his family until I graduated. By then I'd been accepted to the schools where I'd applied. With the scholarship and a part-time job, I could afford to live in the dorm for the first two years. I'd finished the forty-eight hours of class credits I needed to apply with HPD by then, but I figured I might as well keep on going. I shared an apartment with three other guys while I completed my junior and senior years."

"And graduate school?" She seemed completely enthralled with his life story.

"I was already a cop when I decided to go back for my master's."

"Huh." Cassie remained silent for a minute, apparently digesting his words. "What about your mom? Did she agree with your dad, or you?"

"My parents' marriage was based on Dad having everything his way and Mom never crossing him." He shrugged a shoulder. "Bob and I stayed close until a couple years ago, when he remarried. He kept Mom updated on what I was up to, but she wouldn't go behind my dad's back for even a phone call."

Bishop stopped at a light and looked over at Cassie, a thoughtful expression on her face. "Hey, it's fine. I couldn't care less what anyone thinks about my career choices. Not the one to become a cop, and not the one to quit the force. Sometimes you just have to do what's right for *you*. For your health, mental, physical and emotional. Stress can kill you."

Cassie flinched, as though he'd just struck a nerve. A car behind them honked, and she jumped in her seat. "Take a right here. The house is a few miles down the road."

Chapter Nineteen

Cassie strained to see Garrett's Mustang through the windshield. The drizzle that had started during the drive had become a steady rain. She pointed. "There, by the side of the house. See it?"

Bishop slowed to a crawl in the dark. "Barely. By that white truck?" With no traffic on this stretch of road, their headlights would have announced their approach. Bishop had turned them off a mile back. He stopped across from the house.

"That's probably the box truck they used in Resolute. I won't know for sure until I get closer." She muttered a curse under her breath. "I figured if just the Mustang was here, we'd only have to worry about Garrett, maybe one other guy. But with the truck here, too, I'm not sure how many might be inside." Cassie bit her lip.

"They might keep it here because the place is so isolated. Doesn't necessarily mean there will be more guys in there." He tapped his fingers on the steering wheel. "You thinking of calling for backup?"

Cassie met his questioning look. "That would be the smart thing to do if it weren't so complicated. If my brothers or Lonnie get involved, it could cost them everything. Same with my other three deputies. Or it could cost *us* everything if one of those other three happens to be the leak." She pinched the bridge of her nose. "And then there's the fact that I can't officially request backup since I'm not acting as sheriff."

"I'd rather keep it just the two of us, anyway." Bishop rubbed the back of his neck. "The more people in there firing guns, the better chance one of the girls gets killed."

Cassie gave him credit for not making it just about Ashley, even though she was the reason he was here. "We'll hold off on calling anyone. Worse comes to worst, I'll call Lonnie or Adam."

Bishop gave her a single nod of agreement.

"They sure picked a good location." Bishop drifted farther along until he found a wide spot on the shoulder about a hundred yards from the property. "Can't get much more isolated than this."

"It works in *our* favor, too. They won't be able to see us coming." She leaned forward in her seat and looked up at the gray sky. "Just wish the weather was better."

The storm had picked up quickly. Torrential rain now fell, and small trees bent under the force of the wind. Thunder roared simultaneously with a crack of lightning directly overhead.

Bishop reached into the back seat and brought up two folded packages. "Rain ponchos. I always keep extra." He handed one to Cassie.

She grinned. "Don't tell me you were a Boy Scout, too." She unfolded one of the black plastic ponchos and slipped it over her head.

"Nope. Learned this one the hard way." Bishop unwrapped the other one and pulled it on. "You want to split up, or stay together?"

"Let's decide when we get there. Be careful. The place in Resolute had security cameras, back and front. We can't lose the element of surprise." Cassie pulled her poncho's hood up and as far forward as she could, tying the plastic strips beneath her chin. "Your inside lights all turned off?"

"Yep. PI rule number one." He looked at her, his eyes as stormy as the weather. "Ready?"

She gave him a tight nod, her lips pressed together. They climbed out of the truck, eased their doors shut, and ran toward the farmhouse, their jeans, from the knees down, soaked in seconds.

As they reached the edge of the property, they stopped, huddling behind wind-whipped bushes. Cassie tucked her head down and took a few water-free gasps of air. Then she put her mouth right next to Bishop's ear. "Let's check out the truck."

She took point, running in a crouch. Stopping behind trees and foliage along the way, she watched for motion lights and movement near the house. They made it to the truck and checked both sides.

"There's no signage on it now, but this is the one they used in Resolute." Cassie pointed at the damaged rear bumper.

"We need to assume they have more than two men in there." Half of Bishop's words floated away on the wind.

Cassie pointed to herself, then the rear of the house. She tapped Bishop's chest and pointed back the way they'd come, indicating he should circle the house from the other side. With a single nod, he took off, and she hightailed it to the closest side of the building.

Squinting into the rain, Cassie scanned for security cameras but found none. She eased past windows covered by curtains and shades, pausing by each, straining to hear voices. If there were any, they were drowned out by the storm.

When she reached the back corner of the house, she stood with her back flat against the wall and took a quick peek around it. Still no security cameras, so she slid around and moved toward a window near the back door.

The door opened and Cassie froze, her chest too tight

to breathe. Unintelligible voices came from inside, and the door swung closed with no one coming out. Unwilling to take a chance, she ran back the way she'd come, then circled through the trees until she stood behind a chicken coop. From her vantage point she had a clear view of the entire back of the house.

The door swung in again, and this time a man came out on the covered stoop with a lit cigarette. He wore a poncho like hers, and after a minute he pulled up his hood, turned on a flashlight and began a patrol of the property.

Saying a silent prayer that Bishop wouldn't be caught off guard, Cassie pulled off her poncho, balled it up and shoved it under a log. With the wind whipping it up against her face, it hadn't kept her dry, and she could move faster without it. As soon as the man rounded the far corner of the house, she ran back to the window. The curtains on this one hung crooked, and she looked through the gap. Two men, neither one Garrett, crossed her line of sight. *At least three inside, one outside.*

She caught movement in her peripheral vision and spun toward it, hand on her gun. Bishop moved at an angle toward her and a large barn a good ways back from the house. With frantic gestures, he urged her to run, and she did. A beam of light cut across her path and she slid behind the chicken coop.

"Hey!" The light bobbed as the man ran toward her. A gun had replaced his cigarette. "Get out here."

The rain had slacked off enough that Cassie could just barely make out his words. She crouched lower, willing her breathing to slow, and pulled her gun. Boots slogging through mud came closer. Peeking through a cracked board, she watched the man stop, hold up his light and lean forward. His flashlight hit the ground and his gun came up. Cassie dropped flat in the mud as a bullet buzzed past her.

Another shot, this one from Bishop on her left. Then a grunt, and she poked her head up in time to see the guard fall.

"You okay?" Bishop's yell reached her just as the back door flew open and at least six men rushed out.

"So far. You?"

"Yep. Stay down and watch for your chance." Then he disappeared behind the barn.

The men spread out across the yard, all of them armed with shotguns or handguns. None of them bothered to check on the guy Bishop had shot.

"There. Behind the barn." One of the men fired his shotgun toward Bishop's position.

The others joined in, and Cassie took advantage of the distraction Bishop had created for her. She filled her lungs with air and dashed for the front of the house, staying hidden behind foliage as much as possible. Reaching the front door, she listened for the gunfight. Bullets still flew back there.

Cassie tested the doorknob, but it was locked. *Here goes nothing.*

She raised her leg and kicked the door with the sole of her boot. It needed one more kick before it crashed inward. With her gun at the ready, she crept through the downstairs rooms. Empty. Cassie started up the stairs, cringing with every creak of the boards beneath her feet.

The bedrooms were upstairs. She eased open one door and experienced an unwelcome sense of déjà vu. Wall-to-wall mattresses, two girls on each. One leg of each girl was cuffed to a large bolt in the floor by a zip tie. Cassie flipped the light switch and a dim bulb came on. She crouched next to the closest girl and examined her ankle. It was red and raw from the plastic tie.

She moved to the other end of the mattress and felt for a pulse. Thready, but there. The girl's eyes were rolled back in her head, with only the whites showing. Cassie checked each girl on each mattress. Some moaned and looked at her with vacant expressions. Some were out cold. A few raised limp hands to her, begging for more dope.

"I'll be back soon to free you all." The gunfight in the backyard still raged on and she had to make sure the girls didn't stumble into more harm.

As Cassie moved from room to room, each one like the last, the depravity of these evil monsters filled her with stone-cold fury. She repeated her promise to each group of girls as she went. She found Ashley in the third room, near the door. Cassie dropped to her knees and checked her vitals. Alive, but unconscious. She brushed the girl's snarled hair back from her face. "Your Uncle Tyler is here, Ashley. *We're* here." As though Ashley could understand her, she rolled her head toward Cassie and moaned.

A creak outside the door brought Cassie to her feet, spinning toward the sound. Garrett froze in the hall, then took off down the stairs. Cassie followed, catching up with him in the middle of the living room. She raised her gun.

"Don't make me do it." She clenched her jaw in anger. "And don't doubt that I will. On the floor."

Spitting out a string of curse words, he lay down on his stomach and put his arms behind his back.

"So glad you're familiar with the position." Cassie looped a zip tie around his wrists and tightened it. "I think I'll play it safe this time." She cuffed his ankles together, then searched him, removing two pocketknives and small amounts of drugs. "Staying true to form, aren't you? I bet the minute the shooting started, you hid upstairs. I'd think it would be downright embarrassing getting caught running away every single time."

He mumbled something, but with his mouth against a filthy braided rug, it was hard to understand and she really didn't care. Leaving him prone on the floor, Cassie went to the back door. Only two of the traffickers still stood. She let out a shrill whistle and when they turned toward her, Bishop came out from behind the barn.

"Time to lay 'em down, boys." She raised her gun in a two-handed grasp. "You're surrounded."

One started to swing his gun toward her, and Bishop called out, "Uh-uh-uh. You'll be dead before you pull the trigger."

Both men looked from Cassie to Bishop, dropped their guns and raised their hands. Bishop made quick work of the zip ties while Cassie held her gun on them. He herded them to the back door, and Cassie pulled two kitchen chairs around while Bishop frisked them. Then they cuffed their ankles to the legs and their already-cuffed hands to one of the back slats on the chair.

"No more inside?" Bishop asked.

"Just one. He's in the living room, trussed up like a Thanksgiving turkey." She met his hopeful eyes. "She's upstairs. Second bedroom to the right."

Bishop was gone before the last word crossed her lips.

BISHOP TOOK THE stairs two at a time. He raced past the first room, skidding to a stop at the second door. Steeling himself, he looked in at a horror he would never forget.

There, on a filthy mattress she shared with another girl, he found Ashley. Bishop dropped to his knees and took her limp body in his arms. Her head lolled to the side as he brushed back her hair.

"Ashley, can you hear me?"

A low moan escaped her lips, but her eyes remained closed. Bishop laid her back down, noticing needle tracks on the inside of her elbow. He dropped his head into his hands, fighting back tears. "I'm sorry, Little Turtle. I'm sorry it took me so long to find you." Raising his head and scrubbing at his cheeks, he pulled out his pocketknife and sliced through the zip tie cutting into her ankle.

"You're safe now, Ash. I'm getting you out of here." He cradled her in his arms, about to stand, when he looked across the room. Every one of these young women had someone searching for her. Before he could save any of them, even Ashley, there was something he needed to do.

Kissing Ashley's forehead, he rested her on the mattress. Then he stood, curled his hands into fists, and welcomed back the old Bishop.

Cassie was halfway up the stairs when he stormed past her. "What's wrong?" Her footsteps followed him down.

Bishop strode to Garrett, picked him up by his cuffed arms and jerked him to his feet. "You're gonna pay, you little—"

"Is Ashley…she's still alive, right?" Cassie asked from behind him.

"Oh, she's alive. But this piece of garbage doped her almost all the way to death's door. She has needle tracks in her arm and can't even open her eyes." Bishop drew his gun and pointed it at Garrett's chest. He allowed his anger to take control, and it flowed through him, pumping in sync with his blood. In the past, alcohol had been the middleman. Now, sober, he realized the full power of his fury.

"What are you doing? You can't shoot him in cold blood." Cassie stepped next to Bishop. "Let the legal system handle him."

"We've both seen how well the system works. Jessica Santos is dead, and you're not wearing your badge."

Another round of rain pounded the roof and thunder rumbled. Cassie slipped between the two men, facing Bishop. "This isn't you. It's not the Bishop who meditates, does deep breathing, centers his chi."

"Get out of my way, Cassie." Bishop didn't lower his gun.

"I said I'd try things your way. And you were right.

Bending the rules works sometimes." Her eyes pleaded with him. "But I will not allow you to cross this line. Look, I called Lonnie. He'll be here soon. Let him handle Garrett."

"You won't shoot me." Garrett lifted his chin, his mouth twisted into a smug grin. "Didn't last time, won't this time."

Bishop steadied his gun with both hands. "I owe it to Ashley."

"This is the last thing Ashley would want you to do." Cassie rested a hand on his arm, and he shook it off. "Bishop, she has a chance to recover. You think she will if you're in prison because of her?"

At her words, Bishop blinked, the first seed of doubt in his actions creeping in. But he doubled down on his rage, clenching the gun tighter. "You're not a sheriff. You have no say about it."

"I'm not saying this as a sheriff, Bishop. I'm saying this as the woman who's falling in love with you."

"Cassie…" An unfamiliar hitch in Bishop's chest had him relaxing his grip. The previous flames of fury died down to manageable embers.

"You do this," she continued, her hand now resting over his heart, "you'll never come back from it. You'll lose yourself for good. *I'll* lose you for good."

It was the break in Cassie's voice that was his final undoing. He couldn't do this to her, or Ashley, or even himself. He was better than this.

Bishop took a deep breath, exhaled and lowered his gun. Breaking away from the terrified gaze of Garrett Pugh, he met Cassie's loving green one and dropped his head forward on her shoulder.

"You should listen to her," Lonnie said, walking in from the kitchen.

Bishop only had time to raise his head when a searing pain shot through it. *This is getting really old.* And he surrendered to the blackness.

"LONNIE, NO! THAT'S BISHOP!" Cassie dropped to the floor and took his head in her hands, a sticky wetness turning them red.

"Oops. My mistake." Lonnie slipped his gun into his waistband, bent over and wrapped an arm around Cassie's waist, pulling her to her feet. At the same time, he yanked her gun from its holster and tossed it on a chair. Dragging Cassie along, he cut the zip ties that bound Garrett.

"You really are useless, aren't you?" Lonnie yelled at him. "First you kill that girl in Resolute, and now—" he waved his gun around "—all this."

"Hey, none of this is my fault."

"*Everything* is your fault!" Lonnie yelled right to Garrett's face. "None of this would have happened if you hadn't grabbed his niece." Then he spoke as if addressing a child. "Now, pick up his gun, Garrett. Then pick up the gun on the chair. Try not to kill anybody and keep an eye on this dirtbag." He kicked Bishop in the side. "Do you think you can do that?"

Nodding, Garrett scrambled to get both guns and out of Lonnie's way.

Cassie struggled against Lonnie's hold while her mind fought to make sense of what was happening. "You're part of this?"

"I'm so glad you called me, my poor, confused cousin. See, I'm the one they ask for when there are messes to clean up. And whooee, coz, you made quite the mess."

The barrel of a gun touched the side of Cassie's head and her blood ran cold. Inhaling a deep breath, she forced herself to stay calm, ready for a chance to break free. "Why would you do it?"

"You mean work with these guys? Come on, Cass. You think I make enough money as a deputy to support my gambling? I was in debt up to my eyeballs before I started helping them out." He took a step back toward the door, pulling her with him. "Or did you mean the sad end of Wallace Reed?"

Cassie gasped and wrestled against his grip, but he held her too tight. "You killed Dad?"

"He wasn't *my* dad. Y'all never treated me like anything other than an outsider." He stepped back again. "And it was worse at the office. I worked there for years before you, but who gets to be chief deputy? Figured killing him would take care of two birds at the same time. He was getting way too close to figuring out I was tipping off the traffickers. Plus, thought for sure I'd be moved into his position. *And* his pay-check." He chuckled. "Oh well. One out of two ain't bad."

Garrett dropped onto the couch and sneered at Cassie as Lonnie jerked her through the doorway. He dragged her backward toward the trees, both of them slipping in the mud. The rain felt like pebbles against her skin, and its roar drowned out all other sound.

Cassie shifted her weight against him, throwing him off balance, and Lonnie slid down to one knee, still holding on to her. Cassie raised her right leg, then swung it back as hard as she could. Lonnie screamed, and she knew she'd hit what she'd been aiming for. She lurched from his grasp, saw his gun on the ground and scrabbled her way toward it.

He grabbed her ankle as her fingers touched the barrel. She twisted and clawed at the mud, but he held tight and pulled her away from it. Flipping her onto her back, he hauled off and punched her in the jaw.

"That the best you can do?" She spit blood in his face and jabbed her thumbs into his eyes.

Lonnie rolled off her, his hands covering his eyes. Cassie jumped to her feet and ran to the gun. She held it in both hands, aiming straight at Lonnie as he rose from the ground.

"You conniving piece of filth." Lightning slashed through the sky in a ragged line; the thunder that followed shook the earth. "How could you? I loved you like a brother." She dragged her hand across her face, wiping away the rain from her eyes. Rage like she'd never felt before erupted from her very soul.

Another flash of lightning revealed Bishop almost next to her, his gun drawn.

In the next flash, Lonnie reared up like a wounded grizzly, his face unrecognizable with hate and insanity as he rushed toward her.

Cassie shot him.

FLASHING BLUE AND red lights, along with the headlights of more emergency vehicles than Bishop thought existed in Boone County, lit up the night sky. The rain had tapered off, and he held Ashley's hand as two medics carried her stretcher to one of the ambulances. Still too doped up to speak, she gave his fingers a gentle squeeze from time to time.

He'd immediately texted his brother the good news about finding Ashley. Helping her recover came next. He wanted to ride with her to the hospital, but they were doubling up on patients in each ambulance and still making multiple trips.

"You won't be able to see her for a while anyway," the medic told him. "The docs are going to be busy tonight."

Bishop kissed Ashley's forehead. "I'll be there as soon as I can, Little Turtle. But you're safe now." He reached into his pocket, coming out with the turtle key chain he'd carried with him since learning Ashley was gone. He tucked it into her hand, curling her fingers around it.

"I already told you, I wasn't acting in the capacity of sheriff. How many times do I have to repeat myself before you get it?"

Bishop turned toward the aggravated voice. Cassie, a blanket around her shoulders, water still streaming from her hair, sat on the tailgate of his truck facing two tall men in Stetsons.

The Rangers had arrived.

Bishop walked over to stand next to Cassie, glad that she had told him enough about the two men to tell them apart.

"You need to step away, sir," Ward said. "We're conducting an interview."

"You're conducting it on my truck, and since I'm already here, I think I'll hang around. See what's what, if you know what I mean."

Cassie smiled when he threw Ward's own words from the Palmer murder back at him. Bishop returned her smile, the most beautiful thing he'd seen in hours.

"One more time, then we're done." She reached her hand out to Bishop's. "I came here as a private citizen, to help my friend find his niece."

"And leave a yard full of dead bodies," Ward deadpanned.

"Who were killed by legally registered guns while we were defending ourselves."

Mills jumped in. "Regardless of all that, we're going to need you to come down to the station and make a statement." He glanced at Bishop. "You, too."

"No problem." Cassie stood. "Oh, and you're welcome."

"For what?" Ward did not seem happy. Which seemed to make Cassie very happy.

"Oh, let's see. Finding your leak for you."

"Finding the traffickers for you," Bishop added.

"But the girls?" Cassie gazed into Bishop's eyes. "That was all him." She tilted her head as if pondering something. "Think I just might need to call the newspapers about that story."

Ward sputtered as Bishop closed the tailgate and walked Cassie to the passenger door. Before he opened it, he pulled

Cassie close. "How are you doing?" He searched her face. "About Lonnie?"

Cassie closed her eyes for a moment. "I still can't believe it." When she opened them, she looked more lost than he'd ever seen her. "I loved him. My dad loved him. How could he… How could I…" She trailed off, looking unblinking into the flashing lights of a retreating ambulance.

Bishop wrapped his arms tighter around her. "I don't know, Cassie. But I do know this isn't on you. Lonnie lied. Took advantage of your whole family. That's on him."

She sank into Bishop's side. "I just feel so betrayed."

"I understand. But he'll get what he deserves." Bishop kissed the top of her head. "By the way, that was one heck of a shot."

Her lips twisted. "It would've felt good to shoot him in his thigh. Hit his femoral and watch him bleed out like he watched Dad." She sighed. "But I wanted to see him go to prison, too, so I figured I'd get even for my arm."

"I think you got more than even, considering your wound was a through-and-through." He chuckled.

"Yeah, blowing apart his rotator cuff was kind of a bonus." She was silent a moment, a smile on her face as if reliving the moment. But then it faded, and her eyes focused on his. "Ward told me if they have to, they'll offer him a deal so he'll flip on the rest of the trafficking ring." She touched the back of his head. "How's the noggin?"

"Sore." He smiled when she pulled her hand away. "Not *that* sore. Just glad Lonnie didn't hit me in the same spot that he did at Palmer's. I wasn't out long this time." He snorted. "And that idiot Garrett was in the kitchen looking for something to eat when I came to."

Cassie shook her head. "I'm sure he'll be charged with murder, no deals. He's too far down the food chain." She looked him straight in the eye, her brows pinched together.

"How are you doing in here?" She patted his chest. "I can't imagine the mix of emotions."

"It's a lot," Bishop agreed. The image of his niece, lying stoned and half-dressed, would be branded on his mind for a long time. "I'm still angry. Probably always will be. But I'm more relieved that we found Ashley and that she'll be all right. At least physically."

Cassie tightened her hug. "She'll heal emotionally, too. Probably take a long time, but she's got you to help her."

They were silent for a while, content in the comfort they gave each other.

"Hey," he murmured against her hair. "You almost sounded proud of me back there, with the Rangers."

"Almost?" Cassie frowned. "I guess I should do better than that when I *show* you how proud I am." She leaned closer and whispered in his ear, "Because now I'm saving all my energy for the good guy."

Chapter Twenty

Marge had outdone herself with the pies. Cassie set both the cherry and the apple on the dining room table, since there wasn't a spot of empty counter space in the Reed kitchen.

Bishop's deep voice drifted in from the backyard, mingling with her brothers' laughter. Cassie smiled to herself. It sounded right.

Nate came in through the kitchen door. "Hey, sis." He went straight to the fridge and grabbed three beers. "Bishop is great. Glad you invited him to dinner." He disappeared back outside.

Cassie gathered the tequila, a shot glass and a bowl of lime wedges from the fridge. She tossed back a shot, steeling herself for the evening to come. It would be a night of family, laughter, good food. And through it all, she'd be rebuilding the wall around her heart. Protecting it for when she said goodbye to Bishop.

His career, his family, his life were in Houston. She scoffed. Less than a week ago, she was attracted to him because he was just passing through. But then she went and fell in love with him. She'd even *told* him she loved him.

And he hadn't said it back.

She couldn't ask him to stay. Her pride couldn't take the rejection. Her heart couldn't withstand the crushing blow.

Cassie poured herself one more shot, forced her lips into a smile and went out to join the others.

Bishop, talking to Adam by the grill, glanced up as she came out on the patio. He smiled, and she couldn't help but smile back. Covering the space in a few strides, he hugged her and covered her mouth with his. Despite the twins' jeers and catcalls, the kiss seemed to last forever.

He led her to two patio chairs sitting close together. Very close together. As soon as they sat, he reached for her hand. "How'd it go with Frick and Frack after I left this morning?"

Cassie laughed at Bishop's on-the-nose nicknames for the Rangers. He'd gone in to give his statement in the morning, before spending the day at the hospital. "Well, before I met with them, I spoke with Michael Pugh. He was upset that the doctors wouldn't let him see Ashley. I told him he and Billy could stay in their house if he remains in Resolute."

"I hope he decided to stay," Bishop said.

"No, he's going back to Houston and taking Billy with him. He thinks he has a better future there."

"Not with Ashley, he doesn't." Bishop glared at her.

She raised her hands. "That's between Ashley, her family and her doctors."

"Hmph."

"Then I had to apologize to Dave. I'd suspected him unfairly. I needed to set that right."

"He didn't even know," Noah said. "I can't believe you apologized to that—"

"Enough, Noah. We're going to foster better relationships in the department from now on."

"You only suspected him because Lonnie fed you his line of—"

"And enough out of you, Nate. I thought I made it clear, we're not discussing our cousin tonight." She'd suffered enough at Lonnie's hands for too long. He'd killed her dad, tried to kill Bishop at Palmer's house and tried to kill her at least twice. She wanted an evening filled with good memories to hold close after Bishop was gone.

She forced her mind away from Bishop's leaving. "Once I did meet with Ward and Mills, it took a while to give them my statement. Then they tried to make me fill out all of *their* paperwork. I told them a private citizen can't do that."

"I bet they loved that," Adam said.

"First, they apologized for the huge misunderstanding. Then Mills said he'd worked a case with Dad years ago." She swallowed hard over a sudden lump in her throat. "Said he had nothing but respect for him and deep admiration for me."

"He had a nice way of showing it." Bishop stretched out his legs.

"Next, they said the county council had already reinstated me. Turns out my removal was provisional. Then Ward handed me my gun and badge."

"They're cagey, those two." Noah strolled by the grill to check on dinner.

"Not cagey enough." Cassie smirked. "I thanked him, told him as sheriff I forbid the practice of officers not filling out their own reports, and I left."

"Wish I'd been there to see his face." Noah knocked bottles with Adam and they drank.

While her brothers saluted her with beers, Cassie leaned closer to Bishop. "How's Ashley doing?"

His face clouded over. "The good news is that she wasn't assaulted."

Cassie's hand went to her heart. "You must be so relieved."

"You have no idea." His fingers curled and released.

"And the bad news?"

"They shot her up so many times, she's going through withdrawal." He shoved his fingers through his hair. "She'll be in detox for weeks. And then she'll most likely need help to heal emotionally."

"The poor thing. After what she already went through, to have another ordeal ahead of her. Will you stay here while she's in the hospital?"

Bishop shook his head. "I explained all this to Bob, and he's planning to come down here tomorrow on his company's private jet. He'll fly her back to Houston as soon as the doctor releases her."

"Can she handle the flight in her condition?"

"Her doctor says yes, as long as Bob follows all his instructions to the letter." He shrugged. "I can't blame him. He's been worried sick about her since she ran off. If she were my daughter and I had a private jet, I'd do the same thing."

"I suppose her stepmom will be coming along?"

"I seriously doubt it. I was trying to find a tactful way to tell him that Ashley would need some time away from Monique. To decompress, successfully make it through withdrawal, stay clean. He said Ashley won't have to worry about Monica anymore." Bishop chuckled. "The highlight was him not calling her Monique."

Cassie forced a light laugh. "What about you? Are you going back with them?" Her right hand curled in on itself in her lap.

"I'm driving back. I told Bob I'd help get Ashley settled in." Bishop met her gaze. "I leave day after tomorrow."

She forced her eyes from his, afraid he'd see the silent pleading in them. At least she knew for sure. What they had, what she'd *thought* they had, was over. In two days he'd be gone, and she'd never see him again.

Her nails dug deep.

"Dinner's ready. Y'all come help yourselves." Adam

carried platters of steak, chicken and vegetables to their patio table.

"You outdid yourself, bro." Nate pushed ahead of Noah and snagged the biggest steak.

As Cassie took in the special dishes made for Bishop, she met Adam's eyes and mouthed "thank you." He gave her a brotherly wink.

Bishop, coming along behind her, said, "Adam, you didn't have to go to all this trouble." He speared a chicken breast for his plate, then moved on to the vegetables. Grilled corn on the cob, asparagus, mushrooms and zucchini filled the platter.

"No trouble at all. Besides, this whole family needs more—"

"Don't say it," Nate and Noah chimed in unison.

"Vegetables," Adam finished.

Bishop sat next to Cassie at the table, and she poured him a glass of iced tea.

"No thanks. I'm fine. Maybe I'll just get some water." He pushed back his chair to stand.

"Try it. If you don't like it, I'll finish it for you." She gave him a teasing smile.

Bishop took a tentative sip, then shot a look of surprise Cassie's way. "This isn't sweet."

"That pitcher," Cassie said, and pointed to the one nearest him, "is just for you."

"And this," he said before he kissed her, "is just for you."

"Good thing, 'cause none of us want to swap spit with you," Nate managed around a mouthful of steak.

AFTER THE FOOD was eaten, the pies served and the dishes cleared, they sat around a firepit as the stars came out. Bishop watched Cassie avoid his eyes. Her smiles seemed forced, as if she'd tired of his company and was ready for him to be gone.

She'd told him she loved him, and he'd assumed she meant it. Her words had broken through his rage, banishing the Bishop who couldn't control himself. But in hindsight, she probably would have said anything to stop him from shooting Garrett. Probably best that Lonnie had knocked him out before he told her he loved her, too. Things were awkward enough between them now.

"Wow." He tipped back his head and stared at the sky. "Don't see stars like this in Houston."

Cassie looked up. "How can you stand to live where you can't see the stars?"

"I guess I just got used to it." He shrugged. "Same with sunrises. The tall buildings block the view."

Every Reed stared at him as if he'd said something blasphemous. "What?"

"No stars *and* no sunrises?" Noah scoffed. "That's just wrong."

"You need to get out of H-town, man." Nate tipped the neck of his beer toward Bishop. "Move down here where you can enjoy life."

All three Reed brothers nodded. But Cassie stared straight ahead at the fire, only her profile in view. She seemed to be the only Reed who didn't want him to return.

She stayed quiet while Bishop told PI tales, and Adam and Noah shared deputy adventures.

After a while, and a few hilarious stories later, Nate nudged her foot with his. "Cass, you've got the best ones of all. Contribute to the conversation, would ya?"

She stood, stretched and yawned. "I need to get going. It's been a long couple days, and I can barely see straight."

"I should go, too." Bishop rose next to her. "I'll walk you out." He moved around the fire, shaking each brother's hand. "Thanks for the invitation. Can't remember when I've enjoyed myself this much."

"Know how to solve that, don't ya?" Adam asked, brow raised.

In unison, both twins said, "Get your woo-woo self back down here as soon as you can."

Bishop gave Cassie the side-eye. "What have you been telling them?"

"Only the truth." She reached out her arms and wiggled her fingers. "Woo-woo." But this time, she didn't laugh along with her teasing words.

A few minutes later they stood next to her SUV.

"Any chance we can spend more time together before I leave?" Bishop wrapped his arms around her and rested his forehead against hers. "*Alone* time?"

"Tonight?" Her voice was soft, hesitant, as if she wasn't sure.

"I promised Ashley I'd sit with her tonight. She's scared of her own shadow." But Bishop kept trying, determined not to give up on them without a fight. "Tomorrow?"

"It's my first day back as sheriff. There's no way I can play hooky. What about tomorrow night?" Cassie pulled her head back, the invitation clear in her eyes.

His lips met hers, and they didn't stop until the sound of a brother's fake cough cut through the air, followed by the slam of the front door.

Chuckling, Bishop opened her car door for her. "Tomorrow night will be perfect."

CASSIE STAGGERED INTO her house, her arms full of shopping bags and packages. She'd been on the run since the minute she left work, determined to make this a night to remember. After sticking cold items in the fridge and the rest on her kitchen counter, she returned to the living room and started emptying bags on the couch.

She covered her coffee table with new, colorful place mats. From the largest bag she pulled out four huge, poufy pillows, each in a different color, and threw them haphazardly on the floor. Her eye started to twitch and she picked them up, setting them on the couch in a nice, orderly row. *Come on, Cass, you can do this.* She tossed them back on the floor around the table.

Back in the kitchen, she removed chopsticks and small dipping-sauce bowls from another bag. She set plates on two of the place mats, along with forks and chopsticks. She added the small bowls at intervals across the table.

Nodding with approval, she took a quick shower, then changed into leggings and a soft, loose tunic. A quick glance at the clock told her Bishop would be here soon. She dashed into the kitchen and pulled out all her purchases from the fridge. On the extra place mats she set out plates of sushi rolls and sashimi. She removed the top from the container of seaweed salad and sniffed it, wrinkling her nose. *Not so sure about this one.*

A bottle of unsweetened iced green tea filled two wine-glasses. She added them to the place settings, then a bowl of undressed fruit salad for dessert. Cassie stood back and gave the table a critical once-over. She fought the urge to straighten the chopsticks, then gave in and lined them up along the edges of the mats. She'd just set low-sodium tamari sauce on the table and put dabs of wasabi and pieces of pickled ginger in the small bowls when the doorbell rang.

Bishop came in carrying a bottle of red wine. "I may not drink the stuff, but I know red goes better with beef."

"What makes you think I'm making steak tonight?" She maneuvered to block his view.

"Just a feeling." He managed to get past her and saw the coffee table. "I thought you refused to eat sushi? And sashimi?"

The happy look on his face set off a warm glow within

Cassie. She shrugged. "Figured I can't say I don't like it unless I've actually tried it." She took his bottle of wine and set it in the kitchen.

He sneaked up from behind and wrapped his arms around her. When he left a trail of kisses down the side of her neck, she moaned at the hot chills racing across her body. Gasping, she pulled herself from his arms.

"We, uh, should probably eat." Cassie waved toward the living room. "I'm guessing there's a fine line between raw fish and food poisoning."

She took Bishop's hand and led him to the coffee table, then dropped down onto one of the floor pillows. She crossed her legs beneath her.

Bishop toed off his boots in the entry, then sat on the pillow next to her. "Before we start eating, I owe you an apology."

She cocked her head to the side as she met his eyes. "What for?"

"For treating you the way I did when Garrett got away. I'd lost control with him, and you stopped me from taking it too far." He ran his fingers through his hair, and Cassie's chest hitched, knowing how much she'd miss seeing that quirky habit of his. "I should have thanked you, instead of blaming you for his escape."

Cassie laced her fingers with his, noticing for the first time how right their hands looked together. "I appreciate your apology, and I forgive you." What she would never forgive him for was making her love him. "Now, how do you work these darn chopsticks?"

Bishop chuckled as he picked up the salad container. "Have you ever eaten seaweed salad?"

"Do you even have to ask me that?" She gave up on her chopsticks and used her fork to move a couple pieces of sushi onto her plate. "And don't be surprised if I never do."

"You have to try it. You said yourself you can't say you don't like it if…"

She pursed her lips at him. "It's green stuff from the bottom of the ocean."

"You'll love it." Bishop dished some of the salad onto her plate as she was about to slice a piece of sushi with her fork. He reached over and stopped her hand. "You just put the whole thing in, like this."

He demonstrated by filling his mouth with a piece of dragon roll. Sure that she'd hate it, Cassie picked up the smallest piece on the plate and popped it in her mouth.

But as she chewed, she was struck by the flavors exploding in her mouth. "What are the little things popping in there?" She pointed at her mouth.

"You like them?"

She nodded. "What are they?"

"Fish eggs."

Cassie paused in her chewing. She looked more closely at the piece still on her plate. She pointed at the tiny orange balls covering the top of it. "Those things?"

"Yep." Bishop took a swig of his green tea, but Cassie could see the smile in his eyes.

"Huh. They look like the salmon eggs we catch fish with." She looked at Bishop. "But they taste a heck of a lot better."

"You ate salmon egg bait?"

"Tried one when I was a kid. Once was enough."

"Then you can definitely give the salad a shot."

She picked up her fork and looped one tine under a thin thread of seaweed.

"You have to use your chopsticks."

Cassie perked up. "Seeing as I can't pick anything up with them, this shouldn't be too bad."

"I'll show you." Bishop scooted over and sat behind her. He reached around and picked up her chopsticks. After showing her how to hold them, he placed them in her hand and adjusted them. "Now you just move the top one, keeping the bottom one steady."

She tried, but the top one slid out of place. Bishop took her hand in his and moved it to the salad. Together they picked some up with her chopsticks. He slowly moved it to her mouth. She parted her lips and Bishop set the bite of seaweed on her tongue.

Tentatively at first, she chewed the salad.

Bishop scooted around in front of her. "You like it?"

Surprised by the fresh and nutty flavor of the sesame oil dressing, she nodded as she swallowed and licked her lips.

Bishop leaned in and kissed the corner of her mouth. "Not so bad, expanding your horizons, is it?"

"Since it's our last time together…" She blinked at the burn behind her eyes and looked down. She refused to ruin this night with the bittersweet tears of a passionate goodbye.

Bishop lifted her chin until she met his earnest, hopeful gaze. "I planned to ask you later, but…" A sly grin curled his lips. "You think Boone County could use a private investigator?"

Cassie's heart pounded from a whiplash of emotions. "Not sure about Boone County, but I know the local sheriff could sure use one."

They leaned toward each other, meeting in the middle with a kiss that took her breath away.

"Thank you for the amazing dinner," he murmured against her ear.

Cassie straightened her legs and wrapped them around his waist. As Bishop lowered her back against her pillow, she fisted her hands in his shirt, taking him with her.

"Well, you know what they say. The end justifies the means."

Epilogue

Three months later

Bishop grinned and looked at Cassie. "What do you think?"

The shiny new sign on the door read Bishop Investigations.

"*I* think you shoulda made it 'Discreet Inquiries' instead of 'Investigations,'" Marge said, standing on one side of Bishop while Cassie stood on the other side, admiring his new office. "Saw that on one of them English detective shows on TV. Sounded all sophisticated. 'Course, that many letters woulda cost you a goldurn arm and a leg."

"Well, *I* think it's perfect." Cassie beamed at him. "And it's mostly thanks to you, Marge."

"I didn't do nothin' 'cept spread the word about you two and your heroics. There's more'n one way to spice up the food at The Busy B." She cackled. "I bet you're glad to be out of Cassie's extra bedroom and into your own honest-to-goodness office."

"That, I am." Bishop tightened the arm he had around Marge.

"Hey." Cassie poked him in the side. "What's wrong with my extra bedroom?"

Marge stepped around Bishop and next to Cassie. "There's better uses for that room than runnin' a business." She gave Cassie a lewd wink, then slapped Bishop on the arm. "Catch my drift?"

Bishop chuckled. "Slow your roll, Marge. I think Cassie wants to stick to the traditional order of these things. Right?"

"Absolutely. Engagement, marriage and *then* babies. But I'm not in a rush." Cassie leaned against him. "In the meantime, we can turn it into a guest room. I'd love to have Ashley visit."

"I'd like that, too. But I don't think it will happen anytime soon." His niece had made it through detox, but was afraid to leave the house now. "Maybe we can take a road trip to Houston to see her."

"Whatever's best for her." Cassie smiled. "A visit from you would do her a world of good."

"Cassie, be a dear and walk back to the diner with me. It's almost time for the dinner rush, and my leg's been bothering me today."

"Of course, Marge. Do you want me to drive you back?"

"I'm not an invalid, for gosh sakes. I just want someone along in case I fall in the middle of the street. Don't wanna roll around like a turtle on its back until somebody runs over me."

Cassie took her arm and they started down the street. At the corner, Marge looked back and gave Bishop a thumbsup. He returned the gesture, then jogged over to the justice center.

"Good afternoon, Helen." He stopped at her desk, waiting for permission to go past. It had become a game for them.

"Hello, Bishop. Ready for the big event?"

"Working on it. Adam and Noah here?"

"Go on back." She flashed him a smile. "And don't start without me."

"Wouldn't dream of it." He went to Adam's office first. "Can the chief deputy come out and play?"

"About time you got here." Adam checked his watch. "We're cutting it close."

"Then let's get going." They swung past the bullpen, picking up Noah.

"The rest of you guys," Adam addressed Sean, Pete and Dave, "be at the house at six o'clock sharp."

They saluted him and said in unison, "Yes, sir, Chief Deputy, sir."

"They still giving you a hard time about your promotion?" Bishop asked.

"Every day. But I get even with them because… I'm the chief deputy." They laughed as they climbed into Adam's truck. "We need to stop by your place, or pick up anything else?"

Bishop patted his pocket. "Got everything I need."

When they arrived at the Reeds' house, Bishop's jaw dropped. "Holy…"

"You might as well forget that phrase," Noah said. "My sister will wash your mouth out with soap."

Bishop climbed out of the truck and tried to take it all in. A dance floor had been set up in the front yard. Strings of little lights hung everywhere. Long tables for the food stood end to end near the front porch, and more were set up for drinks, both soft and hard.

Nate joined Bishop. "What do you think?"

"I can't believe it." A sudden panic swept through him. "What if she doesn't say yes? I should have done this privately. Not in front of half the town."

"Chill. She's going to say yes." Nate slapped his shoulder. "Go check out the backyard."

Bishop walked through the house, feeling at home. By falling in love with Cassie, he'd wound up with the type of family he had always wanted. He stepped out onto the patio to a rousing cheer from the crowd hiding back here.

He moved through, shaking hands and getting slapped on the back.

"'Bout time you put a ring on it." Doc's cackle sounded a lot like Marge's.

Noah came up to Bishop. "Nice turnout, right?"

"Yeah. But I don't know most of the people here."

"Cassie does. This is her town, and these are her friends, the people she serves, everyone." Noah hung an arm around his neck. "The thing is, Bish…"

"Don't call me that."

"What? It's an affectionate nickname for my future brother-in-law."

"Don't call me that."

Cassie's little brother rolled his eyes. "As I was saying, *Bishop*, in Resolute, we come together to celebrate happy times. Doesn't matter if everyone here knows everyone else. It's the spirit of the thing."

"I like that." Bishop turned Noah a bit so they had the same line of sight. "Who's he? The old, tall guy?"

"That's Charlie. He's the *last* man you want to meet."

Bishop looked at Noah in surprise. "Why's that?"

"He's the town undertaker." Noah slapped Bishop on the back and walked away laughing.

"It's time, everybody." Adam stood on a chair to get the crowd's attention. "Cassie should be here in a few minutes. Nate and Noah are going to take y'all around the far side of the house so you're ready to surprise her."

A loud buzz moved through the group as they made their way closer to the front. Bishop went to the front porch just in time to see Sean, Dave and Pete help Helen carry a gigantic cake out of her car. He held the door open for them so they could hide it inside, then joined Adam near the driveway.

"Nervous?" Adam shot him a questioning look.

"No," Bishop lied. "I'm happy." And he was.

"Good. Then you know it's right."

Bishop didn't need Adam to tell him it was right. He loved Cassie, and that love grew every single day. And Cassie's love, respect and support gave him the strength he needed to be a better man.

Cassie's SUV pulled up and stopped. Marge climbed out of the passenger seat. When Cassie's door didn't open, Marge rounded the hood and yanked it open. "You gonna just sit in there all day? Come on."

"What *is* all this?" She looked at Marge. "You said Nate called with an emergency."

"Maybe I got my messages mixed up." Marge cackled and went off to find a chair.

Bishop walked over to Cassie, took her hand and led her to the center of the dance floor.

Her head swiveled from side to side, a look of bewilderment on her face. "I don't understand."

"Remember that night at the Chute?"

That got a laugh out of her. "Not likely to forget it."

"Well, we never did get to the dancin' part of the evening. So I figured it was about time for our first dance together."

The band, which he'd borrowed from the Chute, stood with their instruments, ready to play. But no one moved. No one spoke. Cassie looked at Bishop, her forehead creased with confusion.

He took a step back. "Sorry. I forgot something." Sliding his hand into his pocket, he came out with a small velvet box. He dropped to one knee, and Cassie's mouth dropped open. Taking advantage of her shock, he captured her hand in his. "Cassie, you've taught me that there are reasons for rules. They might not be good reasons, but they're there just the same."

The corners of Cassie's lips twitched upward.

"When I first arrived in Resolute, I thought it was you who needed to open yourself to new ideas. But I learned that I was the one with a closed mind. We've been through a lot together in a short time, and I'm hoping the adventure doesn't end anytime soon." He opened the box and held it out to her. "Will you marry me?"

Tears welled in her eyes. "Yes," she whispered.

Bishop slid the ring on her finger.

"What'd she say? I can't hear you." Marge's loud, scruffy voice blared from behind Cassie.

Cassie turned, surprise on her face once more at the sight of everyone she held near and dear venturing out from behind the house. "What in the world…"

"Are we celebrating or what?" Noah called out.

Cassie doubled over laughing.

Bishop rose and pulled a still-laughing Cassie to him. "She said yes!" he bellowed, and the whole crowd cheered.

With a radiant smile on her lips and her eyes shining with love, Cassie threw her arms around Bishop. She kissed him like he hoped he'd be kissed for the rest of his life as he danced her across the floor.

* * * * *

CONARD COUNTY CONSPIRACY

RACHEL LEE

For all the people who helped me along this amazing
path, especially my incredibly patient family.

Chapter One

Grace Hall awoke to gunshots in the middle of the night. The sound startled her, causing her to sit up abruptly and twist toward the window. She wouldn't be able to see anything unless she pulled the curtains open.

Her heart hammered. She wondered in her sleep-fogged state if someone was attacking her house. Two more shots. This time she could tell they were farther away. Not right here.

She flopped back down on her pillow, staring up into the inkiness that filled her bedroom at night. She had some security lights outside, bright spotlights on poles, but seldom switched them on because they used electricity she could ill afford.

Tonight she wished she had turned them on. But would she have pulled back her curtains anyway? Not likely.

She lay there, reasoning more clearly as sleep seeped away. Some drunks, she decided. Who else would be shooting into the night? They'd found a wide-open area and had taken advantage of it. That had to be the reason. Too early for hunting season, and anyway, there was no night hunting allowed.

This was one of the few times she felt acutely aware

of her isolation. There had been times after her husband's death when she'd felt it to her core, but she had moved past that. While the huge expanse of ranch land surrounding her sometimes seemed to swallow her, it no longer consumed her. Being alone had brought its own solace.

Her heart slowed down and sleep crept close again. She'd check in the morning for damage, but for now she'd sleep.

THERE WAS A little bit of chicken inside her, Grace thought with mild amusement. She didn't want to go out there even though the Wyoming day was bright.

She dawdled over a breakfast of coffee and scrambled eggs. A piece of toast from a loaf of rye bread reminded her she needed to go to the store again.

Another trip to the store daunted her, but not as much as before. People had realized she didn't like to be asked how she was doing. *Fine* was a lie and they didn't really want to know the truth. Just an empty, meaningless gesture. They asked, she answered and they moved on with their own lives.

She'd let her friends slip away, not that a ranch wife had room for many, because time was at a premium. She'd worked as much as her husband had, caring for their sheep.

She sometimes wished they'd been able to get the goats she'd always wanted. Their antics would be so much more entertaining than the placid sheep.

She and John had never been able to see their way to the kind of fencing needed to keep goats from going walkabout. Those animals could jump almost anything. Plus, they needed special dietary supplements since the grazing here wouldn't provide enough. It was one of those *someday* things they'd never gotten around to.

There'd been a lot of those, she thought as she washed dishes. Too many, like the children they'd dreamed of having. Waiting, always waiting for the right time.

Was there ever a right time?

Eventually the nibbling worry drove her out the door to stand reluctantly on the wide, covered porch. A little more than a mile. A mile where those rowdies could have damaged her fences last night. A walk that would do her good, allow her to check her mail and probably reassure her.

Those guys might have found a great open space to do their manly shooting into the night, joking about firepower and probably full to the gills of the beer they'd been swallowing for hours.

They shouldn't have even been on the roads, but who was going to stop them? While sheriff's deputies drove along here, they couldn't come frequently. Too much area, too few deputies. The department needed more funding.

Random thoughts filled her as she went out the front door. The night's chill lingered but would be gone in a few hours. For now she needed the sweater she wore.

The blue sweater John had given her their last Christmas together. Soft and warm, like a hug.

The morning was bright, the sky a cloudless blue. A range of Wyoming mountains filled the western horizon, not far away. A truly beautiful summer day on the way. She headed for the mailbox.

In the distance she caught sight of the sheep, near the top of a rise. Mitch Cantrell, her neighbor and friend, now owned the sheep and leased her grazing land. Salvation for her, because otherwise she'd have had to entirely let go of the dream she and John had been building. Profitable for Mitch, she gathered. He'd even been able to hire two shepherds, a luxury she'd long ago given up.

The morning began to cheer her up despite everything else. Maybe she should push herself to get back into the mainstream of life. John wouldn't have wanted her to grieve indefinitely.

When she was within sight of her mailbox, about a half mile away, she saw a sheep lying on the ground. They never did that. Was the ewe ill?

She walked closer to the fence. What she saw sickened her.

There was blood all over the animal.

Those drunks last night must have used her as target practice.

She stood frozen for a few minutes, then ran back to the house as fast as she could. No cell connection out here, so she needed the landline. Rage had begun to replace horror. A fury so big she wasn't sure she could contain it.

First she called Mitch. His voice sounded a bit crackly, probably because he was using his satellite phone.

She dropped the news without preamble. "Mitch, a ewe has been shot in the pasture near my driveway."

A moment of silence, perhaps because of the satellite delay. "I'm on my way. Stay inside, Grace."

"I'm calling the sheriff."

"Good. I'm out on the range, but not too far away. Hang in there, stay inside. Thirty minutes max."

Grace called the sheriff. She heard immediate concern from the dispatcher who took her call. To judge by the roughened voice, it was probably Velma.

"We'll get someone out there as fast as we can, Grace. The nearest patrol is about thirty minutes away. Stay inside."

Stay inside? That was what everyone wanted, despite her not having an urge to go out to the sheep again. She did stand on her porch, keeping an eye out down her driveway to the county road. Just in case.

Those idiot drunks might come back to admire their mayhem. She hoped they would. She had a rifle and a shotgun inside and wasn't afraid to use them.

MITCH WAS THE first to arrive. He came in his four-wheel-drive pickup. She guessed he had driven overland instead of taking the road. He did, however, come tearing up her drive, spewing dust and loose gravel, wasting no time.

He passed the sheep, coming to her immediately. He practically jumped out of the truck and trotted up the steps to her.

A hardworking figure of a man, broad-shouldered and browned by wind and sun. Wearing the inevitable jeans and shotgun chaps. He must have been on his horse before jumping into his vehicle.

"You okay?" he demanded.

"I'm fine, but I'm angry enough to explode."

"I don't blame you. Will you be okay if I go out to take a look? I barely saw it as I raced by."

"They're more important than I am." Livestock mattered. They were life and livelihood.

He paused, his gray eyes narrowing. "Don't ever let me hear you say that again."

She'd say it as often as she wanted, she thought defiantly. Because it was true. Even though Mitch owned them now, she and John had worked hard to build that flock. Long summers and cold, dangerous winters. Yeah, the sheep mattered more.

Part of that dream was now in tatters, but it was a part that meant the world to her.

She watched as Mitch reached the sheep and climbed out to look. He'd barely begun his examination when a sheriff's SUV rolled up, five-pointed gold star on its sides. She recognized Guy Redwing as he climbed out to join Mitch. The man had a distinctive stride. Well, so did Mitch, from years in the saddle. Guy was one of the deputies who, when patrolling out here, always came to her door to ask how she was doing. Somehow she didn't mind it when *he* asked.

The men stood looking and pointing, then Guy went back to his vehicle and stood beside it. Probably calling for assistance.

Grace couldn't stand it another minute. Hurrying, she closed the distance and joined the two of them.

"You notice anything?" Mitch asked her.

"Gunshots in the middle of the night. I thought some drunks were out here firing into the air." She hesitated, battling down fury and hating her perceived cowardice. "I didn't dare come out to look."

"Good," Mitch said. "Good. Wise move. Who can predict what a bunch of drunk men might do?"

She hadn't thought of that, but she knew what he was suggesting. Gang rape. All of them ginning each other up. Anger turned into a shudder.

"The techs are coming out," Guy said as he returned from his car. "Don't touch anything."

Flies were buzzing around now, emerging from drowsiness as the temperature rose. The odor began to grow, too. Feeling her gorge rise, Grace turned away.

"You don't have to stay for this," Mitch said almost gently. "My sheep, my problem."

"My land, near my house. My problem."

Let him argue with that. She didn't want to think too much about what had happened, or about what *could* have happened, but she meant to stand her ground. She had been dismissed too often over the last couple of years since John had died.

Nobody of importance. A widowed ranch wife. Sympathy that had quickly blown away like autumn leaves.

Except for Mitch. He'd been her friend and John's after they bought this place He always checked in with her since the funeral. Friendly over a cup of coffee, occasionally bringing a dish over that his housekeeper had made. Always asking if there was any way he could help out.

A genuinely nice guy who had often kept her from feeling totally alone. Letting her know she had a friend no matter what.

But she wouldn't allow him to dismiss her as others had. Too many others. While he never had before, she refused to let him start now.

"Have it your way, Grace."

She thought the corners of his eyes crinkled, suggesting a smile.

She spoke again. "Yes, I will."

"I always thought you were as tough as barn nails."

She didn't know if she liked that analogy, but it would do. She *was* tough. She'd *had* to be tough, except in the middle of the night when she sometimes cried herself to sleep.

But she was still here, still standing, refusing to yield ground in her own driveway.

When the crime scene techs arrived, she faced the fact that she couldn't do anything else. Not that they'd find something useful.

She didn't need a police report to tell her that this crime wouldn't be solved. Shots fired on a deserted road from a vehicle nobody had seen? No evidence.

A sheep was dead. Mitch was going to take the loss. He'd survive it, but loss of livestock was a ding on any rancher's bottom line.

In fact, killing livestock was about the worst thing you could do in these parts. She wouldn't be the only angry person when word got around.

She turned and walked back to her house. It didn't look as much like a refuge as it had yesterday.

MITCH WATCHED HER walk away. He was more concerned about her than about the ewe. Yeah, it was ugly. Even horrifying. Clearly those men last night hadn't been content with a single shot. They'd used that poor animal for target practice. Anger simmered inside him.

But Grace was another matter. All alone out here. Gunshots in the night and no one around to make her feel safe, or help her deal with it. Then this morning, to find this atrocity so close. Not out on a distant pasture, but right near her driveway.

She might stride away with purpose with back straight and shoulders squared, but she wasn't always the brave woman she appeared to be.

No, she was as stubborn as an army mule. Only stubbornness could have kept her out here by herself. Never give an inch. That was Grace's motto.

He admired it, but it worried him, too. She was unlikely to ask for help even when she needed it. She probably never would have mentioned the gunshots last night except for the sheep. Or maybe if her fence had been damaged.

Otherwise, she would have rolled with the blow, as she almost always did.

Hell no. She wouldn't have told him about a broken fence at all. Instead she'd have tried to figure out how to pay someone. Given that he knew she was squeaking by, it would have annoyed him no end to learn she'd done that.

Damn, he had hired help he could send over.

His thoughts needed to be corralled. He'd have to quit imagining things that hadn't happened, and deal with what was.

A dead ewe. Some drunks, most likely, thinking they were having fun. Still, the ewe was dead.

He could absorb the loss financially, but the act itself incensed him. What kind of person got his kicks from shooting up a defenseless animal? Hell, a steer was more of a threat than a sheep.

Guy Redwing wrapped up the investigation, as little as it was. Techs in Tyvek suits bagged and took the remains for examination. Mitch doubted they'd learn much.

"So," he said to Guy as the techs took the ewe, "what's your impression?"

Guy hesitated. "Drunks shooting up the county."

That wasn't all, Mitch sensed. "Got any other cases like this?"

Guy shook his head. "One and only. Maybe others will turn up in the next few weeks."

Mitch studied the man, thinking he was being close-mouthed, but about what?

Was it the savagery? Or something more?

Guy spoke again. "Grace ain't around enough to have made anyone angry. So drunks it is."

Most likely, Mitch thought. Grace couldn't have an enemy on this entire planet.

The techs had had to cut the barbed wire to get to the animal. He pulled out his satellite phone and called one of his hired hands. "I need you and Jack at the Hall place to patch some barbed wire. Today."

When he got the response he wanted, he disconnected and watched the police vehicles drive away.

Then he headed up toward the house.

GRACE SAW MITCH COMING. Unable to help herself, she'd stood at her front window watching the distant activity. She wasn't surprised when Mitch drove his pickup her way.

A tan-colored vehicle with high suspension to get over rough ground, and enough dings to testify to its working life, the truck seemed to suit the man who, despite all, had remained her friend even though she wasn't much of a friend to have.

Sighing, she went to open the door for him, accepting the fact he wanted to help her in some way, but also accepting the fact she didn't want to be alone right now.

This event had jarred her, and not much shook her anymore. The senseless killing of that sheep bothered her at a deep level. Remorseless. Cruel. Those guys probably still laughing about it.

What had a friend once called it so many years ago? Oh, yeah. Testosterone poisoning. She'd found the phrase cute, but over the years hadn't had much call to think of it. Out here, she had met a lot of hardworking no-nonsense men. Men like Mitch.

That didn't mean there weren't any jackasses, but none of them had evoked that phrase in her. Maybe it only applied to *young* jackasses. The idea brought a faint smile to her mouth, a smile still there when Mitch climbed the steps.

"Hey, ranch lady," he said. "Can I beg for a cup of coffee?"

She waved him in. "Always. Let me make a fresh pot."

"Whatever's burning in there will do for me."

She laughed at last. "Sure. Bitter, concentrated. Blech."

She led him to her farmhouse kitchen, a big room from past times, too big for one person. Mitch seemed to half fill it, though.

While the coffee brewed, she leaned back against the counter and folded her arms over her sweater. "They won't catch 'em."

Mitch relaxed against the wall on the far side of the room. He seldom encroached by getting too close to her. She'd begun to notice that.

"Of course they won't catch the guys. Unless they brag about it."

"We can hope they're that stupid."

He passed his hand over his face. "A couple of my men are coming over to mend your fence. Cops had to cut it to get to the remains. Speaking of stupidity, there's that ewe. What was she doing so far away from the flock?"

Her brows rose. "That's a good question."

MITCH WATCHED GRACE as the coffee brewed. She'd always been a lovely woman, but now she was awfully thin. Once she'd been "pleasingly plump" as people would call it, a plumpness that gave a fullness to her curves. All that had vanished since John's death. Well, he could understand it. Her hair was still inky black, her eyes still the bright blue of a summer sky. Her smile was wide and infectious beneath a small, straight nose.

He'd just like to see her smile more. He remembered her before John's death and didn't think John would be happy about the way she was now. In fact, he was sure of it.

He stifled a sigh, knowing he couldn't do a damn thing about it. He turned his attention to a matter that was at least somewhat under his control.

"I need to question my shepherds," he told her. "I hired them to protect the flock, obviously. I'd like to know if they have any idea why that ewe was so far away."

She nodded. The coffeepot finished quickly. She'd evidently only brewed enough to offer him some. She filled a large mug and passed it to him. "Why wouldn't the whole flock have followed her? That's what they usually do, follow each other."

"I don't know. I'll ask Zeke and Rod if they have any ideas." Those were not their real names, coming from Portugal as they did, but those were the names they preferred to be known by. Given how the Portuguese pronunciation was so easily massacred, Mitch understood it. God knew, he'd tried unsuccessfully.

"I suspect she must have been ill." Even sheep could refuse to associate with one of their number who was seriously sick. Protective mechanisms operated at a basic level. He needed to be as sure as possible, though. Strange things were afoot no matter how he looked at them.

Yet he didn't want to make too much of this. He'd

been dealing with livestock his entire life, and weird things happened. Like cows practically dancing with glee when he let them out of their winter pasture, where they lived on hay, alfalfa and some supplements, into a freshly greening spring pasture. All of a sudden those supposedly "bovine" creatures began to run around as if they were spring lambs themselves.

It always tickled him to watch that.

This was definitely not tickling him, however. And worse, tough as she wanted to be, Grace was looking a trifle drawn. Still disturbed. Unwilling to admit to even a bit of weakness.

Damn stubborn woman.

How many erstwhile primary school teachers would take on the dream of a man like John Hall? He'd worked ranches. He'd married the teacher and Grace had quit her job. Then a year later, the two of them had jumped to buy this ranch at a court-ordered auction. John's dream of raising sheep had become Grace's and she'd worked beside him every minute to build this place.

He sometimes wondered if she'd had dreams of her own that she'd relinquished for John. Or if in him she had found the answer to those dreams. That was a question he'd never be able to ask.

He sipped his coffee, seeking another subject to discuss, something that didn't have to do with that slaughtered ewe. Something to turn her away from grim thoughts.

"Thank you," she said presently. "I appreciate you having your men come fix my fence."

That drew a hollow laugh from him. "Your fence, my fence, who cares? It's helping to contain the sheep. I'm hardly going to give them an excuse to wander into a road, and where one goes they all go."

Except last night.

Then a thought occurred to him. "You need to go into town anytime soon? I ought to make a run for provisions. I'm feeding myself, my housekeeper, three hired hands and two shepherds who are pretty good at feeding themselves out in the pasture, but they still need staples."

She knew all this, of course. The problem with the years was that you got to know someone, at least on the surface, and conversation became sporadic. The details had already been shared.

Plus, you knew where all the Do Not Trespass signs were planted. Grace had quite a few, and he guessed he did, too.

Grace's smile was wan, but still a smile. "I was thinking about it when I was making breakfast this morning. I need to stock up."

"Well, then, let's go do it today. Plenty of room in that pickup to carry supplies for a whole bunch of people."

"Thank you for the offer. I'll take you up on that."

A short while later, he departed with the feeling she wanted to be alone for a bit. The princess, returning to her isolation in her tower.

Well, the large landowner, not princess. Fact was, they'd both been recently approached by an industrial farming group that had made an offer for their acreage. Neither of them had had the least trouble in turning down the offer.

It was some damn good land, better than most, with streams that ran sweet well into the summer with mountain runoff, ponds that stayed full unless there was a drought, and some good trees.

Although the cows had nibbled the bottoms of the tree branches until they looked as if someone had come along and pruned them all off at the same height.

His own topiary.

He was glad to see his hired hands Bill and Jack already at work on the fence. Bill touched the brim of his cowboy hat as Mitch drove by.

As he reached the end of Grace's drive, he saw a black sedan turn in. Betty Pollard, Grace's only girlfriend, the only one who came to visit occasionally. He gave a friendly wave, glad to know that Grace wouldn't be alone after all.

Then he returned to his own place, full of questions, with only a few hours to seek answers before he came to get Grace for the trip to town.

GRACE HEARD A car pulling up and looked out her front window to see Betty Pollard. A close friend over the last couple of years since they'd met. Betty had pushed past Grace's reserve, and Grace always enjoyed seeing her.

Except this morning. She'd have preferred a phone call first, because she really didn't want to entertain anyone, not Mitch, not Betty.

The beginning of a cheerful mood in the morning had been dashed when she came across that ewe. She was still shocked that anyone could have done such a thing. Shocked that it had happened so close to her home.

She was getting bluer by the minute. Counting her blessings hadn't worked well since John's death. That particular shock didn't ever seem to quit. It still seemed impossible that a heart defect had killed a young and healthy man like him instantly.

She watched Betty climb out of the black sedan that

looked so out of place. Grace had often wondered how Betty kept it clean, what with all the dust around here. Even now a layer was already starting to build on that shiny black surface.

Betty waved, obviously seeing her through the window.

Grace half-heartedly waved back and went to open the door.

Betty breezed in as she always did, this time without a smile. "I heard," she said.

Heard? Already? That seemed quick.

Betty must have noticed the question in her eyes. "You should get a police band radio, Grace. Never miss out on any of the so-called excitement in Conard County. Tickets. Rowdies at a roadhouse. A drunk staggering around who needs to be led home. Why in the world would you want to miss all that?"

Despite herself, a laugh escaped Grace. "I guess it was more exciting this morning?"

"Believe it. Do I smell coffee?"

"The pot's empty, I'm afraid."

Betty smiled. "Then I'll just make more." She marched into the kitchen. "My God, I can't imagine how you must have felt when you found that. I'd be feeling attacked if that was my sheep."

Grace didn't bother to tell her it was now Mitch's sheep. He hadn't wanted their arrangement broadcast for some reason, so she kept quiet.

"I don't feel personally attacked," Grace answered. "Just some drunk idiots having what they think was a good time."

Betty shook her head as she measured out coffee and filled the machine with water. "I'd be scared to death to live out here if I were in your shoes. Really, you need to think about selling. You need a life."

That wasn't the first time Betty had suggested selling. Every time she did, she set Grace's back up. But Grace was unwilling to get into an argument over it, and she knew perfectly well that Betty would argue when she believed she was right.

"Just think about it," Betty said.

"I will," Grace answered, to end the topic .

"Anyway," Betty said, plopping herself at the table, "let me tell you my good news."

That perked Grace up. "Good news? Do tell."

"I fully intend to. I met a guy."

Grace felt a smile spread across her face. "Just a guy?"

"Well, more than a guy," Betty said impishly. "I mean, it's all brand-new and could disappear by next week, but at the moment he has me over the moon."

Grace had often been surprised that Betty didn't have a trail of men following her everywhere. Blonde and beautiful in every respect, nice to be around. Except she gathered Betty was very picky. A good thing to be when it came to romance.

Inevitably, she thought of John. They had fit together like peas in a pod. A great match, though it had surprised her when it began.

"Anyway," Betty continued, "he's sexy enough to catch my eye. And so far he's been considerate and fun to be around."

"A great combination. Do I know him?"

"I don't think so. He's not from around here. I only ran into him because we were both in Casper at the same time. At the same bar with dancing. We meshed so well I don't think either of us saw another person there."

Grace smiled again. "I'm happy for you, Betty."

"Too soon to be happy. But for the moment I'll enjoy it. Now about you. You need to get out there more, Grace. There are some really nice people in the world."

"You're right. I'm just not ready."

"You will be," Betty said with certainty. "Anyway, I've got to run. Dan and I are meeting midway for lunch at one of the roadhouses. The way it's been going we may close the place tonight."

Betty left after giving her a hug and another suggestion to sell the ranch, leaving Grace with yet another pot of coffee. She turned it off. She felt caffeinated enough to want to crawl out of her skin.

Instead she set about cleaning a bathroom and dusting. Dusting was a perpetual task out here, except during the winter. And it was getting time to pull out her windows and clean the frames. If she didn't do that, they'd get to the point where they wouldn't open or close properly.

Endless household chores. Maybe she did too many. Or maybe she didn't do enough.

Either way, they kept her busy.

BETTY DROVE AWAY, thinking about Grace and her situation. The woman ought to be ready to leave that ranch. She should have been ready a long time ago.

Betty had the feeling that it would take more to convince Grace to move on with her life. If a butchered ewe couldn't persuade her, then what would?

Sighing, Betty pondered the problem. She needed to get Grace to sell.

Chapter Two

Mitch picked up Grace around noon. A trip into Conard City seemed like just the ticket after her morning. He was going to insist on one thing, however. This time she was going to accept his offer of a satellite phone, the only thing that worked out here other than a landline.

It had bothered him for some time that she was all alone, except on those occasions when he could find time to check in with her. Brave and stubborn or not, she needed to take better care of herself.

The first item on his agenda was feeding her. He claimed to be ravenous, so she didn't object when he suggested eating at either the truck stop diner or at Maude's. He gave her the choice, but she was indifferent.

"I'm fine either way, Mitch."

He decided on the truck stop. At least it wouldn't be full of locals, which might inadvertently make her uncomfortable.

Her discomfort with meeting people had become apparent to him. Sometimes he wanted to point out John wouldn't have liked her feeling this way, but he figured it was a lost cause. Everyone grieved in their own way, on their own timeline. It wasn't something that could be marked on a calendar.

The diner wasn't very busy. He supposed a lot of drivers snoozed outside in their growling big rigs. The waitress who came over to take their orders was middle-aged, full-breasted and kindly. Her graying hair was confined in a net, something not often seen anymore.

Grace's order seemed too little, so he ordered extra toast and ham, hoping to tempt her to join him. Damn, this woman needed to eat before she vanished.

"Did you talk to your shepherds?" she asked.

So much for distracting her from the morning's ugliness. "I got a hold of Zeke. He said the flock scattered during the night and they suspected coyotes had scared them but thought it was strange they didn't just knot together for protection. Anyway, after they scattered, he and Rod started rounding them up. He didn't notice a ewe missing until this morning. He also suggested I spring for some herding dogs, and he's right. But they don't come cheap."

"A lot of training?"

"Zeke said most herd by instinct but still need to learn commands so they do what *we* want them to. Apparently one trained dog can train others, even puppies."

"Maybe Cadell Marcus," she offered, mentioning a local dog trainer.

"Maybe. I'll check with him, but I thought he mainly trained police K-9s and service dogs."

"Since he can do that, he might be able to branch out. Then there's Ransom Laird. He's been raising sheep forever. He helped John and me out when we first started. In fact, we bought the beginnings of our flock from him."

"That's a good idea," he allowed.

Breakfast was served and he watched her pick at hers.

He wished he could find a way to increase her appetite, although after this morning that might be difficult.

"How is Betty?" he asked, diverting the conversation.

"She's doing well. Has a new man in her life and seems really happy. And she pushed me about selling again."

"She doesn't give up, does she?"

Grace smiled. "I guess not."

Mitch agreed with Betty. He understood Grace's attachment to the land and the house but also spent a lot of time worrying about her solitary existence. She was practically in the middle of nowhere by herself. What if she got hurt?

That was why he wanted to push the sat phone on her. What if she couldn't reach him, her nearest neighbor, on her landline?

Mostly she needed the phone so she'd have communication wherever she went, like down there to find the ewe this morning. He imagined her running back to the house to call him and the cops.

Nope. He wasn't going to let that continue, but he had to find a way around her stubbornness, and a way to get her to eat. She didn't seem any more interested in conversation than eating. Nothing he could do about that either.

"Let's go, Grace. I need to go to the feed store."

She nodded. " Livestock must be fed."

He headed for the feed store first because he needed horse feed. Several hundred pounds of it, in fact. He wasn't the only person riding horseback around his ranch. After the feed, there was still enough room in the truck bed for some heavy-duty provisioning. He had to care for his employees.

He needed a flat cart to load all the provisions on,

and this grocery provided those carts for the people who came in from outlying ranches with big shopping lists.

Grace needed only a standard-size cart and went her own way in the store. She walked with her eyes straight ahead, as if she didn't want anyone to speak with her.

This was getting out of hand, but he didn't know what to do.

He was glad to see her pausing to speak with the minister. It had kind of shaken the Conard County when a woman was sent to head up Good Shepherd Church, but they'd gotten used to Molly Canton over the last couple of years. A pleasant middle-aged woman who wore black dresses or slacks, with a white collar around her neck. She usually presented a cheery or sympathetic face, and right now she was engaging Grace in a conversation Grace probably didn't want to have.

Molly was stubborn, though, maybe as stubborn as Grace. It was the only way she had survived her initial introduction to this county, which was still trying to live the way it had a century ago. Change didn't come easily.

He moved closer and heard Reverend Molly telling Grace about some social opportunities at the church. Trying to draw Grace back into life. Everything from a quilting group to a Bible study group, with a few things thrown in between.

Grace's answers were polite but noncommittal.

Finally Molly shook her head, saying bluntly, "You know, Grace, building a shell around yourself isn't helpful. Shells can be cracked, and the results can be dangerous. At least think about joining us, even if only for Sunday services. Whether you believe it or not, there are plenty of people around here who still care about you and haven't forgotten you."

Then Molly moved away and began to pick out some produce for her handbasket.

Mitch came up beside Grace. "She's right, you know. Baby steps, Grace. Just baby steps. Betty and I aren't enough."

She looked at him, her blue eyes swimming a bit. "I know," she said hoarsely. "But I still can't."

If she kept telling herself that, she never would. He resisted shaking his head even a little bit and put on a smile. "I think I've got almost enough for my small army."

She looked at his cart. "Where do you put it all?"

"Well, I've got an unheated porch that does pretty well as a refrigerator for dry goods, and a couple of refrigerators and large-chest freezers. You need to come over some time and see how we manage to put it all together."

"Maybe I should."

If so, it would be the first time since John's death. Maybe it was a first baby step.

On the way home, before he could press her about taking the satellite phone, she spoke, saying something that chilled him a bit.

"Mitch, what if it wasn't just some thrill seekers last night?"

It wasn't a possibility he wanted to consider, but it had been stalking the edges of his mind anyway.

Such a brutal, unnecessarily brutal, thing to do. Maybe some drunks or it might be something much more.

WHEN THEY REACHED Grace's home, he insisted on carrying her reusable bags inside for her. He suspected she had purchased more than she had originally intended, maybe to postpone another trip.

Unfortunately, because he had cold and frozen items in his own truck bed, insulated bags or not, he couldn't stay long.

But he *could* address the issue of the satellite phone.

"Grace?"

"Mmm?"

"I need you to do me a favor."

She smiled. "I think I owe you more than one."

"I don't count them, but I'd like this one anyway." He'd brought a spare phone in with her groceries and handed her the brick and charger. "Take this, please. I have a few extra at home, so you won't be depriving me, but you'll give me peace of mind."

She looked at the heavy phone. "Mitch…"

"I know, you want to be independent. I get it. But this morning you could have saved yourself a run to the house to call me and the cops. It's more than that, though. I worry about the rest of the time."

"Meaning? My life is uncomplicated."

Far from it, Mitch thought, but he persisted. "You like to go for walks out there. What if you fall and get hurt, and can't get back to the house? If you think I want to be hunting you three days later, you're sadly mistaken."

She'd been avoiding his gaze, as if she hated to be pressed about anything, but now she looked at him. "I'll be fine."

"Most of the time that's true. It's the one time I'm seriously worried about. Take the damn thing and don't be a fool."

He was always so careful about what he said to her that she appeared taken aback. He'd called her a fool.

Well, it was time she stopped being one about something so simple.

But she still didn't take the phone, and irritation surged in him. "Damn it, woman, you don't have to be so stubborn about everything. Most of the time I understand it, but not this time. All I ask is that you keep it charged and take it whenever you go out. Even to the mailbox, judging by this morning."

She looked down and he figured she was thinking about it. Well, that was a step forward, well past the few times she'd flat-out refused. Maybe this morning had shaken her enough to at least consider it.

Then, to his great relief, she reached out and took it. "You'll have to show me how to use it."

"These modern ones are simple. Hell, if I can use it, anyone can. But I'll be happy to show you."

GRACE DOUBTED HE'D have found it difficult to use the phone, even a more complex one. Over the years she'd seen how handy he could be with darn near everything. He'd taught her and John a whole lot when they'd been neophyte sheep ranchers trying to get their operation up and going.

An endless font of knowledge about the land, the weather, the running of a large operation. Heck, even when they'd been small, with a tiny flock, he'd showed them a great deal that had made life easier. Come lambing season, he'd been on hand, or had sent someone over.

He especially had helped to protect against coyotes who constantly prowled and in larger numbers during lambing. She and John had spent a lot of chilly spring nights out there with shotguns. Not that that was the only time they needed to worry. Eventually when they could afford it, like Mitch, they'd hired some help. With John's passing the work had become more than she could manage without hiring an additional person, and the flock had begun shrinking until she had to let the help go.

Doing it alone proved impossible. Mitch had solved the problem, explaining that he wanted to diversify because cattle were showing less of a profit as the years went by. Like her and John, he wanted the wool, which was still in high demand.

Seemed fair enough to her. She knew the value of that flock, but they had to be cared for. It was impossible for her to do it alone and kept her from having to sell the vestige of big dreams.

She was sure Betty had her best interests at heart, but so did Mitch, and he'd never once pressed her to sell. Instead he'd made it possible for her to stay.

Stifling one of her endless sighs, she began to put her groceries away. She'd bought too much, she supposed, but now she wouldn't need to go to the market for weeks.

That was okay by her.

MITCH HAD PLENTY to do once he arrived back at his ranch. Jeff, another of his hired hands, came to help unload. They trucked the feed over to the barn after dropping off the groceries with Mitch's housekeeper, Lila, leaving her eyeing a pork roast with pleasure.

Mitch nearly chuckled. Usually Lila did the shopping herself, but she tended to be too careful with his money. He appreciated that, but he also understood the appetites of six hardworking men better than she did. For a while she had kept trying to serve normal-size portions and complex recipes. No more.

Jeff had taken care of the horses who appeared to be

content to munch on their feed after spending most of the day on the range or in the corral. Mitch owned six good mares, durable and well-behaved. Believing that none of them should have to work every day, he kept at least two corralled at any given time, rotating them.

Before heading back into the house, he paused to pat each of them and murmur pleasant words. Ears pricked forward, listening, a couple of them gave him a horse hug, pressing their necks to his head.

He decided he'd try again to invite Grace to go riding. Maybe this time she'd accept the invitation. He worried about her, maybe more than he should. At some point the desire to live had to kick in. Didn't it?

Bill picked up the two large dinner buckets Lila had made for the shepherds and jumped onto the ATV to deliver them. Lila at last seemed to understand that two men living on the range couldn't pop in for a snack or raid the fridge. She was always generous.

Greeted by the aroma of roasting pork, Mitch walked through his log home. When he'd inherited it from his dad, it had been little more than a small cabin. The cabin had expanded a bit at a time, always keeping the rustic logs, and now he had a few extra bedrooms and an office for his business affairs, while the mud porch had been enlarged for food storage.

Not a bad accomplishment over fifteen years.

Neither was his herd, which he'd managed to grow considerably despite selling off steers. And the sheep. He was discovering that not only were they profitable, but they appealed to him in a different way than his cattle.

But the house, despite Lila's presence, and the comings and goings of his hired hands, felt empty.

As he stood in his bedroom that night in front of an

open window, he looked out over his life's work. The bunkhouse out back glistened with light pouring from its windows.

Not too many windows, just a few. Just enough of them to give a view of the outside world so this wouldn't feel like a cave. Windows were an expensive luxury in a place with long and cold winters. Maybe someday he'd have more, when he could afford triple-paned glass.

In the meantime he relied on woodstoves and fire-places when necessary.

Oh, cut it out, he told himself. Taking inventory of his house was a diversion to keep him from thinking about Grace.

His growing attraction to Grace made him question his loyalty to John. An attraction that surprised him considering how thin she'd become and how prickly she could be.

And stubborn. My God, the stubbornness. Part of him admired it but it frustrated another part of him.

Grace. Over there alone tonight. Again. But tonight held new fears, fears she was probably determined to dismiss.

Someone had shot up that ewe. In a very visible place. And while Guy Redwing had appeared to treat it like some hijinks gone bad, Mitch suspected Guy wondered, too.

The more Mitch thought about it, the more it struck him like a message rather than a drunken spree.

Who was trying to say what?

His worry for Grace increased.

Chapter Three

Grace had always enjoyed the longer late-spring evenings, especially when she was able to sit on a wooden rocker on her porch.

But this evening felt a little creepy. She had to force herself to go outside, with a blue Sherpa wrap around her shoulders, and rock gently, watching as night slowly stole the last color from the day.

In the late spring there was still plenty of greenery, especially in front of the house, which had never been heavily grazed. It faded slowly into gray as the sky relinquished all but starlight. No moon because of the new moon.

A very odd time for anyone, drunk or not, to be out shooting. The ewe, being fairly white in color, might have been easy enough to see, but what was she doing there in the first place?

That was what worried her. Out of place. An unnecessarily grim event. How could anyone have any purpose in doing that?

She wished John could be here, to share her thoughts, to discuss all this with. To reassure her and calm her increasingly agitated feelings.

He'd been good at that. She'd sometimes told him that

he'd smile into the teeth of a tornado. Hardworking and blessed with a cheerful nature. Nothing got John down.

Well, except when she started wanting to plant flowers and bushes out front. Like they could afford it. Like the dang plants wouldn't probably wither and die when August moved in with its hot, dry breath.

John could read her like an open book and absolutely hated telling her she couldn't have her wish.

"I know it was ridiculous," she said into a night springing alive with a breeze that blew down from the cold mountain heights to displace the warm air over the ranch land.

A lot of things became ridiculous when you were trying to build a future out of nearly nothing. Her desire had been sheer self-indulgence and she wished she hadn't made John feel bad. It had seemed like such a minor thing at the time, though.

Too many things had, and it did no good to think about them now.

Reverend Molly was correct. Grace needed to get out more, to step back into the world.

Except she felt frozen in time, like a fly in amber.

She turned her head and looked over toward Mitch's place. She couldn't see it from here, but she wondered what was happening over there. He might not have a family, but he was surrounded by people anyway.

Maybe he'd gone to bed already. A rancher's day started early. Maybe he sat in front of one of his fireplaces, his feet on a hassock, sipping the bourbon he occasionally liked.

She still had a bottle in her cupboard from when his visits had been more frequent. He and John had liked to shoot the breeze in the front room during icy winter nights. She should remember to offer him some, the next time he came over.

She wished he'd come again soon. She'd been pushing him away, trying to keep her grief to herself.

Nurturing it, she supposed. Indulging. Cherishing.

"Damn it," she said aloud.

There had to be a point when grief was no longer John's due, and a point that life became hers.

She just wished she could find it.

THE MORNING BROUGHT another crisp, sunny day. Having so much help meant Mitch could sometimes take time when he wanted it. After a hearty breakfast, prepared by Lila, he stood, ready to go out.

Lila spoke. "You ought to ask that widow lady over for dinner. Seems like she could use some company."

He smiled. "I've tried. I'll try again."

"You do that."

Indeed, he headed straight for Grace's place. Used to be he'd ride over, weather permitting, but this time he took his truck again. He needed to look some things over.

And this time he didn't drive overland. Instead he followed the road, giving himself a different view of ground he knew as well as the back of his hand.

The image of the sheep was clear in his mind's eye and he wanted to think about the perspective from the road, what would have been the best place for the rowdies to park.

He knew Guy had searched around for some tire tracks but hadn't found anything. Why would he? The county road was paved, however full of potholes. Grace's drive was not.

Why would it be? Miles of paving would cost dearly,

a luxury neither of them could afford. Every spring they had a grader come out to level his and hers off, followed by trucks full of gravel.

He never let Grace know he was paying for part of her costs. She'd have killed him.

Would have had every right, too, he thought. She'd been refusing any kind of charity for a long time now. Woman had her pride.

Each time he thought he might have a decent view of the spot where the ewe had been discovered, he pulled over and climbed into the bed of his truck to take a look.

He'd even brought his rifle with its scope, because, to him, the sheep had appeared to be shot by a rifle, not by a shotgun. That would make sense, too, if you wanted to take more than one shot. Drunks fooling around. A shotgun would have been no fun at all.

Better targeting ability with a night scope. It would allow the shot to be taken from a greater distance, requiring more skill.

He pressed the rifle against his shoulder and targeted the area the ewe had died. Once he'd decided whether it was a good location, he moved on. By the time he had surveyed all the likely positions from the road, he'd covered about five hundred meters in either direction and had found more than a dozen places from which the shots could have been taken.

Would any of them have had the skill to shoot over such distances? Or the desire to?

Frustrated that he couldn't pinpoint a good spot but satisfied he'd checked everything, he stowed his rifle and headed up to Grace's house, hoping she wouldn't think he was being overprotective.

One thing now seemed clear: the shooters hadn't been

that drunk. A stable hand was necessary to sight through a scope.

Hell. What did that mean?

GRACE WAS GLAD to see Mitch. Her night had been restless, stalked by danger she could never see. So weird.

"I haven't had a nightmare in years," she told Mitch as she offered him coffee and a wedge of pecan ring. "You see this? I was up at three kneading dough to let it rise and hunting in my cupboard for a bag of pecans I was sure I had."

She put her hands on her hips. "Think about that. Then I had to warm the oven a bit to get the dough to rise because it was too chilly in here and it might have risen sometime this afternoon. Who does that?"

"A baker maybe. Damn, it's good, though. I'm glad I dropped by." He studied her across the plate and the mug. "Restless with nightmares, huh? Not surprising after yesterday morning."

"Maybe not." She dropped in the chair facing him, propped her elbow on the table and rested her chin in her hand. "Feels like I'm spending most of my time in this room. I've got a perfectly good front room, but here I am again."

Her gaze drifted downward, and he waited, enjoying the pecan ring. He only wished she'd have some, also. She needed it.

"It's John," she said finally, still looking down. Her voice quavered a bit.

"John?"

"We used to spend a lot of evenings in that room, mostly in the winter. I can't sit in there, Mitch. I see him. Hear him. It's… I just sit in there and feel so sad. So sad."

He wanted to reach across the table and take her hand but wondered if he'd cross a line. With Grace he was never sure.

"I don't feel it as much in the bedroom," she said, surprising him. "Probably because about a year ago I threw out the linens and painted. It's a different room now. But the front room?" She shook her head. "If I got rid of every reminder, it would be empty. I don't know if that would be any better."

She sighed and lifted her face. "An empty room might only make it worse."

He hadn't thought about that, but she could be right. A gaping hole where once there had been a life.

"I wish I had answers, Grace."

She smiled wanly. "Me, too. This is all new to me. Still."

He tried to imagine her level of grief and loss but couldn't. Some things had to be experienced and thank God he'd never had to live through this. Losing his parents had been different, maybe because it was expected. They hadn't filled every part of his life the way John had filled Grace's. The two of them had been a tight, compact unit, wrapped up in each other and the ranch. Yes, there had been friends and acquaintances, but nothing like the two of them had been to each other.

He finished the cake, still wishing she'd have some. "How about this," he suggested. "I know the furniture in there is heavy. Most of it was built in the days when a chair or sofa was meant to last generations. But I could help you move things around. Change it up a little. Just think about it."

"That might help. I'll definitely think about it."

He hoped so since he lacked other ideas.

She shook herself a little. "I saw you out there on the road. You kept stopping. At least I thought it was you. It's quite a distance."

"Oh, it was me. Just trying something out."

"Which was?"

He shrugged one shoulder, wanting to make light of it, unwilling to lie, and very much afraid that he might give her another reason to be upset.

"Well, I was trying out vantage points from which to shoot at that ewe."

"Oh." Her face shadowed. "Why?"

Did he want to tell her? If he didn't, she'd probably guess he was withholding. Grace was reasonably intuitive about people, maybe from reading all those kids when she was teaching.

"Just that…well, I don't think it was a shotgun."

She shook her head. "I heard it. A rifle." Then understanding dawned on her face. "A rifle," she murmured. "They couldn't have been that drunk, could they?"

Exactly what he thought, but no need to confirm it for her.

"Then why the hell?" She jumped up from the table and started to pace. The room was big enough to allow it. "This all seems so crazy!"

"It does." He wasn't going to deny it. "Anyway, they could have shot from a bit of a distance out there. I was just looking for the places where they might have done it, but I bet it was from a truck bed, for that extra elevation. You'd have to be *really* drunk or stupid to fire from within the cab. Or to carry a loaded gun inside."

He wanted to let it go at that. Even though Grace might have a new reason for nightmares, he wasn't prepared to ever lie to her.

Once you lost a person's trust, it was damn hard to regain it.

She still paced, although more slowly. "Why would anyone do this?" she asked. "Except as a sick joke."

She turned toward him suddenly. "What about that company that wanted to buy our land?"

SHE'D TRIED TO tell herself that couldn't possibly be, but the suspicion wouldn't go away. This entire incident was almost surreal.

She couldn't imagine that anyone had done this with an eye to hurting her or scaring her. She'd limited her social life to almost nothing, so who could she have offended?

No one knew that Mitch now owned the sheep, so it was unlikely the perpetrator had been angry with him for some reason.

"I need this to make some kind of sense," she told Mitch. "Any kind of sense."

"Me, too. It's not easy to just shrug off."

Grace immediately realized that saying such a thing was pointless. Everyone wanted events to make sense, and sometimes they just didn't and never would. Like when one of her students developed cancer. How the hell could anyone make sense of that?

She returned to the table at last, glad she had Mitch to share her concerns with. Concerns she hadn't wanted to share with Betty, friend or not. Once again Betty had pressed her to sell the place. Grace wouldn't even consider it, no matter how many times someone told her it was pointless for her to remain out here alone. Dangerous, even.

She looked at the satellite phone in its charger, its red light blinking, grateful Mitch had insisted she take it.

He was correct about the phone. Especially when she walked the land, enjoying time in the fresh breeze and sunlight, hearing the distant baas of sheep, which had been a comforting sound for years. She could almost believe the world was right again.

The world would never be right again. Maybe it was time to start rebuilding. But how and where? Diving into a social life at church daunted her. She doubted she could take any groups yet.

At heart she'd always been an introvert living in an extrovert's world. She had managed, but she'd never regretted exchanging her life for a quieter one with John.

She looked at Mitch. "I love it out here. Always have."

"I honestly wondered how much you gave up when you married John."

She half smiled. "Absolutely nothing. I think I was built for this life."

Some of which was gone now, but she had to stop thinking that way. It was holding her down, holding her back.

"I'm not ready to give John up," she blurted, astonishing herself with the bald statement.

Mitch nodded, his work-hardened face softening. "I know. I miss him, too."

"Part of me is beginning to think I've let this go on long enough. That I really need to let go and move on."

"Grief has its own timetable, Grace."

"You're right." But now she felt exposed just for having said the truth out loud. It sounded...over the top, now that she'd heard the words hanging on the air. Nothing, however, changed the facts. She wasn't ready to let go of John. Maybe it was time to put something around that hole in her heart and life.

On the other hand, getting busy might only be a distraction, or a flight from the grief itself. Maybe it needed to burn out in its own time. Although it would never be entirely gone. Ever.

"Want another piece of pecan ring?" she asked, turning the conversation to something less threatening. A brief break from her gloomy thoughts.

"Only if you'll have one."

Again she smiled faintly. "Pressure?"

"Hell no. This is so good you need to taste it. You must have lost twenty or so pounds and are starting to look like someone in severe need of nourishment."

Even as irritation rose in her, it collapsed before becoming fully born. "You're right," she admitted. "Although a pecan ring is hardly nourishment."

"It's calories. Enjoy them."

She retrieved a plate for herself and brought the it over to the table. "Help yourself, Mitch. I'm not going to eat the whole thing. It'll wind up in the compost when it dries out."

"We can't have that." Using the knife, he cut himself a generous piece, then foisted an equally big one on her.

"I never eat that much," she protested.

"Try. Compost, remember?"

A stillborn bubble of laughter tickled her stomach. Laughter was so rare to her these days that she welcomed it. "Taskmaster."

He held up a hand. "Hey, you're talking to the guy who runs a cattle ranch. I never take no for an answer."

"Are you sure the ranch doesn't run *you*?" Man, was she teasing? She'd almost forgotten she could do that.

"It probably *does* run me," he admitted, forking off another bite. "But I like to pretend I'm the boss."

"It's a good illusion."

"That's exactly what it is. But it gives me one advantage."

"Which is?"

He half shrugged. "I was able to tell Bill he's the boss for a couple of hours."

Finally, at long last, the bubble of laughter rose and emerged quietly.

Mitch smiled at her. "I like that sound."

She did, too. It felt good. Maybe it was time to pull out those comedy DVDs that she and John used to laugh at so easily. Time to reclaim something.

The loneliness might come again, but laughter would help.

Then she made a huge decision. "When you have the chance, I'd like to rearrange the living room. But only when you have time."

He nodded. "That's what I have help for. Two of us will come over tomorrow or the next day and make quick work of it. I'll call to let you know. In the meantime, if you can, think about how you'd like to reorder the room."

That wouldn't be easy, but she had to do it. She couldn't keep living in two rooms.

"I will," she answered, as much of a promise to herself as to him.

Then he startled her.

Mitch asked, "Want to come riding with me some morning?"

MITCH THOUGHT SHE was making remarkable progress all of a sudden. He hoped to help keep her going in this direction. He feared her response, and that she would shy away from any more change.

She used to love riding the range on horseback. She'd often mentioned how peaceful it was, how beautiful to be out in the pasture with the sheep. But it might reawaken the very sorrow she was trying to edge past.

Then she astonished him. "I'd really like that. I hated giving up the horses."

And everything else, he thought. The dream, the sheep, the hired hands. The horses.

He'd watched as the financial burdens had become too much for her and had been glad that he was able to take over the flock of sheep. He'd always wanted to try his hand at sheep. Now he had a good excuse to go ahead.

He was grateful he didn't have to watch her struggle to try to do the job alone. It was truly a bigger job than one person could handle. He'd figured she wouldn't be receptive to the idea of him sending help over.

Two birds with one stone. He'd gained something he wanted and she'd been relieved of a huge burden. The latter seemed the most important to him, but he never wanted her to guess that.

Just like he didn't want anyone in the county to know he'd bought her flock. He didn't want people to think he'd taken advantage of the widow. Or worse, that he'd saved her. Yeah, he'd had mixed feelings about doing it. She deserved her pride. Let them all think she was making it, that the shepherds were hers.

He'd encouraged her enough about moving forward for one day. He wondered what she'd change her mind about it.

Well, he couldn't do a damn thing about that, except keep trying gently.

He cared about this woman. A great deal.

Rising, he promised he'd come over in the morning with a couple of mounts, then left quickly so as not to give her time to make excuses.

He just hoped she'd sleep better tonight.

As ugly as the killing of the ewe had been, he couldn't think of a reason why anyone would do it maliciously.

Well, except for using a ewe for target practice.

That was pretty bad, but not likely threatening.

Chapter Four

Fog blanketed the world in the early morning. The fog was surprising in a place where dryness lowered the humidity until it was next to nothing.

Maybe an unexpected cloud was moving in.

Mitch sat on his porch, his booted feet up on the rail, and waited for Bill to arrive. Lila had provided him with an insulated carafe of coffee and a plate full of homemade blueberry muffins. That woman loved to bake and if he wasn't careful she'd add a few unwanted pounds to his frame. Even with hard physical labor, that was always possible.

She mothered him. He smiled faintly into his coffee mug and decided that mothering was a sign she liked working here. She could have made his life hell by reducing her cooking to basics, claiming she had enough to do keeping up with a bachelor's house.

Not Lila. Never a complaint. Well, he *did* try not to ask too much but still. The woman was a workhorse, not only taking care of him but making sure his hired hands and his shepherds were fed.

Those lunch pails were always welcome out on the range, and if his men were closer, all they had to do was run by the kitchen. His shepherds had a specific list of staples they preferred. Things that wouldn't spoil. Those men were pretty much self-reliant.

As he waited for the fog to burn off, he enjoyed watching wisps of it moving slightly on stirring air. Eventually a morning breeze would sweep it away if the sun didn't dry it out.

Despite his plans to ride with Grace that morning, he wouldn't have minded a bit of rain. Rain was *always* welcome out here, greening the pastures and rangeland. Helping to fill ponds and keep creeks running. Most of his neighbors were getting to the point of needing it desperately.

He was blessed in his land and he knew it. John and Grace were similarly blessed, so he understood why that industrial stock company had wanted to buy them out.

He wondered if Grace had begun to think that might be a good idea after the ewe's killing. But no, Grace had a stiff backbone and she'd lost enough already. He'd be floored if such a thought even crossed her mind.

He poured more hot coffee and succumbed to a second muffin. Lila appeared, wiping her hands on her apron, to ask if he needed anything else before she started the eggs and bacon.

"Dang it, Lila, you'll kill me with kindness."

She chuckled, her large bosom shaking slightly. "A hardworking man needs good food. And them muffins ain't that bad for you. No sugar."

He looked at the plate. "Really?"

"I've been cheating on that the whole time and you never noticed." She winked at him. "Tomorrow maybe banana bread."

He groaned and she laughed as she returned indoors.

Grace had dealt with some of her stress by baking,

but it sounded like a slightly irritating task for her. The dough wouldn't rise because the house was too chilly?

The things he didn't know.

Bill should arrive soon, Lila would most likely give him muffins and cook him breakfast, as well. He'd wondered lately if Bill and Lila were taking a shine to each other. They were both in their early forties and seemed to like hard work. A starting point. Lila's cooking could only help.

He grinned, trying not to open a muffin-filled mouth.

The ewe kept bursting into his thoughts, however. He wanted to talk with Zeke and Rod again, get them to be more specific about what had been happening just before the shooting. It still struck him as odd that the sheep had scattered that way. Zeke hadn't looked very happy about it.

Yeah, he needed to get a herding dog. Maybe he'd ask Grace to go with him to find one with enough instinct for Zeke and Rod to finish the training.

Ransom Laird, a guy with a mega flock of sheep, might be able to point him in the right direction. Or Cadell Marcus, the K-9 trainer. Or even the vet, Mike Windwalker.

He and Mike got along pretty well, which was good, because cattle often needed attention, as did sheep. Nonranchers seemed to think you could just put them out on the land and they'd take care of themselves.

Nope. They needed vaccinations, various kinds of treatments, and his cows sometimes had female problems. Not just a "sow them then reap them" kind of business at all. Most animals needed a bit of TLC occasionally.

He often felt he had a bit of connection with his cattle, particularly the cows. The steers, on the other hand, he tried not to get too close to, because they'd be off to market. A reality of his life and not one that especially pleased him. Necessity drove him.

The sheep, however, could be shorn every spring and go back to grazing and making lambs. Well, except for the rams. They could get difficult during breeding season and he needed to keep an eye on them because they'd get into some amazing fights. They needed to be separated from the ewes after they bred, and care had to be taken that they weren't alone. Sheep, like humans, didn't handle isolation very well.

When the lambs were weaned, the ewes could be milked, a surprising source of income.

Sometimes he thought he'd be better off just selling off his cattle and going full-time to raising sheep.

When he considered how sheep needed the company of other sheep, his thoughts turned to Grace. She couldn't indefinitely live alone and avoid social contact. He sometimes was surprised that she'd made it this long.

Before he could delve into his feelings about Grace, Lila called him to breakfast. When he stepped inside, delicious aromas reached him. Nothing like the scent of frying bacon.

He was halfway through his breakfast when Bill showed up. Lila had evidently been anticipating his arrival, because she had his bacon cooked and the eggs already beaten.

Mitch smothered another smile.

"What do you need today, boss?" Bill asked as he tucked in.

"Help me get the horse trailer hooked up, and two horses saddled. I'm going to take Grace Hall riding."

Bill nodded. "Good for her."

"I hope so."

Bill looked up from his plate. "I keep thinking about that ewe. Something ain't right."

"I agree. But what?"

"Danged if I know. I'm thinking Miz Grace shouldn't be all alone out there. I could send Jack or Jeff to keep an eye out from time to time."

"Just make sure she's not aware of it."

Bill grinned. "That one's as prickly as a pear cactus."

Mitch answered drily. "You've noticed."

"Hard not to. After her man died, she chased me off when I hung around a bit to keep an eye out on matters. Furious that I might believe she needed help."

"That's Grace all right."

After breakfast, he and Bill headed out to the barn. The horses had been groomed just last night and were showing signs of restiveness. They needed to be out.

"Maybe corral a little later," Mitch suggested. "A run in the sun would do them good."

"That it would," Bill agreed.

When they'd hooked up the horse trailer, they saddled two mares and led them aboard. Mitch preferred mares for their endurance.

Once the mares were secure, Mitch set out for Grace's house. The last of the fog had begun to burn off, although the sky was getting clouded. Rain, Mitch hoped. Just a little.

Or a lot. But not when he and Grace were riding. He wondered if she'd go out to the flock to meet up with Zeke and Rod. It was worth a try.

When he pulled up in front of her house, the sky started to darken a bit. Not good for riding.

A gust of wind buffeted him, bringing stinging dust with it. The temperature had dropped just since he'd set out.

Grace came out onto the porch to greet him. She even smiled. "Bad day for a ride?"

"Maybe. I suggest we ride a little anyway. If something starts blowing up, we'll head back, but I've got two mares who are saddled and won't be very happy if they don't get out to stretch their legs."

That caused a laugh to escape her, a delightful sound. He'd been missing it.

She was dressed for the ride, wearing cowboy boots, jeans and a light jacket, her black hair caught back in some kind of elastic thing. What he didn't know about women's clothing would probably fill a book.

The horses never liked backing out of the trailer. They performed the act on pure trust, like jumping a fence they couldn't see when they got too close. They knew Mitch and backed down the ramp one at a time, seeming to know he wouldn't let them stumble.

He gave the reins to Grace to hold while he closed the trailer.

"Mount up," he said and paused a minute to watch her swing upward into the saddle easily. He didn't mind the view of her bottom, either. He wondered if that was disloyal to John, then decided not. Grace was a free woman now.

Daisy sidled a bit with her signature prance as she felt Grace's weight and the promise of a ride to come. Dolly responded almost the same way when Mitch mounted.

The weather was still okay, and from Grace's response on the porch, Mitch believed she was looking forward to this as much as the horses.

Or as much as him.

TWO MEN WATCHED through binoculars as Grace and Mitch passed through a gate and struck out for the range.

"Well, hell," Larry said to Carl. Both men looked scruffy, their clothes a bit dirty because they didn't have enough to change very often. Their beards were also a few days past the two-day unshaven look that was so popular. Larry still had a few biscuit crumbs stuck to his chin.

"What do you think it means?" Carl asked.

"What do *you* think?" Larry said sarcastically.

Carl shook his head. "That Mitch guy hasn't been spending that much time with the woman. This might be just neighborly."

"We should be so lucky," muttered Larry. "This was supposed to be easy."

"If shooting that ewe didn't scare the woman, we need to come up with something better."

"She's not going to be as easy to scare if that guy is living in her pocket now."

They took another look through their binoculars. Magnification made the riders appear much closer than they were. There were too many glances from the guy to the gal to please Larry, who tended to be pessimistic about most things.

"Hell's bells," he said, more emphatically.

"Oh, take it easy," Carl retorted. "One horseback ride doesn't mean he's moving in with her. We can still frighten her, regardless."

"Yeah? How?"

Carl rolled onto his back, hating the way the brush poked at him. "Well, there's fire. Since killing a sheep didn't upset her very much, we maybe need to get stronger."

"We've got limits on us," Larry responded. "The boss doesn't want us to go too far."

"No murder. Well, there's a lot we can do short of that. Let me think."

Carl didn't think fast. He knew that. Thinking wasn't his strength. His strength had been herding cattle. Repairing fences. Riding a fence line to check for breaks. Long nights under the stars, listening to the restless stirrings of hooved feet, gentle lows as the cattle spoke to each other in their indecipherable language. Yeah, he thought of them as talking.

He'd loved that life. The current situation with the beef market had cost him the only thing he loved: being a cowboy.

"You know them shepherds?" he asked presently.

"What about them?"

"Furriners. Taking our jobs. Come all the way from Portugal instead of people hiring hardworking Americans."

"Yeah," Larry answered. It ticked him off, too. "But we ain't shepherds, Carl."

"What difference does that make? It's herding animals, right?"

"Yeah," Larry agreed after a bit. "Looks easier than herding damn cattle, too."

"So what's she need them damn Port-a-gees for?"

Larry thought about that. Good question. "No killing," he said.

"I know, I know. But we can make them look so damn stupid they get fired."

"How's that going to scare the woman into leaving?"

"Cuz she can't run the place alone."

Larry thought about that, too. "It'd make me happy, but don't mean the woman will up and leave."

"I don't see why we can't work this deal for us."

Larry nodded, turning over to stare up at the graying sky. "We're gonna get wet. I wanna think anyway."

Together they rose and trudged back to their camp, an army surplus tent and a couple of sleeping bags that had seen better days. Bedrolls. They'd just about worn them out over the years.

As much as the boss wanted that ranch, the two of them wanted to have jobs sleeping under the stars again.

It was enough motivation for them, and the cash they'd been promised only made it better.

Yeah. Now they had to figure out how to get it done.

GRACE HAD EXPECTED to be saddened by the ride, had expected to recall the many times she'd ridden like this with John. That didn't happen.

Riding beside Mitch had shifted everything somehow. The sun, the breeze, the movements of the horse beneath her, the creak of saddle leather… Perfection. A fine day, with great companionship.

They surmounted a rise and saw the flock in the dip beneath them. Grace reined in and watched. She and John had worked so hard on that flock, but without a hired hand, without John, she simply hadn't been able to do it by herself. She'd begun to lose sheep.

She'd run into the wall of her own limitations. Perhaps she needed to find something that expanded her limits, to remind her that she was capable, not a failure.

Mitch, too, seemed to be enjoying the ride. "I miss the time I used to spend on the range herding."

"Why would you do it less?"

He looked at her with a rueful smile. "Because some things have to give way to being reasonably successful in this business. In any business, I suppose. I'm making decisions that I didn't use to have to, for one thing. Have to organize more for so much livestock. Tend to more medical problems. Round and round. Hell, everything is taking more time."

"I hadn't thought about that."

"Your flock is growing. You and John used to spend nights out here protecting lambs from coyotes. Now it takes four of us. Not a lot of time for riding."

She nodded, knowing he was right. Wouldn't John have been pleased to see how the flock had grown? Mitch's flock now.

She sighed, and Daisy sidled beneath her.

"What?" Mitch asked.

"Just thinking of what might have been. Pointless now. You're doing a great job taking care of the sheep."

"I've had to learn a lot. Intensive course."

She looked away from the flock toward him. "John and I learned the hard way."

Mitch shook his head. "You guys were doing pretty well."

"How are your shepherds doing? And why from Portugal?"

He shrugged. "Talking to other people who raise sheep, I was told that a lot of Portuguese shepherds are well practiced with tending flocks. Better than someone we'd have to train here. I took the advice, and so far I've been really pleased. I mean these guys rarely leave the flock, and if they do it's one at a time. I had cowhands who were less conscientious."

She'd had some experience with that.

"Wanna go down and meet them?"

She did. Together they rode down from the rise toward the flock who had gathered close, although not in a knot. She loved seeing them, their mostly gentle ways, the beauty of their now shorn wool, although that would be growing back soon enough.

Mitch spoke. "I had some little kids out here last spring. One girl, about three, pointed and said, *'Blankies!'* I believe she meant blankets, and I still think of it."

"That's adorable!"

"I thought so. Through the eyes of a child the world becomes a magical place. Have you ever wished you could regain that sense of wonder?"

"Sometimes. Adulthood kind of squashes it."

"Maybe, but it doesn't have to kill it."

Didn't it? Responsibilities took over, ugly things happened, the wonder and magic vanished, left to youngsters who could still feel it. That was one of the things she'd enjoyed about teaching, how the younger kids could get so excited about little things. That mostly disappeared with the assumed worldliness of middle school, but until then, life was bright, shiny and new.

She doubted she'd ever experience that again. Life had carved it out of her.

But she could still enjoy approaching the flock, watching the two shepherds who still used crooks. She'd never expected to see that.

The flock parted to let their horses through, and the two men approached with smiles.

"Something up, boss?" asked one of them, a swarthy man with shaggy hair. The other man looked like his brother.

"Nothing, Zeke. I just wanted to show Miss Grace the flock."

Zeke smiled her way. "They're doing well," he said

with an accent, but not so much Grace couldn't understand him.

Mitch said, "I've been thinking about that sheep dog you want."

The other man drew closer. "Yes," Zeke said excitedly. "Good protection against the coyotes. Good way to keep the sheep moving where we want them."

"When do you want it?" Mitch asked. "It might take some time. And what exactly are you looking for?"

The two men spoke to each other in Portuguese.

Zeke faced them finally. "We use Komondors at home, but there are good breeds more easy to find here. Australian shepherds. Border collie. Many more, I think."

"Probably. About the training…"

Rod bobbed his head and spoke in Portuguese again. Zeke translated. "One dog part-trained. We can make better. Then puppies."

"Puppies?" Grace asked, surprised.

"Puppies learn from older dogs. Easy."

Grace hadn't considered that. An interesting idea.

Mitch spoke. "So once you get an older dog trained to your liking, puppies can just learn. How many puppies?"

"One or two," Zeke said. "Two are better. Two dogs herd better."

"I'll definitely see what I can do. After that ewe was killed… You still don't know why she left the flock?"

Zeke shook his head. "Sheep run all over. Don't do that 'cept wolf or coyote gets in flock. No wolf, no coyote."

Mitch lowered his head, pondering. "It's so strange. Please keep thinking about it. Something had to make those sheep run like that."

Grace spoke again. "Snake?" she suggested.

"Nighttime," Mitch answered. "Snakes don't move fast at all when it's cold. Zeke and Rod would have found it."

Zeke nodded emphatically. "No snake."

After a few more minutes of casual conversation, she and Mitch turned their mounts away, heading back up the rise. "So you're going to get herding dogs?"

"That ewe made me nervous. I guess I really need to think about it, expense be damned. The flock is getting so big now that I doubt Zeke and Rod could round them up easily if they scatter."

"True," she answered, "but it's still a mystery."

"Yup. And maybe we're both worrying too much. Shouldn't happen again, but if it does, then we can worry."

That made sense to Grace, much as she'd like an answer. It wasn't easy to say, *Oh, well*, about something like that, but right now it would be wise to let go. Worrying never got a person any closer to answers. It just used up time and energy.

"It won't happen again," Mitch said.

"You sound more determined than convinced."

He laughed.

Grace gave herself over to the pleasure of swaying in the saddle. She'd missed this. The sun had risen high enough that she felt its touch prickling her back despite the slowly darkening cloud that still moved in. She unzipped her jacket, planning to remove it but quickly felt the remaining nighttime chill in the air. Later, then.

Mitch spoke as they approached a small copse of trees that grew beside a creek. "How's a picnic sound?"

She looked at him. "Wouldn't that take a lot of time?"

He shook his head. "Whatever makes you think Lila

would let me head out without a full saddlebag of food? I don't have to make it, just eat it."

It was her turn to laugh, this time more easily. "Sure," she said.

"I know she didn't give me peanut butter sandwiches."

"Hey, what makes you think I'm opposed to peanut butter?"

He flashed a grin. "You don't know Lila."

They dismounted under the trees. The breeze was freshening, and the brief visit from the sun was over. Clouds were thickening, more than earlier, and hanging low.

"We might have just enough time," Mitch remarked. "It's beginning to look like we're in for more than a light rain."

She agreed, turning to look out over the range toward the mountains. Those clouds seemed to be sinking as they crested the high altitude, possibly heavy with their burden.

She wondered if it would hold off until they got back, then realized she didn't care. It had been a long time since she'd been out in the rain, growing wet and cold. Right then it seemed like a great prospect.

She turned around again and saw that Mitch had spread a blanket and was putting out plastic containers and paper plates secured by real silverware.

"What did Lila do? Send an entire restaurant?"

"Well, she knew I was going to have company." He winked. "I'm sure there's something for every taste."

"I'm not picky," she protested.

"Maybe it's high time you were. Anyway, sit down and let's enjoy as much of this feast as Mother Nature will allow."

It certainly was a feast, Grace thought as she watched him open containers. Fresh-made potato salad. Sandwiches thick with roast beef and cheese. More sandwiches with ham. A container of carrot sticks. A dessert that looked yummy enough to eat by itself. A thermos of coffee and several bottles of water.

"This could feed an army!" she exclaimed.

"Never too little from Lila, not anymore. What would you like?"

She settled on a ham sandwich and a small spoonful of potato salad along with carrot sticks.

"Don't be afraid to ask for more," Mitch said. "The less I bring home with me, the less trouble I'll be in."

She had a hard time imagining Mitch in trouble with anyone.

After Grace had eaten a bit, she said, "Everything's so fresh!"

"That's Lila. She believes in keeping a roast in the fridge and baked ham. And don't talk to her about store-bought potato salad."

"I'm surprised she doesn't make her own salami."

Mitch held up a hand. "Don't give her any ideas."

Grace smiled. She was enjoying this morning. She'd feared it might awaken memories of John, but it hadn't. Not really. They'd spent a lot of time out here on horseback, but this was somehow different. She leaned back on an elbow as she finished her sandwich.

Looking up, she saw the clouds had swallowed the whole sky. "We don't have much time," she remarked.

He followed her gaze and nodded. "Nope. I'll start packing up while you finish your sandwich."

She watched him seal the containers and slip them

with practiced ease into his saddlebags. She felt the first icy drops of rain as she stood while he folded the blanket.

"Let's go," he said. "With any luck we'll make it to your place before the deluge."

A deluge sounded good. A dark, rainy day, a perfect day to be indoors. Wrapped in warmth and snuggly clothes. Yeah, she could enjoy that.

They didn't follow an easy pace as they made their way toward her house. The horses seemed glad to cut loose and break into a full gallop. The wind blowing through Grace's hair felt refreshing, even as it grew damper.

The day had begun to turn wild, and so did she. Soon she wanted to grin into the teeth of the storm. It had been so very long since she'd allowed herself to be this free.

The skies opened up just after they passed through the fence to her driveway. Another couple of hundred feet took them to her barn. Mitch jumped down to open the door and Grace rode through. He followed behind with his mount.

Luckily, Grace hadn't thrown away much when she gave up her own horses. The girls, as Mitch called them, stomped and snorted, possibly because they could still smell the previous occupants. Or maybe they were getting cold.

She helped Mitch remove the saddles—she could still do that!—and place them on the padded sawhorses. Then came the comb and towels to dry them as much as possible, followed by blankets.

Daisy and Dolly settled quickly in the stalls.

"I've got some hay in the loft," Grace said. "I don't know if it's still good for them. And a bag of oats in the back."

"I'll check."

Mitch ascended the ladder at a quick pace, and soon forkfuls of hay began to fall.

"So it's still good?" she called up.

"I wouldn't be pitching it down if it wasn't."

She knew exactly what to do with it. She pitched hay into the stalls and more into their feeding troughs. Daisy and Dolly appeared quite happy with their improved circumstances. Using her muscles this way brought a sense of contentment to Grace. She might be stiff later, but that was okay.

She'd missed so much over the last two years.

The time arrived to dash into the house even though Noah's flood continued to pour. Mitch dug out an old tarp she'd nearly forgotten and threw it over them. They ran huddled together to the front porch and shed the tarp to stare at a gray curtain of rain.

"Can't see a thing," she remarked. The warmth from caring for the horses was rapidly diminishing.

"Let's go inside," she said. "I don't know about you, but I'm starting to freeze. How are you going to dry off?"

He shrugged. "If you don't mind, a towel or two will be enough. I'm used to this."

Once she'd been used to it, too. Not anymore.

She dashed to her bedroom, reluctant to keep him waiting out there cold and wet. It would be inhospitable, even more so after the morning he'd spent with her.

She returned wearing dry jeans, a heavy shirt and socks. In her arms she carried the towels he'd asked for, as well as a spare comforter. "You're not going anywhere soon," she remarked.

"I could call one of the guys to come get me. Leave the horses here for a bit."

Astonishingly, her stomach plunged. "In a hurry to go?"

He shook his head as he used the towels to get rid of the worst soaking, then wrapped the comforter around his shoulder. "No rush," he answered. "But I left the bottle of coffee out in the barn with my saddlebags."

"Well, heck," she said, placing her hand on her hip. "I've been known to make a pot. I may even know how to do it."

"That's not what I meant. I don't want to impose."

"Damn it, Mitch, stop worrying about that. You just showed me a wonderful morning. How could I feel imposed on? You need to warm up." She tilted her head a bit. "Come to think of it, so do I."

That pulled a smile from him as she waved him to a chair and he sat, still wrapped in the comforter, a Southwest pattern she'd always liked.

The minutes ticked between them in silence, as if they couldn't find a safe thing to say, as if casual conversation seemed pointless.

Finally Mitch said, "I'd like to leave Dolly and Daisy with you for a few days, if you don't mind."

She brought the carafe and two mugs to the table. "Why?" she asked simply.

"I think they'd like a few days of TLC rather than being workhorses most of the time. You could let them out in your corral when the mud dries a bit. Now, I *know* they'd like that, running around without a saddle."

She nodded, smiling faintly. "I guess they would."

"I'll come over to help care for them. Clean hooves, pitch hay, muck out stalls. That kind of thing."

She waited, hoping there'd be more but unsure what that might be. Then it occurred to her that he was offer-

ing her something to do besides mope around this house
and think about all she'd lost.

She loved horses. She loved everything about them.
It would be nice to have them around again, for however
little or long Mitch wanted. He couldn't do without them
indefinitely, but a few days maybe? She liked that idea.

"I'd be happy to keep them here. As long as you want.
I miss horses."

He nodded. "Most of us would. Anyway, I'd appreciate the help."

Perhaps he was seeking an additional reason to come
over. The thought danced through her pleasurably. Mitch
had always been there for her. Mostly he'd given her
space. He didn't tread on her healing and grief.

Fat lot of healing she'd done. Plus it would definitely
be nice to see more of Mitch.

"It's a sealed deal," she told him. Now all she had to
wonder was just how much she'd agreed to, then decided
there was no point in worrying about it.

Mitch would be coming over every day. She could
deal with it.

AN HOUR LATER, Mitch asked Bill to have someone to
come get him. He wanted to leave his truck and horse
trailer here for ease of a return journey with his mares.
Or in case Grace needed to take the horses somewhere
for some reason. He didn't want to leave her high and
dry.

Rain still poured in sheets, making the driveways a
bit hazardous even with the gravel. "Do me a favor," he
said to Bill. "Don't get stuck."

Bill laughed. "You still got them two horses. They
can pull."

"Not if I can help it. Mind yourself."

Bill laughed again.

Typical of Bill to laugh, Mitch thought as he disconnected. Bill wasn't just a handyman and range boss. This country was bred into his blood.

"The creeks are going to be running high after this," he remarked to Grace. "Not too high, I hope."

"Me, too."

Mitch handed her the towels and comforter. "Sorry for the laundry. When Bill gets here I'll grab my saddlebags. Lila will be wanting her precious containers back."

"Precious?" Grace asked.

"Don't let one of them disappear. The wrath of a dragon."

He left Grace smiling and went out to the porch to wait for Bill.

It had been a good day. Not only had Grace seemed to have enjoyed their ride and picnic, but she appeared delighted by having horses around again.

The way to a man's heart might be through his stomach, but the way to a woman's was through a horse.

The thought still had him grinning when Bill pulled up. In the four-wheel. Of course. They drove over to the barn so Mitch could get the all-important containers, then headed back to his ranch.

He never felt the eyes trained on him. Never thought the sheep hadn't been the end of what was going on.

It was all so senseless he had no real reason to suspect anything else.

Except part of him didn't quite believe that.

FROM THE FAR side of the road and protection of brush, Carl and Larry watched.

"Well, hot damn," said Carl to Larry. "The guy's leaving."

"It's effing wet out here. And still daylight. Who cares the man is leaving? No use to us."

"Later, after dark, it might be."

"Not if it's raining like this. All we'd do is leave footprints."

Carl couldn't argue. He sighed and pulled his poncho hood tighter around his face. "We'll think of something."

"We have to. The boss ain't happy."

Carl shook his head. "No kidding. You'da thought the sheep would be enough to scare a widow off. Nobody around to help her."

"That rancher ain't too far away."

"Far enough. Eff it. I want a fire, something hot to eat and coffee."

"How you gonna build a fire?" Larry pointed to the rivulets running down the slope beneath them.

"Time to break out the tent. I brought a surprise in the back of that side-by-side."

"Yeah?" Larry looked interested. "What's that?"

"A propane camp stove, idiot."

Larry sat up. "Guide me to it."

"I figure our brains will work better when we ain't starving."

"And when we warm up a bit. Let's go."

Pitching a tent wasn't unusual for either of them. Line shacks were practically a thing of the past, so they had that basic army surplus tent, heavier than they would have liked, but sufficient. Damn, the thing was so old it still had wooden pegs.

However, inside it was dry and, with the front flaps open, safe to turn on the stove. They set it up on its short stand, then turned on the blue flame. The heat was a draw all by itself. The dried food they'd brought would heat up in a little of that rainwater. They set a couple of tin pans outside to collect it, along with their aluminum coffeepot.

Neither of them had any difficulty with the old-fashioned utensils. The coffeepot might be banged and dented but could still perk the coffee.

"One advantage to this damn rain," Larry remarked. "We don't have to carry water from a stream."

That pulled a chuckle out of Carl. "Got that right, man."

When they'd at last drunk plenty of coffee and filled their guts with reconstituted beef and potatoes, they leaned back to smoke a cigarette. A bit of a challenge given how damp everything was, but the stove helped. They left one burner lighted for the heat it provided.

"Got no ideas," Larry eventually said.

"Keep thinking, man. After this rain stops, some things'll be easier."

"Mebbe."

Wisps of smoke rose to the top of the tent. Some even twisted their way out the open flap.

Carl spoke. "Shouldn't be too hard to scare that widow woman off."

"Seems like that's what we thought when we took this job. Now shut up and think."

Both reached for the pack of cigarettes at the same time. For once they laughed.

Yeah, they weren't stupid, Carl thought. They'd come up with something.

STRANGELY, THE RAIN gave Grace a sense of security in a different way. Sheets of falling water blocked the world out completely.

In her bedroom there was an old-fashioned chaise that she'd inherited from her mother. Curled up on it with a blanket across her legs, she opened the newest novel she'd ordered online. She still liked printed books, most especially hardcovers.

Only one page in, she realized she wasn't focused on it. Her thoughts kept trailing back to Mitch, to the wonderful morning he'd shown her. He'd given her back good memories of riding on the range. And the picnic. She and John had sometimes done that, but nothing quite so nice and relaxed. Those picnics had always been a bit rushed because of all the work they needed to do.

She liked that this had been different. Mitch's attention had been entirely focused on her, not on some next task that awaited. The pressure wasn't there.

Of course, Mitch's life couldn't be like that all the time, considering what a huge ranch he ran, but he'd spared her the time anyway.

He'd made her feel special.

What was more, he'd reminded her that there could be hours without unending pressure. Without a weight on the shoulders. As her and John's flock had grown, so had the workload. Success carried its own price. She suddenly was glad to be free of it. In the early days it had been a romantic adventure, building their lives, making plans, visualizing the future.

At some point responsibility had edged most of the romantic dreams out and had left reality. She didn't regret it, but, well, today had been a nice change. More like the early days.

Tucking her knees up under her chin, her book forgotten, Grace ran back through her memory. She wouldn't have traded it, not any of it, if that would have meant giving up John.

But was it so wrong to realize the degree of freedom she had now?

Her thoughts turned back to Mitch, as if tethered to him by a spring.

A good-looking man. A capable man. A very kind man. One who'd been willing to devote a chunk of his day to making her smile and feel happy.

Hugging her knees, she smiled again. Mitch was breaking through the cocoon that had swallowed her for so long. That was a positive thing, right?

MITCH RECALLED HIS morning with Grace pleasurably. It had been enjoyable, if nothing fancy. He hoped he was right to think that he'd drawn her out a bit. Damn, he'd been worrying about that woman since John had died.

John had been a close friend, but so had Grace. Those winter evenings stretched out before the fire, shooting the breeze, playing cards, talking about similar problems that arose from raising stock. They'd shared a lot.

But Mitch's secret, one he'd almost buried successfully, was his attraction to Grace. She had a way of smiling that could light up her face, a laugh that rang on the air almost like a bell. A serious face that caused her brow to knit. An anger that occasionally sparked in her blue eyes.

What had caused him to bury his response to her as a woman had been the glow on her face almost every time she looked at John.

He wondered if John had truly realized how fortunate he was. He hoped so. Grace had deserved his appreciation and love.

For all she said otherwise, Mitch still suspected she'd given up a lot for John. For love.

Grace had no background in farming or ranching. The daughter of a small-town family in Maryland, she'd had no connection with life out here on the rangeland of Wyoming. Then, upon graduating with her degrees, she'd been employed to teach at the reservation for two years. Next thing, she'd taken a job here in Conard City.

He'd never asked about her time teaching on the reservation, and she'd never volunteered much. He suspected she'd run into a lot of pain there.

Why wouldn't she? It was not as if he hadn't had the opportunity visit the rez. Some tribes had done well over the last couple of decades, but they had to be on a road to draw traffic, at a good destination. Reachable. Up north, here on the prairies, everything seemed to be out of the way to everyone except long-haul truckers.

The forgotten people on the forgotten lands. Gutted by European invasion, then gutted by the way they'd been treated for so long. Trying to put themselves back together after they'd been stripped of almost their entire way of life.

Yeah, he knew, and could only imagine some of the sorrow that had followed Grace from that job.

Two years had probably been enough for her. Surrounded by so much sorrow...a whirlpool that sucked you in.

He wondered if her parents were still alive. Probably not, given that she never spoke of them, they never came to visit her even in the time since John's death. All alone in every respect.

Cripes, he had cousins within a couple of days' travel time. Not the closest family, but close enough they kept in touch, mostly by email. His mother's alcoholism had somehow stunted the family unity that others had. Then her liver had killed her and his father hadn't been far behind. Grief? Or had his father worked himself to death? This operation certainly hadn't been prosperous until after Mitch took over.

He wondered if he could get Grace to talk about herself more. Maybe let her question him beyond the casual talk that had filled most of their conversations over the years. They needed to establish a connection somehow.

Or was that just his own need?

Hell. Standing on his porch he watched the continuing deluge and wondered how to occupy himself with something besides bookkeeping.

Delightful smells had begun to seep through the screen door behind him. He guessed Lila was dealing with the dreary day by cooking up a storm.

The image made him laugh. *Cooking up a storm?* Hah!

He wondered how Zeke and Rod were doing out there amid this, then decided it was a waste of his time. Those two seemed utterly self-sufficient even in the dead of winter.

Unlike most ranch hands they didn't take a Friday night to go get into some trouble at a roadhouse. Every month he took their pay to a large bank. Maybe to save it for a rainy day. Maybe to send it back to their families. None of his business.

There was so much he didn't know about the people in his life. Like Lila. She'd taken this job after leaving a ranch over near Boise. After a divorce that he suspected had been bitter. Maybe the guy had been abusive. She'd sure come a long way to escape.

He sighed. He could go pitch out some stalls. Check the condition of tack. Look for some repairs to do.

His problem was that Bill and the others had probably dealt with all that. They were making him a superfluity in his own life. He'd better watch it or he'd become one of those guys who sat behind a desk for the rest of his days.

The thought amused him. He'd never be that guy. Nope, when this weather cleared, he'd be back out on the range. Not even three hired hands could take care of everything now that his herd had grown so much.

Reluctantly, he went inside to his office. Paperwork always waited. He hated the never-ending task but it had to be done.

Grace trailed along with him. As did the dead ewe. He absolutely preferred thinking about Grace.

The rare smile he'd seen on her face.

The rain let up during the late afternoon. Bill, Jack and Jeff trailed in, leaving sodden ponchos and boots on the porch.

"Hey, Miz Lila," Jack said. "Thanks for the dinner invitation."

Lila shook her head. "Seems stupid the three of you eating out in the bunkhouse on a day like this. I was in a cooking mood anyway."

Mitch watched with a faint smile as Lila fussed over all three of them, seating them at the big farm table, insisting on serving them herself.

Yep, Mitch thought, there was a special spark between Lila and Bill. Next thing he knew, she'd be cooking in the bunkhouse instead of in here.

Not that he thought she'd willingly part with all the fancy cooking gear she'd accumulated. Never had Mitch thought he'd become familiar with catalog stores that catered to chefs, but he had. If she mentioned she wanted something, Mitch went hunting for the best. Copper clad pots hung from a rack overhead. A wooden block was filled with every expensive knife made. Only the best. Now, lately, Lila had been talking about a magnetic rack for those knives. He guessed he'd better look for that soon.

He suspected she watched cooking shows on the TV in her room.

The conversation didn't remain lighthearted for long.

"That ewe?" Bill said. "We been talking."

Mitch looked up from his chicken piccata. "Yeah?"

"Yeah," said Bill. "Funny thing, that."

Mitch didn't think he meant funny as in humorous. "Any ideas?"

The three men exchanged looks.

Jeff answered. "Feels like a message."

Mitch stiffened. "Why?"

"Because it don't make no sense," Jack answered. "None. Middle of nowhere. No other such things anywhere."

Jeff nodded. "Feels directed."

Mitch put his fork down, and Lila began fussing.

"You three! Let the man eat his meal before you go getting him all upset."

Mitch shook his head. "It's okay, Lila. I'm ready to hear anything about that ewe because it's bothering me, too."

"Like anybody could know," she sniffed but went back to checking something in the oven.

"Nothing else makes any sense," Bill said. "Question

is who's sending a message and who they're sending it to. Awful close to Miz Grace's place."

Yeah, it was. That wouldn't stop nagging him even though he couldn't think of a passable excuse why anyone would want to frighten Grace. A more inoffensive woman had never lived, and she'd barely been off that ranch in two years. Had she bumped someone at the grocery with a shopping cart? He couldn't imagine she'd done anything worse.

"Give me a reason," Mitch said. "One good reason why anyone would want to upset Grace."

The three other men exchanged looks. Bill, his range boss, answered. "Because they think she hired them two Portuguese shepherds?"

Mitch sat up straighter, his dinner forgotten. Could someone really be so disturbed by that? Just two men, not an invasion of foreign workers. Far from it.

Equally disturbing was the possibility that his insistence on keeping the sale of her sheep private could have opened her to so much anger.

"Just spitballing," Bill said after a bit. "Sounds crazy even to me."

Mitch nodded. Aware of Lila's disapproving gaze, he resumed eating. After another couple of mouthfuls, he said, "You guys are keeping an eye out her way, right?"

"Much as we can," Jeff answered. "Don't seem like much going on over there."

"I hope not. I left Daisy and Dolly over there with her, along with my truck and trailer. Just in case. I'm planning to ride over and clean out stalls for her. Maintenance."

"We can do that, boss," Jeff replied.

"Let me do it at least the first few times. She doesn't

really know you guys and I want her to feel comfortable. I'll introduce you more over the next couple of days."

The men seemed content with that and dinner continued without any more unpleasantness discussed. They talked about the cattle, mostly, how well they were fattening. Soon enough some steers would be off to market.

Which reminded him to check the prices at the stockyards. That could have a big impact on whether he chose to ship.

Business must go on, or there'd be five other people looking for work.

Chapter Five

Grace woke in the morning to sunshine. After breakfast, she decided to go out to the barn to check on the horses. The idea filled her with pleasure.

She'd missed having horses. Even missed their scents and the way they made the barn smell. Their neighs and their whinnies, their hooves clomping on wood and hay. Everything about them, including the work of caring for them.

Unfortunately, the ground was still muddy. Not an ideal time to let them out into the paddock. She didn't want their hooves to soften up. In the meantime, she could curry them after cleaning their stalls and laying fresh hay.

She wore her rubber Wellingtons rather than her work boots and was soon glad as the mud grabbed at her feet and splattered her lower legs. Practically time for hip waders, she thought with amusement.

Inside the dark barn, she turned on the work lights, glad to see none had burned out from neglect or age. The horses nickered as soon as she stepped inside, then Daisy neighed and tossed her head.

Ah yes, horses. Loving and magnificent. Didn't ask for much. Pats on their necks, good feed, a dry place when the weather was bad and plenty of exercise. Take care of them, win their loyalty and they'd run themselves to death for you. Not that she ever wanted to see that.

Made her think about the mustangs she and John had considered adopting. No guarantee they'd ever make quality mounts, but they'd be safe. Too many people thought they were nuisances, swearing they ruined prime grazing land.

Grace and John had never seen them that way. They were gorgeous, running free in their herds, somehow symbolic. As for their hooves, they turned the ground, true, but grasses grew in their wake. Their grazing didn't take too much since they moved so often and quickly.

Maybe she ought to get a couple of those mustangs. She'd have to clear it with Mitch, though, since he leased the land.

Daisy found some hay and chewed placidly while Grace brought out Dolly. Then she returned and began pitching everything out of their stalls. That manure and dirty straw could go on the compost heap out back of the barn. Speaking of which, it probably needed to be turned soon.

One thing at a time. Her back and shoulders had just started to ache when a sound drew her attention to the wide-open barn doors. Her heart skipped a beat.

A shadowy figure, astride a horse and beneath a cowboy hat, sat there. As well as he could sit, however, on a mount that would rarely hold entirely still. Full of vigor, the horse sidled, tossed its head and stomped a foot with impatience.

Grace caught her breath, thinking he could be an image right off a book cover or out of a movie.

"I said I'd help with that," Mitch remarked.

"I need the exercise and I like being around the horses."

He laughed. "I figured. Well, let me help anyway."

He swung down from the saddle with practiced ease and tied his horse to a stanchion. "This is Princess," he said. "Mainly because she thinks she's one. Hey, where are your work gloves?"

She looked down at her hands and realized she was going to have some blisters. Why hadn't she thought of that? "Too eager, I guess."

"You're going to need bandages by nightfall if you keep this up. Where are the gloves?"

"I think on a peg by the tack room."

He strode back there, then cussed. "What am I going to do with you, Grace?"

She stiffened. "What the hell are you talking about?"

"They shouldn't have been left out here. They're open at the cuff. Do you know what could be in there? Like a poisonous spider?"

Oh, heck, he was right. She lost her resentment.

"You're off duty until these get replaced. Don't think I'm criticizing you. A lot on your mind."

True. After she sold her horses, she'd never thought again about work gloves. No reason to blame herself, but she felt vaguely ashamed anyway. Too much around here had gone to hell.

Mitch set to work without another word. He moved with practiced skill and plenty of strength while she perched on an old sawhorse.

When he was almost done, and ready to open the back door, he asked, "Wanna keep the girls for a few more days? I doubt they've had a run in the paddock yet."

"Too much mud."

He nodded. "Another day for that, mebbe."

He carried out a few forkfuls of hay and manure before saying, "That compost pile is getting a little too hot. I'm going to have two of my men come over to turn it."

She wanted to argue, but given the state of her hands, she decided against it. She had a lot to relearn. A whole lot. "Thanks, Mitch."

"Glad to do it. You need to take care of those hands, anyway. You got some spare work gloves?"

"Somewhere in the house. Maybe."

"Then find 'em but wait a few days. If you got blisters...well, I don't need to tell you about that."

No, he didn't. Infection could set in fast. "I wanted to ask you a question."

"Sure. Just let me get this last bit out of here."

When he finished and had used a big broom to sweep the remains out the back door, he pulled off his gloves and came to stand facing her.

Dolly and Daisy stirred restlessly, nickering quietly as if to say, *When do I get my breakfast?*

Grace nearly laughed at them.

"So, what's the question?" Mitch asked.

"What would you say if I got a few mustangs?"

He tilted his head, thinking. "You know most of them are impossible to break."

"I don't want to break them. I just want to give them a place where they won't be considered nuisances. But that's up to you."

He nodded, still clearly thinking. "I'm not opposed," he finally said. "But let me think about logistics. They sure are magical running across the range. But I don't want them to be giving my mounts any ideas."

Now she *did* laugh. "You think they could?"

"I need to check into that. I don't think there'd be a

problem but I'd rather know before we have to make a hard decision."

"I have to agree with that." She hugged the possibility to her heart. It would feel like a new lease on life. Something to look forward to.

MITCH SAW THE expression on her face and ardently hoped he could make this happen for her. Grace so badly needed to plan again, to have hopes and pleasures laid out before her.

The Bureau of Land Management would probably be glad to turn over two or three horses. The mustang issue was becoming big, and so many horses had been rescued by the BLM that culling was under discussion. He hated to even think of it.

To him horses were one of God's gifts to the world and should be treasured. Not raced, not overused as beasts of burden, but treated with gratitude. They were helpmeets more than they were tools.

Probably an unusual attitude for many people, but that was the kind of man he was. To him, animals were not simply stock on a store shelf.

At Grace's suggestion, after they curried the horses he joined her for a brief cup of joe and a piece of that pecan ring, a lot of which was still left. She should have eaten more of it.

He knew better than to mention it. He'd already pressed her enough about the gloves. He wished he could get past her prickliness so she'd let him help more.

"I'll send over one of the guys to turn that manure pile either this afternoon or tomorrow."

She bit her lower lip. He knew what was coming. "You all must be so busy. I don't want to take your time."

"Screw that," he said bluntly. "Trust me, I won't harm my operation by having one of my boys do a few hours of work. In fact, knowing them, they'll be glad of the chance to do something helpful. I know they love riding the range, but not all the time."

He leaned forward, as if sharing a confidence, which he guessed he was. "If you ask me, Bill would like to spend some more time with Lila. So if I give him a few hours of work that'll bring him home at the end of the day, he'll be grateful. Right now, riding herd keeps him away for days at a time."

She smiled. "He's getting sweet on her, huh?"

"That's how it looks to me. One of these days she's going to be cooking in the bunkhouse and bringing me my dinner in a can."

That pulled a small laugh from her. "She wouldn't."

"Probably not. She'd hate to leave all those expensive kitchen tools behind." He grinned. "You'd never guess, but I've become an expert shopper for chef's equipment."

"Now, that's fascinating. Lila did that to you?"

"Believe it. She loves to cook, she's great at it, and every time she mentions how nice it would be if… Well, I get around to finding it for her. I don't know how much more she can put in that kitchen, but I'm sure she'll let me know."

He left Grace with a smile on her face.

Very big step, he thought. Now he'd better look into those mustangs.

BETTY POLLARD DROPPED in to see Grace around midafternoon. Grace was glad to see her, and offered her some of that everlasting pecan ring.

"Mmm, this is good," Betty said as she sat at the table

and ate. "Could I move into the living room with this? It's so much more comfortable."

Grace nearly froze. She avoided that room like the plague. She couldn't step in there without remembering John, without seeing him there.

"Betty..." She paused. Maybe it was time to stiffen her spine and just face it. No single room could contain John anymore. She liked to think he was everywhere.

"Sure," she said after her moment of reluctance. "Help yourself to any chair. Want me to bring the last of this cake?"

"I think my waistline can stand it."

Betty carried the plates and mugs while Grace followed with the coffee cake and the nearly full pot of coffee.

She was relieved to see when she entered the room that Betty had chosen the couch, not John's chair. For her part, she avoided her own and joined Betty on the couch with the cake and carafe on the coffee table.

"Now, isn't that much nicer?" Betty asked with a smile.

Depended on your perspective, Grace thought. After a minute or so she didn't feel the sorrow quite as strongly. Sitting on that couch with Betty felt different.

Grace spoke. "How's it going with the yummy mystery man?"

Betty's smile widened. "He's gone past yummy to scrumptious."

"That's great. I'm happy for you."

"We'll see how it goes. I haven't had the best luck with men. Anyway, he works on a ranch farther out, toward the north edge of the county. Can you imagine me with a cowboy?"

"Maybe that's the change you needed."

Betty laughed. "You might be right. I can hardly wait to see him on a horse."

Inevitably Grace thought about the image of Mitch in the barn door that morning. She understood what Betty meant but didn't want to say anything. Mitch wasn't interested in her that way.

She couldn't help feeling a little tingle in her heart, then almost immediately felt guilty.

"You need to find someone," Betty said. "It's been two years, Grace."

"Maybe someday," Grace said stubbornly. She'd know when the time was right, if it ever was.

"I'll drop it," Betty answered promptly. "I've just been worried about you."

Grace blinked. "Why? I've been doing okay for a long time now."

"Depends. I'm especially worried about that sheep."

Grace's mood darkened. "It was just some drunks," she lied. She didn't want to discuss the possibilities.

"You may be right, weird as it sounds. But I keep thinking about it, and you know I've been wishing for a long time that you'd just sell this place and move into town where you wouldn't have to be alone so much. God, it'd take twenty minutes for the cops to respond out here. At least that long for EMS. You need to think about those things, damn it."

Well, that was the strongest statement she'd heard from Betty on this subject. Did she really think the ewe was that important? Maybe some kind of warning?

A chill passed along Grace's spine, but she caught herself. If it was a warning, it had failed. Totally.

"I'll be fine," she insisted, "but I'd promised I'd think

about it and I will." A promise she didn't intend to keep. She was so tired of this discussion. She knew Betty cared for her, but the pressure was irritating. Especially since she was far from ready to give up this dream of hers and John's. She'd already lost too much.

Betty moved on to talking about her new man. "Would you believe he likes to dance? How many men like that? Not many, I can tell you. He not only likes it, he's good at it. He's taught me a bunch of new steps. I was kind of meh about it. I like the closeness of having a man's arm around my waist, moving back and forth and hoping he doesn't step on my toes."

Another laugh escaped Grace. Was she changing somehow? Regardless, Betty's description was a riot. "That's a man for you."

"Sho' nuff," Betty answered and grinned. "Most of the time I'm happy to sit on the side, but not with Dan. He likes it and I'm learning to like it, too. Country-style dancing. I didn't know it could be so much fun."

Betty stayed about an hour, then excused herself, saying, "I've got to get ready for tonight. I'm not sure which roadhouse we're going to, but I'm sure it's a good one."

She paused on the way out. "Grace, don't forget what I said."

"I won't." Although she intended to forget immediately. Leave the house she'd shared with John? The wide-open country she'd come to love?

The implication in Betty's mention of cops and EMS still bothered her. Was something going on? No way to know, and very unlikely anyway.

A little while later, Deputy Guy Redwing arrived. Grace invited him in and offered him coffee, an essential invitation on the ranches. When someone came this far out of the way, you offered hospitality however limited.

"Thanks for the coffee, Miz Hall."

He had a nice smile, Grace thought. Amazing that he still racketed around as a bachelor.

"I come with bad news," he said as he sipped. "Well, not bad but disappointing."

He added the last quickly as if he realized he'd opened the conversation with exactly the wrong words.

Before Grace could ramp up her feelings, she settled down. "Disappointing how?"

"No solution to what happened to your ewe. There hasn't been a similar case in the county, not anywhere. There also wasn't any evidence that might help us track the perpetrators."

"I kind of expected that," she replied. "Mitch suspects it was done with a rifle, maybe with a scope, from the road."

Guy nodded. "I agree, much as I'd prefer to give you some useful information. Seems like a weird time of year for a hunter to be practicing, but you never know."

"That's probably all it was," she said after a moment or two. "Maybe a kid with a new fancy rifle."

"That would make sense. Couldn't wait for autumn. Anyway, we're going to keep up a more frequent patrol for a week or so."

Grace felt almost guilty. That was using a lot of county resources. On the other hand, it *would* make her feel safer.

Not that she wasn't safe, she reminded herself as she watched Guy drive away. A kid with a shiny new rifle or scope or both. Yeah, that was the likeliest explanation.

It was time to make dinner. God, she hated cooking

only for herself. With John it had been fun. Most nights they'd cooked together, with a lot of laughter.

But it did her no good at all to think about that.

"THE BOSS AIN'T HAPPY," Carl said to Larry as they lay on their backs and looked up at the stars.

"Surprise," said Larry.

"Yeah."

They fell silent for a while, maybe pretending they were back on the range. It couldn't work, though. The sounds were all wrong. The smells were wrong, too.

"So what's the boss want now?" Larry asked.

"Something scarier."

"Oh, that's easy."

"We're kind of limited."

"By *her*," Larry pointed out. "Scarier, huh? I'd sure like to know why she's so determined to frighten the widow lady."

"That ain't gonna make our job any easier."

Considering that, they continued to look up at the stars.

"We'll think of something," Carl said finally. "We ain't stupid."

That was something they both agreed about. They just had to put their brains to it.

Because there must be more frightening things they could do.

Chapter Six

During the night a week later, Grace awoke from a night-mare so jumbled it had terrified her. Her heart hammered wildly and she couldn't catch her breath.

What the heck? Life had returned to its bland nor-malcy, nothing had happened...

Then she saw a red glow at her window, reflected dimly by her ceiling. Fire.

Oh my God. There'd be no help. No help at all be-cause the fire department was so far away. Leaping out of bed, she jumped into her jeans and a sweatshirt, hop-ing it wasn't the house. *Please, God, not the house.* That would kill her.

When she reached the kitchen, she knew it wasn't the house. The barn was in flames.

There were horses out there.

With no other thought than to save those animals, she stuffed her feet into boots and ran out, straight to-ward the fire. Give her time to save those horses. Please.

MITCH WAS WAKENED by his sat phone ringing insistently. Jack and Jeff were out on the range with the cattle. What had gone wrong?

He sat up and grabbed the phone, pressing the button.

"Yeah?" he said, his voice still rough with sleep.

"There's a fire over at the Hall place," Jeff replied.

Mitch hit high gear immediately. "Bad?" he asked as he pulled on clothes with one hand.

"Big," Jeff answered. "Jack and I are riding over as fast as we can."

It was dark out there, Mitch thought. They had to take care with their horses. "I'm getting the four-by-four," he told Jeff.

Not fast enough for a fire. Not even the fire department. Ranchers out here were pretty much on their own.

They at least had some firefighting equipment of their own. Big hoses attached to pumps that fed from the ponds or a well, depending.

His heart slammed repeatedly as he raced toward Grace's. What if it was her house? What if she hadn't wakened in time to get out?

Waking nightmares followed him through every mile.

GRACE REACHED THE BARN. It was burning from the sides. Old dry wood was acting like tinder but at least it hadn't reached the roof yet.

Ignoring the heat of the barn door handles, she pulled them open, feeling her hands burn. She heard the horses screaming from inside as terror shook them, cries loud enough to be heard over the roaring, crackling flames. The doors were heavy, seeming to move in slow motion.

Her overriding purpose was to open the stalls and drive the horses toward the barn door if they didn't run on their own. They might not realize that safety lay out in the dark night because they were so panicked.

The fire created a hellish light inside the barn. Smoke made the air almost too thick to breathe and see through.

Luckily, she knew every inch of that barn and could

have walked it blind. She knew exactly where the stalls were; she just had to get to them as she pulled the neck of her sweatshirt up to cover her mouth and nose. It helped a little.

She reached Dolly's stall, feeling almost breathless, weakened by the smoke-filled air. She fought to open the heavy gate with its steel bars on the top, glad the horses weren't tethered inside the stalls.

Dolly continued to scream and buck, unaware of her freedom.

Grace couldn't take one horse out at a time, for fear the roof would catch and collapse on them all. She hurried as fast as she could to Daisy, who was rearing repeatedly. Ignoring the hooves that might kill her, trying to stand behind the stall door, she called the horses.

"Daisy. Dolly. Outside."

Whatever the horses had previously understood, they didn't understand it now. With no choice, Grace chanced those rearing hooves and stepped in to grab Daisy's halter. It was impossible with the horse bucking in terror.

Giving up, she risked the rear hooves and slapped Daisy hard on the hindquarter. The whites of Daisy's eyes were showing, but the slap caught her attention. Grace slapped her again, harder.

At last Daisy galloped toward the door. A few seconds later, a panicked Dolly followed the run for freedom.

Thank God, Grace thought as she staggered after them. Smoke had robbed her of coordination. The barn had grown so hot she could feel her skin beginning to shrivel.

MITCH ARRIVED TO find the barn going up in flames. He saw the horses dashing out and running far away. Only one way they could have gotten out: Grace.

His heart stopped when he didn't see her immediately. Jumping from his vehicle, he ran toward the barn. The roof had begun to burn and he feared she was unconscious from smoke. Could he drag her out before that roof caved in?

It was as if he moved in mud. A small distance had just become miles. Before he quite reached the barn, his face already burning, he saw Grace come stumbling out.

At last his speed returned. He raced toward her, dragging her away from the raging death. No telling how far that fire would spread when the roof came down.

He picked her up like she was as light as eiderdown and began running again, getting her as far as he could from the conflagration.

Just as he neared her house, Jeff and Jack came riding up at nearly a full gallop.

"Everyone's out," he shouted. "Get the fire!"

It DIDN'T TAKE long for the two men to find the rolled-up fire hoses and the pump. Mitch was less concerned about the barn than he was about Grace.

Her eyes fluttered as he carried her inside the house and put her on the bed. Her face was seriously reddened and when her hands flopped at her sides he saw the beginnings of blisters.

God in heaven. She'd risked her neck to save the horses and now she was a mess. He pulled the satellite phone off his belt and called for firefighters and medics. She needed care. Bandages. Oxygen. He felt so damn helpless.

Then she groaned. "Mitch?"

"I'm here."

"The horses?"

"Damn it, woman, they ran for the hills faster than you did."

"Good. Barn?"

"My boys are fighting the fire. Medics are on the way. Can you breathe okay?"

She drew a shaky breath. "Yeah. The air tastes bad."

"I'm not surprised."

"The fire, Mitch. Go help."

He hated to leave her, but she was right. A prairie fire might take more than her barn. "I won't be long," he promised.

"I'm not going anywhere."

Humor in the midst of this. He'd always known Grace was tough, but that beat everything.

Jamming his hat on his head, he went out to help.

BY THE TIME he got out to the barn, Bill had arrived and the three men were spraying the fire hoses on the ground around the barn, and at its sides.

They weren't going to be able to save a damn thing. Except Grace's house. They had to prevent it from spreading toward her house and igniting the prairie. Nothing would stop those flames once they escaped.

Mitch joined his men, helping to hold the hose that Bill struggled to manage alone. While they didn't have the full pressure of a fire truck's pump, the flow of water was still enough to make controlling the hose difficult.

Round the building they moved, spraying every bit of ground for six to eight feet around. The entire barn roof now shot roaring flames to the sky.

Mitch prayed that the building would collapse downward into itself and not to the side, where it could kill two of them and spread the fire farther.

When he heard a loud groan from timber, louder than the surging flames, he shouted for his men to get back. "It's falling!"

They all heeded him, hurrying backward with hoses that still spewed toward the barn. Barely audible over the beast they were fighting, he thought he heard sirens.

Thank God.

As the fire trucks screamed up, the barn roof collapsed. Other than the groaning of wood, like a howling beast, it was surprisingly quiet. As if the roof had already lost most of its weight to fire.

The firemen unwound the hoses from the tank trucks, like the well-trained team they were, and began drenching the barn and the area around it. Four others took the hoses from Mitch and his men, relieving them and their aching muscles.

Then all Mitch could do was stand back and watch as the fire unit worked to drown the fire.

At last two ambulances arrived and he turned from the fire, hurrying over to them, to take them to Grace.

"You don't look so good yourself," one remarked.

"Don't worry about me," Mitch said as he led them into the house. "I'm a little scorched. Grace is burned."

He stood near as the EMTs bent over Grace and began assessing her. First came an oxygen mask. Before long, they wound gauze bandages around her hands and forearms and spread some kind of gel all over her face.

"I want to see the barn," she said weakly, her voice muffled by the mask.

"You don't," Mitch said.

One EMT was on a radio, talking to someone. Maybe a doctor?

Then the man turned to Mitch. "We're taking her to the hospital. Now. You should come along, too."

"Later," Mitch said impatiently.

"Mitch?" Grace's voice was still weak.

"Don't worry about anything, Grace. Just let these guys take you to the hospital. I'll handle everything else."

Then they brought in the stretcher.

After he saw her aboard the ambulance, he spared a few seconds to watch it race down the drive toward the road, sirens screaming. They didn't think a slow ride was going to be good enough.

That sight enhanced his fear for Grace. Then, because he'd said he would, he turned back toward the barn.

He didn't believe for one minute that this had been an accident.

The fire was mostly extinguished before the sun had climbed much above the horizon. Two more tanker trucks had arrived to help.

The barn was now a smoldering skeleton of ruin, black ribs reaching toward the sky. Smoke still rose from the blackened heap and the few standing stanchions. Water still gushed from fire hoses. The job would not be done until the fire team was sure there was nothing left that was hot enough to nurse another flame into conflagration.

Burned earth surrounded the barn but at least it hadn't spread.

He couldn't stop worrying about Grace, wishing he could be with her. He wondered if this would be one blow too many for her.

He wondered how bad her burns were.

He'd have liked to race to the hospital, but he'd promised her he'd take care of this. Taking care meant assuring the fire was truly out, that her house was safe.

Another couple of hours passed before the firefighters entered the gutted building. Using axes and industrial thermometers, they worked their way through the mess, trying to be certain that no remaining chunks of wood might harbor significant heat that could later burst into new flames. Evidently the crew didn't trust that thousands of gallons of water had quelled everything.

Then one of his smaller trucks pulled up. Lila emerged with huge insulated bottles of coffee, the kind of bottles she often sent out to his workers when they were out herding or checking the fence. She also brought big steel containers of food, freshly made bread, enough sliced ham for an army, mustard and mayonnaise. He even caught sight of her homemade donuts.

She marched over to him with his own bucket and coffee, ordering him to eat something "for God's sake."

Then she pulled a folding table out of the back of the small truck, set it up, and encouraged the fire team to come eat. They came in shifts, grabbing paper plates and loading them. Coffee went into more tin cups than Mitch had realized he owned.

Lila evidently thought ahead. She had probably started cooking as soon as she heard about the fire. Amazing woman. He hoped he'd never lose her.

Now that the fire had been nearly contained, he thought constantly about Grace. He imagined her in the emergency room, being assessed and given any treatment she needed immediately. Then she'd be moved to a room by herself. Medicated for pain, he hoped. Because at some point she'd start to feel her burns. All of them. He had no idea how badly injured she was.

He needed to know. Impatience began stalking him. Waiting for the firefighters to finish up this last part majorly frustrated him. He should be driving to the hospital.

But Lila was standing over him. He accepted the fact that he wasn't going anywhere until he'd eaten as least some of the bounty she'd brought.

"I'm not hungry," he said.

"I made them sandwiches just the way you like them. Now eat one before you leave for the hospital. When you get there, have them check you over, too. That looks like more than a sunburn on your face Last I heard nobody gets sunburned in the middle of the night."

Hell. He didn't want to eat. He could have pushed past Lila and left for town, but he didn't want to suffer her wrath, especially when it might include Lila quitting her job.

So he ate the ham sandwich fast, barely tasting it or the Swiss cheese he normally loved. Heck, he couldn't even taste the spicy mustard.

The fire crew had begun to roll up their hoses, signaling an end to their part. He was about to be free.

He finished choking the sandwich down and drank a cup of the piping hot coffee. Then rose. "I gotta go, Lila."

"I know you do, but they ain't no reason not to take more food and coffee. Waits can be long at a hospital."

He couldn't argue with that. He paused long enough to tell his three men where he was going, and to turn the reins over to them. "I've got my phone. Call me if anything important happens."

Then he set out for the Memorial Community Hospital, driving much faster than the speed limit. He couldn't wait to get to Grace.

He kept remembering those moments when he feared

she'd been overcome in the barn, that the roof might cave before he could find her and drag her out.

The instant when he'd seen her staggering out of there alive still hadn't been quite enough to puncture his fear.

That fire was no accident. He was sure of it.

So who had it in for Grace?

MITCH LEFT THE extra sandwich in his truck, taking only the coffee bottle. The hospital machine coffee was good only in a moment of desperation.

Not that he cared about that. All he wanted to do was check on Grace, and in a relatively short time he learned that he couldn't. Not family. No authorization. He couldn't even find out how bad she was.

He was on the verge of punching a hole in the wall when Mary, one of the previous sheriff's daughters, approached him.

"Mitch?"

He'd met her many times over the years and tried to smile as he turned toward her. A social nicety when he didn't at all feel like smiling or being nice. Not when he wanted to chew steel and spit out nails. "Hey, Mary."

"You're here for Grace Hall, right?"

"Yeah, but they won't let me see her."

Mary nodded understandingly. "Rules, you know. To protect a patient's privacy. Anyway, doctor said she can't have regular visitors until tomorrow."

"She's got no one else. I'm her neighbor, I lease her land. We've been friends for years."

Mary looked around and drew him into an unpopulated alcove that appeared to have been set up as a small adjunct to the waiting room. Quite an empty waiting room, but he didn't have a thought to spare about how unusual that was.

"I can't take you to see her," Mary said. "She's heavily sedated and can't tell us to give you privileges."

"But how is she?" A word, just a few words before he lost his mind.

Mary touched his upper arm. "She's got burns on her hands that require some treatment. Otherwise it's all minor. She's going to feel a lot of pain for a while, though, so I can't tell you how soon she might wake up and want to give you access to medical information."

He nodded, accepting it. At least now he'd learned *something*. "I'm going to sit right here," he announced. "I need to know."

"You do that. I'll keep on it. But, Mitch, you really need to get something to eat. It's going to be a long haul." She started to turn away, then looked at him. "You really need to see a doctor, too. You might not realize it, but to my eyes it looks like you might have some noncontact first-degree burns on your face. If you haven't felt it yet, I can promise you're going to when the adrenaline wears off."

She left him to his own devices.

First-degree burns? He'd had them before and figured he could sit it out. It'd hurt, she was right about that, but nothing he couldn't tolerate. Last thing he needed was some doctor filling *him* full of painkillers or sedatives. What use would he be to Grace then?

He sat with his coffee, not hungry. Hell, for once in his life he didn't even want coffee.

Instead he thought about Grace, and how intertwined their lives had become over the years. All the time since she'd married John he'd felt attracted to her. An attraction he'd buried deeply because it was wrong. She was another man's wife. The wife of a good friend. He'd known John before he met Grace.

John had been a ranch manager before Grace, before they bought the this place. It hadn't seemed strange to Mitch that John had wanted his own ranch. What still seemed strange was that Grace had so quickly abandoned her teaching job for a life as a rancher's wife.

He knew how good Grace was at ranching, how hard she had worked right beside John. He got the attraction to the life, he understood the joys of it, but it still surprised him how well she had settled in. Town didn't often blend well with country, but in their case it had.

They had been deeply in love. No one could miss it. It was there in every glance, every smile, every light touch. He'd envied them because that kind of love had never visited his life.

Much as he perhaps understood her prolonged grief, he understood something else as well. Grace needed a life for herself. She needed to stretch, to find new activities, to make more friends. He and Betty Pollard couldn't possibly be enough in the long run.

Thinking about Grace inevitably led him back to the same question: Was someone out to hurt Grace? Was the barn fire deliberate?

He believed it was, but he couldn't know for certain until the arson investigator had a chance to look it all over. It might be days until the investigator could conclude the cause.

In the meantime, he had to put all those thoughts in the back of his mind, because Grace needed someone to care for her right now.

He was damn well going to do it, whether she liked it

or not. He admired her determination, but it just wasn't safe for anyone to be as alone as she was, not out there in the wide-open spaces. Too many bad things could happen, and help was far away.

Like with her barn. If his men hadn't seen it, God knew what might have happened.

Sometimes he wished he could shake some sense into her.

OUT AMONG THE TREES, two men with binoculars scanned the burned-out barn.

"The boss is going to like this one," Carl said with satisfaction.

"If not," Larry answered, "I don't know what the hell else we can do."

"If she don't like it, she's crazy."

Larry snorted. "She's already halfway there. But yeah, if that don't send that Hall woman running, she's as crazy as the boss."

They'd already decided the boss was nuts. What the hell was so important about moving that Hall woman out of there? They guessed they'd never know. Not that they really needed to.

It was a job. Just get it done.

IT WAS EVENING before Mary showed up again. Mitch was stiff from the lousy waiting room chairs. After telling the desk where he could be found, he'd paced the parking lot. The rest of the time he'd watched patients come and go. Nothing serious.

Mary smiled. "Grace wants to see you and she verbally gave us permission to talk with you."

He jumped up. "Thank God."

"I'll warn you she's still groggy on morphine, but she's talking and somewhat alert. She may fall asleep on you, so don't worry."

Mary led him to the door of Grace's room. She opened it and called in cheerfully, "Look who's been waiting all day to see you."

Mary nodded, leaving him along with Grace. He crossed to her bed, not wanting to startle her, and saw her blue eyes blinking at him. She looked half-asleep and he was grateful for that. He couldn't imagine the pain she'd feel from her hands if she'd been fully conscious.

"Mitch," she whispered.

"I'm here, darlin'," he said, slipping up. He tensed, then decided she wouldn't remember. Morphine was like that, he'd seen a few times.

"How bad?"

"The horses are fine. Jeff and Jack are out looking for them but are pretty sure they ran for home. Only a fence would keep them from making it."

"Good." She sighed, her eyelids drooping. "The barn?"

"Gone."

She swore faintly, something he'd rarely heard her do.

"Barns can be rebuilt. You and horses not so much."

The faintest of smiles reached her lips. "My face hurts."

"Not surprising. They've got you pretty well gooped up. Anyway, you don't need to worry about your pretty face. It'll be there when you leave here."

"Yeah." She inhaled deeply, as if she still needed to draw more air.

He'd have to ask Mary about that when he had the

chance, away from Grace's hearing. He didn't want her to worry about anything else.

"My hands are bad. Lots of bandages. I don't feel them yet."

Maybe the morphine? "That's probably a good thing."

Her eyes were almost closed now. He wondered if she wanted him hanging around in her room, or if he should wait outside. He didn't want to ask her, not when she was clearly having a hard time talking.

Then a nurse came into the room. "Time for more morphine," he said cheerily. "Dreamland for you, Ms. Hall."

"I'll be waiting when you wake up," Mitch said. "You just go to sleep now."

The morphine was already running into her IV line. She started to speak but fell into the arms of Morpheus before she could do more than make a sound.

Thank God. When she *could* feel her hands again, it would be awful. He'd seen them. Not quite raw meat, but close.

He stepped outside and looked around for Mary. Five minutes later she found him.

"I need to know" was all he said to her.

"Of course. Let's step into the waiting room."

Once again it was empty. "Quiet night?"

"We all need one sometimes."

They sat side by side, and he asked impatiently, "Well?"

"Second-degree burns on her palms. A lot of skin is lost but not enough to require any kind of graft. It was blistering, nothing deeper. They'll be fine, but it's going to take a while. Face has first-degree—no problem there except discomfort. She was in shock when she got here, typical of burn cases."

"That's it?"

Mary shook her head. "Not quite. She had a lot of smoke inhalation, which we treated with bicarbonate. It's going to take a few days to get her blood acids back to normal."

He nodded, taking it all in.

Mary reached out and touched his arm again. "Mitch, she's going to be fine. Completely fine. She just needs some recovery time."

A coiled spring deep inside him began to let go. "Completely?" he repeated.

"You have my word on it. You can come down off the ceiling now."

She smiled. This time he returned it and blew a long breath as tension released its hold. "Thank you, Mary."

She rose. "Take my advice and get back to your ranch. Eat something, rest a little if you can. She's going to sleep most of the night. Come back earlier if you can't catch eight hours. I'll tell the desk you have Grace's permission to visit and get her medical info. You won't be locked out."

That was another relief. He couldn't have tolerated coming back here to find someone guarding the gate. "Thanks," he said again.

Then as she walked away he put his head in his hands, ignoring the tenderness of his own skin. God, how close it had been. Too close.

He had to find out who was behind this before they struck at Grace again. Determination filled him, making him sit up straighter. Someone was going to pay.

Feeling marginally better, he took Mary's advice. He'd

be no good to anyone if he were sleep deprived. He also needed to talk to his men, check out the entire situation. Then maybe he could snag a few hours in the sack.

BACK AT THE RANCH, he found a couple of worried people, Bill and Lila. They were all over him almost before he got in the door.

"How is she?" Lila demanded even as she dragged him toward the kitchen for food and a drink.

"I need a shower first."

"We need news first," Bill said. "Plus, damn it, you need to eat. You look like hell, boss."

"Thanks a bunch."

Mitch quit arguing and soon had a meal fit for a king spread in front of him. Lila and Bill joined him at the trestle table with cups of coffee. Lila shoved two fingers of whiskey in front of him.

After a bite or two, Mitch discovered he was ravenous. That seemed to please Lila, who sometimes appeared determined to fatten him up like a steer headed for auction.

"Okay," he said presently. Never had he possessed a more attentive audience. "She's going to be all right. Hands are a mess, but they'll heal. She had smoke inhalation. They're going to keep her for a few days. I talked to her briefly and she was concerned about the horses and the barn. Of course, she wouldn't be in this mess if she hadn't saved those horses. You should have seen her stagger out of that barn."

"Damn, she's brave," Bill said.

"Damn straight," Mitch agreed. "Whenever they release her, she's going to need some help, though."

"Consider it done," Bill said.

Lila offered, "I'll go over and cook and clean for her. That's if you don't mind."

Mitch shook his head. "I don't mind. Like I said, she's going to need help. I doubt her hands will find it comfortable even to hold a cup of joe or a fork, but I know damn well she'll try. Well, I don't want her doing any more than that."

They both nodded.

"As for the horses," Bill volunteered. "Came this way like we thought. Couldn't pass the fence. I think they're both happy to be bedded down in their own stalls, though."

"Wouldn't you be?"

Mitch ate until he couldn't hold another bite, then reached for the highball glass holding his whiskey. "Thanks, Lila. That was a truly great meal." He then downed half the whiskey.

"Don't I always feed you this way?" Then she laughed. "I'm so glad everything is going to be okay."

"Except the barn," Mitch remarked.

"About that," Bill said. "Had a few of our neighbors stop by this afternoon. I think we might be having a barn raising almost before you know it."

Let Grace stick that in her craw, Mitch thought with amusement. She was going to get help even if she didn't want it. That was what neighbors did in these parts. "That's really great. The four of us could do it, but it'd take us a lot longer."

"Plus me, Jack and Jeff aren't the best carpenters. We'll have plenty of help. Might get it done over a weekend, if enough folks show up."

Mitch eyed Lila. "You up to cooking for an army?"

She grinned. "I kinda think we'll have a lot of wives showing up to pitch in."

Maybe, thought Mitch as he left the remaining whiskey in favor of that shower. Part of the tradition, for the wives to get together to help feed all the men at an affair like this.

He didn't care if that sounded sexist. That was the way things were in these parts. If some of the women wanted to join in the building part, they'd be welcome. And any of the guys were welcome to cook.

He was hardly interested in how folks chose to split the labor.

In the shower, the events of the last day finally, truly hit him. He placed his palms on the tile and shook, water pouring over his head. His chest squeezed so hard he could barely breathe.

He'd come so close to losing Grace. He couldn't bear the thought.

The words that came out of his mouth were more prayer than cussing.

He *had* to find the person behind this. He *had* to or Grace would never feel safe again.

Chapter Seven

Mitch arrived back at the hospital in the wee hours and sat by Grace's bed while she slept. From time to time he walked to the uncovered window and looked out at the surrounding town.

It seemed not so long ago that buildings hadn't reached out this far, but during a brief time the semi-conductor plant had brought people to town and provided local jobs. There'd been a spurt of growth. Gone now, but the signs remained.

He doubted the community college provided enough jobs for all those houses. Or maybe they did. He didn't much care. His ranch was still mostly empty land, giving him an unobstructed view of rolling prairie and mountains. Just the way he liked it.

He turned back to Grace's bed and resumed his watch in the chair.

A nurse came in and drew some blood, then checked the IV. Something was tweaked, then she left without a word.

Probably trying not to disturb Grace.

He couldn't even reach out to hold her hand, to let her know in the depths of sleep that she wasn't alone.

He turned his thoughts to something that didn't make

him feel as bad. A barn raising, huh? Nothing like that had happened recently. There'd been one years ago when that tornado blew through. Most of the damage had been to roofs, but one barn had taken a lot more. Too much damage to save.

He'd helped that time, wouldn't have dreamed of not doing it. He could still remember, however, the great scar that storm had left across his own land. Fifteen feet wide, it had cleared the ground of grass and everything else. He was still grateful that none of his herd had been there. Unlike that movie, it wouldn't have been funny.

"Mitch?"

He leaned forward in his chair. "I'm here." The sound of Grace's wispy voice filled him with joy.

"Everything? The horses?"

She couldn't remember what he'd said earlier. Good. He didn't want her wondering uncomfortably about that *darlin'* that had escaped him.

He cleared his throat, to make his voice as calm and reassuring as possible. "The horses are fine. They ran home, like you'd expect."

"Good." As hard as it must be for her to talk right now, she managed to sound satisfied. "I was so worried about them. God, they were so terrified. I can't imagine being trapped in that fire."

He didn't want to imagine. "And you," he said. "I saw you stagger out of there. You could have died, Grace. The roof collapsed just a little while later."

"I'm okay," she repeated. Then her voice began to slow again. "The barn must be gone."

"Yeah. Don't worry about that now. There'll be plenty of time to deal with that when you feel better. I'm just glad it wasn't your house."

"Me, too…" Then her voice began trailing away. "Go home, Mitch. You've got work…"

Then she disappeared into drug-induced sleep. Better that way. She didn't need to be awake for most of this.

One of the nurses stopped him outside Grace's room. "She'll sleep most of the day. Come back this afternoon."

The sun had begun to rise, casting a dim, golden light outside. Yeah, he had to get back to the ranch. To see the damage in the light of day.

NEARLY AN HOUR LATER, he pulled up Grace's drive. Even at this distance he could see equipment waiting.

Wasn't it too soon to be starting a new barn?

He saw several front-end loaders in a line. Probably getting ready to clear the land.

Then he saw the arson investigator standing with a clipboard and a case full of chemical sniffers and other tools of her trade. She was looking at the heap of rubble, burned pillars that pointed crookedly at the sky.

It was Charity Camden, the department chief's wife. An arson investigator with a lot of experience before she'd come here on an investigation and met the chief. She'd stayed.

"Hey, Mitch," she said, smiling. "How's Grace doing?"

"She'll recover. Her hands are a bit of a mess. Also, smoke inhalation."

Charity screwed up her nose. "Been there. No damn fun."

"I wouldn't think so. Got any ideas?"

"Absolutely. An amateur's job. Kerosene on four sides of the barn. I guess they, or he, didn't much care if we could tell."

"Just kerosene, huh?"

She nodded. "Spread around. The barn was dry, right?"

"And old. No rain for a while except last week. Not enough, I guess."

"At this time of year? Nothing stays wet for long." She shook her head. "A firebug? Or just someone who's mad about something. Grace got any enemies?"

It was Mitch's turn to shake his head. "She's hardly been out of the house since her husband died."

"Well, damn. I hope we don't have another fire. I absolutely hate arsonists, and those who repeat? They all ought to be in prison for life. Lives are at risk in every fire."

He couldn't disagree with that. "There were two horses in that barn. Grace got them out before the thing collapsed."

Charity drew a sharp breath. "My God. No one told me that. Most people couldn't make themselves get that close to a raging fire."

His answer was simple. "Grace loves horses."

"I guess so." She bent and started packing her equipment. "This was easy for me. I've got everything I need for a report. You can tell your neighbors to get at it."

That was when he noticed a group of men standing farther out, smoking cigarettes. Now he knew why those loaders were sitting there.

As Charity left, he walked over to them, shaking hands with men who'd been ranching around him his entire life. They all had faces marked by years in the sun and wind and by hard physical labor. "Thanks for coming, guys."

One of them tipped a water bottle over his cigarette

butt to put it out completely. "We gotta clear the land, Mitch. Can't start a new barn with all that there. That is, if we got the go-ahead."

"You got it," he said. "Grace has a few more days in the hospital."

That made the man, Edgar, frown, but then he smiled. "Might have a nice surprise for her. Folks are talking about getting started tomorrow."

"That's fantastic."

One of the other men, Orson, spoke. "Least we can do. Man, you look like you need a meal, some coffee and some sleep. Just go home. We can clear this mess between us. Hear?"

He was so grateful to his four friends he wished there were words. But they didn't need them. All of them understood.

Orson especially, since he'd lost his barn to that tornado.

When Mitch drove away, he heard the loaders rev up, then their roar as they started scraping debris out of the way, making the land level.

Lila served him a huge breakfast and most of a pot of fresh coffee. "How's Grace doing?"

"Still mostly knocked out on morphine. I'm going back later."

Lila nodded. "Jeff and Bill are heading over to her place to see what they can do to help. Jack'll keep an eye on the herd. And, of course, you got them shepherds to look after the flock."

All neatly sewn up. He might start to feel extraneous. "There are four men out there clearing up the rubble. They're talking about starting to raise the barn tomorrow."

Lila nodded her satisfaction. "Good. Who are they?"

"Edgar, Orson, Tom and Jim."

"Good men. I'll talk to their wives. They might have some idea of how many will be there tomorrow. Meantime, I can take lunch out to the ones we got."

"I'm sure that'll be welcome. Charity Camden was out there when I arrived."

Lila sat down. "What did she say it was?"

"Arson. Someone poured kerosene around the outside of the barn."

"With the horses in there? For God's sake, what is this world coming to?"

"Beats me," Mitch answered as he took more of the thick slice of ham. "Hey, this is good."

"Always is, and don't talk with your mouth full."

He'd have laughed if his mouth *hadn't* been full.

Lila was silent for a minute or so. "I'm scared what this might mean. For Grace especially."

Mitch took a long swallow of a glass of milk. "Me, too," he admitted. "Very much so. But I can't think of anyone who'd want to hurt her."

"Except maybe those folks who wanted to buy these ranches."

He started to shake his head. "Why, though? Big companies don't need to stoop to this. Anyway, they could afford a better arsonist."

Lila frowned. "That could be the point."

Mitch felt a punch in his gut that killed his appetite. "Dang, Lila, you have a devious mind."

"Comes from having a devious ex. Get your appetite back, boss. When Grace wakes up this time, she'll probably really need you."

Then she winked. "I need you to take her some of my cinnamon buns. I'll even pack a couple for you."

"Junk food," he teased.

"Not my cinnamon buns. Look, the hospital gives her the healthy stuff if she can eat it. She needs something tasty."

"I doubt she could pick up one. Her hands are bandaged."

"That's why God made you. You can feed her pieces."

He laughed for the first time since the barn caught fire.

HE REALLY DID need some sleep. No avoiding it. After a shower he hit the bed, his mind still racing over all of it. Not for long, though. His body demanded its due, and soon he was carried away on dreams of Grace that at least weren't filled with threat. Sleep brought him a short span of peace.

IT WAS LATE afternoon when he at last climbed into his truck with the promised cinnamon buns in a plastic container beside him.

He detoured over to Grace's place and was amazed. Those men with loaders had done quite a job. The ground where the old barn had been was flat now. The last bit of detritus from the fire had been carted away some distance. Out of the way, soon to be out of sight. It wouldn't be long before something grew among the rubble, turning the ugliness into a small, living hill.

Nature was a wonderful thing.

AT THE HOSPITAL, he found Grace considerably more alert, although not her usual self. Still groggy, but awake. She couldn't be comfortable.

She managed a small smile when she saw him. "Mary

said you were here most of yesterday and this morning. Mitch, you've got better things to do with your time."

"Nothing more important than you."

"I'm probably blushing, but you can't see it. Red like a lobster already. Sweet of you to say that."

"Just the plain truth. Are you hurting much?"

"Mostly my hands but they won't let me wake up enough to start screaming. Might scare the other patients."

He grinned. "That's my Grace. Say, Lila sent me with a bunch of cinnamon buns. She thinks you need something tasty."

"I do," she admitted. "Jell-O and something like cream of wheat, ugh. Hard for me to eat, though. Spoon only." She held up her hands. "I can't eat one of those buns, Mitch. Couldn't hold one."

"That's what I said until Lila reminded me that God made me to feed you pieces of bun."

A quiet laugh escaped her. Probably didn't want to stretch her face too much.

"She's a gem," Mitch said. "Keeps me in my place."

"Can't be easy."

Mitch laughed. "Nope." He was so damn glad to see her spunk returning he could have done a jig right there. Except he didn't know how.

The door opened and in walked Betty Pollard. "My God, girl," she said without preamble. "I heard about the fire. How are you?" Only then did she say, "Hi, Mitch."

"Betty."

Grace held up her hands. "Pretty good, all things considered."

"How did you get burned?"

"Saving the horses," Mitch answered.

Betty frowned. "I didn't know you had horses."

"They were mine," Mitch answered. "She's damn brave."

"More than brave," Betty agreed. "I don't think you could have gotten me that close. I hate fire."

"Most of us do," Grace answered. "I'm going to be fine."

"I hope so," Betty said sincerely. "But when are you going to listen to me? Out there all alone, now you're burned and how long did it take for help to arrive?"

Grace shook her head slightly. "Only as long as it took Mitch and his men to arrive. I was already coming out of the barn."

A prettier picture than he would have painted, Mitch thought. He remained silent, however. This was Grace's story to tell, and since Betty was *her* friend, Grace had a right to say what she wanted .

"I'm serious, Grace. You need to be in town. Even Mitch is too far away."

"I don't think so," Grace replied. "I'm tired of talking about it, Betty. I don't want to leave my ranch."

Betty frowned but fell silent a beat or two before saying, "Your decision. I just worry about you."

Mitch leaned forward to look at Grace. "I can leave if you two ladies want to talk."

"There's nothing private," Grace said. "Stay, Mitch."

It almost sounded like a command, which surprised him. Well, maybe she wasn't in the mood for pressure from Betty.

Remembering the cinnamon buns, knowing Lila had probably packed enough for six, he said, "Anyone want a cinnamon bun?"

Betty rose. "Thanks, Mitch." Then she moved closer to Grace. "But I have to go meet my boyfriend."

"Sounds like you two are getting serious."

Betty smiled. "Time will tell. I'll come by and see you tomorrow, okay?"

"Sure. I'd like that."

Grace didn't speak for a while after Betty left. "Damn, I wish she'd stop pressuring me to move to town. I know she means well, but lately she's been ramping up. Now, after this, she'll be impossible."

"Can't blame her."

Grace frowned at him. "You, too?"

"Nope," he answered honestly. "I worry, sure. That's why I kept pressing you to take the satellite phone. But everything else is your decision."

Grace sighed. "Thank you. I'm not a baby. I can make my own decisions, even if they're not smart. It's my *right* to be stupid."

Mitch had to laugh again. "I've never heard it put that way before."

"Well, it's true. Making mistakes is how we learn, and we learn better from them than things that go right. I didn't do anything to burn my barn down, so that wasn't even stupidity on my part."

"No, it wasn't," Mitch agreed. He was determined not to tell her about the arson until she got out of here. Assuming Charity didn't show up with questions in the meantime.

He opened up the box of cinnamon buns. He'd been right. There were six huge ones in there. "Now I get to perform my God-given purpose. You ready for some pieces of bun?"

She gave him another small smile. "They *do* sound good. Very good."

"Then hush and save your mouth for eating."

The process was crumbly, spreading crumbs on the front of her gown, but she ate and even laughed once when a larger piece fell on her.

"Woman," he said, "you're going to need a broom and dustpan at this rate."

"Maybe you need to reconsider your purpose."

"Damn, you're something else."

The evening nurse appeared eventually. "How are you feeling?" she asked Grace.

"I hurt," Grace admitted frankly.

"I thought you might. Doctor cut your morphine in half, and it's time for another dose. But if you feel you need more, let me know and I'll call her." Then she injected the morphine into the IV port. "That'll make you groggy. Probably won't knock you out, but it'll probably make you care less."

"That might be good right now."

Mitch waited until the nurse finished checking everything, even brushing crumbs off Grace. He hadn't wanted to do that himself considering where they had landed.

"Mmm, that smells good," the nurse remarked.

Mitch held up the plastic container. "Help yourself."

"You're the devil's right hand, Mitch Cantrell. I'm on a diet. I'll live with just drooling over the aroma."

"Wow," Grace said when the woman had departed. "From a God-given purpose to being the devil's right hand. Quite a fall."

"That's me. Up and down all the time."

It wasn't long before Grace began to doze and told

him to go home. "You can't sit here like my babysitter. Enough other people are getting paid to do that."

"I'll see you in the morning, then?"

"I wouldn't miss it."

He went home, feeling considerably better.

Chapter Eight

Midmorning, after getting himself filled in on the state of the ranch, Mitch drove over to Grace's to check on the house and make sure no pipe had broken or anything else.

Houses left alone could become a serious headache if no one was there to notice little things.

Before he could go into the house, he noticed a beehive of people around the bare earth where the barn had been. Turning off his ignition, he headed on over and was astonished.

Piles of lumber were already stacked in several places. He guessed some of Grace's neighbors had been out getting the wood while the others had cleared the detritus.

He wouldn't have expected anything that fast. His heart swelled. Good neighbors. The best. He walked over to talk with the crowd, to thank them. None of them wanted to be thanked, however.

"Least we could do" seemed to be the common sentiment.

Maybe Olson said it best. "Neighbors gotta come together when there's trouble. We're no earthly use if we don't."

Mitch stayed with them awhile, looking over the

plans, having little enough to add. The guys knew what a barn should be, and they were about to give Grace the best.

"You go on to the hospital," Sam West said. "She must be needing a friendly face."

Sam was right, but Mitch hated to leave these folks. They were being so generous, and he wanted to pitch in. He was Grace's neighbor, too.

They seemed about as determined as Lila to get him over to see Grace, and he was glad to go. His worry remained, even though it had been eased. He'd been around too long to believe that matters couldn't go awry.

He smiled, though, as he approached the hospital. Thinking about the barn raising made him feel good. It wouldn't have been surprising if no one had wanted to do it, because Grace rarely needed a barn these days.

He guessed her need didn't enter into it. A neighbor had experienced some major trouble, and they were doing the best thing they could think of to help.

Which made him damn proud to be one of them.

He stopped in the hospital gift shop and bought Grace some flowers, hoping to cheer up her sterile room. While he rode the elevator to her second-floor room, he wondered if he should tell her about the barn. Then he decided against it. It might come better as a surprise, especially since he was convinced she'd object.

He entered Grace's room with a smile and was delighted to see the head of her bed raised, and the blue eyes he liked so much looking bright again. Not as much morphine today.

He carried the flowers to her and set them on the bedside table. "How are you today?"

She smiled back at him. "Much better. The flowers are beautiful, Mitch. That's so sweet of you."

"Momma didn't raise no idiots."

The made her laugh and the sound of it tickled him. "You *are* much better. How are your hands?"

She held them up. They didn't appear to be quite as heavily bandaged. "Painful, but they could be a lot worse. They might let me go home tomorrow."

"That would be wonderful if you can. Lila says she'll come over to look after you."

"That's really not necessary," she argued.

He sighed. "Listen to me. For once in your life, let someone help you. Lila wants to. She offered. If that's too much for your cussedly independent soul, you can come stay at my place. I've got more than enough room."

"But…"

"No buts," he said sternly. "I'd be very surprised if you're out of those bandages tomorrow, and even if you are it's going to be awfully painful to cook or feed yourself. Just, for heaven's sake, let people help you. Have you ever considered that it might make *them* feel good?"

She blinked, clearly taken aback. "Really?"

"Do them a favor. Make them feel good. I doubt they'd like their caring to be rejected, either."

She closed her eyes briefly, then looked at him again. "I hadn't thought of it that way."

"A lot of people don't. They don't want charity, but they forget it's rarely offered grudgingly, and when it's accepted, others can be happy, too."

"Wow," she said quietly.

"Yeah, put that in your pipe and smoke it. Meantime, I'll just sit here and bore you to tears with talk of cows and sheep and horses. About my limit."

She shook her head. "Don't put yourself down. It's like a new mom apologizing for talking endlessly about diapers and feedings and spit-up... All of us talk about the most important things in our lives."

He shook his head. "I ought to make time to start reading books again. Or watching some TV. Then I could tell jokes about the latest reality show."

"You don't watch TV?"

"Occasionally. So occasionally that I can't remember how to operate the clicker."

She laughed.

"Books, on the other hand... I've always loved them, but for the last few years all I seem to have time for is keeping up with journals about the best way to raise cattle and sheep. A bunch of stuff from veterinary schools. That kind of thing."

"Lots of new information?"

He cocked a brow. "Seems like there's always someone with a harebrained idea about how to do something better. It might be better, but I'd like to suggest they come out here and try to apply it to a huge herd of cattle on the range."

She laughed again. "You've still got your sense of humor."

He looked around. "Wasn't aware that I lost it."

GRACE WAS SORRY when Mitch left, but she understood. He still had a ranch to oversee. He couldn't possibly sit here for hours trying to amuse her.

But she missed him. Her nurse, Mary, appeared with a pain pill. No more morphine, which was fine with Grace. She hated the way it kept her asleep, even though she had needed it. She didn't like the odd dreams it gave her, though.

Before the pain medication could take effect, she raised her bandaged hands and studied them. They really hurt, and the earlier bandage change along with the ointment they put over her skin hadn't helped. If anything, the pain had become sharper.

Closing her eyes, she hoped the pill would bring some relief.

Which gave her plenty of time to think about events. The barn. The horses. She wanted to cry. She couldn't believe it was an accident, but who would want to do that?

It seemed extreme for some juvenile mischief. Which left what? Who?

She kept coming back to that industrial farm company that had wanted to buy hers and Mitch's land last fall. Would they actually try to burn her out?

She could think of no one else who might want to do such a terrible thing. She lived such a quiet life that she couldn't imagine anyone wanting to do such a thing to her.

It wasn't that terrible things never happened in this county, but other than a few times, the worst she'd ever heard of was a couple of drunken guys getting into it at one of the roadhouses and shooting guns at each other. That was angry, all right.

But overall, folks around here didn't seem drawn to seriously violent acts. Not that they couldn't happen.

She remembered the high, leaping flames. The sound of the horses' terrified screaming. She hoped she never heard that sound again. She hoped that Dolly and Daisy would get over it. They could be as traumatized as people.

Animals didn't forget; they just moved on quicker.

Which might be a good lesson for her.

Mitch was drawing her out. After the last two years, his constant patience and understanding were beginning to pull her out of the dark well she'd fallen into with John's death.

That was something else she'd never forget. Noticing John was late to dinner. Going out to the barn to discover what had preoccupied him.

Finding him dead and already feeling cool to her touch.

The agony that twisted in her gut, the guilt because she hadn't been there. What if she could have helped him?

Even though the doctors said it had been instantaneous, that no one could have done anything, she couldn't quite believe it.

John had been healthy and strong. How could he have been carrying a genetic heart defect all his life? It defied understanding.

Questioning it didn't help one damn thing.

John was gone, and now her barn was gone, as if life were stripping everything from her.

As the pain pill began to take effect, easing her discomfort, she fell into dreams more pleasant than the ones she'd had on morphine. Mitch. Riding a horse with him.

Not everything was bleak.

Sometime during the night, she woke with tears running down her cheeks.

Weeping for the old dreams lost. Weeping for the new ones that couldn't be born.

Chapter Nine

Two days later, Mitch picked up Grace from the hospital with her hands still bandaged and a bottle full of pain medication.

"I guess the new rules about pain meds don't apply when you're burned," she remarked as she studied the bottle once they climbed into his truck.

"Haven't you heard?" he asked. "The CDC revised its advisory, saying it was never meant to keep doctors from treating patients as required by good medical practice."

"I guess that means this bottle is okay."

He laughed. "I wouldn't worry about it, Grace. Your doctor prescribed it. Best medical practice in your case."

She returned his laugh with a smile. "I won't argue that it keeps me from screaming sometimes."

"There you go."

He could hardly wait for her to see the barn. He'd helped some with it yesterday and had enjoyed how fast it was growing. They'd probably get to work on the roof today. Amazing what you could accomplish with a large group of determined people. With people who laughed, joked and even sang sometimes, turning the work into a party.

Then there was the food. The long folding tables were

never allowed to become bare. Fantastic home cooking filled them. Maybe Grace would try some. The cooks would undoubtedly press her to eat. That was part of hospitality.

As they approached her ranch, he heard her draw a sharp breath.

"Pain?" he asked immediately.

"No. Mitch, what's that near my house?"

"Well, your neighbors decided you needed a new barn."

"Oh my God," she murmured, her voice barely audible over the roar of his engine and the rattle of everything else. "Oh my God," she repeated more loudly.

"Remember after that tornado years ago? Folks turned up pretty fast to build Orson a new barn."

"But I…"

"What? Your neighbors are giving you a gift."

Grace fell silent and he let her admire the construction as they drew nearer. She probably felt overwhelmed.

As he'd expected, women swarmed the truck as he parked near the barn. They didn't give him a chance to help her out, and insisted she come over to a folding chair near the tables, from where she could see the new barn.

"I can't… What can I say?"

"Nothing," Jenny Wright answered. "We all know what it means. Now, what are you going to eat, Grace? You must be starved after that hospital food."

Mitch was relieved to hear Grace laugh. Overwhelmed or not, she'd decided to enjoy the generosity. The crew high up on the barn called greetings down to her.

"Leave some food for us," Edgar Cruz shouted. "Almost lunchtime, Grace."

She laughed again as Margie Cruz pressed a full paper plate into her lap. "Can you handle a spoon or fork?"

"I think so. Margie, I can't eat this much."

"Sure you can," Jenny answered. "Just take your time. Nibble away all afternoon. Drink? We got lemonade, iced tea, coffee and some cranberry juice someone sneaked in here."

"Coffee, please. The stuff at the hospital was worse than the food."

Soon a smaller folding table was set up in front of Grace so they could put her plate and drink on it.

"Now, you just relax," Margie said. "Need anything, wave. Enjoy the show. These guys are cutups."

Grace looked at Mitch and he saw the sheen of tears in her eyes to go along with her smile. He asked, "Mind if I go help the crew?"

For once she didn't remind him he had work back at his ranch. He kinda figured his cattle and sheep were capable of grazing without help for a few days.

Soon he climbed a ladder to help with the beginnings of the roof. The labor felt good.

GRACE HAD TROUBLE believing her eyes as she gazed at the new barn and struggled with a spoon to eat the best potato salad she had ever tasted.

These people were amazing. Why had she been avoiding them for so long? She hadn't before John had died, although most didn't have much time for socializing. Too much work.

Their generosity made her eyes well up again. Some of them she'd never had time to get to know much at all, but here they were. Mitch was right—this was a gift.

She didn't deserve it, but that didn't seem to matter to these folks.

And a barn raising seemed to be a party as well as work. They joked as they moved along at astonishing speed. Once they even broke into song, a simple melody that she didn't recognize. At least it made it possible for everyone to join in.

At lunchtime, they didn't all descend to the waiting food, but came in waves as the others continued sawing and pounding nails. They said "hi" or "howdy" to her as they came to the tables and filled paper plates and cups. Then they were happy to settle on the ground to eat, talking about the barn and whatever came next. From time to time smaller knots of them burst into laughter.

Jenny pulled up a chair beside Grace. "They're all having a good time," she remarked. "Not much excuse for a party like this, except for weddings and funerals. You need something else to eat? Maybe you're ready for a piece of cake or cobbler?"

Grace glanced at her plate. "There's still a lot of food."

"So I'll put it in a container for you to eat later. Now, how about that dessert?"

Something sweet sounded great to her, so she opted for the blueberry buckle with a crumb topping. It was a bit difficult for her to eat, unlike the food she'd been able to take on a spoon, but it was soft enough she made her way through it, a bit at a time. Her hands began to hurt seriously again.

Mitch climbed down from the barn. It must be his lunch shift. First he came straight over to her and squatted. "How are you doing?"

"I'm floored. Think I need a pill."

He nodded. "In your bag in the truck, right?"

"Yes. Thank you."

He trotted away. Jenny eyed Grace. "He's a good man."

"I can testify to that."

Mitch came back with her pill bottle and put it on the table.

Jenny rose. "Water or something else? Lemonade?"

"Water, please." Grace looked at Mitch. "I'm about to get a little groggy."

"That's fine. Just enjoy the show. If you get too groggy, let me know. I'll take you home with me. Lila is really impatient to look after you."

Then he left her, going to get his own lunch.

He was indeed a good man.

She swallowed her pill with some of the water Jenny gave her. She followed Mitch's instructions and enjoyed the incredible show.

"HELL," CARL SAID to Larry. "This ain't gonna convince the woman to move."

Larry agreed as he stared through the binoculars at the quickly rising barn. "Damn," he said. "What was the point of burning it?"

"She *did* have to go to the hospital," Carl said after a minute or so. "Maybe that's enough."

"I wish. She's got nine lives like a cat."

"Boss ain't gonna be happy," Carl grumbled.

"Then maybe she damn well ought to work some on this," said Larry, a layer of taut anger in his voice.

"If she wasn't paying us so good, I'd walk away."

"Yeah," Larry answered. "Are you sure she's gonna give us that money? I don't trust her."

"She'll be one sorry fool if she don't pay up. We can deal with her."

Larry nodded. A look of satisfaction crossed his face. "Yeah, we can."

MIDAFTERNOON, MITCH TOOK Grace home with him. She not only looked weary, she appeared to suffer quite some pain. Tomorrow would be better. Bound to be.

Right now she wasn't very far from a bad burn on the very tender palms of her hands.

"I want to go home," she said.

"We can talk about taking you home when those bandages come off." He saw her bristle, then relax. Damn, that woman really bridled when someone else tried to take charge.

When they started up the bumpy drive to his house, she remarked, "I'm supposed to change these bandages every day. No one told me how to do that."

"We'll manage."

"They sure gave me enough rolls of gauze and that gel." Then her head drooped onto her chest.

Mitch smiled faintly. She was more tired than she realized and he was damn glad to be taking her to his house. Lila would mother her despite any protests. His housekeeper could be a bulldozer when she wanted, a quality he didn't always appreciate. But it was what Grace needed now, whether she wanted to admit it or not.

He was willing to bet that somewhere inside that plastic hospital bag were discharge instructions. He and Lila could ensure that Grace got everything she needed.

How had that woman ever thought she could go home by herself?

Because she could be mulish, pigheaded and so damn independent. All qualities he enjoyed in her. Usually.

Right then, he wasn't admiring them. He kept seeing the fire in his mind's eye, kept seeing her staggering out of that conflagration. He'd have hated it if those horses had died, but he'd have hated it even more if Grace had died.

An ache filled him at the mere thought. He understood why she went in there. Hell, he'd have done it himself. That was somehow different. His heart hurt every time he remembered.

There was no doubt in his mind that Grace would experience another wave of grief as she emerged from the suffering of the last few days. Grief over the loss of her property. Then she'd be afraid, because who would want to do that to her? Finally she'd get angry. Furious.

Rocky days lay ahead.

MAYBE TWO OF those pills at a time was too much, Grace thought as Mitch helped her wobble into the house. But oh, they helped the pain. Perhaps tomorrow she'd try to cut back to one. If she was brave enough.

The way she'd been hurting earlier, she doubted it. There were times when courage failed her, and maybe this time it should.

Inside, Lila appeared instantly. "Put Ms. Hall on that recliner nearest the living room door. Unless you'd rather go to bed, dear?"

"No, really…" She wasn't ready for bed. She'd had enough bed in the hospital to last her for a while. "No bed."

Mitch laughed. "Tired of that, huh? Here we go."

He steadied her while she walked into his living room, then helped ease her into a chair and reclined it.

It had been a long time since she'd been in here, but she remembered the warmth of the decor. She didn't know who had chosen to cover the walls with horizontal knotty pinewood planks, and the floor with darker planks, but the room was inviting. Mitch had a couple of plaid recliners in dark green and burgundy, as well as a few other chairs upholstered in hunter green.

A huge fireplace dominated, surrounded in natural rock with a thick, rustic piece of wood serving as a mantel. The room had a very Western feel to it unlike the living room in her own house, which sported some very old wallpaper. Their homes spoke of very different tastes.

Both were welcoming.

Lila soon placed a hot cup of coffee beside her, and tossed a light knitted throw over her legs. "You'll get a bit cold if you're not moving around."

"I feel wrapped up like a baby," Grace said.

Lila smiled. "Good. Now you just rest a bit. I need to finish making dinner."

GRACE WASN'T SURE what time she woke, but she knew one thing: her hands hurt as if they were burning all over again. She couldn't prevent the groan that escaped her.

She opened her eyes, longing to escape everything. Then Mitch appeared, bending over her. Without a word, he slipped his arm behind her shoulders and lifted her to a seated position.

"Hold this," he said quietly.

She looked down and saw an open bottle of water. She took it between her hands. It was wet and her mouth felt as if she'd been eating dust. She raised it quickly and drank deeply, ignoring the water that dripped down her chin. She must have drained half the bottle before she took a breath.

"Now, here," he said, holding her prescription bottle in front of her. "I know you can take these with some effort, but why don't you just let me pop them in your mouth?"

She opened her mouth to say she could do it, but immediately felt two pills on her tongue. Well, now she *had* to drink.

With the pills washed down, she said, "You're the devil after all."

He chuckled. "Guilty. You want me to raise the back of the chair?"

As she felt his arm slip away, she wished he'd continue to hold her. How long had it been since anyone had held her?

As soon as she met the back of the recliner, she knew the answer to his question. "Up, please."

He reached for the control switch on the end table beside her and raised her as smoothly and easily as if she was on a hospital bed.

How had she missed that earlier? Probably because she'd been so weary.

Mitch backed away and tugged one of the upright chairs over so he could sit facing her.

"Hurting?" he asked.

"A little," she allowed, then wondered why she was lying. He'd just put two pain pills in her mouth. He already knew the answer. "I hurt like hell. When I woke I wanted to run from my body."

"That's awful," he said. He leaned forward, took the water bottle from her and placed it on the end table. Then he put his elbows on his knees. "Just take a few to wake up and let those pills start working. Then we can discuss dinner."

Dinner? The last thing she felt like doing was eating. The pain from her hands seemed to be shooting up her arms, like a living monster. This hurt worse than when she was in the hospital. Then she realized she'd probably been on something stronger than what was in the prescription bottle.

"It shouldn't take longer than twenty minutes for the pills to start working," Mitch said. "God knows I've had them a few times myself."

Seeking distraction, Grace asked, "What for?"

"You really want the laundry list?" He sounded amused.

"I don't know much about your life before we met."

"True, I guess. I'm mostly forward-looking. Well, let me see. There was the time I got thrown by my mount, landed on some rocks and broke nearly half of the bones on my left side. I was twelve at the time, stuck in a bunch of casts, needing some surgery to put in pins."

She drew a breath. "That bad?"

"I was good at accidents around that age. One of the worst was when I fell from the barn loft and broke my wrist. Damn thing was at an angle no arm ought to be. To get it back in line to be set, they had to put this torture device on me, pulling all my fingers hard while I did some caterwauling." He shook his head. "That's on the top of my list for miserable experiences. Cracked ribs hurt pretty bad, too."

"It sounds terrible." She felt the first stirrings of relief from the medicine. Thank God. "Accidents, huh?"

He shrugged. "Let a young boy loose on a ranch, and he'll find some trouble. Fell into a pile of barbed wire once. Took my dad and two of his men close to an hour to cut me loose."

"How in the world did that happen?"

"I was running and tripped. I also wasn't being very cautious. Should have picked a better place to run."

"Like you'd have been thinking about that when you were so young."

"That's how the young get some sense," he answered. "From mistakes. My dad took it in stride. Mostly. The time I got thrown he wasn't completely sympathetic. A boy on a ranch ought to know how to keep his seat better. Doesn't matter if a snake terrified the horse."

"So you fell near a *snake?* And I suppose you were too hurt to move?" The idea was scary.

Another smile appeared. "My mare kinda took care of that. Wasn't much snake left after she trampled it good."

"So that's why the horse was bucking?"

"Yup. She saved both of us by killing it. Then she nuzzled me a time or two. My memory isn't completely clear. After that she took off hell for leather back home. Let my dad know I was in trouble, then brought him to me."

Grace thought about that as the pill begin to soften her pain. "I always suspected horses were smarter than we know."

"I couldn't agree more. She was a good old mare. And my dad was right about keeping my seat. It kinda stung when he said I didn't have as much sense as my horse."

Grace laughed. "That *would* sting."

"When you're twelve? Yeah. I had to admit Baby was getting skittish and I didn't pay attention, just kept guiding her into danger. More sense than me for sure."

"Horses will die for us," she remarked.

"They sure will. Run themselves to death if we demand it. Go straight into battle." He paused. "Feeling any better?"

"Think so. I'm getting a bit muzzy."

"How about some coffee? Lila always has a fresh pot. After, we can talk about what you feel like eating."

Coffee sounded good. It might even keep her from falling asleep. "Please."

She hoped she'd be able to hold it between her hands. It had worked earlier at the barn raising She'd even managed a spoon. Basically she was working with two hands formed into claws.

Much as she hated to admit it, she was very glad Mitch had brought her home with him. She couldn't imagine taking care of herself right now without help. She just hoped having her here wouldn't burden anyone.

Mitch returned in quick order with a brushed steel mug. "It's insulated, so be careful when you sip. The coffee's a little hotter than my tongue would like."

"No more burns for me, thank you very much."

She was able to hold the mug between both her hands and draw in the aroma. Rich and nutty. He was right about the heat, though. She could feel it as she carried the cup closer to her face.

"It won't cool as fast in that mug," he said. "You already know that. Whole reason I got a cupboard full of them."

"I have a few, too. But they have tops."

"So does that one, but I didn't want you to take a swig before you knew what you were getting into." He pulled a top out of his breast pocket. "When you think it's cool enough, I'll put this on."

He was so considerate, Grace thought. Little seemed to escape him.

A few minutes later, she brought the mug up and tested it with her lip. "I think it's ready."

He took the cup and pressed the top on it. "There you go."

She accepted it and tasted the coffee, savoring it. Just what she needed.

"Now to dinner," he said. "Lila made a great one, but she always does. She was thinking of you, too. Not much that you can't eat with a spoon."

All this caring might overwhelm her. She said so.

"Like I care? Damn, woman, I'm just thrilled you're alive. Let me know when you're ready to eat."

A while later he said, "Lila went over to your house to get you some night things and a few fresh changes of clothes. She also said when you're ready she'll give you a sponge bath."

"Oh my God," Grace answered, her cheeks heating. "That's too—"

"Too much," he interrupted. "I know. Let me remind you she's taken care of a family and she volunteered. Besides, in a day or two you're going to start feeling like something that needs to be mucked out of a stall."

That actually made her laugh. "You're awful, Mitch."

"I work on it." He flashed another grin. "Much better than Lila telling me I have a God-given purpose. I don't see ranching that way. It's a job, like any other. I'm just luckier than most."

She shook her head. "You do a great job looking after your animals. That's not all luck."

"Maybe not, but I've got this big spread. My great-granddaddy left it behind. Dad and I always felt lucky. You gotta have the land and this is damn fine land."

She knew it was true. Her own place was blessed with

enough water unlike so many around here. She and John had definitely been lucky to get it at auction for such a good price. Otherwise they'd never have had their flock, their life together on the land.

A wave of sorrow passed through her, then released her. She sipped more coffee and realized she wasn't getting as sleepy on the pills as before. Getting used to them?

Then she noticed she was getting hungry.

As if reading her mind, Mitch asked, "Getting hungry now?"

"Amazingly, yes."

He nodded. "Good. Lila would be upset if you didn't eat at least a little of her chefery. I can recommend the stone soup. Easy to eat with a spoon."

"Stone soup? Really?" There couldn't be stones in it.

"That's what she calls it. A bit of most of what she has in the fridge and the cupboards. Trust me, it's always an adventure and surprising how she can make all that taste good."

He frowned a little, evidently in thought. "There's some mashed potatoes. Some fruit salad that has pieces small enough to eat with a spoon. That salad is the best. She makes it from fresh fruit."

Grace was impressed with the splendid smorgasbord he offered her. "You choose," she said after a moment. "I can't decide. Everything sounds good, even stone soup."

He chuckled at that. "I know. Really? All right, I'll come back with the first course."

He paused in the doorway, looking back at her. "Like I said, she was thinking of you when she made dinner. Small pieces."

Grace was touched, if a little embarrassed that the

woman had gone out of her way. This was the kind of thing she always tried to avoid.

Mitch returned with a deep bowl, not a soup plate, putting it on a TV table in front of her. Beside it he placed a napkin and spoon.

"Don't worry if you dribble a bit," he said. "Whenever I eat soup, I always swear there's a hole in my lip."

That relaxed her because she shared the feeling. Before she began to eat, she took the napkin and tucked it in to her collar as best she could.

"Good idea," Mitch remarked. "I've often talked about finding an adult-sized bib."

The soup was every bit as delicious as he'd promised. Grace had no idea what Lila had cobbled together, but it was the best soup she'd ever tasted.

Shortly after she finished, however, she fell asleep sitting up.

Her day was done.

Chapter Ten

Over the next few days, Grace came to accept that she couldn't have gone home by herself. Lila took over her bandaging according to Grace's discharge instructions, patiently smearing on the gel. At last the day arrived that her fingers could all be bound separately. What a relief!

Lila would sit with her for a while, chatting about irrelevancies, then head back to her domain, the kitchen. Marvelous food came out of that kitchen, every kind of baked good, from croissants to pies and cobblers. Grace was sure she was going to plump up.

Mitch went out every day to look after his operation and to help finish her new barn. She still couldn't get over that. How had she come to have such good neighbors?

"It's simple," Mitch answered when she mentioned it. "You're part of the ranchers' family. All of us are."

Mitch had taken to eating his meals with her. As she had begun to back off her pain medication, she joined him in the kitchen, sometimes with Bill and sometimes with all three of the hired hands. Conversation was generally light, mostly talk about cattle. Grace listened eagerly, feeling she had stepped back into part of the life she had lost.

Then Bill said, "Grace, your new barn is finished. I hope you'll get to see it soon. It's so great that I'm thinking we ought to burn down ours."

"Don't you dare," Mitch said with a laugh.

Bill and the others laughed with him.

The roast beef was perfectly done, the mashed potatoes a scoop of heaven and the broccoli impeccably cooked. "You're a wizard, Lila," she offered sincerely.

"Just you wait until I really rev up. Bet these guys never expected to eat fancy cooking."

"This is pretty fancy," Bill remarked.

Grace watched Bill and Lila, thinking that Mitch might be right about the two of them. Something in the way they looked at each other. She dipped into the food on her plate again, savoring every mouthful and enjoying having nearly functional fingers again.

The mess on her hands, which she saw every time Lila changed her bandages, was bad but healing. She suspected that they were going to be tender for some time to come. That was down the road, however, and she was enjoying being able to hold a fork again, even if not the way she used to.

"Tell me about the barn, please," she asked when the conversation flagged. The four men were clearly on a wavelength together, an easy flow of talk between them. She enjoyed listening but was still curious.

"It's something to behold," Jeff said. "Don't see too many new barns in these parts. Almost a shame it'll have to be painted."

Painted? Grace hadn't thought about that, and her stomach sank a bit. Paint for a building that big would be monstrously expensive.

"Or," Mitch interjected, "she could just let it age awhile. Maybe until the wood silvers a bit."

Jack laughed. Bill answered, "Boss, you know how long it takes for wood to do that?"

"I do. I also know how a freshly painted barn would look in these parts. Like a damn lighthouse."

Grace laughed, too. He was right about that. Her own barn, the one that had burned, had been all silvered with age but still usable. How many years ago had it been built? She had no idea.

Jeff spoke again. "Aw. Here I was thinking we could gussy it up with some bright red paint. White trim."

Jack looked at him. "You want to go all New England?"

"Hey," Jeff answered. "These days most new barns look like Quonset huts, all built out of steel. Which doesn't last as long, you ask me."

"Don't believe I did," Jack retorted.

Another round of laughter ringed the table.

"Well, I never did like rust all that much," Jack continued. "Whatever they make them barns out of, it still rusts eventually. Like those the ones you got to park all the heavy equipment and vehicles in."

"Then don't burn my wood barn down," Mitch said. "Otherwise you'll be patching metal more of the time."

Jack feigned a frown. "I stay on a horse better than a ladder."

More laughter. Grace thought about how easy it would be to slip into this camaraderie and forget everything else. It wrapped around her like a warm blanket.

After dinner, Lila settled her back in the recliner with a hot cup of coffee and a piece of peach pie. Grace wished she could help the others with cleanup, but that was impossible right now.

Still, she apologized to Lila. "I'm sorry I can't help with the dishes."

Lila put her hands on her hips. "I got four healthy men out there taking care of it, and well they should, if they want me to keep cooking. Besides..."

Lila's face softened. "Honey, you ain't gonna be doing much with those hands for a while. Even after the bandages come off, they won't like hot water. And I *really* don't want my pots and pans washed in cold water. Like I need to tell you that."

Lila sailed away, probably to spend more time around Bill.

Grace looked at her hands. Lila was right. She'd had burns before, much smaller, but hot water was like holding a match to them. God, would she ever be able to stand on her own two feet again?

TIME PASSED, ALTHOUGH far too slowly for Grace. The days fell into a routine: breakfast in the kitchen, usually with Lila and Mitch, then Mitch setting out for a day of work. Before long, Grace would be settled in the living room with a cup of coffee, the TV remote and a book.

Despite what Mitch had said about watching TV so rarely he couldn't find the remote, there was a large flat-screen enthroned over the fireplace. Not that she'd ever seen Mitch turn it on, and she wasn't inclined to. Daytime TV rarely offered her anything she cared to watch. She knew because she'd tried it for a while after John's death, seeking distraction. However, it hadn't provided any.

Her own channel selection had been limited, but

Mitch had a satellite dish out back that looked big enough to track the stars.

The thought amused her. A remnant from years past, she supposed, that still worked.

Time dragged anyway. Holding a book fatigued her sore hands rapidly. She still took a pain pill from time to time but they no longer made her sleepy. God, why had she never appreciated how much hands did? How often they were needed even for the simplest things.

She had begun to take walks outside. Sitting around so much was weakening her, and stretching her muscles felt good. The sun kissed her skin with heat, the breeze tossed her hair around, but before long her eyes began to water. The sun was too bright. Damn, she needed a cap of some kind. Sunglasses. Blue eyes sucked when the sun was really bright. An eye doctor had told her once that they didn't block the light as well as darker eyes.

Before, she'd been mostly content with solitude. Now she found herself eagerly anticipating Mitch's appearance in the late afternoons. He'd shower, then come to keep her company.

The amazing thing was that he hadn't become bored with her. Instead he'd sit with her, telling her about his day, asking her about hers. She rarely had anything to offer, but he could make amusing stories out of the mundane matters of operating a cattle ranch. Or some story about what the sheep were up to.

Listening to Mitch, she wondered why she'd never noticed the sheep antics he reported. Maybe she hadn't been paying close enough attention.

"The spring lambs are developing a real sense of adventure," he told her. "Into everything, according to Zeke and Rod. You'd think they were young goats."

"Really?" she asked. "I never noticed that."

"You aren't Zeke and Rod. They live with that flock. They've had to rescue youngsters who tried to leap barbed wire."

Grace sat up a little straighter. "That's hard to believe."

"Feeling their oats, I guess. Their wool is growing in and they get caught easier. Zeke said the ewes are forever trying to round them up, but this group is really adventurous. He says they aren't moving with the flock, the way sheep usually do. He and Rod are getting frustrated. I got the word again that they need a dog. Sure sounds like it. You can't run fast enough to keep up with that crowd."

"Amazing. I never guessed."

"Neither did I, and I've been watching over that group for a little more than a year now. I get them enjoying running around, burning off all that youthful energy. Kinda like puppies. But trying to jump fences?" Mitch shook his head in disbelief. "I wonder if a goat or two got in there during mating season. Although I have no idea where a goat could have come from."

"Me, neither. I always wanted goats, but we couldn't because they need special fencing so they can't get out. Plus the cost of supplements was just too high. Maybe we should have just put up the fence anyway."

Mitch flashed a grin. "I'm thinking they'll settle down. I hope they will. And I've still got to look into a herding dog or two. I talked to Ransom Laird and he has some puppies who are being trained by his older dogs, but it'll be a little while yet before they're ready."

Grace nodded. "Didn't you use to have some dogs?"

"I still do. Out on the range. Mainly they keep wolves and other predators away. Never trained them for sheep."

"Was there ever a wolf problem here?" She'd never heard anything about it.

"Not in my lifetime. Some ranchers closer to Yellowstone claim to see them once in a while. Frankly, wolves aren't overpopulating the place. More trouble from coyotes, especially with spring lambs."

"That was our experience, too." She hesitated, gnawing her lower lip. "Mitch?"

"Yeah?"

"I've been trying not to think about it, but why would somebody burn down my barn? Or maybe more important, who would want to? I honestly can't quite believe it was the industrial farming company. They must have better ways of taking over land."

He nodded slowly. "I can't get it off my mind, either. I also can't figure it. Unless some firebug just wanted a big blaze."

Grace didn't like that idea at all. The randomness of that disturbed her deeply. Maybe because she needed a reason for most everything. "Coming so soon after that ewe was shot only bothers me more."

"Me, too," he admitted.

Grace was glad he didn't dismiss her worries. Much as she'd been trying not to build a massive case of anxiety, the anxiety remained anyway.

She closed her eyes briefly, remembering that night, the impossibly high flames, the screaming horses. She shuddered. "I'm going to have some bad dreams for a while."

"Understandable." He'd brought the inevitable cup of coffee in with him, and reached for it now, taking a couple of swigs. "It feels like beating my head on an invisible brick wall. I want answers. Seems like I'm not going to get any soon."

"I hate that," she admitted.

"You ain't the only one." He paused. "I've got all my men keeping an eye out for anything suspicious. I'm not ready to move on as if this is nothing but chance."

"I don't think I can."

His gray eyes met hers. "Grace, understand that I'll do anything to protect you."

The words caused her breath to catch in her throat, followed by the burn of unshed tears. His concern wrapped around her, answering an ache she hadn't even realized was there.

She looked away, swallowing hard. His statement had opened something inside her. It had been a long time since she'd felt such honest concern. Maybe Mitch had been offering it all along and she hadn't been paying attention.

Why would she? Grief had consumed her. Her entire life had become one of fighting to save what she could of her dream, leaving no room for anything else. She'd been obstinate and blind in her determination to stand alone, feeling she owed it to John.

Words couldn't convey the unexpected, hungry need that roiled inside her. How much had she missed having someone give a damn about her feelings and her needs? These moments told her that while she was mostly introverted, she still needed something more in her life.

Mitch's kindness reached beyond an ordinary friendship. He was offering something a whole lot bigger.

"Thank you," she answered, her voice thick.

"Hey," he said quietly. "I didn't mean to make you sad."

"You didn't." She turned her face back to him. "You... just made me feel special."

He smiled slightly. "Good. Because you're one hell of special woman. Stubborn as hell, but still special."

That drew a choked laugh from her. "I was just thinking about my stubbornness."

"I hope we've gotten you a little past that. The new barn and all."

"And taking care of me here."

He feigned astonishment. "I value my skin. Lila would have taken a piece of my hide if I'd done any less."

He'd lightened the moment, for which she was grateful. She seemed to be losing her balance somehow. Falling off the tightrope of emotion she'd been walking for so long.

Maybe she ought to excuse herself. The barn, her injuries, her steady but slow recovery, the mess all this had made of her usual life... Plenty of reason to feel shaky emotionally.

It wasn't just that. Who would have guessed that emerging from long stasis could feel so painful? Far from feeling as if she were coming out of a long nightmare, she felt as if her protective layer was being stripped away. It hurt.

"Ah," Mitch sighed. A few moments later he rose. "More coffee? Mine's cold. Or something stronger?"

"Coffee, please." She wasn't sure how alcohol would mesh with the pain pill she'd taken two hours ago. Because her dang hands had started to seriously hurt again. As if the bandages were irritating them now.

She rested her head back against the chair while he went to the kitchen, trying to quash the feeling that he'd just offered her a gift she wanted badly to accept. All he'd said was that he'd do anything to protect her.

Simple words, a strong promise, leaving her exposed like a raw nerve ending. Worse, she now had to face the gaping holes she'd dug in her own life. Not just missing John, but burying herself alive.

Damn, she couldn't deal with this right now. No way. Bad enough that she was wondering who had hung this sword over her head and what might be coming her way.

Because deep inside, she didn't believe the barn was the end of it.

"You GUYS GOTTA do better," the boss told them over the phone they'd put on speaker. "I don't see any sign of the Hall woman hightailing it."

"She ain't home," Carl argued. "She's living with that Cantrell guy now, and she ain't showing any sign of going home."

"Damn Cantrell," the boss said. "Damn him to hell. Why is he getting involved?"

Neither Carl nor Larry had an answer for that.

The boss nearly snarled. "You gotta scare her more. Figure it out. But not too soon. Too soon and we blow it. Just remember, if she doesn't leave, you don't get paid the rest."

Both Larry and Carl were aware of the money that she'd dangled before them. A small down payment to be followed by an appreciable sum when their job was complete. But damn, this was taking an awful long time. Who'd have thought some damn woman could be this stupid. Or this stubborn.

It wasn't at all the way that Larry and Carl thought of gals.

As THE EVENING DEEPENED, Grace circled around once again to her fears. Or maybe concerns. She'd rather not think she was afraid.

"Someone had to have done it," she said yet again. The uneasiness wouldn't back off.

"The fire, you mean? Well, yeah."

She nearly sighed. "And the ewe. You know what I'm talking about. They could be linked."

"I know."

He didn't dismiss her worry and she was thankful. Over the years, being a woman, she'd been dismissed many times, especially when something bothered her. As if her feelings didn't count.

She spoke again. "I keep thinking of that industrial operation. I can't get it out of my head, even though I also can't quite believe it. Great way to get me to sell and leave you their only problem."

He nodded slowly. "I've been thinking about them, too. Doesn't make sense to me, but they keep popping up. Thing is, I've been too busy worrying about you lately to do what I should have."

Her heart quickened a bit. "What's that?"

"Call the sheriff and tell him I've got this suspicion. If anyone can find out if that company has left a trail of fires or anything else shady in their wake, the sheriff's office can."

"I hope so. I wouldn't know where to begin. You don't have to worry yourself over me."

He spoke firmly. "Someone has to."

Again that rending inside of her, opening like a door closed too long. Squeaky and creaky as it pulled away from its frame on unoiled hinges.

She cleared her throat. "Thanks for not thinking I'm being silly."

"Why in the hell would I do that? The ewe incident might have been one jerk being stupid beyond belief. But the barn? One plus one equals two. Or three, depending on how you count on your fingers."

That made her laugh again. "Thanks."

MITCH WAS ENJOYING having her in his house, and definitely enjoying how she was laughing more. The sound had been absent from her for so long. Her face lit up and she became more than pretty. She became beautiful. Sometimes he just wanted to feast his eyes on her but resisted the urge. He didn't want to make her uncomfortable.

Why would she suspect that he might find her silly for her worries? Even had he not agreed with her, he never would have thought that. There was nothing about Grace that anyone could call silly.

He wished he could heal her hands with a magic wand. It hurt him to see her bandaged like that and to know that when the bandages came off her hands would be painfully tender. It might be a while before she could do simple things, like hold something heavy, or endure her palms rubbing on anything. And forget hot water.

He focused instead on the courage that had led her into a burning barn to save the horses. Amazing woman.

Thinking about that night led him to say, "I've got some free time in the morning. Want to see Dolly and Daisy? They're out in the far paddock."

"I'd love to see them!"

He smiled. "Then we'll drive over to see your new barn. You can also decide if you want it painted."

She laughed again. "I take it no red?"

"Only if you want to become a local landmark."

Her grin widened. "I think I already am, given that there aren't too many newly constructed barns out there."

"Eighth wonder of the world. You'll be attracting tourists before you know it. Crowds will come from all over the county, rarely having seen a brand-new wood barn."

The idea clearly amused her.

"How are your hands feeling?" he asked.

She waved one at him. "Painful. I'm sure sick of the bandages."

"I can imagine. Consider them to be protective gloves."

She frowned a little. "I hate to think what it's going to be like when they get unwrapped for good. I've had burns before."

"Yeah. Well, since I don't have a magic wand, how about you stay here for a bit? You're not going to manage well on your own for a few weeks." Then he added, "I'm still astonished that you ran into that barn."

"I couldn't do anything else." Her expression turned sober. "Mitch, it would have been awful to let those horses burn. I couldn't do it. I'm sure you'd have done the same thing."

"Maybe. I've never had to. Probably a reason I'm not a fireman."

She shook her head. "Quit being so modest."

At least she didn't pursue that. He doubted he could have stood the embarrassment.

Needing to change the subject, he asked, "Wanna watch some TV?"

She dropped her somber mood and her face relaxed. "Hey, aren't you the guy who said he didn't care for it? The guy who said he couldn't find the remote?"

He pointed to the table beside her. "I think Lila found it when she was cleaning."

"Does she find everything for you?"

"More than I'd like sometimes. Seriously, it was up on the mantel. I've got little use for it."

"You, the guy with the huge satellite dish out back."

He laughed. "Blame my dad. Man, he wanted those sports shows come the weekend. That thing is a dinosaur."

"Bet it picks up radio signals from distant galaxies."

"I've never checked, but maybe I should donate it to the Smithsonian."

"Or to some observatory," she teased.

God, it was good to see her spirits this high. Tread carefully, he warned himself. Don't say anything that might sadden her again.

He knew that she was always tipping toward grief. Always. That was another thing that made him wish for a magic wand. With John she had been happy most of the time. He could understand why John's death had gutted her. Eventually, though, everyone had to move on.

Grief would always be with her, but it didn't have to smother her. It didn't have to penetrate her every day and control her. But how did you make someone see that?

Only Grace could do that. When the time for her was right.

Later she dozed off. Clearly still recovering from her harrowing experience and her burns. He found a throw and gently draped it over her. His mother had crocheted that throw, one of the good memories about the brief time he'd had with her. She'd died from breast cancer when he was six, but he could still remember her sitting in her rocking chair and working that crochet needle all evening while talking to him and his dad.

He walked quietly to the kitchen to grab a beer, then came back to the living room to stand at the front window. It had never been covered with curtains because this far out, the likelihood of anyone traipsing here to peer in was minuscule.

Next, he grabbed a few of his journals and magazines from his office and settled in to read.

Oh, yeah, he thought. The dogs. A couple more months, Ransom Laird had said. By then autumn would be creeping in with winter hard on its tail. The sheep would be heading to their fold as the cold winds began to blow. The shepherds had a small house for protection and warmth as they continued their duties. And the dogs? He'd have to ask about that.

This sheep thing was still very new to him. He was grateful for a couple of guys from Portugal whose knowledge appeared to be bottomless. Best investment he could have made.

Mitch almost laughed at himself as he sipped his beer. Those guys allowed him to look confident whenever he was asked about the venture. But mainly they prevented him from doing something stupid that might harm the sheep.

Then there was Grace, whose pretty head probably held a wealth of knowledge about sheep. He should have asked her but didn't want to jar her into unhappy memories.

He turned to look over at her as she slept. He wouldn't mind that view for a long time to come. Then he forced his attention back to his reading material.

Chapter Eleven

In the morning, Grace was eager to take the drive Mitch had promised.

Well, of course, Mitch thought. She must be awfully tired of the inside of his house and walks around the outside of it. His front yard wasn't much of a yard, rather a scrubby patch that hadn't been good enough to graze.

Out back were the barely discernible remains of his mother's kitchen garden, once always brimming with vegetables throughout the growing season, followed later by endless days of canning and freezing. Now it had become a weed patch through which could be seen the vestiges of once-neat rows.

One of his favorite memories was of the end of the growing season when she'd say, "Get out back and eat some of them tomatoes, boy. Can't can 'em all."

Nothing, he believed, could quite measure up to a warm, sun-kissed tomato right off the vine. He ate himself sick. Then it was over, cold weather moving in again.

He recalled the year when she let him choose any vegetable he wanted to grow, and how astonished she'd been when he'd picked radishes.

What had sent him down this particular path of memory? Over scrambled eggs and bacon, he watched Grace chat with Lila about inconsequential matters. He enjoyed her animation, her hands gesturing as she spoke. He hadn't seen her like this since his last visit before John died.

He wished the mood would last.

A short time later, she got into his pickup truck with him and they set out on their minor adventure. "We'll go see Dolly and Daisy when we get back."

"Okay."

He suspected she was about ready to bounce on her seat.

After twenty minutes or so, her barn emerged from behind the rolling land.

"Oh man," she said quietly as she took it in. "Oh man."

He unbuckled her seat belt, then leaned across her to open the door. As soon as she could slip out of the truck, she hurried toward the barn.

It was a beautiful construct, rising as high as her old barn, maybe higher. As soon as he caught up to her, he opened the huge door to let her in.

"Oh man," she said again. Six stalls, three on each side, stood ready for horses. At the back could be seen a work room and a tack room. Overhead, a loft for storage.

Grace spoke again. "Smell the wood. Oh, I love the smell of fresh lumber."

He did, too. He inhaled the scent and thought his neighbors were a pretty damn good bunch of people.

When she looked at Mitch again, there was no mistaking the sheen of tears in her eyes. "It's beautiful. How do I ever thank everyone, Mitch?"

"I believe they know without being told."

"I sure hope so. Maybe when my hands are better I can hold a barbecue."

"They'd like that. Everyone out here loves a good excuse for a shindig and a day away from work. You must remember that."

She whirled around with her arms extended. "It's more than beautiful, it's perfect." Then she laughed. "I need some horses in here. Well, maybe not for a while."

"And a decent pair of work gloves," he reminded her.

That drew another laugh from her. "They even put in some small windows."

"Well, ya gotta be able to see in here. At least when the sun is bright. You don't want to be burning lights all the time."

"I wish…" She fell silent.

He knew what she wished. That she could share this with John. Hadn't this woman been kicked around enough, at least for a while? He ached to make her life better, happier.

For now, she *was* happy. Thrilled even. And it hadn't taken a piece of fancy jewelry and a dozen roses to make her feel this way. No, a barn, and one that she really didn't have use for at present.

The glow in her face was lovely. He hoped it would remain a little longer.

She ran the length of the barn and back, as excited as a kid on Christmas. "I can't believe this."

"Believe it. Touch it if you have to."

She just shook her head, joy written all over her. "Let's go to the house," she suggested. "I need to make sure everything's okay."

"Lila's been over here every few days."

"I know, but I still need to look around."

That made sense to Mitch. It was her home, one she and John had shared for nearly a decade. The sights and smells would be familiar and welcoming.

They walked together over to her house, leaving behind the smell of fresh wood. There was still a spring to Grace's step, for which Mitch was grateful. At last something had truly cheered her up.

He followed her more slowly, wanting to give her time to feel at home again. Like most folks around here, she probably hadn't locked her door.

The he heard her cry, "Oh my God, oh my God."

Mitch hit a full run, reaching her door in seconds. Grace had collapsed on her floor, and his heart started skipping wildly. The front door was busted in.

Then he saw her living room and, through the open doorway, her kitchen.

Her house had been trashed.

Chapter Twelve

Mitch hurried to Grace, instantly worried that the fall might have harmed her. "You hurt anywhere?"

"No…" Her voice broke, barely audible as she gasped for air, and a huge tremor ripped through her.

Mitch picked her up, holding her close and hugging her tightly. Her body shook as she sobbed violently. She'd reached her breaking point. His mind skittered around uselessly, desperate for a way to help her.

"Why, Mitch? Why?"

He couldn't answer that. There was no answer he could give that wasn't a lie. She clung to him as best she could, but he had no intention of letting her go. Giving her comfort with his embrace was all he *could* do.

"Let's go outside," he suggested when her sobbing began to ease.

"I need to look," she said brokenly.

"We shouldn't touch anything. I'll call the cops. Please, Grace."

She let him keep an arm around her waist, to steady her. Her feet proved unstable and he wondered how much her hands were going to hurt after falling on them. Right then she was in too much shock to notice.

Anger burned in him once he had her settled in one

of the chairs on her porch. Who the hell would do something like this? Remembering all the things that had happened to her, he decided it felt like a siege. But why?

Then he did the only thing he could. He pulled the satellite phone off his belt and called the sheriff.

Velma, the dispatcher, answered immediately.

Mitch spoke right away. "Someone trashed the inside of Grace Hall's house. It may have been a robbery."

"Fifteen or twenty minutes," Velma answered promptly, wasting no words. "Don't touch anything."

He squatted, placing a hand on Grace's shoulder, feeling the tremors that still rippled through her. Whatever was going on, it was snowballing, racing down a mountainside. He hoped like hell that there wasn't more to come.

Next, Grace would want to stay to clean up. He knew this woman. Ten years of friendship had taught him a lot about her. She'd emerge from this shock with her backbone stiff and angry determination driving her. She wasn't going to leave after this. No way. She'd want to protect her house. The ragged ends of a dream.

The thought of leaving her here alone was more than he could bear. She wasn't going to feel safe, maybe never again, unless they caught whoever had done this. Hell, he wasn't going to *believe* she was safe until this all got sorted out.

Anger simmered in him until it erupted into rage. At this point he could have cheerfully killed the perp without a bit of guilt.

He had something more important to think about. He dropped to his knees beside her. Tears still rolled down her cheeks. His rage turned into a deep-seated ache for her, a compression of his chest so powerful it hurt.

"Don't leave me, Mitch."

"I won't." Not ever, but certainly not right now. He dared to squeeze her forearm gently. "I'm right here. I'll be here as long as you want me."

She nodded, closing her eyes as more tears fell. "What did I do wrong?"

Oh, God, he didn't want her to think that way, to blame herself. "Nothing," he said firmly. "Not one damn thing."

"I must have done something!" Her voice broke.

"How could you have done anything? You've locked yourself away for damn near two years. Anyone who had a grudge would have long since cooled down. I seriously doubt you and John could have upset anyone. You were both tied up most of the time with your sheep."

Ranchers of any kind rarely went to town except to get supplies or go to church. The rest of the time they kept their noses to the grindstone. John and Grace had been no different. Even back when they'd been able to afford a couple of hired hands, they didn't leave for long. There was too much work to be done. Always.

Grace calmed down, a little at a time, and finally fell still and silent, staring out over the open land toward the mountains. From here they looked closer than they really were, their purpled slopes looming over the county.

Mitch got off his knees and sat cross-legged beside her, waiting for whatever came next. Anger, now accompanied by fear for Grace, whipped at him. What would come next?

He knew Grace would be hit with a whirlwind of reactions when the shock passed. Fear was going to lash her, the way it did him. But Grace wouldn't knuckle under to it. Not Grace. She'd try to turn her back on it, and nurture her anger the way she had her grief. She'd want to get whoever had done this, not allowing anything to halt her.

She would certainly see that the killing of the ewe couldn't have been isolated, nor the barn fire, not when compounded with the ransacking of her house. She would feel she was being targeted and he wouldn't be able to disagree.

She'd wonder why forever, and so would he. The damn cops better solve this one. He didn't want her to be shadowed by this, nor did he want her to run away, giving up everything she'd been hanging on to.

At last he heard sirens coming their way. Sirens seemed a little much given that no life was in danger and the back roads around here were pretty much empty most of the time. Still, they were coming as fast as they could.

Because most of them knew Grace, knew of her troubles and her solitariness out here. They wouldn't allow her to sit amid the shambles if they could arrive faster. The flashing blue and white lights turned into her driveway, sirens silenced. Three cars and a crime scene van. The perpetrators better not be hanging around anywhere nearby.

He rose, remarking uselessly, "They're here." The silence had grown too long and too deep. The rustling of the endless wind didn't fill it.

The vehicles pulled up fast. Guy Redwing was the first to climb out, and from the second came Gage Dalton, the county sheriff. Mitch was surprised to see him. Gage didn't often answer calls anymore. Back in the day when he'd headed up crime scene investigations, he'd been out and about more, but since taking over as sheriff, he'd been buried in management and politics. Everything came down to politics sooner or later.

Several other officers arrived and began fanning out around the house, probably seeking evidence. But Gage and Guy came up the steps to the porch.

"Grab me a chair, please," Gage said without addressing anyone in particular.

Guy quickly dragged a wooden chair over and Gage sat. "Not the way it used to be," Gage remarked. "That damn car is a torture device."

Used to be? Mitch wondered. Gage had been so seriously injured by a bomb during his DEA days that Mitch doubted he'd had a single pain-free day since.

"Ms. Hall," Gage said. "You okay?" His scarred face reflected intense concern. "You weren't here?"

Grace shook her head. "I'm okay." Then she asked, "What's okay?"

Gage gave her one of his patented crooked smiles. "Not much right now. So you weren't here?"

Grace looked up at Mitch.

He answered for her, since she seemed to want him to. "We'd come over to take a look at her new barn. She's been staying with me because of her injuries in that fire."

Gage nodded. "Believe me, I heard about that. Fire inspector said it was arson. We have people working on the case."

"I know you do," Mitch agreed. "Anyway, we thought a trip out to see the barn might make for a brighter day. It did until Grace went inside her house."

"Ransacked?"

"If there's anything in there that wasn't tossed, I'd like to see it."

Mitch sensed a shudder running through Grace, and he reached up to touch her arm. "We'll get through this, Grace."

She nodded jerkily, but another big tear ran down her face.

"Do I need to get medics out here?" Gage asked. "Shock."

"No...no," Grace said. "No. I'll be...okay, whatever that is."

Mitch could tell that she was floundering, trying to fit all this into a permanently changed worldview. This had to be earth-shattering. Well, he wasn't doing too well with it himself. The enormity of all this felt beyond human ken.

Who the hell? And why the hell? They both needed answers, and if the techs didn't find any clues, there wouldn't be any answers. How did they deal with that?

Four crime scene techs, wearing white Tyvek suits and booties, their hands gloved in blue, entered the house. Grace turned her head and watched them without expression.

"I hope they find something," Mitch said.

"Me, too," Grace answered.

Mitch looked at her, sensing she was edging out of shock, reconnecting with all this in a different way. She was coming back. He hoped that was a good thing.

Gage leaned back in his chair, wincing. "Doesn't this all beat hell? The ewe, the barn and now this. Damn it, Grace, if someone wants this place, why destroy it? Why not make an offer on it?"

Which reminded Mitch. "Earlier in the spring we had

an industrial operation out here who wanted to buy both our places."

Gage stared at him. "You have any information about them?"

"I think I've still got the leaflet they left with me."

The sheriff nodded thoughtfully. "I want to see it. You both have some of the finest land in this county. I'm not surprised someone would want to buy it. But this?"

"It does seem like a long shot."

"Maybe. You get me that information, Mitch, and we'll find out everything we can about them. I'm going to know what the boss uses to wipe his nose."

"When can I go back inside?" Grace asked, out of the blue.

Gage replied. "Not for a few hours, I'm afraid. When the techs are done, we'll need you to go in and tell us if you notice anything major missing. If not, you can add items later. Knowing what was taken can help with the investigation."

She nodded slowly, and a sigh escaped her that sounded pent up for a long time.

Mitch walked to the far end of the porch and used his phone again. "Lila? Grace's place was trashed. We'll be over here for a while with the sheriff."

He listened to Lila's exclamations of horror, then asked, "Can you bring over sandwiches and coffee? It's looking to be a long day."

"Absolutely. How many?"

He looked around, counting. "Including Grace and me, we've got nine altogether. Maybe more coming."

"Give me an hour. I'll get Bill to help."

Then he disconnected, hanging his phone on his belt. Life was sure going to hell in a handbasket.

GRACE DIDN'T KNOW what to do. The first shock was passing, and she needed action of some kind. Sitting around doing nothing had never been her forte. Not even during the endless two years since John had died. She probably had one of the cleanest houses on the planet, outside of a hospital. Make-work, mostly, that kept her moving.

She was itching to get inside and clean up the mess. She'd definitely need help. Some heavy stuff, like her furniture, had been upended.

She looked at Gage again. "It was more than a robbery," she told him.

He nodded. "Why do you think that?"

"Because it looks like a tornado whipped through there."

"That's unusual," Gage agreed. "But we'll have to wait and see. Drugs might cause someone to go to that extreme."

"Really?"

"Yep. Trust me, I know recreational drugs inside and out. What's more, they don't affect everyone the same way. I've seen rages that are terrifying, and not necessarily directed."

The idea that some junkie had done this was easier to swallow than the other ideas that started to circulate in her mind. She couldn't imagine that anyone *wanted* to attack her this way, but with this break-in following the barn being burned…well, the fear was inescapable.

She ransacked her mind, trying to think who might want to harm her, and came up empty. None of this made sense. None of it.

And while Mitch had again mentioned the people who wanted to buy her land, that seemed outlandish.

A big company had a lot to lose from doing something like that. A whole lot.

The drug addict idea felt better to her, but then why both the barn and the house?

She'd stopped crying and shaking, but her insides still roiled. The way the house was trashed, her one overwhelming sense was that it had been vicious. Even more than the barn.

Her barn had practically been tinder, old as it was. It had been empty a long time and might have appeared attractive to a firebug. But the house? It made no sense at all.

She couldn't stop linking them, nor apparently could Mitch. He'd even suggested the ewe had been part of it, too. Like a warning of worse to come.

She shuddered and tried to drag her mind away from her worst speculations. If she was going to get through the next days and weeks, she couldn't afford to harbor such ideas. She needed to deal, not sit around worrying.

Time seemed to be moving through sludge, holding her captive. She wanted those techs to be done so she could get in there and assess the damage for herself. When she thought of all the keepsakes from her marriage, the photos of John, her stomach turned over and she felt she might vomit.

Those were the only important things in that house. They'd better still be there and be okay.

Lila pulled up in a truck like Mitch's and hopped out. She'd brought Bill with her, and after a wave, she and Bill started setting up a folding table and bringing out large plastic containers.

"Coffee?" Mitch asked her. "I'm sure Lila brought enough for an army."

She looked up at him and tried to manage a smile. "Thanks. But I'll just go over and see if I can help Lila with anything. I sure don't want to sit here and brood."

As if she hadn't done enough of that. She shook herself, rose to her feet and hurried over.

Lila greeted her with a hug. "Poor honey," she said. "Poor, poor girl. Somebody needs to meet the business end of my long meat fork."

"I wish," Grace answered. "What can I do to help?"

Lila pretended to size her up. "With those hands? I don't want my sandwiches spilling." Then Lila gave her a big smile. "You just sit here, sweetie. You can keep me and Mitch company. Looks like those guys are going to take forever."

It sure seemed like it, Grace thought. Maybe with the mess in there, their job needed to take longer.

Mitch trotted down from the porch with a couple of folding chairs. He urged Grace into one. "Let me get you that coffee, then Lila can start ordering me around."

"I'd never do that, boss," she said, a twinkle in her eye. "I don't need to anyway. That's what I have Bill for."

Bill feigned a sigh. "Yeah, she's training me good."

Lila gave him a look then told Mitch to sit down, too. "You keep Grace company."

"Yes, ma'am."

Lila handed them both coffees, then lickety-split put out sandwiches and paper plates for everyone. "I hope," she said as she finished layering the sandwiches on several big plates, "that those guys can eat, too. Else we're going to be eating sandwiches for a lot of meals this week."

"Damn, it looks like a party down there," Carl grumped to Larry.

"Didn't look so good earlier. That woman was scared, I tell you."

"Maybe so," Carl muttered. He looked through his binoculars again. "She *did* call the police."

"Well, yeah," Larry answered. "Like she was going to walk in there and ignore it. Which we didn't want her to do, did we?"

"Hell no. So okay, maybe all that food is just neighborly."

"Most like." Larry peered through his own binoculars. "Them sandwiches look good. Wish I had me some."

"Fresh bread, too, I bet." Carl's mood wasn't improving. He got heartburn every time he thought of their boss. Her demands were beginning to chap his hide. Nothing was enough to make her happy. Or at least to satisfy her. *Witch*.

"I hope we didn't leave nothin' behind," Larry remarked, giving Carl another dose of heartburn.

"You better not," Carl retorted angrily. "We talked about it before. Gloves, hats… What could be there?"

"Nothin'." Larry hated these moods of Carl's. When they got going, Carl just got darker and angrier until they blew past. Lately they'd been almost constant.

"I hope she's satisfied now," Carl grumbled. "Damn, what more can we do? Shoot the Hall woman?"

"Murder's out," Larry reminded him.

"I *know* it's out. But what more is there?"

"Not murder," Larry said. "Not that."

"Hell's bells."

Now they both stared glumly at the scene below. It

did look like a party. And when had the woman, who was almost always alone, got herself so many friends?

Everything just kept getting more and more complicated.

THE INSTANT THE techs cleared out, after they and the deputies nearly cleaned out the food, Grace was allowed into the house. Gage Dalton had gone back to the office, but Guy Redwing and Sarah Ironheart remained behind to accompany her as she sought any missing items.

As if she could see any, given the mess in the house. She headed straight to the bedroom where she kept photos of her wedding to John, as well as photos of him, in frames on her dresser.

She gasped with horror as she saw the photos had been tossed around. Lifting a couple of them with her bandaged hands, she felt huge relief as she discovered that while the glass was broken, the pictures remained unharmed. She could deal with that. New frames and they would be ready to place again.

Her dresser, a piece of very heavy and very old furniture, had been left untouched, except for a few drawers that were open, her underthings and a couple of sweaters hanging out. That worried her less than the one drawer at the bottom.

She knelt, needing to open it, but her hands wouldn't allow her. Then Mitch was beside her, brushing her scrabbling hands away.

"Let me," he said. With one easy move, he pulled it open and she nearly collapsed again. Huge tears rolled helplessly down her cheeks. The mementos were all there, from her short bridal veil to the plastic-wrapped ornament from the top of their wedding cake and John's ring. Even the bouquet of red silk roses looked back at her.

She found the diamond studs that John had given her for their first anniversary. She'd never understood how he'd afforded them. She'd never asked.

The important thing was that all the reminders of her time with John she'd saved over the years hadn't been touched.

"It's all here," she whispered. "Thank God."

She spent several minutes staring into the drawer, so glad the looters had left this alone. Nothing else really mattered.

Then she had to face the rest of the damage. Together with Mitch and the two deputies, she walked through the entire house, reaching a scary conclusion.

"If anything is missing, I can't tell."

Sarah and Guy exchanged looks.

"Weird," Guy said. "Well, if you notice anything later, give us a call."

She promised to do that, then was alone with Mitch and the destruction of the rest of her life.

"How am I going to clean all this up?" She asked the question of herself, but Mitch answered.

"You're not. You've got help. And wouldn't this be a good time to rearrange that living room?"

She looked at him, conscious of a brief sting of annoyance, then remembered their earlier conversation. "You're right," she answered, feeling her shoulders stiffen. "A good time. I don't think I ever again want to see this place as it was."

Late afternoon had arrived. Mitch spoke. "Lunch was hours ago. I think if we don't get back to my place soon, Lila might get upset for ruining another of her excellent meals."

She was ready to close the door on all this. Before Mitch could secure the broken door behind her, something she rarely did, Betty Pollard drove up.

"Oh, God, not now," she muttered.

"I thought she was your friend."

She looked at Mitch as Betty strode toward them.

"She is, but I'm not up to being lectured about how I need to get rid of this place. I understand her concern, I should appreciate it more than I do, but I'm tired of it."

"I'm starting to agree with her," Mitch said.

Grace felt almost betrayed, but she bit her tongue as Betty reached them.

"Let me guess," Grace said before anything else. "You heard it on your police scanner."

"Of course I did. I would have been here sooner except I was out with Dan. Priorities, you know." She flashed a smile, then passed Grace before she could protest, and entered the house.

"Oh man," Betty said. "Oh man."

Grace had to agree, but she wanted to escape. She'd already spent enough time in there, studying the wreckage.

Betty emerged quickly, saying, "I don't want to look. How can you stand it, Grace?"

"I don't have a choice."

"Guess you don't." Betty closed the door firmly behind her. "God." She reached out and hugged Grace. "I can't believe it."

"I'm having some trouble with it, too."

Betty evidently wanted to remain, but Grace had reached her limit. No polite chitchat, not now. She felt all roiled inside and couldn't have stood any inanities.

"I'm just going to say one thing," Betty said firmly.

"I know. I should get out. I told you I don't want to hear that anymore."

Betty looked a little offended. "I almost didn't come to the hospital after the barn burned down because I thought you didn't want to see me again. But this is beyond enough."

"Meaning?"

"The ewe. The barn. And now this. If you don't feel hunted out here, then you should."

Betty reached out to hug her once more, murmuring, "Stay safe."

After a farewell to Grace and Mitch, she left with a wave.

"That was frosty," Mitch remarked.

"On my part. I suppose I should feel guilty."

Mitch looked at her. "For what? You're entitled to your feelings, and I can understand why you don't want to be bothered right now. Anyway, let's go home. If you want to yell at me, do it there. Lila will probably join in."

"What would she yell at you for?"

"Being late to dinner. Although in fairness I gotta say that Lila doesn't yell at me. She can give me looks, though, to put me in my place."

WHILE MITCH HONESTLY agreed with Betty—it did feel as if Grace were being hunted somehow—he understood why Grace didn't want to hear it. Especially now. As she came out of her shock and horror, she was going to defend her life choices, especially the one about keeping her home and her memories there.

Betty's common sense didn't stand a chance against that.

He could have sighed but refrained. Grace might hear him, even over the growling and squeaking of his old pickup. He didn't want to have to explain that he agreed with Betty.

Grace had always been a bit difficult to deal with, especially since John's passing. Stubborn, opinionated about some things, and totally refusing to let go of any part of her grief.

Stubbornness had probably gotten her through a lot, but now here she was, being obstinate at exactly the wrong time. The only thing that consoled him was that she couldn't return to that house until her hands were well enough for her to take care of herself.

He had no doubt she'd race right back as soon as she thought she could manage. But he wasn't going to let her go alone. Not now. Not after all this hell that had been visited on her.

Back home, Lila greeted them with delicious aromas and a smile. "Go wash up, boss. But not you, girl. You get yourself right into the kitchen and get your saliva running. I want to see you eat a big meal."

Grace spoke quietly. "I don't feel very hungry."

"Of course you don't. But you get in there and smell yourself into hunger. Nobody can resist my food for long."

"I'm sure of that," Grace said. She looked at Mitch.

"Go on," he said. "I can find my own way to the bathroom sink."

"I hope so. You've only been living here your entire life."

Teasing. A very good sign. Maybe she'd emerge from this grimness faster than he'd thought possible.

But of course she would. Grace was remarkably resilient, except for one thing.

John.

Chapter Thirteen

Three days later, Grace stood in her house, directing the arrangement of her living room. Bill and Jack were there to help, a good thing considering the weight of some of those pieces.

Rearranging the room was harder than she had expected, but Mitch nudged her along, suggesting different placements. Left to her own devices, Grace might have put everything back in the original arrangement.

But Mitch was right. She needed to claim this room for herself.

"I should clean the rug," she remarked as the room fell into order.

"Are you sure that rug would survive it? Wasn't it already here?"

"Yeah." It had been one of the economies she and John had practiced, using most of what had been left in the house. With a tax sale, nobody came in to clean the house out.

It had sure served them well.

She smiled. It felt good to smile again. The anticipation of change had lifted her spirits some. "I never asked, but did you know the previous owner? I never even knew who he was because the deed came from the county."

"Not well. Crusty as I recall and I don't think I ever knew his name. Not the friendliest of guys, which probably explains why no one tried to help him out of his tax problems. Or maybe no one knew about them. I don't remember that I ever did."

"Shame that he lost it. That would kill me." She sighed. "Well, it turned out to be a blessing for me and John. Hardly seems fair, though."

"What's fair about life? The man didn't pay his taxes for at least five years. The county let him run longer than most would, I suspect. I thought about buying it myself."

She turned toward him. "Why didn't you? You could have bid more than we did."

"Because I saw your face at that auction. Bright and hopeful. Couldn't take it from you."

Her heart jumped. "Oh, Mitch…"

He shrugged. "Not a big deal. I got you two for neighbors, then I got your land anyway."

That made her almost laugh. "You're awful!"

"Never denied it. Hey, Bill?"

"Yeah, boss."

"Put that ugly old chair in that corner."

"Ugly!" Grace couldn't resist, although she'd often thought so herself. Horsehair, too, which was impossible to sit on with bare legs. Over the years it had been mostly useless.

Mitch eyed her. "I'd send it to the junkyard, myself. Or to a charity. Someone else might be desperate enough to buy it."

"Desperate?" Grace had to laugh at that one.

"That's what it would take. Lot of new upholstery, too. Maybe a charity would be too picky to want it."

Now the laughter rose all the way from her belly.

Troubles seemed to slip into the background. Man, he was good for her.

"You want it here?" Jack asked, grinning himself. "Reckon we could take it out to the truck right now."

Mitch laughed. "Don't steal the lady's antique."

"Antique?" This was too much. "It can't possibly be that old."

"My guess is a hundred years. Not that that feels like much, the old century being so close."

He had a point there. Suddenly, this furniture rearrangement became an adventure. Like a fresh wind blowing through.

Grace drew a deep breath, then nearly choked on the musty smell that had risen from that long-unused chair.

"Oh, take it out," she begged. "I can smell it, and it's not good."

"Happy to oblige, ma'am," Bill answered, tipping an invisible hat. "Some things just aren't meant to be. Where to, boss?"

"Our burn pile, or some charity. You guys decide."

"Burn," Bill and Jack said simultaneously.

Bill added, "The smell must be in the cushions. Ain't nobody gonna want that in their house."

Mitch's hired hands grunted as they carried the chair out into the sunshine.

Bill groused, "Might make good target practice."

"Beer?" Grace asked when they returned. Both Bill and Jack were sweaty. "You'll have to get it yourselves." She waved her bandaged hands.

"I think I can manage that," Jack assured her. "Mitch?"

"Yeah, that sounds good. Worked up a bit of a sweat myself, overseeing all this."

Another joke. Grace had watched him work as hard as the other two. Mitch was no slacker.

She was also glad that Mitch had brought over a couple of six-packs when she and he had come over this morning. She could act the gracious part of all this when she couldn't help.

But it was just acting. A whole lot of her life seemed to be acting. Damn, she needed to get out of the hole of self-pity.

Quit pretending, she told herself. Things were *not* okay and might never be again. *So cope.*

"Now we gotta refix things," Bill said. "Nothing balances."

"That's a point," Mitch agreed as he popped the top on his longneck. "But is balance important?"

"It is to me," Bill replied. "The lady decides."

Three pairs of eyes settled on her.

"I need to think about it. Maybe I'll have a beer, too, while I study it."

Mitch brought her a beer and opened it for her. "Take your time," he suggested. "We might get into another longneck before we're ready to get on with this."

The two hired hands went outside to sit on the front steps and argue about how they were going to get the "dinosaur" onto the truck bed.

"Wanna sit outside?" Mitch asked her.

Given the smell that still permeated the room, and the dust that had been stirred up by all the moving, she definitely did. Amazing what accumulated when you didn't move furniture for a while. As for that old chair, she'd never been able to move it at all.

She and Mitch settled into the wooden rockers on one

side of the porch. John had been so pleased with himself for building them during long winter nights.

"Beautiful day," Mitch remarked.

Indeed it was. Bright sun combined with the steady wind into perfection. Rocking gently helped soothe her, carrying her away from the mess inside her house and what it might mean.

"I'm so grateful to you guys," she said.

"Hell," Mitch said. "None of us could have done this alone."

"Especially that dinosaur."

Bill and Jack had come over to join them with their own beers. The "dinosaur" still sat on the ground behind the pickup truck. "Let me guess," Bill said, leaning back against the porch post. "You never got rid of that chair because it weighs a ton."

Grace had to laugh, although at the moment she didn't especially feel like it. "You're right," she admitted. "Besides, it filled a bare space."

That brought laughter her way.

Mitch smiled with his eyes. "A bare space, huh. So you arranged the whole room around it?"

"I guess so. As time went by, we added a little here and there, but we were too busy most of the time to be thinking about decorating."

Busy indeed. Once they'd started the flock, there weren't enough hours in the day. They had a good time together, though. She doubted they would have made it if there'd been nothing but work.

She'd tried so hard to keep that flock, but she was glad Mitch had taken over. It was definitely too much for one person as the flock had grown larger. Two hired men had been required along with John, who'd told her to take it easier.

Because they'd hoped to have a child, and he believed that her working so hard might be hindering that. Then he had died, and shortly after she'd had to let the two hired men go because she couldn't afford to pay them.

At first, doing everything herself had occupied her enough that grief had remained in the background. Then she'd had to face the reality that she could not go it alone.

She had to deal with the fact that John would never return. Grief was one hell of a roller coaster, but she seemed to have left the anger behind. And the bargaining. Nothing she could do, say or promise would bring her husband back.

She sighed, dragging herself into the present moment. Retracing those steps wouldn't help anything. It certainly wouldn't help her move forward in a world without John.

It was a wonder Mitch hadn't washed his hands of her long ago. Steadfast, he'd become a rock for her. When she had let him.

Like now, helping her to clean up this mess. A lot of detritus from the break-in was gone, but there were still plenty of things to put right. Like the living room.

Oddly, as she watched it take new shape, a kind of relief started to ease through her. Maybe she should have asked for Mitch's help sooner. Keeping most of the house like a museum wasn't changing a thing. It certainly wasn't making anything better.

She looked down at her hands, still bandaged, although not as thickly. She was supposed to be flexing them now to avoid stiffening. Tomorrow she'd visit the doctor again and find out just how much more she could do. When she could get rid of these bandages. Just their mere presence had become seriously annoying. Thank goodness for Lila, because Grace sure as the dickens couldn't have cared for herself the last few weeks.

She even suspected that she still wouldn't be able to do much once the bandages were gone. Through the layers, she could feel tenderness.

Meanwhile she was beginning to feel as if she had a target on her back. She hadn't mentioned that fear to Mitch because she didn't want to appear silly, but this had just been too much. A fire and now this?

She couldn't help but feel stalked.

As she scanned the world beyond her porch, she wondered if she was being watched right now. A shiver passed through her even though the day was warm.

Who then?

She guessed she had to wait for the sheriff's findings to be sure, and she and Mitch *had* felt there was a link between the events. But they hadn't discussed how this was making her feel. Or him, for that matter. She'd shied away from talking about it. Conspiracy theories had never been her thing. She had always resisted them.

But this?

Bill and Jack had finished their beers and now started discussing how to move the chair onto the pickup.

"It's not that heavy," Bill insisted. "Maybe three hundred pounds and it'll be split between us. We're strong enough to do that."

Mitch set his bottle on the porch beside his chair and went down to them. "I'll help. Then nobody will break a back."

"Thanks," Bill said. "I was thinking about making a ramp but dragging this damn thing will be as hard as lifting it, maybe more."

"I absolutely agree," Mitch said. "We just gotta be careful to balance it or somebody's gonna take it on the chin. Find a spot to grab, guys."

"I'll count to three when we're ready," said Jack.

"Just one thing," Mitch said. "Everyone counts to three, but no one ever says whether to lift *on* three or just after the number is said."

The two other men exchanged looks.

"Good point," Bill said. "Okay, right on three, the number being the lift when it's spoken."

On the porch, Grace had to smile. She'd never thought about that. Count on Mitch not to miss a detail.

All three squatted down, feeling around as they sought purchase on the wood frame.

"It's gonna want to tip," Mitch said. "Toward the truck, so you guys lift your ends a little higher than me."

Which was going to put more weight on Mitch, Grace thought, but didn't say anything. Mitch knew what he was doing.

Two minutes later they had the chair loaded. Bill and Jack said they'd take care of tying it down, so Mitch came back to sit with Grace.

"No major injuries," Mitch remarked.

"And that's why I never moved it. Is your back okay?"

"It is. Now that chair will go to its FRP."

She raised her brows. "Its what?"

"Final resting place." He gave her a crooked grin. "Maybe you don't have the problem, but I've noticed that when you set something down it almost never moves again."

"I like that." In fact, it tickled her.

"At least the guys won't have any trouble getting it off there. A couple of good shoves and it'll tumble away."

The afternoon was waning as the two cowboys drove away. A little coolness had entered the breeze, feeling good. The wind caught wisps of her hair and she had to shove them away from her face. Despite her uneasiness earlier, she began to relax. It was so beautiful here with the western mountains changing color throughout the day and she hadn't been noticing for a while.

But she needed to bring the subject up. "Mitch?"

He turned toward her. "Yeah?"

"I'm feeling watched."

She saw him sit bolt upright, his face creasing with concern. "Since when?"

"Today. Just today. Well, maybe a few times before the barn burned."

"Hell."

"I can't imagine where anyone would be hiding."

He could. There were a few copses of trees out there. And then there was the side of the mountain, not too far out of reach for a good pair of binoculars. "Why didn't you mention it before?"

"Because it sounds crazy. Totally off the wall. This is the middle of nowhere, and it'd be hard to hide around here."

He hesitated, then said, "Let's go home. Dinner will be ready soon, and we can talk about this later. And trust me, you're not crazy."

She'd begun to wonder. She'd cut herself off from everything since John's death. She'd allowed Mitch to show up from time to time, and she'd made friends with Betty.

But still, without much to wind her mind around other than grief, she wondered if her mental wheels had come off the rails.

Time would tell.

No, MITCH THOUGHT as they drove back to his place, it wouldn't be impossible for someone to watch without being seen. Especially if no one was looking for it.

Watched? He hadn't thought of that part. No one would actually have to watch Grace to do these things. The barn had burned while she was there. She'd been home so rarely since her release from the hospital, anyone could have done this at almost any time.

Except for Lila's visits to pick up clothes or other items Grace wanted and her checks on the house.

Someone would have to watch to figure out Lila's schedule, to know for sure when the house would be empty. A truck sitting out front didn't mean much, especially since he'd put Grace's pickup in the new barn to protect it. It could have been *her* truck out there.

Regardless, someone had to watch to be sure when Grace's house was empty.

Someone who needed enough time to get into the house and trash the place thoroughly.

"Nothing was taken," he said aloud as they drove up his drive.

"Nothing I can tell."

Which made this even weirder. "We'll check again tomorrow to make sure nothing else is missing."

"I have a doctor's appointment at three."

"We can do both. Besides, there's more cleanup I can help with."

Jack and Bill had ridden out to check on the herd, and Lila said they didn't plan to be back for a couple of days.

Mitch wasn't surprised. The cattle had been needing attention and they always needed to be watched for problems. Jeff couldn't do it all single-handedly, although he'd sure as hell try.

All three of his hands were good men and he was lucky to have them.

Speaking of which, it was getting on time to check on his shepherds and take them the staples they'd need, including a little extra that Lila always baked for them. Plus the hot meal he'd carry in the pails.

Since Grace had come into his care, he'd been letting matters slide a bit too much. Especially his bookkeeping. The longer he let that go, the more of a headache it became.

As Grace made her way to the living room after dinner, he stepped outside into the long twilight of summer. Scanning the view, he wondered if someone was really hiding out there.

Grace had felt watched, and that sense was often true. Not often, but too often to be ignored. Well, there were groupings of trees all over the land since he and Grace had enough water. Easy to hide in one of them.

Or on the side of the mountain as he'd thought earlier. One really good pair of binoculars would make that possible.

But how could anyone ramble around too much without being noticed? The folks around here made a tight-knit group. A stranger would be noticed, maybe remarked on. Well, more than maybe after that barn fire. No one had caught attention.

Weirder and weirder.

Night crept slowly in, starting to reveal some of the brighter stars. He kind of missed the days when he'd slept out there with his bedroll, his horse and the cattle. The sounds they made had been his lullaby.

He shook his head, deciding he might take a look around

Grace's place the day after tomorrow. But first the doctor. He hoped she'd get the news she could stop bandaging.

Not that that would help her discomfort.

Hell, he thought. Just hell.

He was a man who liked to be in control as much as possible. Life didn't always allow that, but right then he felt totally helpless. Helpless to solve this problem. Helpless to make Grace safer. Helpless to make her feel better.

Tired of his rambling thoughts, he went inside to join Grace. At least this evening he could make her comfortable and make her safe.

He should have guessed what was coming, but he knew Grace well enough that he shouldn't have been surprised.

"I'M GOING HOME," she announced as they drove from the doctor toward his place. Her hands, freshly unbandaged, still looked red and sore. Those blisters had been really bad.

She was ready to take up the reins of her life, and he had no way to stop her except by argument. When had a disagreement ever stalled her? Never, of course.

Stubborn. Cussedly stubborn.

"When?" he asked after a minute or so.

"I'd like to go tonight."

"Grace…"

"I know," she answered. "I know. Okay, tomorrow but no later."

"Of course not."

"Mitch, I can't leave the place unattended any longer. Look what happened because I wasn't there."

True, but it was also a signpost she was choosing to ignore. It could get worse.

The idea clamped his stomach into a knot.

How to handle this? He wondered why she'd let him do anything at all. There'd been very little she'd allowed him to do since John had died.

He stifled a sigh and kept driving. He had to figure out a way to stop her. But he doubted he could.

GRACE HAD GONE from frightened to furious. If someone was attacking her for any reason, he was going to meet the business end of her shotgun. She knew how to use it and wasn't afraid to.

Especially not now. Shock after shock had knocked her back on her heels, but no more. It was time to stand up for herself against this shadowy threat. Time to reclaim her life and protect her ranch.

No one was going to get away with doing this to her.

She sensed Mitch's disapproval and wasn't surprised. He'd spent the last two years trying unobtrusively to look after her. He'd be wanting to make her safe right now.

Except he couldn't do that. No one else could make her safe. She was absolutely certain that if he could find a way to stop this and protect her, he would.

There were no answers to this conundrum. What could he do? Camp on her porch? He had important duties on his own ranch and couldn't afford to let matters go. She knew he'd been doing a lot of that while she stayed under his roof.

Enough. Short of abandoning her ranch to more mischief, she had to stand up for herself.

In a way, the idea pleased her. She didn't like being weak, and this threat was weakening her because she wasn't facing it squarely and standing guard.

"Can I borrow a horse?" she asked.

"Oh, for Pete's sake."

"No, then. I can understand why after the barn."

"Damn it, Grace you saved those horses and risked your life doing it. It's not that I'd be afraid for a horse."

"Then what?" she demanded,

"I'd be afraid for you."

That silenced her.

MITCH KNEW WHAT she was going to do. She was going to get on that horse and start riding around, looking for any evidence of a campsite or a campfire on her property. Looking for traces of the perp.

She'd be out there all alone, a perfect target for a serious mishap. The idea that he'd convinced her to carry a sat phone didn't make him feel any better.

Worse, if he'd ever found a way to divert her when she was set on something, he didn't know it. Even John hadn't been able to. As far as Mitch knew, John had only been successful when it came to the goats she wanted. And knowing Grace, John had been obliged to sit down and show her the numbers.

Not just the cost of a fence, either. But the reality that there wasn't enough forage for goats, who didn't graze the same greens as sheep. Which meant nutritional supplements and additional food.

Want them or not, they could become very expensive out here if you had more than a few. As near as he could tell, goats bred, too. Then what?

He might have laughed about it all if Grace hadn't decided to do something that he considered remarkably foolhardy in these circumstances. But he could also understand her desire to protect what was hers and put any threat to bed.

He'd have felt the same himself. Except he had hired hands to stand with him. She had no one but him.

Oh, crap. He could see the storm coming.

Chapter Fourteen

Two mornings later, Mitch took Grace over to her house and helped clean up some of the last of the detritus because he didn't want her overworking those hands.

He also didn't lend her a horse.

"You simply can't go riding with your hands in that condition. No way."

He wouldn't budge, either. Part of the truth was he didn't want her riding alone when there might well be someone out there watching her, possibly with worse intentions that just messing up her property.

He needed to go to town for some feed, but she didn't want to accompany him. Of course not. She was determined not to leave her property unprotected.

He got that. Totally. But however strong and brave she might be, she was still *alone*.

He dealt with that by asking one of his men to keep a distant eye on her.

And whether she liked it or not, he was coming back with his own shotgun to stand guard with her. He'd have skipped going for the feed except he'd let that go too long while spending more time with her.

The devil and the deep blue sea, he thought. That famous rock and a hard place. Scylla and Charybdis. The problem was so common to life that there were any number of references to it.

He was not a happy man as he headed out. He didn't want Grace mad at him, and he didn't want her alone. He couldn't completely fail to take care of his cattle, however.

He could have asked one of his men to run for the feed, but he was getting uneasy about his animals. Whatever was after Grace might extend to *his* herds. Especially if this turned out to be that operation that wanted his land, as well. A brief gallop by one of his men over to check on her would be okay, but he didn't want to reduce the watch on his cattle for too long.

Hell. He hurried into town as fast as he could. The feed store was ready for him and loaded his truck bed quickly.

Another reason for the trips to town was to grab something at Maude's diner. It always gave Lila a break from making him lunch and dinner and he thought she appreciated it.

Grace wouldn't be able to cook right now. She might be able to manage a peanut butter sandwich, but no more.

That decided him. He dropped into Maude's and placed a very large takeout order. He could cook for both himself and Grace, but she'd probably get edgy as twilight deepened, and he didn't want her standing out on her porch.

Hell, he thought for the second time. Maybe he needed to get a horse over to Grace's for himself. Maybe if *he* rode around, he could ease her mind on that score.

Or, he might just make her mad.

He sighed. You couldn't deal with a prickly pear cactus without getting stung by spines. Grace would just have to get over it.

Maude quickly delivered him a couple bags full of his order as if she sensed his urgency.

Then he had another thought. He couldn't drop the feed off at his own place. Not without leaving Grace alone for longer. Another cuss word escaped him. He gave in to need.

So he called Bill. "I've got the feed, but I need to stay with Grace. Can one of you bring me a horse and get the feed?"

Of course they could. He thought once again how lucky he was in those three men.

When he reached Grace's, he carried the bags inside to discover she'd managed to make coffee. She'd also found it necessary to bandage her palms again.

"Hurting?" he asked as he put the bags on the counter.

"A little," she admitted. "Not quite ready to have things brush against my hands."

"Hardly surprising. You know they'll be tender for a while. Well, I brought us some food. No cooking for you. Whenever we're finished eating this, *I* can cook. Believe it or not, I know how, and while it'll be simple fare, it won't require an outdoor grill."

That made her laugh, and his heart lifted a bit.

"Jack of all trades?" she teased.

"Cooking on the range and, for a while before Lila, cooking for myself. If it's easy I can do it."

"I feel so useless."

He looked at her. "Don't. You've been injured. You didn't cause any of this. Anyway, I like being of use myself, so live with it."

He paused, hating to bring the gloom to her again. "I need to go out and get my shotgun."

Her small smile vanished. He detested that, but he'd be of no earthly good to her if he wasn't prepared to defend her homestead alongside her.

He might try, but there was no way he could turn this into a fun campout. Sooner or later the darkness would have descended anyway.

"Thanks," she said, her voice small.

This seemed to be his cussing day. While he went out to his truck to get his shotgun and a box of ammo, plus the pistol he always carried to put a sick or injured animal out of its misery, he muttered a few choice words.

He had to hope that he could really help Grace, that he could put someone behind bars so that she could breathe easy again. All he needed was some concrete evidence to pass to the sheriff. Although it would make him feel a whole lot better to hold the guy at gunpoint for a while before the sheriff arrived.

Inside he found Grace seated at the table with a cup of coffee. She didn't look even remotely happy anymore.

He'd done that by reminding her of this god-awful situation. Well, that made him feel about two inches tall.

He put his shotgun in a corner, and his locked pistol case on the counter.

"Guess what I brought to eat?" he asked, trying to cheer her a little.

She looked at him.

"I went to Maude's. I must have made her happy since I ordered at least two meals worth of most items, plus some big pieces of strudel."

That perked her interest. "Strudel? That's a beast to make. I'm surprised she bothered."

"Maude's always a surprise, except when she's slamming dishes on the table."

That brought back her smile. "Too true. The clattering you hear in any diner doesn't reach the decibels in Maude's."

"I'm amazed she has a whole dish left, honestly."

Still smiling. Thank God. They'd get through this mess somehow. "Are you getting hungry?"

She didn't have to think about it. "Famished."

"Good. Maude would be appalled if we didn't eat while it's mostly fresh."

"Just don't tell her if we don't."

"She'll never know," Mitch pointed out. "Unless you want to tattle on me."

TWILIGHT BEGAN TO creep over the land, flattening the shadows, making the land darker even as the sky remained blue overhead. One of the beauties of the mountains. They swallowed the sun before they stole all the light.

Grace decided to sit on her porch with her own shotgun cradled across her lap. Mitch joined her soon with fresh mugs of coffee.

"To keep us awake," he said as he passed her one.

For all she resented not being able to take care of all this herself, she was terribly glad of Mitch's company. It struck her again that she'd been keeping him at a distance for a long time.

Why? Because he was a supremely attractive man? Because noticing that might be a betrayal of John? All she could be certain of was that she was drawn to Mitch and it didn't feel like a major crime.

As if it ever had been. Even when she was married.

She'd seen John notice other women, a very male thing to do. Well, she was a female and she was noticing Mitch. The sight of his backside in jeans was enough to make her heart skip a beat. The narrowness of his hips reminded her of his masculinity. Almost constantly.

Mostly, just then, she was glad he was here. The coming night didn't quite seem so scary.

Anyway, it wasn't the night that scared her. It was what it might conceal.

"It's probably too soon to expect anything more to happen," he remarked. "There were a few weeks after the ewe, and between the barn and the home invasion. Moving slowly. A rapid blast wouldn't give enough time for the threat to sink in."

She nodded, basically agreeing. But not certain by any means. She supposed he wasn't, either, or he wouldn't be here.

"You're just trying to make me feel better, Mitch."

"Probably," he admitted.

"But you called it a threat."

"Hard to see it any other way now."

The evening breeze was shifting direction a bit, bringing a colder breath to the land, washing the air, cleaning it for another day.

Grace drew in the familiar scent of sagebrush. She loved the aroma. Nature had a beauty all its own, even out here where many might find the vast expanses dull and the dry summer colors boring.

The land rolled gently, trees grew everywhere they could find enough water. There were wildflowers in the spring, delicate beautiful blossoms. Sometimes as winter approached, she even caught the smell from the evergreens on the mountains. If you were quiet enough, you could see deer who'd jumped the fence and grazed.

It was a beauty many couldn't appreciate, but she certainly did.

A sigh escaped her.

"What?" he asked.

"I was just thinking how much I love it out here. I'm not going to give it up, Mitch."

"Me, neither."

After a bit she remarked, "You had Bill bring you a horse."

"Clearly. But not for you. Your hands..."

"I know about my hands," she said querulously, then wished she had softened her tone. "I got a whole introduction to what I can't do today. After you left, I tried to clean up some more. No go. At least I could make that coffee."

"Small victories. Take them when you can. Look, those hands you're angry about are a badge of honor."

Her head swiveled toward him. "What do you mean?"

"You burned them risking yourself to save two horses. That was brave. Take your badge or medal or whatever you want to call it, because you deserve it. You could have saved your hands by letting those horses die. You didn't."

She couldn't very well argue with that. "Well, I couldn't have let them burn. Period. So I didn't really do anything special."

"Most people are too afraid of fire to go into a burning building. Welcome to the reality and courage of one Grace Hall."

"You think so?" Inside her, an icy knot began to warm

for the first time since John's death. Courage? She hadn't been showing much over the last two years.

"I know so," he replied firmly.

As the last light began to fail, he reached over and took her hand. It was a careful, gentle touch that caused her no discomfort.

Well, except for the leaping of her heart and the almost forgotten tingle that ran through her. Within herself she could feel creaky doors opening wider, letting in fresh air, sweeping away dust and even the fog that had shrouded her.

A new day was beginning.

If she could just tunnel through this mountain of trouble.

She looked at Mitch again, seeing his face in shadow, and wished she knew how to close that last bit of distance between them.

It wouldn't be easy, not after that way she'd built her self-protective wall between them. Keeping them at the level of friends and colleagues.

If she wanted to go that way—and she wasn't yet certain she dared to take the risk—she might have to make the move herself, knocking the barrier over.

But still there were the other things, the ugly things that seemed to be pursuing her. Her needs versus her wants. Dangers of two different kinds that couldn't possibly mesh just now.

While she tried to deal with it all, warning flags were spinning around her head like disembodied demons. It might be wiser to solve the big problems before adding the possibility of another to the list. What if he wasn't interested? What if he just saw her as a friend, or as a sister?

Oh, God, could she take the humiliation?

But she couldn't deny he was waking her from her long slumber in the depths of despair. Pulling her up from the mire that had been in danger of becoming comfortable.

She drew a deep breath of the cooling air that cleansed her physically. Maybe she was cleansing herself inside, too?

"We ought to go in," Mitch remarked. "Unless you want me to go get you a jacket."

That was Mitch. Caring. Always caring.

"Let's go in," she decided. Because as night crept in, with all its mysterious shadows, a threat felt as if it were sneaking closer.

She couldn't imagine what it might be, but knew it existed.

This was not over.

Chapter Fifteen

The upstairs of this two-story farmhouse was empty. Grace and John had used it for storing a few things, but otherwise it had been extra, unneeded space. Bedrooms they had once thought would eventually be filled with children. If they'd had children, they'd have moved their bedroom up there, too. Plenty of room.

But there was a room downstairs that was adequate for them, and they'd used it as their bedroom. A much smaller room had been given over to a tiny office of sorts, now filled with papers and loose-leaf binders and boxes, all holding the inevitable documents for running any kind of business. Over the years the stacks had grown, and since John's death had been mostly untouched.

As a business, Grace was practically nonexistent. She recorded the sale of the sheep to Mitch, diligently recorded the payments he made on the land he leased from her, recorded a rare expense that fell to her.

Then she always closed the door on it all. Leaving it in the dust.

Grace and John had had little in the way of savings, only socking away what they could for emergencies. So far, she had managed to survive on the proceeds of his life insurance. That wouldn't last forever, but it had gotten her through. Sooner or later she was going to have to face economic reality. Mitch's intervention had merely postponed it.

The unwanted thoughts wafted through her head in the morning when she rose. Mitch had spent the night in the living room, sleeping on a recliner. John's recliner. It somehow felt right.

He was already up and dressed, standing in the kitchen. He wore his shotgun chaps over his jeans, topped by a chambray shirt with snaps. The sleeves were rolled up. On his feet were cowboy boots, not work boots.

"Coffee's ready," he remarked. "As if you couldn't smell it coming down the hall. I recommend a piece of Maude's blueberry buckle for breakfast."

"That sounds great." She hadn't even showered yet, and was still wearing an old terry cloth robe over her nightshirt. Feeling suddenly embarrassed, she pushed her hair back and hoped it didn't look too much like a rat's nest. Heck, why had she stumbled out here before taking her shower, cold as it would have to be because of her hands?

He placed a mug of coffee on the table and motioned her to a chair. "Sit, milady, and sip."

A surprised laugh escaped her as she slid into the chair.

He turned back to the counter to open a container and pulled a couple of plates out of the cupboard.

Which gave her a nice view of the worn seat of his jeans that cradled him oh so perfectly.

She blinked, shocked by the turn of her thoughts. *Really, Grace?* Fearful he might read her mind, she yanked her attention elsewhere.

"Boots and chaps?" she asked as he brought squares of the blueberry buckle to the table. "I haven't seen you wear chaps often."

"That's because, lately, I haven't been riding into brushy areas." He sat, facing her.

"Are you planning to?"

He shrugged one shoulder, as if trying to minimize. "I thought I'd ride around and look for trampled brush, spots under the trees, things like that."

Anxiety swooped in like a hawk. She had to swallow hard and drink some coffee. "I should do that with you."

He cocked a brow at her. "Really."

It wasn't a question and she flushed. "Mitch…"

"I get it," he interrupted. "You want to do something, anything. You don't want me taking over. I know how independent you are."

She opened her mouth to answer, but he forestalled her.

"Well, I've got a job for you, if you're willing."

She quelled an instinctive burst of resentment. This was her homestead, *her* problem, and she ought to be managing it. But the instant the irritation flared, it subsided. There was a difference, she reminded herself, between being stubborn and being reasonable. She certainly wasn't capable of doing what he was proposing he do. Her damn hands.

"What do you need?" she asked after another sip of coffee and a stab at the cake with a fork.

"Guard the place. Just sit out front with your shotgun. The sight of that ought to help any miscreants decide to go elsewhere."

Half an hour later, outside the barn, Grace watched Mitch mount a palomino named Joy. Leather creaked, a sound she had long loved. She handed him his shotgun and he slipped it into the saddle holster. Just like a cowboy of old, he wore a gun belt, his pistol safely sheathed. He crammed his battered Stetson with its stampede string onto his head.

Not a show cowboy, but a working one.

Iconic image, she thought, as he touched the finger of a gloved hand to the brim of his hat then rode out with the jingle of harness. She'd never become immune to that sight or those sounds over the years.

Grace spared a sigh, then returned to the house. She filled a tall insulated mug with coffee, then returned to her porch with her shotgun. The single barrel held six shots. No hasty reloading required.

The ceaseless wind blew, stirred to wakefulness by the rising warmth of the summer day. The humidity was so low that she considered rubbing moisturizer into her face, but let it go. Now that she was alone, the shadows that haunted her seemed to be rising even in the sunlight.

Almost too much to comprehend, she thought.

She was alone now, as she had been since John's death. But this time the loneliness was enhanced. Mitch's absence presented her with a whole new emptiness.

A FEW HOURS LATER, she spied a vehicle turn into her driveway. Distant though it was, she quickly recognized Betty's car.

She and Betty had been friends for a while now. Betty was one of the very few people she'd allowed into her life since John's passing, and in the past, Betty's visits had always been welcome, pleasurable.

Lately she'd found her friend annoying. Why? She couldn't really say. Even Betty's repeated suggestions that she needed to move couldn't be all of it. It wasn't as if Betty had done more than suggest, and even Mitch had said he kind of agreed.

But Mitch didn't bring it up, and certainly not repeatedly.

No, Mitch just kept coming around to look after her. Man, she was a mixed-up mess. Both Betty and Mitch were trying to protect her, and she sprouted sharp quills any time they tried.

The look at herself was uncomfortable. It wasn't as if she were the only solitary widow in the world. She certainly didn't need to get her back up every time someone cared for her.

As Betty climbed out of her car and approached, Grace summoned a smile and a wave. "Howdy, stranger," she called.

Betty waved back and grinned. "It's been a while. I'm still not sure I'm welcome."

"Of course you are. It's just been rough lately."

"So I hear."

Grace leaned forward, ready to put her gun aside. "Coffee, blueberry buckle?"

Betty waved a hand. "I know my way around your kitchen. I'll get it myself. What about you?"

Ten minutes later, they both sat in wood rockers, coffee on the wooden end table between them. Betty had helped herself to blueberry buckle on a small plate.

"Catch me up, as in why you're sitting there with a shotgun," Betty said, then lifted a forkful of cake to her mouth. "Tell me nothing else has happened. Lately I've been feeling like every time I turn up, it's the worst time imaginable. You're entitled to a break."

Grace balanced the shotgun across her lap and surrounded the mug of fresh coffee with both hands. "You'd think. But no, nothing else has happened except Mitch's men got rid of that horrid, heavy chair from the living room. They were calling it the dinosaur."

Betty laughed. "Great description."

"I hate to admit how long I've loathed that thing. It's as if it was rooted to the house and would never move."

Oddly, she thought she saw a faint shadow pass over Betty's face.

"That it did," Betty said after a couple of seconds. "Why didn't you and John ever get rid of it?"

"Too heavy. Neither of us thought it was important enough to struggle with. Boy, did it smell when the guys moved it."

"Age does that," Betty remarked. "But I'm not here about the furniture. I'm here about you. Had enough yet?"

Grace felt herself bristling again and tried to stamp down on it. "Meaning?"

"Just what I said. God, Grace, it's been one thing after another. You're sitting there holding your shotgun, for heaven's sake. This goes way past what some might call karma. Besides, you've never done a bad thing in your life."

That drew a quiet laugh from Grace. "Everyone has, Betty. I'm not ready for sainthood."

Betty grinned. "Well, I can't say I can argue with you. I've been so bad lately. And I'm loving it."

"Tell, tell. I need something good to think about."

"I figured you might. Well, the boyfriend. He happened."

"You told me."

"But not that he moved in with me."

Grace drew a surprised breath. "Really? *Really?*"

Betty nodded with a satisfied smile. "Really. We're not talking marriage or anything, but it's starting to look long-term." She sighed happily. "I was beginning to think this would never happen to me, Grace. Usually one of us figures out that it's not working, pretty quickly. Usually me, since I'm so picky."

Grace tilted her head a bit. "Picky is important in relationships. You know that."

Betty leaned toward her. "No kidding. Worse to become picky after it's too late. Anyway, I figure I'll give him a workout. Does he do dishes? Laundry? Can he mop a floor? Because I swear I'm not going to turn into Suzy Homemaker for any man."

"Good for you."

"I mean, look at you," Betty said, waving a hand toward her. "You got married and started working on a ranch. Raising sheep. Pitching hay or whatever. I suspect all the cooking and household chores didn't fall on only your shoulders."

"No, they didn't. John and I were shoulder to shoulder with everything. He was also tall, so that gave him some added use."

Betty laughed loudly. "He was a stepladder?"

"One of his amazing talents."

This was the way it had been before, the easy camaraderie that the two of them had often shared. Grace relaxed.

After a bit, Betty spoke again. She eyed Grace. "Have I stepped into the Wild West?"

Grace's gaze snapped to her. "Meaning?"

"Girl, you're sitting there with a shotgun across your lap. Old West for sure. You didn't really explain."

"Or modern West," Grace answered, feeling her mouth twist a bit.

"You're on guard, then?"

"Wouldn't you be?" It looked so peaceful out there that even Grace had trouble believing that so much bad had happened lately.

"Well, you look ready for anything. Did you find much missing after the break-in?"

Grace shook her head. "That makes it even weirder. Like someone got all they wanted by tossing the place. A mess, but anything that matters is still there."

"Strange." Betty frowned and leaned back, rocking gently.

Grace tensed in expectation of Betty's usual insistence that she needed to dump the ranch. It didn't come this time.

Betty spoke again eventually. "At least you've got those guys to look after the sheep for you."

"Yes." Grace said no more, mindful of Mitch's desire that no one know of their arrangement. "They do a good job."

"I'm glad. But why Portuguese?"

"They're famous for their shepherding. Breeders all over the country hire them. Maybe because it's impossible to find anyone else willing to actually live with a flock."

Betty pursed her lips. "No kidding. For a while most cowboys were coming from south of the border. People who didn't mind working for a pittance and living on the range. Not so much anymore."

"Things change with the times and there are few enough cowboys who need to herd on horseback."

Betty giggled. "It's all about ATVs now."

They chatted a while longer about Dan, about romance, about the summer that was coming to a slow but steady close.

When Betty left, Grace still smiled. At least one part of her life had recovered some order.

But she still felt incredibly alone and wondered how long Mitch would be gone.

MITCH SCOURED EVERY place he thought it might be possible for someone to watch Grace's activities, where someone might find a decent launching place from which to attack her property.

He'd wondered if someone could be observing from the western mountains, but maybe they could camp up there, then come down here when it was time to act.

He didn't like it. None of this. Not only the attacks themselves, but the shadowy person and purpose behind it. Uneasiness was becoming his constant companion, as he was sure it had for Grace.

He barely wanted to think about anything else, and was leaning heavily on Bill, Jack and Jeff to handle most of his ranch. Then there were the shepherds, Zeke and Rod.

They were farther out, too far away to be at a good watching point, but the two of them were out here most of the time. They might have caught wind of something.

He widened his circle until he heard the sheep and finally saw them over a rise. And there were Zeke and Rod, not far from their charges.

He rode up, and they both stood immediately. They'd been sitting around a small propane stove, brewing some coffee, and instantly offered him some. He declined.

"You guys doing okay?" he asked.

They smiled. "Yes," Zeke answered. "The dog?"

Mitch laughed. "I'm working on it. A couple of puppies, later this summer, trained by their mommas and papas, if that's okay."

"Best kind," Rod said approvingly.

"Great. Listen, I wanted to ask you if you've seen anyone out here. Maybe near Grace Hall's place? Or camping?"

The men exchanged looks. Then Zeke said, "I would tell them to go away. This *your* land. No camping."

"That's good. Just keep a sharp eye out. Bad things are happening."

"The fire," Rod said. "Very bad."

"Very bad indeed. You men need anything?"

As he rode away, the westering sun told him it was time to head on back, with or without information. Grace would begin to wonder and he didn't like leaving her alone for so long.

GRACE WAS RELIEVED to see Mitch's silhouette approaching, but alongside relief came a huge dollop of excitement. She let it come, allowing herself to take pleasure in the joy she felt.

About time she permitted even a small amount of happiness to enter her life. Well past due.

He waved as he approached, heading straight for the barn. Carrying her shotgun, she followed him, not wanting to wait until he finished tending to Joy's needs.

He was removing the palomino's saddle as she entered the darker space inside. Her eyes needed a few seconds to adapt to the change, but then she saw him clearly.

Still iconic, she thought wryly as she approached.

"How'd your day go?" he asked as he settled the saddle on a long-unused leather-padded sawhorse. His saddlebags already hung there. He pushed the Stetson off his head and allowed it to dangle on his back by the stampede string.

"It was good," she answered. "Betty came by for a visit and for once she left the elephant alone in the room."

He laughed. "The elephant being wanting you to move away from here?"

"I'm not aware of any other one. Maybe she left it alone because she's so happy in her new relationship. The guy evidently moved in with her."

"Big step," he remarked. The saddle blanket joined the saddle, the halter settled on a hook at eye-height, reins draped back around it. Then he reached for the roll of farrier tools that occupied one of the saddlebags.

"I wish I could help," Grace admitted wistfully.

"That day'll come."

She perched on a stool to watch as he began to clean and, as necessary, rasp Joy's hooves. The real question trembled on her lips, but she was afraid to ask it. Either answer wasn't going to please her.

Regardless, it was a pleasure to watch him as he bent and lifted each hoof, cleaning and caring for that horse as kindly as he would a baby. Each time he rose, he patted the side of the palomino's neck.

The best place to show affection for a horse. John had taught her that. "You know how they show caring?" he'd asked, pointing. "They kind of wrap their heads over each other. I read that's not only affection, but soothing. Calming."

The horses sure seemed to like it when she did it that way. Of course, they didn't seem to mind a pat to the flank, either.

"Well," Mitch said when he'd finished with the hooves and reached for the curry brush. The horse looked as if she were in heaven. "Wish I had something useful to report. I might have missed it, but I couldn't see any places where someone had been hanging out. I checked with Zeke and Rod, and they haven't noticed anything, either. They'll keep an eye out."

Grace had known that news either way wouldn't be cheerful but felt deflated anyway. She'd rather have had some kind of starting point.

"What now?" she asked.

"Tomorrow I'm hoping to check out the far side of the road. I'll call Burt Stiller tonight and make sure it's okay to poke around."

She nodded. "That's a good idea."

"Oh, I'm just brimming over with ideas. No call from the sheriff?"

"Nada."

"Hell." He remained silent as he finished currying Joy. Then he led her into a stall and loaded her up with hay and a mixture of feed. A huge bucket of water followed. "Those guys didn't overlook a thing when they built this barn."

"It's beautiful, all right. Still takes my breath away."

He smiled as he stripped off his gloves. "Can a man get some coffee and leftovers?"

MITCH MADE ONE more circuit of the house and barn before joining Grace inside. She'd made fresh coffee and brought out the remains of his trip to Maude's. Plenty enough for more than two people. The microwave went to work.

Mitch still wore his chaps and grimaced when they

creaked as he sat. "Time for another oiling. So Betty provided a high spot in your day?"

"She did."

But there was another elephant in the room, and Mitch knew they were avoiding it. There didn't seem to be much they could say, however. No new information. Just another night ahead of watching the stars. Of standing guard. The frustration just then was powerful. He wasn't a man who could live comfortably without answers, and lacking answers to something this dangerous nearly maddened him.

Grace looked better, however. Maybe she'd needed a day of sitting in the fresh air and chatting with a friend. She sure didn't need to be sitting around here worrying nonstop.

Her color was higher, her movements more comfortable. And unless he missed his bet, she'd put a little of those missing pounds back on. Her face had softened, although he didn't want to get into measuring her head to foot. That struck him as both rude and dangerous.

Not that he could entirely avoid it. Grace was attracting him more with each passing day, and there was no good reason to ignore it as he had when John still lived. Not anymore.

Not that he'd pounce on her or press her in any way. She deserved more respect than that. Still...

He almost smiled at himself. The rock and the hard place again. He might as well resign himself to living there at least for a while and ignoring her charms. She had plenty of them.

Their ad hoc supper was a perfect finish to the day. Then they moved outside to keep an eye on the place. An insulated bottle of coffee sat on the table between them along with a small plate of the remaining blue-berry buckle.

The strong breeze swept across the darkening land, bringing a variety of scents, from the pines up on the mountains to the distant smell of cattle and grass.

Grace spoke. "You'll be bringing in the hay again?"

"In a couple of weeks. The alfalfa and clover aren't ready yet. The heads on the hay are a ways from ripening, so we're safe for now."

Familiar, easy front-porch conversation. Anything but the elephant. It was such a beautiful, peaceful evening it would have felt criminal to invite the ugliness in again.

But it waited anyway, just a little to the side, but not gone.

He was sure that she was wondering how long they were going to have to keep this up. He certainly was. They couldn't even be positive that anything more was going to happen.

What *had* happened couldn't be brushed off. Too much to think it was some rowdy kids getting their thrills.

He smothered a sigh, not wanting her to hear it. She must have felt it, though.

"Mitch, you can't camp here every night. You've got important things to do. Heck, you even have a life you need to look after."

The words hit him oddly, making him realize that Grace had become a big part of his life. The distance he'd tried to keep in response to her obvious wishes, in response to his own desire not to thrust himself where he wasn't wanted, was gone.

"Are you throwing me out?" he asked lightly, though

the question wasn't light at all. He nearly held his breath waiting for her answer.

"No!" She sounded shocked. "Not at all. Lord, Mitch, you've been my salvation through all of this."

Well, he didn't want to be her salvation. Or anyone else's for that matter. "Just being neighborly." A bald-faced lie.

"Yeah," she said quietly. "You've said."

Neighbors always helped one another, standing shoulder to shoulder as necessary. It was the way. He wouldn't have dreamed doing anything else.

Depending on the threat, there simply wasn't time to wait for the authorities to arrive if anything happened again. Yeah, he was standing guard, and that was how it was going to be.

The night remained quiet, peaceful. The stars wheeled overhead as they had for millions of years. A waning gibbous moon was setting in the west.

A thought struck him. "How's this all fit in with the phases of the moon?"

"What?" She sounded startled.

"Maybe nothing. Maybe a touch of my lunacy. Just wondering if these events have been tied in any way to the phases of the moon."

"Lunacy?" she asked dubiously.

"Not what I mean, not sure I even believe in it, other than that most animals get more active as the moon brightens. No, I was just wondering if these guys are waiting for moonless nights. Nights when it would be harder to see them."

"I hadn't thought of that."

"I half wish I hadn't. It sounds crazy in a world brightened by flashlights."

She rocked steadily, clearly thinking about it. "I was home the night of the barn fire. Flashlights might have given them away if I'd looked out a window. So the moon would have had to be bright that night, wouldn't it?"

"Like I said, crazy thought."

"I'm not sure it is. The moon is waning right now. It would have been bright when they broke into my house, assuming they did it at night."

"True. I was just spitballing, because for a fact they needed light to do either thing. So clearly they wouldn't be waiting for new moon."

She laughed and he joined her.

"Crackbrained thought," he admitted.

"Not really."

"Okay then, backward. I'm thinking of all this happening in the darkness, but you're right. There's some bright light at night."

None of this was really useful, however. Just spitballing, as he'd said.

"We're getting tired," she remarked. "Too much running around like hamsters in a wheel over this. I guess you want answers as much as I do."

"Believe it." Mostly he wanted to be certain of her safety.

A while later, he walked the perimeter again, checking the barn, checking around the house, checking a little farther out. Peaceful. Probably too soon for the next action.

When he returned to the porch, he said, "You go in and get some sleep."

"That's not fair to you!"

"Fair enough. We'll split the night if you want. And I can holler for you if anything happens."

It took a few minutes, but she finally agreed. "Just make sure you wake me for my watch."

He watched her go inside, then settled in the chair once again.

He'd wake her all right. Mainly because he didn't want her to become furious with him. But not as early as she probably expected.

Watch the coddling, he warned himself. She'd hate it.

ONCE INSIDE, GRACE unwrapped her hands and indulged in a shower. Yes, the warm water hurt the tender skin, but she couldn't stand feeling dirty. Anyway, the light bandaging had gotten to the point where she could bind her hands herself if necessary. Not as neatly as Lila would have, but neatly enough.

She was reluctant to get into bed wearing only a nightgown, though. What if she needed to run outside, or run across the ground? She settled on a pair of pajamas as a compromise and found her thickly soled slippers that had loop and hook closures. That would have to do for quick response.

When she climbed into bed, however, sleep escaped her. So many thoughts swirled in her head. Unanswered questions about what was going on.

Thoughts of Mitch. Many thoughts of Mitch that seemed to counterbalance all her worries, at least for a short time.

He was steadily becoming a part of her life, taking up space in her mind. Not necessarily a bad thing, since it gave her some relief from fear, but another discomfort to plague her.

Desire for him was slowly growing, and even as she

lay in her bed, she squirmed a bit from the direction her mind kept taking.

How could she not wonder how it would feel to kiss him, to feel his hard body against hers? How it would feel to run her hands over his skin, and how it would feel if he ran his hands over hers? What culmination would be like.

Even in the dark she blushed. As her face heated, she pulled her hands from beneath the covers and pressed them to her cheeks. The gauze prevented them from doing much to cool her face. The heat did seem to drive downward, spiraling ever closer to her center, making her *need* to feel a man's weight on her.

It had been so long and, strangely enough, she didn't feel at all guilty. During the last few weeks her grief over John had steadily eased. It would never leave, but she had begun to doubt it would rule her life.

She knew John would have wanted this because she would have wanted the same for him. To move on and build a new life, preferably a happy one. She never would have wanted to deprive him of that.

All these troubles seemed to have kicked her into gear, pushing her out of neutral, out of stasis.

That was a good thing, right?

While she might daydream about Mitch, she had no right to expect him to feel the same. He was already doing too much for her, entirely too much.

She couldn't stand alone. She knew it. Whatever was going on, there was no way she could face this solo. That annoyed her and scared her. Problems too big to handle on her own. She hadn't had them before, not really.

Except with the sheep. She'd been forced to face reality there, as well. One person couldn't do it on any useful scale. She'd had a choice: sell them or pare the flock down until they were essentially pets. Neither solution would have helped her keep the ranch.

She was grateful to Mitch for the way he had stepped in. He'd made it clear he wanted the sheep, all without her mentioning her increasing troubles, but as part of the deal he'd insisted she lease him most of her pasture and would sell him her hay crop.

"How am I supposed to graze the animals without the land?" he'd asked her.

Good question. The answer, she thought, was good business for them both.

Now he was stepping in again, this time with no apparent motive except to protect her. His concern warmed her but also worried her. She didn't want to become dependent.

She didn't want him to step back once again, either. Like it or not, she was growing dependent on his company.

That could be a very bad thing.

Eventually sleep snuck up on her and carried her into some surprisingly pleasant dreams. The nightmares didn't reach her.

Chapter Sixteen

Mitch waited to wake Grace until the first very early gray light began to wash out the stars. He hadn't had the least trouble staying awake and he hated to rouse her.

He also figured her wrath wasn't worth letting her sleep. He went to her bedroom door and called her gently, not wanting to frighten her.

"Huh?" she asked drowsily.

"Your turn on watch. I'll go make you some coffee and rustle up some food."

If she woke up, good. If she went back to sleep, not his problem. Hah!

He needed some breakfast, too, and looking in her fridge he found eggs and some shredded cheese. A promising start. He opened the breadbox beside the stove and discovered English muffins. Good accompaniment. Plenty of butter in the fridge. Hidden in her pantry was an unopened jar of raspberry preserves.

He could already taste the food to come.

He turned his head as he heard her behind him.

"I can cook," she said.

"I know you can."

"You must be tired. And you let me sleep too late."

"Late is a matter of perception, I can sleep just as well

during the morning, and look, lady, I *can* cook. So just sit yourself down and enjoy the service."

Hell, she didn't look fully awake yet. Mitch suspected she hadn't slept very long.

The coffeepot finished brewing just as he was cracking eggs into a bowl. "Scrambled okay?"

She nodded, her chin on her hand. "Thanks." Her eyelids kept drooping, which amused him. Yeah, she was awake. Barely.

He poured her a big mug of caffeine to help, then set about toasting bread and whipping the eggs with a dash of milk and a lot of cheese. "I am such a skilled cook that I'll take your breath away. Well, not really. I warn you, I couldn't begin to hold a candle to Lila."

That drew a weary chuckle from her. "I don't think anyone could."

"I think it helps that she loves cooking. Me, I'm a survivalist when it comes to that."

"I think I've pretty much become one, too. Feed me before I faint."

He laughed. "I read you."

ACROSS THE ROAD, in the foothills of the huge mountains where pines towered and a few cottonwoods succeeded, Carl and Larry lazed in the warming day, awaiting their next assignment—if one was needed.

"I'm going to town," Carl announced abruptly.

"You sure you should?"

"Look, I'm sick of eating out of cans. I want me some decent food. A burger and some fries. A milkshake. You sure as hell can't make a milkshake over a camp stove."

Larry didn't put up a fuss over that. "Milkshake sounds good," he admitted. "Beer's getting cold enough in that stream, but you're right about anything colder. Hell, I'd just be glad of the taste, even melted."

"You see? I'm gonna get us something decent."

Larry rolled over and looked at Carl. "What about the boss?"

"She ain't asked us to do one damn thing except at night. I'll be back before then. You can take a message... if she ain't done with us."

IN HER SMALL apartment in Conard City, Betty Pollard brushed her hair. Dan was a figment, an imaginary boyfriend to throw a concealing cloak of normalcy over her real plan for Grace.

All these years later, Betty still grew furious at the chain of events that had ripped that ranch from her father. So what if he hadn't paid his property taxes? Did that mean a man should lose everything?

She ignored the other debts that had mounted, debts she didn't know about until it was too late. Most ranchers and farmers ran an open line of credit to deal with major expenses. Her dad had eventually stopped paying those, too.

The foreclosure had come from taxes and that lien was filed first. Since the county wasn't trying to make a profit, and the lenders had accepted the newer equipment for collateral and not the land, the auction had been for peanuts. Peanuts! That whole damn place was worth a hell of a lot more.

But Betty had only been a high schooler. She'd learned about the taxes but hadn't been able to do anything because she didn't have any money. She'd told her dad to sell off a parcel, but he refused.

"It'll get better, honey. It always does."

It had in prior years. But this time he'd let it go too long, and the county foreclosed well before Betty expected it. As soon as the lenders had heard about the foreclosure, they'd moved in to take anything of value.

Then her father had died, with nothing left to live for, and Grace and John had bought the homestead for a song.

Betty didn't have a personal grudge against the Halls, but she wanted her childhood home again. She wanted it with an enduring ache and unrequited fury.

Thanks to a legacy from a nearly forgotten aunt, she now had the money to pay a fair price for the ranch. A decent price. She wasn't trying to rip anyone off.

Without John, it seemed crazy for Grace to hang on to the land and the house. It was fair for her to be reluctant about selling, but managing the ranch was entirely too much for one person alone. Hell, as near as Betty could tell, Grace was having trouble keeping up. Of course, she had those two shepherds but Betty sensed an opportunity.

Betty sighed and poured herself a double shot of bourbon. She tried to contain her anger, but since John's death her self-control had grown increasingly difficult.

While she didn't want Grace to see that anger, it simmered in her anyway. She had finally gotten to the point of trying to scare Grace away.

Nothing that would actually hurt Grace. She didn't want to do that. She felt terrible about Grace's burns but she hadn't known there were horses out there, and apparently neither had the men she had hired for this job.

But if Grace didn't fear that she was being targeted, then she was stupider than Betty would have believed.

So why wasn't she hightailing it to town? Away from the repeated threats?

Betty finished off her bourbon and poured another. It was too soon to demand that Larry and Carl do something else to scare Grace.

Give it time to sink in, Betty decided. Let the threat linger longer.

Then she would tell those two idiots to get going and warn them again about not hurting Grace. Hell, she was paying them enough with a bonus at the end. And they were despicable enough to do it. The whole barn-burning, while it had seemed like a good idea when those guys proposed it, still made her sick to her stomach. What was she paying those men for? They should have known there were horses in that barn.

But the break-in should have been enough to drive the point home to Grace. Especially when nothing had been taken but an old computer and TV.

"Hell," she said, this time aloud. Then several times she repeated the word emphatically.

It made her feel only a bit better.

MITCH SLEPT UNTIL nearly noon, which was fine by him. He expected the worst of the danger would come at night, that the mornings were free of the threat. The earlier events had given him reason to think so.

He sat up, closing the recliner, ignoring the stiffness that came from not being able to move much in his sleep. Well, it was better than bedding down on rocky ground.

He could hear Grace on the porch, so he took the opportunity to shower and change. He'd brought extra clothes with him, enough for a few days, and the change was welcome.

By now he must have the same stench as a barn animal. His chaps still hung over the back of a chair, needing that oiling he couldn't give them just yet. They'd do okay for a while.

And now he'd do okay smelling more like shampoo and soap. Only thing he regretted was that he must be smelling like a field of lavender.

Funny he hadn't noticed that aroma when it lingered around Grace. But maybe it had been part of her all this time, like her wide smile, her pleasantly curved figure, her light and enchanting voice.

Oh, boy. He was getting it bad.

Then he realized he also smelled bread. He sniffed with pleasure, then stepped outside to find Grace, her shotgun nearby, leaning against a stanchion and surveying the property toward the county road.

"Do I smell bread?" he asked.

She pivoted and smiled. "Gotta do something during this stakeout."

"But bread? That's a lot of work, especially with your hands."

She raised her arms. "More like a workout for the upper body. It felt good. As for my hands, we've come to an agreement. They're going to hurt regardless. Anyway, four more loaves coming up since the remaining ones are getting stale."

"Four?"

"If I was going to do one, I might as well do more. Same mess. The kneading part is great exercise. Cleaning flour off the whole damn kitchen, not so much."

A grin emerged, stretching his face. "You're a messy cook?"

"More like a messy baker. I might do drop biscuits later."

"I love biscuits."

"Who doesn't?" Grace resumed her watch. "Nothing. I even walked around the house and the barn to see if I could catch sight of anything at all."

His heart skipped. "Grace—"

"I know. Skip it, Mitch. I went alone because I've been doing it for years. If someone wants to take a potshot at me, then this whole thing wasn't going to end well anyway."

He could see that stiffening in her backbone. Not a good time to press her. The obstinate Grace was out in full force.

"I'll make us some coffee. Want some?"

She nodded. "Thanks. I guess it's almost time for lunch."

"I'll take care of that. I have this delusional idea that I can be good for something."

At least that drew a laugh from her. "Good for a whole lot, Mitch. Like staying here when I need some help."

"Such a sacrifice," he joked. No sacrifice at all. He had people he could rely on for his ranch. She had no one else.

Besides, he was seeing parts of her that he hadn't seen since John. He liked them.

MITCH HAD RUSTLED up sandwiches made with cold cuts, lettuce and mayonnaise. He brought them along with coffee out to Grace.

"Thank you," Grace said as she accepted a paper plate. She looked at the thickness of the sandwich and asked, "Did you use up all my cold cuts?"

"Yup. I like 'em hearty. Don't worry about it. Lila will replace them and more. Just enjoy."

Enjoy enough for two people, she thought, surveying the size of the sandwich. Gamely she bit into it and decided his choice had been a good one. "Delicious," she said.

"I'm sure the bread would have been better if it was yours."

She glanced over her shoulder. "Believe it. It must be close to done with the final rise, so I need to check on it after lunch."

"Making bread is a mystery to me."

"It was to me, too, until I made my first loaf."

A songbird seemed have taken up residence on the porch roof and provided a happy accompaniment to the meal.

THE WORLD STILL sounded cheerful, Grace thought as she listened to the bird. And the food and coffee still tasted good. She needed to hang on to those things, to remember the beauty nature offered. The beauty of having a friend make her a stupendous lunch.

She was seeing Mitch so much differently now, more than a friend and neighbor. As a man. Her first real inkling was when she had watched him mount his horse to set out on a hunt for the transgressors. Now she felt it even more.

A man. An attractive, weather-hardened, work-hardened man. A stand-up guy. If he had any real failings, she hadn't encountered them. Or at least none that bothered her enough for them to rise to her awareness.

The bird continued to tweet happily as the sky overhead darkened. The wind shifted a little, bringing new scents to the world.

"Rain soon," she remarked.

"Smells like it. I hope it doesn't blow over. I saw some dry patches in the pasture when I was out yesterday."

Amusement struck her. Such a prosaic and ordinary conversation between two ranchers. As if the weather and the state of a pasture were all that mattered. As if the threat of danger didn't lie in every shadow.

A comfortable rhythm, however, dredging up memories of many conversations over the years, with John and neighbors. In ordinary times, such thoughts were essential. They usually led to conversations about livestock, feed, pasturage, crops, the most important thing in most lives around her. Common ground indeed.

It still felt odd to be having such a conversation in these circumstances. Both of them sitting there with shotguns ready to blast away. Both of them scanning the countryside for any sign of threat.

A jarring counterpoint.

As soon as she finished her sandwich, she rose to go check on her bread. Almost ready for the oven, she decided. The rising could be slow or fast depending on ambient temperature. Today, inside, there was a coolness that probably lingered from the night before and she wouldn't have expected the dough to rise so fast.

She turned on the oven, set a timer, then headed back to the porch with the coffeepot. "Top you off?"

"Sure. Thanks." He held out his mug.

She topped her own mug, then placed the pot on the table between them. "This," she said as she sat again, "feels too much like an ordinary summer day."

"It is," he said.

"Oh, yeah."

His gray eyes twinkled as they settled on her. "Well,

apart from that. Let's enjoy it. In a bit, I'll walk around, maybe ride out again to look for problems."

"Did you get Burt Stiller?" she asked.

"I got his voice mail. He's probably out on the range."

"Yeah." The idea deflated her a little. Mitch would go out to cover the same territory he'd covered yesterday and learn exactly nothing.

The timer inside beeped and she returned to the kitchen to put the loaves in the oven. Four, side by side, just like she used to bake when…

She cut that thought off. She couldn't let every damn thing carry her back to the past. Today was a new day, one that carried its own set of problems. Time to deal with here and now.

She set a timer for the bread, then went outside again in time to see a pickup coming up her drive. "Who's that?"

"I guess we'll find out." Mitch stood with the shotgun cradled in his arms. A warning to whoever.

No warning needed. Out of the car stepped Jenny Wright, a ranch wife Grace had once known but hadn't seen again until the barn raising. A lot of things had disappeared after John, mostly her own fault.

"Hey," Jenny called with a cheerful wave. "Thought it was time to be a good neighbor, so I brought you my famous chicken and green bean casserole. The beans are from my kitchen garden and while you'll taste the white wine, it won't make you drunk." She grinned almost ear to ear, then leaned back inside her car to bring out a very large casserole dish. She carried it up to the porch. "At least enough for several meals, even with a hungry cowboy around."

"Thank you so much!" Grace was touched. How had she pushed people like this away?

"I'd give you a hug of greeting, but I'd like to set this down somewhere it won't draw flies and other critters."

Mitch spoke. "You ladies go on inside. I'll stay out here."

Inside, Jenny placed the casserole on the counter. "Mmm, I smell baking bread. Got ambitious this morning?"

"I did," Grace agreed. "Stay awhile and I'd be happy to send you home with a loaf."

Jenny shook her head. "I'd love it, but I have to get back. I left three boys with an overwhelmed husband who would rather be herding cattle."

Grace laughed. "Three now?" She seemed to remember Jennie had been pregnant way back, but hadn't thought about it.

"Yup, and they're all hell on wheels. The youngest, Timmy, is way too young to ride yet, except on a pony, so the older boys can't go ramming about on their horses because Daddy can't take 'em out. Because of Timmy. Hell, they say the youngest child is always spoiled, but Timmy will never get the chance thanks to his older brothers."

"Tough on him?"

"Oh yeah. They also don't much like it when he keeps them from doing stuff because he's so young. Not that we let that happen too often, but you wouldn't believe it because of the way they complain."

"Oh, I can believe it."

Jenny raised a brow. "That's right, you taught elementary school. Lots of experience."

"Enough to know that many boys are more active and

adventurous than most girls their ages. I've often wondered if that was social."

"I'll let you know if I ever get my daughter." Then
Jenny frowned. "Grace? I heard about your break-in. Are
you getting scared? I would. First the barn and then this?"

"I'm not scared, at least not yet," Grace said with determination. "I'm angry, though, angrier than hell. Scared
might come in the middle of the night if this keeps up."

Jenny nodded thoughtfully. "It seems like an awful
lot. At least you have Mitch here. I wouldn't want to be
alone just now."

"I'm grateful I don't have to be," Grace admitted, although it felt a little like weakness to lean on someone
else. It had been different with John. They'd leaned on
each other. Mitch didn't seem to need anyone to lean on.

Jenny stayed long enough for Grace to make another
pot of coffee, then they joined Mitch on the porch. Jenny
sat where Mitch had been perched and looked up at him
as he leaned against the porch railing.

"What do you think is going on here?" Jenny asked
Mitch.

"Damned if I know."

"But you don't think it's over," she said, pointing to
his shotgun.

"Don't dare to. Not yet. All of this is moving closer
to Grace."

Grace drew a sharp breath. She hadn't thought of it
that way. That she might be targeted, yes. But that the
threat was moving toward her, like a shark circling in
the water? The idea went past property crimes, and for
the first time a nearly overwhelming fear filled her. She
also felt a little stupid for not thinking of this in such a
way, not when it was as plain as the nose on her face.

"Do you really believe that?" Grace asked Mitch.

"Like I said, I don't dare to assume it's over. We both already knew that, though."

Yes, they had. The threat hadn't disappeared for her personally, not yet. It had been against her property, all of it. She had been convinced that it was all directed against scaring her, not against hurting her physically. But she hadn't noticed the fact that it was indeed moving closer to her. All the way down the driveway, then the barn, then the house.

Jenny finished her coffee just as the bread finished baking. It was too hot to send a loaf with her, so Grace said, "Another time?"

"Any time you get another yen to do all that work, call me. I'll be over as soon as it cools."

Smiling, giving another friendly wave, Jenny departed. Grace watched her car pull away, and the darkening day seemed to grow darker.

The air delivered the strong smell of rain and the faint scent of ozone. The storm was coming.

"I need to get out and ride around again," Mitch said.

"Are you sure you should? Lightning."

"I haven't seen any, nor heard any rumble of thunder. I promise I'll take shelter under a tree if I see or hear any."

Grace gaped at him. "You wouldn't!"

Mitch laughed. "Gotta go. As many times as I've been through it, I still hate getting drenched."

Feeling even lonelier, she watched him ride away. At least he had an oiled leather duster for protection.

SHE PULLED THE bread out of the oven and dumped each loaf onto a cooling rack, then set them upright. Pretty darn good, she decided as she looked at them. She hadn't forgotten how. Then she went back out to keep watch.

Gusts of wind blew rain every which way, driving Grace indoors. The day had darkened until it seeped through the world like approaching night. Inside was even darker, and she didn't want to open curtains, advertising to any watcher where she was in the house.

Which sounded paranoid, but that was where events had taken her.

In times past, she had always enjoyed storms like this. Unless she and John had been out with the sheep, the graying, wind-and-rain-lashed days had felt cozy. Time for a cup of hot chocolate, lots of laughter, and lovemaking.

That part of her stirred awake again. She wondered if she should be disturbed or feel disloyal. No. She knew as sure as she was walking around her house that John wouldn't have wanted that. He'd been a generous man and, while his death had been totally unexpected, she knew him well enough to believe he would not have wanted her to spend the rest of her days in lonely grief. In emptiness.

Inevitably, her thoughts turned to Mitch and the desires that had begun to take on life. She had no idea if he might be feeling the same toward her. No idea at all.

But maybe he sensed he might be transgressing. Hardly surprising considering the distance she had placed between them.

She started the casserole heating for supper, the entire dish. It would be more than the two of them could eat, but she had no idea how hungry Mitch would be after riding in this rain. Rain was always cold. Almost icy.

When the squall line finally passed—it had sure taken

a sluggish path over the house—the wind settled to more usual levels and stopped driving the downpour in every direction. Excuse enough to return Grace and her shot-gun to the porch.

It would have been an opportune time, with the dark sky and flat light, for someone to have approached.

As she was emerging from her cocoon, she saw Mitch ride up to the barn. A wave of relief filled her. Knowing Mitch would take care of his horse before anything else, she went inside to heat water for instant cocoa. With a bit of cream, it tasted almost like the real thing.

Finally she heard Mitch's boots on the porch. She ran to open the door and saw him dripping despite his duster.

"Did you go swimming?" she asked lightly.

"I thought I might need skin diving gear. Listen, I want to strip out here, so if you wouldn't mind bringing me the bag I left on the mud porch so I have dry clothes, I'd appreciate it."

She hurried to get the bag for him, along with a towel. "Dry off, too."

He flashed a grin. "Now get inside unless you want to see me as naked as the day I was born."

She wouldn't have minded that at all. In fact, she quickened between her legs. But he deserved his privacy, so she went back to the kitchen to wait. She could imag-ine the sight well enough anyway, and a sigh escaped her.

While she waited, the phone rang. Guy Redwing was on the other end.

"We researched that big cattle operator who tried to buy your operation earlier this year."

"And?"

"Their business practices appear to be aboveboard. No complaints anywhere from property owners. In fact, no complaints or disputes about their contracts, either. Whatever hijinks they might be up to are buried within the corporation itself."

Grace's stomach sank. She had hoped for information the sheriff could work on. "I wish I could say that's good news."

Guy sounded sympathetic. "I hear you, Grace. We'll keep looking. You know that. We want to solve this problem as much as you do."

The nice part of living in an underpopulated area was the attentiveness of police. She was sure they wouldn't drop this because they couldn't immediately find good information.

Although how they would, she couldn't begin to imagine.

Mitch entered the kitchen barefoot but otherwise covered in dry clothing, a khaki safari shirt with faded jeans.

"I'm going to let my stuff hang out front to finish dripping, then I'll beg for the use of your laundry."

She smiled. "What would you do if I said no? Of course you can use them."

She turned to the boiling water on the stove, switched off the gas flame, waiting for it to cool just enough so she wouldn't singe the dry milk in the mix. "Cocoa?"

"Sounds great."

She heard the chair slide away from the table as he sat. She didn't turn around immediately because she was having just a bit of trouble breathing and she didn't want to devour him with her eyes.

Dang, where had this come from? It was rising in her like a powerful tide. She needed to resist it for Mitch's sake. What if she embarrassed him? A good friendship might die.

At last she felt comfortable enough to sit with him. She avoided his gaze for a few minutes longer, though.

"This is good," Mitch told her after he'd sipped. "A package mix made this?"

"Cream helped make it richer."

"I'm sold."

What a mundane conversation. "Guy Redwing called. Nothing about the company that approached us seems problematic."

He sighed. "I should have been smarter than to hope it would be that easy."

Now she *did* look at him. "Then what?"

"I don't know. I'm running out of suspicions, not that I had many to go on at the start."

A grim prospect indeed. Where did all of this go from here?

Nothing seemed promising.

MITCH INSISTED ON cleaning up the cups and pan. When he turned around he found Grace right behind him.

He saw the heat and longing in her gaze and was almost afraid to believe it. Good God, was it possible? And why *him*?

No, it wasn't possible. He didn't dare risk the fragility of whatever was growing between them. Too quickly, too soon.

Then she leaned into him, wrapping her arms around his waist.

"Don't hate me," she whispered. "Just hold me."

Hate her? That could never happen. Without a word, he surrounded her shoulders and held her close. He would have held her even closer except he didn't want it to feel like a squeeze.

But his body, damn his body, was reacting to her in the most obvious way possible. Her face rested against his shoulder, a trusting gesture, and he half expected her to break into tears.

She didn't, though. She turned her face up to his and said one simple word. "Please."

Chapter Seventeen

Mitch's head nearly exploded in response to this unexpected development. He could feel her shaking like a leaf against him and couldn't mistake how much courage that one word had required of her.

All he could do was tighten his hold. "You sure?"

"Yes," she murmured.

Grace might be using him to make her first step back to a fuller life, just a stepping-stone, but he didn't care, not at this moment in time, with her leaning into him. Regardless, he couldn't reject her, no matter how gently, and leave her feeling unwanted.

Well, he didn't want to reject her. Not at all. Barely formed desires had erupted inside him and he wasn't going to walk away. If persuasion of some kind was needed afterward, then, damn it, he'd worry about it then.

He doubted her steadiness, so he lifted her in his arms to carry her back to her bedroom. She was too light, too much like a bird in his arms. Fragile.

He was almost afraid he might hurt her. He was equally uncertain of himself. It had been a while, and he feared he might be rusty.

Sitting her on the edge of her bed, he knelt and gazed into her blue eyes. They appeared almost smoky just then.

He had to know before he laid a finger on her. "Grace. You can say no. Now or later."

She gave a jerky nod but did nothing to send him on his way.

His own hands shook a bit as he reached for the top button on her simple checked shirt. He wished they were snaps but opening the buttons one at a time gave her another opportunity to back off. She didn't. Instead while he released the buttons, she lifted her hands to his shoulders. Inviting him.

He was leaping off a cliff with no idea what lay below.

His worries soon slipped away as he revealed the beauty hiding beneath her shirt. Her full breasts were encased in a lacy confection that surprised him. She was always dressed in work clothes, and he hadn't expected to find she had a secret liking for special undergarments.

His mouth dried a bit as he pushed the shirt from her shoulders and reached behind her to release the clasp of her bra. More beauty filled his gaze, large pink nipples rising from the smooth skin of her breasts. So enticing.

He murmured her name, overwhelmed by the desire that pounded through him. How long had he wanted her? It was a question that needed no answer, even as the longing began to be answered. All that mattered was that he wanted her now, and that she seemed to feel the same.

He brushed his thumbs over the peaks of her breasts and wished his hands were smoother, as she surely deserved. Glancing up at her face, he saw her eyes closed, her entire face growing softer than he'd ever seen her look.

Her breath came faster, too, another lure that wrapped

around him like a spell. Ensorcelled, he could be stopped by nothing now, except a protest from her. But she didn't protest, merely leaned back on her hands, welcoming and inviting.

Too much. He rose and began stripping away the clothes that he'd donned such a short time ago. Her eyelids fluttered open and she smiled sleepily as she watched.

Heaven had just entered the room along with rising musky scents.

GRACE WATCHED HIM STRIP, her heart jumping and accelerating until she was sure the last air had been sucked from the room.

He was gorgeous, she thought hazily. More gorgeous than her imaginings. Hard muscle from work created a captivating body, so masculine and perfect in every way. A few scars nicked him here and there, but they only added to his desirability.

He was ready for her. So ready.

She throbbed achingly at her center and could hardly wait for his weight to cover her. She needed nothing further to make her eager, and resented the delay.

But there was more. He knelt again, leaning forward to take her nipples into his mouth, sucking so strongly that the pleasure dived through her, coalescing in her core.

His fingers reached for the snap of her jeans, and she didn't appreciate the last impediments that needed to be removed. He pulled her jeans down until they rode her calves, then pulled her boots off in swift, easy movements. So strong!

At last her jeans were gone, and only a wisp of panties stood in their way. Once again, he pulled back to look at her.

"Damn, you're beautiful," he muttered. Then he reached for her delicate panties that matched her bra.

The moment she was naked, she basked in his hungry eyes, in his faint smile. Then he moved between her legs, teasing her breast with his tongue, reaching out to stroke her petals with gentle fingers.

The last of the world was lost in an explosion of magic so powerful it hurt.

Need. She became a needy vessel, impatient for him.

"Mitch," she groaned.

With a slow, steady movement he slipped inside her, carrying her ever upward to the stars. She fell back, giving herself completely over to his ministrations, so thrilled by the feel of him deep inside her that she came close to losing her mind in pleasure.

He pumped into her, caressing her sensitive nub with his finger, driving her upward to heights that felt new to her, fresh, as if she had never visited them before.

"Grace..."

Her name reached into her, filling places she'd hardly been aware of.

Need. She was needy and rose ever higher until she trembled on the peak and tipped over, a climax so strong it nearly hurt.

MITCH FELT THE exact moment of her culmination, and drove one more time, hard, so hard he could barely stand it. Then he followed her into the slow fall on the far side.

He fell forward, his face resting on her midriff, satisfied as he was sure he'd never been satisfied before.

Then, at last, some strength poured into his muscles. Just enough.

He rose, lifting her until she was under the comforter on her bed. Moments later he fell beside her and took her into his arms, hugging her tightly.

He felt blessed.

MINUTES PASSED. MAYBE HOURS. At the moment, time no longer mattered to Mitch. When Grace stirred, he asked huskily, "You okay?"

"Better than," she whispered in response. "Far better."

Happiness flooded him. Joy. When had he last felt as high as a kite? He couldn't remember. Life so seldom left room for it.

"Me, too," he answered. "Me, too."

She snuggled closer, offering him a trust that made his throat tighten.

"Grace," he murmured again.

Her fingers touched his lips. "Shh. Let perfection be."

Perfection? The word crashed through him like thunder. Then he realized she was right. Perfection. She shared the feeling with him. He couldn't have asked for more.

EVENTUALLY, BECAUSE EVENTUALLY always came, they rose and dressed. Hands touched lightly, a few kisses were exchanged but reality had begun to creep into the room once more.

There might be a threat out there, and neither of them could ignore the possibility for long.

MITCH WENT OUTSIDE again to check around the house and barn. Reluctantly, Grace watched him go but knew he was right. They had to keep an eye out. Rain still fell, but lighter now. Even the leaden gray of the sky had changed to a lighter color, announcing it had dumped most of its watery burden.

She touched her loaves of bread, surprised to realize they had cooled. Had they made love for that long?

She blushed faintly, guessing they must have. It had seemed to be over too soon, but time had faded in Mitch's arms.

It had been beautiful. Whatever happened between them now, she decided she didn't care. The past hours had been so fantastic she wouldn't have missed them for anything.

Regardless of what she told herself, there was a nugget inside her that hoped for more than the friendship they had shared. Much more.

Another tumble in the hay? She almost giggled aloud. Oh, she had it bad. She needed to brace herself, though. As she'd long since discovered, life rarely turned out the way one hoped.

MITCH WALKED AROUND in the gentle rain, hoping it would cool him down a bit. Damn, he wanted that woman again, and he wasn't at all sure she'd welcome another advance.

Maybe she'd just been overcome by stress. Maybe she had reached out for comfort and not for him in particular.

Maybe she regretted the sex they'd just shared.

One thing he knew for certain: he didn't regret it. He hadn't lived a celibate life but he knew when sex was special. This had been, beyond his wildest dreams.

Facing yearnings he'd been denying for a very long time, he accepted that he was drawn to Grace for reasons that had nothing to do with sex. Something deeper had rooted inside him, and he might need a tiller to pull it out.

Leaving a gaping hole behind, with no way to fill it in.

"Now what do I do?" he asked himself as he continued his patrol. The rain didn't give him an answer.

But a surprising roll of thunder did. He looked up at the sky and saw it blackening again. Cripes, one squall hadn't been enough? Two in a row?

Climate chaos, he thought. God knew he'd been seeing enough of its effects on his ranch. You couldn't wander around as much land as he owned without noting steady changes. You could try to remain blind until life-long observation told you that you had your head in the sand.

Or this might just be an isolated incident. He wanted to hope so.

He hurried his survey but contented himself that no threat hovered yet. How long did they have to wait for the next one? Because he believed there would be a next one.

He wished he could imagine why Grace was being targeted this way. It would have at least given him a direction to pursue.

At last he headed back to the house and entered, hoping Grace might give him a slab of that fresh bread. Preferably with a thick coating of butter.

She greeted him with a smile, but he didn't miss the faint touch of heightened color. Was she embarrassed? Uneasy?

Not knowing what else to do, ignoring his slightly dampened state—even the duster hadn't been able to keep him completely dry—he walked to her and gave her a tight hug.

"Missed you," he admitted. And it hadn't even been that long.

"Missed you, too." She sighed and returned his hug.

They separated, as if neither was sure how to continue.

"It's still raining," he remarked. "That's no big deal, but there's another squall moving in."

"Really? That's odd."

"The sky is mad at us, I guess. Now, how do I beg for a big piece of that fresh bread?"

She laughed, sounding easier. "You sit at the table and wait for me to cut it. How hungry are you?"

"Well, I could probably eat half a loaf, but I'll be polite."

"Polite is eating up all my bread. If you stop after one slice it definitely won't be polite."

His turn to laugh. He was feeling better by the minute.

She must have taken him seriously, because she *did* cut him a couple of thick slices and passed him the butter dish along with the butter knife.

"Have at it," she said. "And tell me what you think. It's been ages since I made bread."

He spread the butter thickly, then bit into the soft bread with its crunchy crust. "To die for," he announced, even though he hated that phrase.

"I detest breads where you can't taste or smell the yeast."

He hadn't thought about that. All he knew was that he liked it a lot.

She sat facing him with her own, thinner, slice of bread. "So nothing outside?"

"Nothing I could detect. It's a miserable day out there, and about to get worse. Colder, too, I expect."

"Good. I hope the bad guy is out there and is freezing and wet."

A surprised laugh escaped him. "I never dreamed you could wish ill on anyone."

"Well, I can, and this guy deserves it. Maybe he'll even get hypothermic."

Mitch grinned. "Remind me never to get on your bad side."

Then she surprised him again, saying softly, "I don't think you could, Mitch."

"I'm no saint," he protested.

"Neither am I. As you just saw."

She finished her bread and rose. "Want more?"

"A couple of slices just like these."

She cut them for him, then began to wrap the loaves in plastic. They went into a large breadbox. "Jenny's casserole for dinner?"

"Sounds great."

"Save some room. She brought enough for an army."

Then she pulled back the curtain at the kitchen window for a minute. "I'm scared Mitch. Someone is out there and I don't even know what he wants."

"Maybe to scare you," he said slowly, repeating a concern they had shared.

"But why?"

He wished he could answer. They *both* wanted that answer.

CARL HELD THE satellite phone away from his ear as the boss shouted at him. Larry could hear it, too.

"What is it with you two," she yelled. "I'm paying you to do one simple thing!"

She was going nuts, Carl decided. Losing her marbles. What was eating her? They'd done some pretty bad and dangerous things for her, now they was getting screamed at?

"We can't *make* that Hall woman do a damn thing," he retorted, his own voice rising as anger triumphed over his perplexity. "You want her out of there, *you* go do something."

"Like hell. You're getting money for this. You'd better think of something soon."

"Not too soon, you said. Give her time to think about it, let it eat at her, you said. Well, you get your freaking butt out there and *you* do something."

Silence greeted his words.

"I thought so," Carl spat. "You keep wanting us to risk jail or death, then you can just put up with this. Alls I want to know is do you want us to speed up or wait like you said."

More silence answered him.

Carl continued his rant. "You ain't got no idea what's going on. That woman's got a guy with her and they's patrolling the place with shotguns as if they was military."

Then her voice returned to the earpiece. It sounded steely as all hell, throwing some icy water over his indignation.

"Just remember, you don't get your money until this job is completed. And I don't mean halfway." Then she disconnected.

Carl listened to a different kind of silence before he closed his end of the call.

"Man, that was some yellin'," Larry said after listening to a godforsaken and lonely bird calling another of its kind.

"She ain't happy," Carl said needlessly.

Larry lost interest in the singing when the bird flew away. Damn thing needed to find a mate for hisself. Good luck. Not that Larry had had much luck with finding a woman, and it kinda soured his view of romance. Or sex. Whatever. He didn't know the difference and he didn't care.

"What now?" he asked.

"We follow our orders for a bit. Wait and see. Then we's gonna worsen it."

"How?" asked Larry, who'd about given up trying to think of something new to do.

Carl didn't answer for a minute. "Somebody gonna die," he said. "We tried it her way too damn long."

GRACE AND MITCH felt safe. Briefly. The time between incidents had been long and neither of them expected one immediately.

Maybe, thought Mitch, their patrolling with guns could hold the threat at bay. For a while. He didn't expect their guns to be a permanent magic charm, and he couldn't help wondering how long he and Grace could keep this up.

As long as necessary, he decided. If he had to go back to his own operation for a short while, one of his men could come and stand watch.

Because he was damned if he was going to leave Grace alone.

She joined him on the front porch with a carafe of fresh coffee. When she sat, she picked up her shotgun.

The sky remained leaden, still pregnant with rain. It would be surprising if the clouds dumped again because the rain shadow of the mountains generally caused rain to fall farther east. Summers here were usually dry. Well, drier than this one was turning into.

Grace spoke. "You don't think they'd kill anyone, do you?"

The fear was uppermost in his mind, too, although he was reluctant to voice it. But now she had.

"I don't know." Never lie to Grace. His guiding star.

"I don't know either, obviously. I shouldn't even have asked."

"Why not? It's impossible not to wonder at this point. Worry is buzzing inside both our heads like angry bees."

She nodded, shooting him the smallest smile at his comparison. "I wish the sheriff had found something about that company. A word might have been enough to make them back off."

Now they were staring into a black hole with no idea if there was a bottom. Not an easy place to exist.

"We're doing all we can," he reminded her.

"You must need to get back to your life."

He almost said she had become the most important thing in his life, but after the time they'd shared in her bed, he suspected she might scamper away like a frightened rabbit. He had little doubt that the specter of John would swim to the forefront of her mind, making her feel disloyal. Lucky man, John, to have known Grace's love.

"Not yet," he told her. "Not yet." He said no more, giving her room to escape if she needed it.

Nothing permanent. Maybe her reference to him getting back to his own life had been her first attempt to push him away. God, he hoped not. The attraction to her that he'd buried during her marriage to John, that he'd buried in the face of her widowhood, had sprung to full life. She was beautiful, to his eye anyway, but she was even more admirable in so many ways.

Stubborn, yes, but tough and loyal and so lost over the last two years. He wanted to put the sparkle back in her eye for longer than a brief spell. He wanted to put it there most of the time.

He nearly sighed as he realized he'd wandered away from their purpose, the most important purpose. Keeping Grace safe.

Rising, he announced that he was going to take another walk around.

"No coffee first?"

"When I get back. That carafe will keep it hot enough." Then, gun in hand, he stepped off the porch and began to walk his mental perimeter, not only looking for a man, but looking also for anything out of place.

Soon he'd need to ride out again, even though his men were keeping an eye out for any indication that a stranger had been there, camping on his ranch.

He still hadn't heard from Burt Stiller about riding around his land. Stiller wouldn't mind, but it wouldn't be neighborly to just go ahead. And Stiller must be out somewhere on his own ranch, a big spread that sometimes needed a lot of attention. As they all did.

Chapter Eighteen

The next week passed without any threatening events. Grace began to suggest that it might be over.

Mitch didn't accept that. The barn-burning and the break-in had been designed to terrify her. Directed at her. Why else would someone do those things if they didn't want her shaking in her boots? And clearly she wasn't shaking.

She'd become as immovable as a post sunk six feet in the ground. Which was good for *her*, he supposed, but it wasn't good for *him*. If she'd wavered at all, he'd have swept her off to his house, left her in Lila's competent charge and waited with a whole lot less fear for her until the next thing happened.

It would be a helluva lot harder to frighten Grace in his house. Too many people around, and Lila was a deadeye marksman.

Not something anyone would expect from a housekeeper.

Of course, the other side to that was that the threat might indeed move to his place. Not that he was worried if it did—he could deal with whatever—but he doubted it would. He could imagine no upside to coming after him. Besides, if there was a target in this madness, it certainly wasn't him. But it would sure trouble Grace and convince her to return to her own land to protect *him*.

Inwardly he fumed about the entire mess. Without a direction to pursue, there could be no useful action.

Then there was the immovable steel that was Grace. She hadn't shown any desire to repeat their memorable hours in her bed.

John, he thought. Or maybe he just wasn't a good enough partner to make her want another round—despite what she'd said.

Aw, hell. He couldn't remember ever having felt so many rats scrambling around in his brain. This way or that way? Hah! Damn fool.

Peace of any kind had escaped him.

As he watched Grace rocking on her front porch, shotgun across her lap, he wondered if he just needed to approach her himself. Maybe she interpreted his reluctance to mean he didn't want to have sex with her again.

How was he supposed to know? And as the days dragged by, making them both edgier about the possibility of more trouble, he felt less inclination to distract either of them with time in the sack. He knew from their one time together that a bomb could have exploded beneath the bed and he wouldn't have noticed it. Lost to the world with her in his arms.

He stopped pacing around the house and settled beside her on the porch. The inevitable carafe of coffee sat there with two mugs. He didn't think he'd drunk as much coffee in his entire life as he'd swallowed in the last few weeks.

But it jazzed him enough to keep him from fatigue, which he supposed was Grace's idea. So he poured another cup.

"You should go home," Grace said again. "You must be sick of being here."

Far from it, he thought. Given his choice, he'd tear the fences down between her land and his and move into her house with her. No way to say that, though.

"I'm fine," he answered. "Damn well fine."

She looked at him and he was relieved to see her smile. If she could still do that, she'd be okay.

"That sounded like you're aren't, Mitch."

"Believe what I do. I'm here. My choice. I'm just furious about the situation. You should be wanting me here, not needing me. Anyway, I sure as hell don't want to be anywhere else."

How could he not be sure? The witch had cast her spell and he had no desire to dispel it. The description amused him.

"You're sure your guys are handling everything well enough?"

"I trust them or I'd fire them. Hell, they're probably managing so well that I'll feel useless when I get back. My secret fear, that the ranch doesn't really need me."

She laughed quietly, then startled him enough to almost lock his breath in his throat. "Mitch, what you said—do you want to be needed or need to be wanted?"

His neck suddenly stiffened. He had a bit of trouble turning his head to look at her. "Both," he said finally. "Who doesn't?" Brushing it off when he felt it was truly important.

She nodded and returned her gaze to the wide-open spaces, beyond which mountains loomed. "Once I had both."

He nearly stopped breathing. Here it came again. John. Not that he could blame her, but he nevertheless sent some silent words heavenward. *Let her go, man. You loved her. Love her enough to let go.*

A selfish thought on his part. All about him.

Then she surprised him again. "John wouldn't have wanted me to grieve for so long like this. I know I wouldn't have wanted him to."

"Meaning?"

Her voice grew soft, wistful. "Before all this I'd just started letting go of the past."

"Then this."

She nodded. "The thing is, I was just beginning to think about the future. Just thinking that maybe I could have one. Then this."

"And now?" He was emotionally on the edge of his seat, expecting her to say that the grief had risen again.

"This? This makes me so angry there aren't words. Someone is trying to steal my future."

Slam. Like a body blow. He hadn't thought of that. "You can still have a future," he insisted.

"Not if I'm sitting on my porch all the time with a gun in my lap. This has to end. Maybe it already has."

He poured some coffee and sipped the hot brew. He needed to think carefully before he blundered into the wrong words. He chose a quiet response, rather than an impassioned one.

"We can't afford to think that way, Grace. Give us another six months."

"That's an awfully long time to be on guard with a gun."

"Try the military."

Thank God she laughed again. "Good point."

At least he'd pulled her into a less despairing mood. He just had to hope it would last.

DURING THE NIGHT, three gunshots sounded on the air. Mitch bolted upright from the porch chair. They'd come from a long way, carrying better on the cold air, but they were still an ominous sign.

He heard clattering feet behind him and turned. Grace emerged from the front door clad in pajamas, armed. "What was that?"

"I don't know. It came from a distance."

"God!"

He was already pulling the sat phone off his belt. After a very long minute or two, he heard Bill's voice. "You hear that?"

"I sure did. Jack and Jeff are riding over that way from the cattle pastures and I'm about to follow as soon as I get saddled up. It may take a while, hard to tell where the sounds came from. I'm thinking the sheep. Again."

"Damn. I'm going to ride that way, too."

"Not necessary, boss. You keep an eye on Grace. In case. Lila says she's getting a rifle and will keep an eye out here."

"Let me know."

"Like I'd keep it secret. Relax, man, we got three guys to check it out."

He disconnected. "See, I'm useless. My guys are heading out to look into the shots."

"Mitch, you can go if you want."

He faced her. "I'm not leaving you alone. Most especially not after gunshots." Bill had been right. He'd have been more useless out there than he was here.

"But…"

"No buts. Well, except one. If you want to keep watch with me, I wouldn't mind it."

Grace hesitated. "Shouldn't you be over there watching your own house?"

"Bill tells me Lila is getting a rifle. I wouldn't want to be at the wrong end of it."

Yup. They didn't need him. But the thought didn't sour him. He was grateful to those men, and to Lila. He had a family of his own, built of four people who'd earned not only his trust, but his strong affection, as well. Now he was going to worry about them, too.

"They mean a lot to me," he remarked even as he was debating whether to patrol around the house and barn. The moon was practically gone now, providing lots of cover. Now he knew. This criminal worked in total darkness. Night vision goggles?

Hell's bell.

"Your men and Lila seem almost like a family," Grace remarked.

"They are. I was just thinking that."

"So now you have someone else to worry about."

"You're very intuitive," he replied.

He saw her shake her head, even though there was no light but starshine.

"Nothing intuitive about it. I lived with all of you for weeks. I saw it. I also envied it."

That touched him and made him ache for her. She was feeling the loneliness. And here he'd thought her impervious.

"I'm going to make my rounds," he told her.

"I'll go get us some coffee—are you getting sick of it yet?—and something to eat. Anyone comes in that kitchen and he'll be dead."

He waited long enough to see her disappear inside, to see the kitchen light come on, then started his march again around the buildings. He didn't expect to find anything, but it was possible those gunshots had been a distraction. He couldn't risk it.

As MITCH HAD PROMISED—had it only been a week ago?—Lila had brought over a generous load of supplies.

"I know how much that man eats," Lila had said. "He'll run through all this in no time at all. I'll bring more next week."

Lila had also brought two of her pies and a coffee cake. Evidently, Mitch had something of a sweet tooth.

The coffee cake sounded best to her, so she opened the airtight container and put it on a serving plate. There was enough sugar there to keep them both alert for hours.

The coffee didn't take that long to brew, and soon she was carrying the carafe outside. Another trip and she had the cake on the table along with a couple of small plates.

When Mitch at last returned, she was ready.

"Nothing," he said. It was becoming a refrain to their days.

"Damn," she answered. "Well, eat."

He sliced into the cake and slipped a wedge onto one of the plates. "I wish to God one of my guys would call."

"They probably haven't found anything yet. There's a lot of open land out there."

She understood his uneasiness, though. Livestock and shepherds. Plenty to shoot at out there. She just hoped it hadn't been directed at the shepherds. Bad enough to kill more sheep, but men? A shudder ran through her.

She was also sure this hadn't been directed against Mitch. Nobody knew he owned those sheep but he'd been specific about that and she sure hadn't told anyone.

"Mitch?"

"Yeah?"

"Why didn't you want me to tell anyone that the sheep now belong to you?"

"Because I sure as hell didn't want anyone thinking I'd taken advantage of you."

"But you didn't! I was going to have to sell them anyway."

"No one knows that. You didn't tell anyone. I also know how hard you fought against selling them."

She had, she acknowledged. Perhaps ridiculously so. Part of a dream she could never hope to maintain. She'd been relieved when Mitch made his offer. The sheep wouldn't leave—they'd remain on her land. They wouldn't go to slaughter but would continue to produce wool for years to come.

She understood the realities of raising livestock. Mitch couldn't hope to keep that many steers without sending them off every fall. The only alternative would have been dairy farming and in this dry country that would have been a bad bet.

Nor did she believe he was doing anything wrong. People ate meat. They'd been eating it for thousands of years and there was only one way to get it.

But the sheep...ah, that was different, and she liked that fact. So did Mitch, from everything he'd said.

"Thanks for taking my flock."

"No thanks necessary. I ought to be paying you royalties on all that wool."

She would have chuckled except something dark was waiting out there and it wasn't the night. Something ugly.

It was impossible not to notice that ugliness was stalking her. Ugliness beyond her imaginings. No rhyme or reason to it. It just was.

They had to stop it somehow.

TWO HOURS LATER, Bill called Mitch. "The shepherds have been shot. One of them managed to return fire. They're both alive. We bandaged them as best we could, but you should be seeing the helicopters coming soon."

"You get someone over here," Mitch said sharply. "I'm going to the hospital."

"Take Grace with you," Bill said. "I'll be responsible for her property but not her life."

"What?" Grace asked as soon as disconnected.

"The shepherds, Bill said. The rescue choppers are on their way. You're coming with me to the hospital. Bill is going to watch your property."

He tried to forestall an argument with her, but he wasn't sure it would have been necessary. Grace's values weren't in the least warped. She clearly thought the shepherds were more important.

"I feel responsible," she said as they climbed in her truck.

"Now how the hell can you blame yourself? You didn't pull that trigger. You didn't make that decision. Stuff a sock in it."

At least he'd made her smile faintly.

But *he* couldn't smile. He was beginning to wonder if he'd ever genuinely smile again.

A FEW YEARS AGO, local people had built a helipad and a wide cement path to the ER doors. They'd wanted to help, to end the necessity of carrying people from the outlying airport, which took time. Possibly precious time.

A blue sign stood near it, telling the world, Built and Donated by the People of Conard County.

Memorial Community Hospital had grown a bit over the intervening years, but it was still small. Given that it served relatively few people, many scattered over huge distances, the county was lucky they hadn't lost it.

But the hospital had resisted buyout efforts by large companies that wanted to make a profit from health care, mainly because the taxpayers continued to support it.

The two medevac choppers had already landed, so Grace and Mitch hurried through the emergency doors.

Mary, the nurse, greeted them. When she heard why they were there, she said, "I'm sorry, you can't see them."

"But how are they doing?" Mitch demanded. "Will they be okay?"

"How are you related?" Mary asked.

Grace stiffened, hearing in those words a refusal arising from patient privacy. That was why she'd had to give Mitch permission, unlike a regular visitor. She could only imagine how much more annoyed Mitch must be than she.

"They work for me," Mitch said, his voice growing edgy. "Whatever relatives they have are in Portugal."

Mary raised a brow. "In that case... They're going to be okay. The men who found them gave them some excellent emergency aid, and they got here in time. Both will need surgery. If you want to wait, it might be a few hours."

"I'll wait," Mitch answered. "And send the bills to me."

Mary shook her head. "You aren't legally responsible and we don't charge patients who can't pay."

As she walked away, Mitch gave a low growl. Grace reached out to touch his arm. "They're going to be okay."

"And I'll pay the damn bills."

She followed him into a nearby waiting room, convinced he wanted to do the only thing he could by taking care of the bills. He must not only be worried but totally frustrated that he'd been able to do nothing at all.

Angry that the shootings had happened on his watch. Furious that while he'd been protecting Grace two men had been shot, probably by the same criminals.

Grace was upset, too. If someone wanted to scare her for some reason, they'd just kicked up the level of her fear. Was everyone else merely an obstacle to what they wanted?

What if they went for Mitch? That was her greatest fear. She didn't care nearly as much for herself, but whatever was going on, innocent people shouldn't be targeted because someone was after her.

The whole situation sickened her and her stomach kept rolling over.

For a long time, Mitch kept tapping his fingers on his thighs, probably to release some of his tension. Eventually he stopped and simply leaned forward with his elbows propped on his legs.

He remained silent. Grace didn't much feel like talking, either. No words they could say would help. Hell, she thought, there weren't any words for this horror.

Two men shot. Shepherds. All those guys were doing was taking wonderful care of a large flock of sheep.

Mitch spoke eventually. "Where are your parents now? I don't think you ever mentioned."

"They're both dead." Her heart squeezed even though it had been ten years. "They were on a vacation and died in a mudslide in Oregon."

She couldn't say any more than that without reawakening the horror she'd felt when she'd heard *how* they died. She'd had nightmares for months, and days where she couldn't think of anything else. She still missed them, and always would, but she couldn't afford to think about *how* they'd died. Nor did she want to explain her reaction to anyone.

"That's awful," he said. "Not natural. That's so much worse than the usual."

Amazingly, he had intuited part of her reaction. The other part was imagining them being suffocated by mud. All she answered was "Yeah."

Two sheriff's deputies, Guy Redwing and Connie Parish, showed up to take their statements. Not that they had much to say. Mitch sent them along to talk to his men. "The three of them found the shepherds. All I know is they were both shot."

Connie leaned toward Grace before departing. "We're going to get to the bottom of this."

Grace wished she believed it. So far no one knew anything about who might be behind all this mayhem.

The waiting resumed. Though it was only three hours, it felt like eternity. Then the nurse appeared with news.

"They're in recovery," she announced with a smile. "Maybe another hour or so and you can see them, but they're both going to be just fine."

Grace sensed pressure escape Mitch, like a balloon that had been overfilled. Relief came over her. Despite what Mitch said, she still felt responsible.

"Thank God," he murmured. "Thank God."

Instinctively, Grace reached for his arm and squeezed gently. He moved and clasped her hand in his.

"This is almost beyond belief," he said. "I'm going

to catch whoever is responsible and they won't like the consequences."

Grace didn't doubt it.

SEVERAL HOURS LATER, Mitch drove them home through the deepening night. He stopped for about fifteen minutes at Maude's diner to get breakfast for the two of them, and for Bill, as well. Since they hadn't known when they'd be getting back, Mitch suspected that Lila wouldn't have brought over an emergency meal.

Both shepherds had spoken briefly with him, but as usual they didn't say much. They never said much. He thought that was because of their limited knowledge of English.

There had been anxiety in their eyes, however. Obviously there was. They'd been shot. He suspected some of that fear grew out of apprehension that they'd been attacked because they were immigrants. Too much of that type of violence going around these days.

But he couldn't reassure them. Not about that.

He hoped they wouldn't quit when they got back on their feet, but he wouldn't blame them if they did. He wished he could make them safe. Make them *feel* safe, but that might never happen again.

After all these hours, there was one thing he still needed to know. "You okay, Grace?"

"Sure. I'm not lying in a hospital bed with a nasty hole in my body."

Well, that was one way to look at it.

Damn it all to hell. He had to find some way to put an end to this. There had to be a way.

Even though he hadn't expected it, he wasn't surprised to arrive at Grace's house to find Lila basically in residence and cooking up a storm. She greeted him with a hug and looked at the bags he was carrying.

"Put them on the counter," she ordered. "I'm not gonna let Maude's food go to waste." She turned to hug Grace. "You okay, girl?"

"I'm okay." Grace's smile was thin.

"Like hell you are," Lila said. "You and the boss set your butts down at the table. Coffee's fresh. I bet you didn't drink much at the hospital. I know what that stuff tastes like."

Mitch chuckled. "You got that right."

"Of course I did," Lila answered with a sniff.

"Where's Bill?"

"He's out riding what he calls a patrol." She waved to the corner. "Don't worry about me. There's my long gun and I know how to use Grace's shotgun. I just wish the bastard had showed up."

"I wish he had, too," Grace told her as Lila put two mugs of coffee on the table.

"I'd have fixed his wagon, all right. Then I'd have nailed his hide to the barn wall."

Mitch almost spewed coffee, then he laughed. "My God, Lila, you're something else."

"Been working on it for forty years. Think I've done pretty well, too." She started buzzing around the kitchen. "So, boss, you want Maude's food or mine?"

"Yours beats anything this side of heaven."

"Well, Maude's pretty good, too. I can heat this up tomorrow."

Mitch watched her put Maude's food in the fridge, then go about heaping two plates with eggs and home fries.

"Eat up," Lila said. "I'll eat mine whenever Bill gets back."

Grace looked at Lila as she delivered the plates full of food. "Are you and Bill an item?" It was really none of her business but she had to ask.

Lila sniffed again. "You ask Bill that question. He's never said so to me."

Mitch spoke. "Then maybe I should kick his behind."

Lila roared with laughter. "I'd like to see that."

LATER, LONG AFTER a new night began in, Grace and Mitch sat out on the front porch. Inside, Lila and Bill shared a meal of turkey slices and gravy over Grace's bread. She had served Grace and Mitch the same meal a little earlier.

"I think I'm about to pop," Grace volunteered. "I ate way too much."

"That happens with Lila's cooking."

"So how do you keep from gaining weight?"

"With difficulty." He shook his head. "And some nights I go for very long walks."

She laughed quietly.

He missed those walks, he realized. And he would have liked to take them with Grace. "Grace?"

"Yes?"

"Are you regretting those hours we spent in your bed?"

He heard her swiftly indrawn breath. "No! I thought you were."

Boy, had he read the situation all wrong. "I didn't regret them at all. I thought you did. Hell."

She gave the most relaxed laugh he'd heard from her in a while. "Think of all those hours wasted since then. Not that we could have felt that relaxed very often."

The specter of the two shepherds rose before him. "No. I think I got too lax, though."

"How?" she asked. "How? Who would have ever thought…?"

She didn't finish the question. She didn't need to. The question he was asking himself, however, had no easy answer. They'd known Grace was being targeted. Why hadn't he thought that men believed to be her shepherds might have been targeted, as well?

He felt like a damned fool.

CARL AND LARRY were gloating. They'd been told not to murder anyone, but the boss hadn't said they couldn't shoot someone. The night felt fine to them, and they toasted it with a couple of beers, feeling terribly smart.

After this, that Hall woman would run for the hills.

When the boss called later, they expected to receive a heaping helping of praise. Instead they got her wrath.

"Damn it, I told you not to kill anyone."

Carl answered. "We didn't. We just shot 'em. They're still alive."

"You asinine idiots. That's *attempted* murder!" She was shouting again, loud enough for Larry to hear.

The two men exchanged looks. "We didn't kill no-body," Carl argued.

"Maybe not, but this is exactly what I told you not to do! I ought to fire you stupid fools!"

Carl clenched his jaw, fury enveloping him, then said, "You better not. We got a pretty story to tell the cops."

Silence greeted him, then an empty connection.

Larry spoke. "You got her, Carl."

"By the short and curlies," Carl said.

"Uh, don't that mean a man?"

"She's got short and curlies, too."

Larry lay back with his third beer. Yeah, he guessed she did. He savored the image.

BETTY POLLARD WAS even angrier than Carl and Larry. Their threat of telling the police had struck her with her first fear since she'd started this operation.

Walking around with a glass of scotch, she drank faster than she should have, the wheels spinning in her brain. They wouldn't tell the police, she assured herself. They'd only make things bad for themselves.

But given the dubious intelligence of those two, they might forget this was a damn conspiracy and they were as deep in it as she was.

Charges began to flicker through her thoughts. Conspiracy, certainly. Accomplice, maybe. Attempted murder? Well, she had specifically told them not to do such a thing, so they couldn't charge her for that. Maybe.

For the first time since she'd set this all in motion, it occurred to her that she never should have thought she'd skate through this undetected. From the moment she had hired those goons, she'd opened the possibility they might squeal. But she couldn't do it herself.

She blamed Grace for not getting out of Dodge. If Grace had just fled, the way she should have, most of this never would have happened. So yeah, it was Grace's fault. *All* her fault.

That didn't comfort Betty because *she* had been involved in the wrongdoing, not Grace. That was going to be a bright line if her scheme came before a judge.

Damn. Maybe she should abandon this all right now. Pay off those guys and get rid of them before they could start talking. That might be the best way.

Yes, it would. Because she'd explicitly told them, as part of this deal, that they had to vanish with the tidy little sum she still owed them. They'd clear the county and leave her safe.

And she'd have to start all over again, trying to move Grace.

"Hell," she swore savagely at her empty apartment. "Hell."

Another two fingers of scotch went down easily. She continued ruminating because there had to be a way to fix this. To let Grace know this wouldn't end as long as she remained on that property.

Maybe she could give those stupid men an order to do one more thing. Betty would have fled by this point, so why wouldn't Grace?

Shooting those shepherds hadn't been a direct attack on Grace. Maybe she didn't realize it had been a warning to her.

So Betty would wait a little longer to see how this developed. If Grace still wasn't frightened enough to leave, then another incident would be required.

She'd leave it up to those fools. But this time she'd make it clear that no one was to be shot. Apparently the first warning hadn't penetrated. Next time she'd make it crystal clear.

Maybe that would get through to these dimwits.

Chapter Nineteen

A week later, Zeke and Rod had settled into Mitch's bunkhouse. Neither was in the best shape. Zeke still sported a sling from being shot in the shoulder. Thank God, it had missed the artery. And Rod hobbled around on crutches, his thigh having been hit. Both men had been seriously injured enough to require blood transfusions, and they still appeared wan. They also tired easily.

As Mitch had expected, all of Lila's mothering instincts came to the fore. She seemed to be in her element between looking after Grace and caring for the two shepherds.

How she managed it all, Mitch had no idea. He was grateful, however, for every single thing she did.

Bill came over once to stand watch while Mitch went to visit his shepherds. Grace refused to be budged. If she'd needed a last straw to pile on her stubbornness, the shooting was it. That woman had a spine of steel.

Admirable but frustrating, too. She needed a break from being constantly on guard, but she wouldn't take it.

When Bill arrived, he talked about Zeke and Rod. "They may not be getting around too well, but they've given the three of us volumes of information about watching the damn sheep. Guess they're worried."

"I kinda thought they might be." Mitch smiled.

"Oh, and one other thing. They were asking about a dog."

"I've been waiting on two herding dogs from Ransom Laird, but maybe a couple of guard dogs would help sooner. If they'd had them, it's possible that creep wouldn't have gotten close enough to shoot."

"Good idea." Bill turned to look toward the mountains. "Oh, yeah, I saw Burt Stiller in town yesterday. He'd been out of pocket on a trip to see his wife's parents. He said go ahead and ride his range. You want one of us to do that?"

Mitch tilted his head. "How are the three of you supposed to handle all this? You're looking after all the livestock, you've added the sheep to your load, and now you want to go riding the Stiller place to look for signs of a watcher."

Bill answered wryly. "It'd give one of us a break."

Mitch laughed. "I hadn't thought about that. But I'll do it tomorrow, Bill. I need something to sink my teeth into or a throat to wrap my hands around. As long as I'm back in the afternoon, Grace should be fine."

"Nah," said Bill. "I'll be over here with her." He raised a brow. "But you knew that already, didn't you, boss?"

Mitch smiled. "I had a hope, that's all."

NOTHING EVER WENT according to plan. Carl and Larry hatched their own plan, and they didn't want any bull from *their* boss.

"Screw the waiting," Larry said. "She's nuts. If she din't make us wait so often this coulda been all over."

Carl thought about it. "You're right. Faster mighta got rid of that Hall woman sooner."

"You betcha," Larry answered. "Damn screwed-up plan. Ain't no way the boss figgered this right."

"No way," Carl agreed. "She been making me madder 'n' a wet hen. Right now, I don't freakin' care if we get the rest of the money."

Larry didn't like that idea. "No way. She's gonna pay us, man. Or we talk. Just send a letter to the sheriff or something, then get the hell out of here."

Carl nodded. "Okay, then. I don't wanna tell anybody what *we* done."

Larry scratched his chin. "Wish I'd never hooked up with her."

"It's a lot of money."

Larry shook his head. "And that's why we're in this mess, ain't we?"

Carl frowned deeply. "She got us by the short and curlies, too. We gotta take care of this, get paid and skedaddle. Or maybe if the heat's on, we just skedaddle anyway. But I did like shooting them Port-a-gees."

"Yeah," Larry agreed. "Did my heart good. Them furriners, stealing our jobs. I don't care that we shot 'em."

"I wish we'da killed 'em."

Larry made a sound of agreement.

"So think," Carl demanded. "Figger out how we do it and soon."

MITCH TOOK THE first watch again. The duty was beginning to feel useless. Maybe they were scaring the perp away. Their visible presence, always armed, might be acting like a flashing warning beacon on a road at night.

Or maybe it was over, never to be explained. Given that they had no idea of the purpose behind this, they were stuck with fear of more.

He hadn't been kidding Bill when he'd said he wanted to get his hands around someone's neck. At this point he couldn't even swear he wouldn't kill the guy.

He was feeling far too murderous for his soul's good.

Chapter Twenty

Mitch rode back to Grace's late the next afternoon, shot-gun and rifle in their holsters in case he needed some-thing more precise than a shotgun. The sun painted the wisps of cloud in the sky with a reddish alpenglow. A truly beautiful evening, and he gave it some moments of appreciation.

He felt decently satisfied. He'd discovered three places where someone had camped among the trees on Still-er's land, three places from which Grace's property was visible. Whoever it had been, they'd moved on, leaving nothing behind but a few beer bottles buried in the duff. He'd already called the cops, giving them the GPS loca-tions he'd noted on his sat phone. He hoped they could find some prints on those bottles.

But now he had to relieve Bill and take care of Grace. He enjoyed taking care of Grace, and just wished the cir-cumstances were happier. As it was, he had to be content with his discoveries.

When he reached the foot of Grace's driveway, he felt an internal shudder. The impression of wrongness overpowered him. He couldn't put a finger on it—maybe eyes watching?—but it caused him to touch Joy's sides with his heels.

Joy needed no other encouragement. She took off at a full gallop along the gravel road, crossing the mile to Grace's house rapidly. Not rapidly enough for him, but Joy went all out, lathering before they reached the house. She seemed to feel his worry and probably wouldn't have stopped if he had tried to rein her in.

Where was Grace? She should have been on the porch, especially upon hearing the swift pounding of Joy's hooves.

Joy skittered to a stop just before the front porch, sliding and spewing gravel into the air.

"Grace?" Mitch bellowed her name. "Bill!"

Nothing answered him.

His heart pounded as hard as Joy's did. Swinging his leg over the saddle, he dropped to the ground with a jolt, shotgun in hand. Releasing the reins, he left it to Joy to cool herself down. She wandered around the yard, then headed for the trough near the barn. She knew what to do for herself.

Not that he had time to think about that. He hadn't been shot at yet, so he didn't care about the racket he made running up the steps, across the porch and into the house.

"Grace! Bill!"

Nothing. No answer. He could scarcely breathe as his heart pounded, as terror filled him with renewed strength.

Then he heard a hammering from the back of the house. Racing toward it, he found Bill bound and gagged with duct tape, sitting in a corner of the room. Bill's eyes pleaded with him as his booted feet banged the floor once more.

Mitch crossed the floor in two strides and ripped the

tape from Bill's mouth. Bill barely reacted. "Two men," he said. "They took Grace."

"Where?"

Bill shook his head. "No car. I'd have heard a car. Cut me loose. We can track them."

Mitch yanked the ever-present bowie knife from the sheath on his belt. With quick swipes he cut the tape binding Bill's hands and feet.

Bill struggled upward, clearly stiff. "Twenty minutes. Let's go." Then he grabbed Grace's rifle, which stood near the front door, checked the load. "Ready."

Mitch hardly waited. "Joy practically killed herself getting me here."

"S'okay. Got two mounts in the barn, unless they were taken."

Mitch didn't even ask why Bill had two horses here. Explanations could wait. They ran to the barn to quickly saddle Daisy and Joy. Both horses were a bit restive, but quickly calmed to receive saddles and harnesses.

"Jeff brought us two horses this afternoon," Bill said as he swung the saddle up onto Daisy. "Ms. Hall was hell-bent on riding around the property, so I got the horses. We locked up. Damn. We rode a bit, then brought the horses in here. How the hell were we to guess two guys were waiting inside? We didn't see no one while we were riding."

"Don't blame yourself." Mitch tightened Joy's cinch, patted her neck. The he slipped his shotgun into one saddle holster and his rifle into the other. He mounted. Bill wasn't far behind.

"They had to have left some sign," Mitch said as they rode out of the barn, more to reassure himself. "Especially if they didn't take her in a truck."

"Surely something," Bill agreed.

"Call the sheriff. I already found three campsites on Stiller's land, and they might be headed that way. We need the cops over here."

While Bill made the call, Mitch turned Joy in a tight circle, looking for any sign of how the men had taken Grace away.

Then he saw it: crushed grass, unmown this summer, deep enough that the passage of the two men and Grace might have paved a road. Bill followed.

"Twenty minutes," he repeated. "Not far."

"Unless," Mitch said, "they got her into a truck farther away. Grace wouldn't have made it easy on them."

Bill snorted. "That woman is a force of nature."

Then they fell silent, intent on the ground ahead of them. Even from the height of Joy's back, Mitch saw signs that Grace had dug in her heels. Fighting every step of the way.

God, he hoped they hadn't hurt her.

GRACE WAS MORE furious than frightened. She struggled against the arms that dragged her backward, ignoring it when their grip hurt. At every opportunity, she dug in the heels of her boots, making them move slower.

She worried about Bill, left behind and bound. She worried about Mitch arriving at her house to find this mess. She noted the red glow fading from the sky, promising darkness that would make all this easier on her captors by concealing them.

The duct tape held her mouth in a tight grip, but that didn't stop her from forcing her tongue between her lips and trying to loosen it.

Adrenaline poured through her system, but it

couldn't make her strong enough to break free. All she could do was make this as difficult as possible for her abductors.

She had no idea what these men intended to do to her, but this was a far cry from burning her barn or ransacking her house. Did they intend to kill her?

She realized she no longer cared. She could no longer tolerate living in constant fear, standing on constant watch. Her life had become that of a soldier standing unending sentry duty in a dangerous zone.

She was more worried about Mitch. Her panic led her to diverting her thoughts down ridiculous paths. At least her death would set him free to return to his own life instead of letting everything go in order to watch over her. It was too much to ask of him.

He deserved to go home, to take care of his own affairs. Sure, he'd grieve, but nowhere near the endless sorrow she'd felt for John. Nor should he. She was merely a friend he'd cared for. Because she was a duty he believed he owed to a neighbor.

Their lovemaking hadn't changed a thing. It didn't matter that she'd been longing to repeat it. That was selfish.

She struggled harder against the kidnappers, wishing she'd changed out of her cowboy boots on the porch so she could have dug her heels in deeper.

Mitch, she thought, *go home. Let the police deal with this. Risk no more for me. I'm not that important.*

But that didn't keep her from fighting. It was not in her nature to give up, despite how it had appeared during the years she'd grieved for John. She hadn't given up her heartache, and she wouldn't give up her life without a struggle. Then they dropped her to the ground.

MITCH FOLLOWED AN entirely different line of thought. He might as well die if he couldn't find Grace alive. She'd become the center of his existence, more important than his livestock, than his entire ranch.

He *had* to save her.

"There," he said suddenly to Bill. Drag marks mashed grass and showed deep score marks in the underlying ground.

"Yup," Bill answered, turning his mount to follow Mitch.

Mitch pulled out his rifle, ready. Bill followed suit.

"Twenty minutes," Bill said again.

"She can't be too far from here." Hope spurred Mitch to a faster pace. Dolly agreed with him.

Concern for the horses on the rough ground gave way to urgency. Neither mount stumbled as night blanketed the world.

Please, God. Please. He had no idea if he spoke aloud, but he knew all too clearly what he feared finding. He hadn't heard a gun report, but that didn't mean a damn thing. Knives. A garrote.

Suddenly, even in the night's darkness, he saw her. Crumpled on the ground. Dead? Alive?

He slid from Joy, rifle at ready. Bill stood guard from horseback.

Then he fell to his knees. "Grace? Grace."

She stirred and his prayer of gratitude rose to the heavens as he began to strip tape from her.

"Mitch." The first word from her mouth. "Get them. Leave me. Get them. *Please.*"

"You…"

"I'm okay. *Go!*"

He mounted Joy so fast that she sidled. "I'm going," he said to Bill. "Stay with her. Protect her."

"You got it."

Mitch holstered his rifle and pulled out his shotgun. Now he wanted the widest spray possible. He was going to take those sons of bitches down. He wanted them lying on the ground, bleeding from every pellet of birdshot he could pump into them.

Rage could have blinded him, but he refused to let it.

Then he saw them, black shadows running through deep grasses that impeded them. He never hesitated as he sighted them and pulled the trigger.

Both fell screaming to the ground.

Mitch's satisfaction knew no bounds. Astride Joy, he kept the shotgun pointed at them.

"Don't try anything. I got five more shells in this."

They didn't move except to writhe.

The sheriff's men arrived at remarkable speed on their four-wheel-drive SUVs. Two cops took over the scene. Two more loaded the wounded men in the bed of their vehicles to carry them to approaching ambulances.

Mitch lifted Grace into the passenger seat of one of them, even as she protested that she was fine.

"I'll be riding alongside," Mitch promised. "Right here. Now, dammit, quit being so stubborn."

At last she subsided.

BACK AT GRACE'S HOUSE, as the two men were loaded into ambulances, a surprising sight greeted them. Betty Pollard, on the porch, her hands cuffed behind her.

Grace froze, staring at her friend. "Betty?"

"I came to confess to you. It's all my fault," the

woman said, tears running down her face. "I told them not to hurt anyone, most especially you."

"What?" Disbelief nearly made Grace deaf.

Betty poured out her plan to frighten Grace off the ranch, her reason for doing so. "But they weren't supposed to *hurt* you!"

That didn't seem to make any difference to the deputies who hauled her off and shoved her into a car. All Grace could do was watch, then turn to Mitch. "Did that make sense?"

"Unfortunately, yes. Now let the EMTs look you over."

"I'm fine." But no one was listening to her. They took her inside and began treating scrapes.

"All we can do about the bruises is let them heal," one said. "But you're going to be sore, very sore. We're giving you some muscle relaxants or you won't sleep tonight."

Grace felt too revved up to care. It was going to be a long time before she slept again.

Mitch changed all that. He carried her to her bed and gently removed her remaining clothes, then covered her with the blanket. It was easy to relax into his arms as he lay beside her, despite all her bruises. She needed him close.

FOR A LONG time he said nothing, hoping she would drift into sleep. She didn't and he could understand it. She'd had more than one shock tonight.

"Bill is okay?"

"Okay enough to ride with me to find you."

"Good. You came out of the night like an avenging angel."

He laughed quietly. "I felt like one. All I had was a gun when I wanted a flaming sword."

"The gun did well enough." She sighed, then groaned faintly as she wiggled closer. His arms tightened gently.

"I could get you some ice for those bruises," he suggested.

"Probably too late now. I was thinking when I was out there how much I've messed up your life."

That was more than Mitch could bear. "You know what I was thinking when I hunted for you?"

"What?"

"That you've become the center of my life. That you've become all that really matters to me."

She drew a swift breath. "Mitch...no."

"Grace, yes. I was thinking that I couldn't live without you. Grace, I love you. I realize you're not ready..."

"Oh, shut up," she answered, startling him.

"Huh?"

"If you start backing off what you just said, I may shove you out of my bed. Damn it, Mitch, are you going to keep me from loving you, too?"

Shock slowly gave way to a deep-seated warmth that filled him from head to toe. "Love as in marriage?" he asked tentatively.

"Of course," she replied promptly.

His heart soared. "Kids?"

"I always wanted them. I always wanted to see my kids riding ponies and laughing. You?"

"You bet," he murmured, then kissed her deeply. The heat that rose in him was entirely inappropriate given how sore she was, but he let it grow anyway.

"How soon?" she asked.

Damn, that was Grace. "How big a shindig do you want?"

"Just get Reverend Canton over here. How much more do I need?"

"Ah, man, Grace. Do you really think you could keep the neighbors away?"

She laughed then. "Tell them to bring their own barbecue."

It was his turn to laugh. "I love you, Grace Hall. Heart and soul."

She snuggled a tiny bit closer. "Don't ever let me go, Mitch."

"Never," he promised. "Never."

* * * * *

COMING SOON!

We really hope you enjoyed reading this book.
If you're looking for more romance, be sure to
head to the shops when new books are
available on

Thursday 3rd
February

To see which titles are coming soon, please visit
millsandboon.co.uk/nextmonth

MILLS & BOON

THE HEART OF ROMANCE

A ROMANCE FOR EVERY READER

MODERN

Prepare to be swept off your feet by sophisticated, sexy and seductive heroes, in some of the world's most glamourous and romantic locations, where power and passion collide.

HISTORICAL

Escape with historical heroes from time gone by. Whether your passion is for wicked Regency Rakes, muscled Vikings or rugged Highlanders, awaken the romance of the past.

MEDICAL

Set your pulse racing with dedicated, delectable doctors in the high-pressure world of medicine, where emotions run high and passion, comfort and love are the best medicine.

True Love

Celebrate true love with tender stories of heartfelt romance, from the rush of falling in love to the joy a new baby can bring, and a focus on the emotional heart of a relationship.

Desire

Indulge in secrets and scandal, intense drama and plenty of sizzling hot action with powerful and passionate heroes who have it all: wealth, status, good looks…everything but the right woman.

HEROES

Experience all the excitement of a gripping thriller, with an intense romance at its heart. Resourceful, true-to-life women and strong, fearless men face danger and desire - a killer combination!

To see which titles are coming soon, please visit

millsandboon.co.uk/nextmonth

LET'S TALK
Romance

For exclusive extracts, competitions
and special offers, find us online:

 facebook.com/millsandboon

 @MillsandBoon

 @MillsandBoonUK

Get in touch on 01413 063232

MILLS & BOON
Desire

Indulge in secrets and scandal, intense drama and plenty of sizzling hot action with powerful and passionate heroes who have it all: wealth, status, good looks…everything but the right woman.

MILLS & BOON
MEDICAL
Pulse-Racing Passion

Set your pulse racing with dedicated, delectable doctors in the high-pressure world of medicine, where emotions run high and passion, comfort and love are the best medicine.

MILLS & BOON
True Love
Romance from the Heart

Celebrate true love with tender stories of heartfelt romance, from the rush of falling in love to the joy a new baby can bring, and a focus on the emotional heart of a relationship.

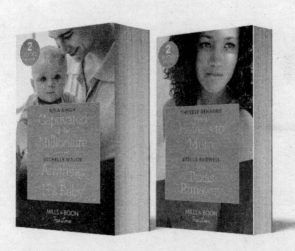